KU-400-754

THE WARTIME SINGERS

London, 1914. Sick and injured servicemen are returning home and Lizzie Kellaway and her godmother Margaret Penrose are determined to do their bit to help them. With Lizzie's beautiful singing voice and Margaret's talent for the piano, concerts in hospitals and convalescent homes offer the perfect opportunity to lift the spirits of men who have suffered so much.

When Polly Meadows's fiancé rejects her and leaves for the war, she doesn't hesitate before travelling to London to be with her childhood friend, Lizzie. It isn't long before she's persuaded to join their efforts to entertain the troops. At least while performing Polly can forget her troubles and open her soul to the joy of singing.

With all three women facing struggles, one thing is certain: these wartime singers will need each other more than ever before . . .

LESLEY EAMES

THE WARTIME SINGERS

Complete and Unabridged

MAGNA
Leicester

First published in Great Britain in 2021 by
Aria
an imprint of Head of Zeus Ltd
London

First Ulverscroft Edition
published 2022
by arrangement with
Head of Zeus Ltd
London

Copyright © 2021 by Lesley Eames
All rights reserved

This is a work of fiction. All characters, organizations, and events portrayed in this novel are either products of the author's imagination or are used fictitiously.

A catalogue record for this book is available from the British Library.

ISBN 978–0–7505–4952–3

BRENT LIBRARIES	
AF	OUT
00134503	

Dedication

To my beloved daughters, Olivia and Isobel —
my inspiration and my joy.

1

January 1909

Witherton, North-West England

There were no curtains at the window of the attic where Lizzie was forced to sleep, so even as she sat on her bed, she could see that outside all was cold, winter darkness. Down in the hall the grandfather clock began to announce the hour. Counting each heavy chime, Lizzie felt nervousness flutter inside her like winged creatures suddenly taking flight.

. . . Six, seven, eight o'clock. In another few hours she'd leave this house secretly and alone for an uncertain future. She was terrified, but the alternative was . . . No, it couldn't be borne.

Until she left, the pretence of normality had to be maintained. Not that anyone was likely to check on her, but it would be foolish to take unnecessary risks. Lizzie changed into her nightgown, though she kept her stockings on because the sheets would be icy. Plumping up her pillow, she got into bed and sat back to wait.

But it wasn't long before restlessness overwhelmed her. Lizzie got up again and stuffed her feet into her boots. Her old bedroom downstairs was carpeted, but here where Susan Monk had banished her, there were only bare floorboards. No fire either.

Slipping her coat over her nightgown, she crossed to the window. The sky was inkiness upon inkiness

1

until the clouds thinned to allow a hint of light to appear. A moment later they parted to reveal the moon. Not a full moon, but almost. Lizzie tried to take heart from it, as it enabled her to make out shapes in the garden below . . . the gateposts, the shrubbery, the flower bed that was cut into the lawn . . .

Moonlight would help her to see where she was going. Of course, it might also make her visible to others, but she'd keep to the shadows where possible.

She looked in the direction of St Paul's church and identified the steeple as a dark finger against the sky. It was in St Paul's churchyard that Mama had lain buried for the past year. What changes her death had brought! Feeling the old outrage burn inside her, Lizzie's thoughts rolled back in time . . .

* * *

She wasn't allowed to attend the funeral. Apparently, her father forbade it, much to Lizzie's distress. Mama deserved to have someone who actually loved her present instead of just the town's finest citizens . . . there for the sake of appearances — and the husband who'd scared her.

Edward Maudsley was a stern, irritable man who'd rarely even spoken to his wife. Poor Mama had grown timid whenever he was near and it had troubled her that she was leaving Lizzie behind with such a man. 'I love your spirit, darling, but promise you'll do your best to rub along with him peacefully,' she'd urged.

Lizzie had never provoked him on purpose, but even laughter in the garden, a cough at the dinner table or a burst of cold air when she ran into the house after one of her tramps across fields could bring a

2

frown to his face. Otherwise, he'd ignored his daughter even more than his wife.

'Of course, I promise,' Lizzie had said, desperate to spare Mama from worry, though full of doubt over how the promise might be fulfilled.

But after Mama left the world, a strange thought slid into Lizzie's head. Was it possible that the death of a kind, gracious wife like Mama could work a change in Edward Maudsley and make him actually crave his daughter's companionship? After all, Lizzie had reached the age of twelve and that was surely old enough to provide both comfort and conversation. If he just took the trouble to know her . . .

A feeling like hunger stirred in the hollow space of her stomach though it wasn't a yearning for food. Hope stirred too, but the day after Mama's funeral brought unexpected developments. Lizzie didn't know where her father was going when he left the house in the carriage but seized the chance to slip out to say a private goodbye at Mama's graveside, intending to slip back in with no harm done.

Not wanting to be seen walking out between the front gateposts she pushed through the hedgerow at the side of the garden onto Amesbury Lane and made her way to the churchyard from there, kneeling beside the sorry heap of brown earth and sobbing with grief for the woman who'd meant the world to her.

Shy, tender-hearted Mama hadn't enjoyed the society of Witherton's starched and critical matrons, and she'd educated Lizzie at home, so they'd spent most of every day together. How was Lizzie to bear life without her? Loneliness stabbed at Lizzie's heart as tears stung her eyes like red-hot needles.

But she had to bear it. Somehow.

In time she got up and wiped her eyes on a handkerchief, promising Mama all over again to do her best to get along with Papa. She was pushing back through the hedgerow from Amesbury Lane when he returned in the carriage.

Ducking behind a laurel bush, she watched in surprise as he helped a woman down onto the gravel drive. She was a tall, thin, handsome woman, but her lips were narrow and her eyes were sharp. And, oddly, she looked up at Briar Lodge with a triumphant expression, almost as though she were thinking, *I'm here at last and it's mine now. All mine.*

Unease seeped into Lizzie's skin like icy water. Who on earth was this woman?

The gardener came to take the carriage away and Betty the maid opened the front door to Papa and his visitor. Lizzie waited a few minutes longer then made her way to the rear door that led into the passage between kitchen and scullery. From here she could take the back stairs to her room. Or she could have done if Betty hadn't caught her.

'Heavens, Miss, I was just going to fetch you.' Betty looked flustered.

'Has the visitor upset you, Betty? Who is she?'

'Her name's Miss Monk. That's all I know, but you're wanted in the drawing-room. Hurry along, but go up to the landing and come down the front stairs like you're supposed to. I'm to fetch tea.'

Lizzie started up the stairs. 'Miss, your boots!' Betty wailed. 'Your dress too!'

Amesbury Lane had been muddy. After a quick and not very thorough clean-up, Lizzie descended the main stairs with neat steps, as befitted a young lady brought up by a mama who had once been Miss Grace

4

Sophia Kellaway of Harrogate. The drawing-room door stood open, showing Miss Monk sitting stiff-backed in a chair and looking around the room as though taking an inventory: *That ormolu clock is mine now. So is that magnificent mirror, those silver candle-sticks, the china . . . Mine, mine, mine . . .*

She was a little older than Mama, with none of Mama's angelic softness. This face had a hard, greedy look to its handsomeness.

Lizzie took a deep breath and knocked on the door.

'Enter,' Papa called, turning from the window.

Lizzie walked in.

'This is my cousin, Miss Monk. Susan, this is Elizabeth,' he said, but he barely glanced at Lizzie.

She was disappointed. Worried too. And more than a little confused, because she'd never heard mention of a cousin. She'd always understood the family comprised just Papa, Mama and herself.

But she set these uncertainties aside temporarily, stepping forward to execute a small curtsey before holding out her hand and saying, 'It's a pleasure to meet you.'

Susan Monk looked unimpressed. She left Lizzie's hand floating in the air and raked her up and down with her gaze, those sharp eyes lingering momentarily on the still-messy boots and damp dress. 'Dear me,' she said, as though her worst suspicions had been confirmed. 'I see I have a lot of work ahead of me.'

Lizzie turned a questioning face to her father, but he didn't rush to defend her. Mama had considered her daughter to be a gift from Heaven after several years of childlessness, but Papa looked as uninterested as ever. Time might still change that, though.

'I'm not usually this messy,' Lizzie said. 'Today is

5

just . . . unfortunate. You can call me Lizzie, if you like.'

'I do not like. Lizzie is the sort of name kitchen girls have. Not young ladies of twelve years old who are supposed to be a credit to their papas.'

Mama had called her Lizzie all the time: *My clever Lizzie . . . My strong, spirited Lizzie . . . My Lizzie with the dancing feet . . .* This woman was insulting Mama. 'I prefer being called Lizzie.'

'Well!' Miss Monk said. 'What a badly brought-up girl you are, talking back to your elders like that.'

Horrible, hateful woman. How dared she insult Mama's way of raising her daughter? Still Papa didn't speak.

'If that's your opinion of me, I'll be sure to stay out of your way during your visit,' Lizzie said, but an awful fear washed over her, a fear that explained the possessive way Miss Monk had looked at the house and the lovely things inside it.

'You misunderstand.' There was malice in Miss Monk's satisfied tone. 'I'm not visiting. I'm here to keep house for your papa.'

She looked at him with a smile that invited him to confirm it. He nodded brusquely, as though the conversation bored him.

Betty arrived then, struggling to balance the tray and knock on the open door at the same time. Lizzie moved to help her, but Betty stopped her with a warning look.

'Enter,' Miss Monk called, like a queen holding court.

Betty placed the tray on the table.

'Dismissed,' Miss Monk told her then.

Betty glanced at Lizzie again and looks of dismay passed between them.

6

An idea suddenly formed in Lizzie's mind. Mama had educated her at home, but had sometimes asked, 'Am I being selfish, keeping you here with me, darling? You're far too clever for anything I can teach you, and perhaps you'd be happier at school with friends of your own age. I have fond memories of my time at school.'

Lizzie had loved Mama far too much to want to leave her alone with her cold, unfeeling husband, but circumstances had changed. 'Perhaps I should go away to school,' she suggested. 'Mama attended an academy for young ladies and—'

'Pert *and* opinionated,' Miss Monk said, pursing her lips in disgust. 'You have a lot to learn, Elizabeth, but I don't see why your papa should be put to the expense of a school when I'm more than capable of educating you.'

'You're going to give me lessons?' Lizzie was appalled.

'Most certainly I am. Those lessons will include discipline and respect. Now go to your room. I'll be up shortly and I'll expect to find you both clean and usefully employed. Be warned, Elizabeth: I've tamed far stronger spirits than yours.'

★ ★ ★

The grandfather clock chimed again . . . Seven, eight, nine o'clock. Not long to go now. As long as Lizzie's courage didn't fail her. But no. She couldn't allow that to happen.

It was freezing cold by the window. Lizzie got into bed but kept her coat on as she let her thoughts drift back into the past.

7

Dismissed by Miss Monk that first day, Lizzie went to her room and took a book from the shelf. After a while she heard voices out in Amesbury Lane. She got up to investigate, opening the window despite the winter chill. There were two children in the lane, though the hedgerow meant she couldn't see them properly until they reached the place where the old sycamore had stood before being struck by lightning. Here the bushes were thinner.

One child was a dainty, fair-haired girl; the other a strong-looking boy. Lizzie had seen them in the lane before and heard the girl singing sweetly as she walked. But they were poor children who moved in a different social circle. They laughed at something one of them said, then the girl broke into a run and the boy chased after her.

It must be pleasant to have a friend. Lizzie knew a few other children but saw little of them as, despite being every inch the lady, Mama preferred to stay at home. Lizzie didn't mind because Clara Bland was sly, while the Mayford sisters were given to whispering secrets, and Alice Payne was only interested in embroidery, shrinking from the very thought of the sort of tramp across wet fields that Lizzie found exhilarating. Mama hadn't liked tramping either, but understood Lizzie's need to burn up excess energy before her lessons.

These poorer children looked as though they had a lot more fun, and —

'So this is how you spend your time.'

Lizzie whirled around but the book slipped from her fingers and plummeted to the gravel drive outside.

Miss Monk stood in the room like a cobra preparing to strike, pleased to see Lizzie discomfited. 'I should have guessed I'd find you idling.'

'I was reading!'

'Humph!' Miss Monk thrust Lizzie out of her way to look down on the fallen book. 'I see you're very careless with your father's money. Books are expensive.'

It was the second time she'd mentioned Papa's money. What business was it of hers?

'Go down and retrieve that book now. I'll be waiting.'

Lizzie ran down for the book and carried it back upstairs, dusting powdered gravel off the pages. 'Let me see,' Miss Monk demanded.

'It's fine.'

'The jacket is scuffed!'

'Those scuffs were there before. It's an old book.'

Miss Monk picked up a ruler. 'I was minded to give you six smacks. Now you've answered back disrespectfully, you'll have twelve. Hold out your hands.'

Vicious woman. She brought the ruler down hard, and Lizzie blinked at the stinging pain.

'Let that be a lesson to you. It's my job to undo the over-indulgences of your mother and bring you up as a girl who doesn't disgrace her father. I take that job seriously and, as you've just discovered, resistance will only result in punishment being doubled.'

She looked around the room at the pretty embroidered white counterpane and pillows, the beautifully-dressed doll, the dolls' house, the flowery china trinkets . . . Her mouth pursed resentfully. 'Where do you have your lessons?'

Lizzie willed her voice not to crack. 'Mama taught

9

me downstairs.'

'That will never do.' Miss Monk stared at Lizzie's bookcase and pulled out a history book. She leafed through the pages until she found one that she approved.

'Here.' She pushed the book into Lizzie's face. 'Learn the names of all the kings and queens of England, and the dates they were on the throne. There'll be no lunch for you today because children who are impudent to their elders deserve no lunch. Fail in this task, and you'll have no supper either.'

A mean smile curved her lips. 'Spare the rod and spoil the child, that's my philosophy. And you've been spared too much. I don't know what your mother was thinking, but from what I've heard about her . . .'

It was all Lizzie could do not to spring at the woman and scratch that hard, pinched face. Miss Monk removed the temptation by removing herself.

For the next several hours Lizzie heard bustle and commotion as Miss Monk's things were carried up to the best guest bedroom and she barked out demands for the furniture to be rearranged, showing no concern for the strain she was putting on the staff.

Lizzie already knew most of the kings and queens, so had merely to sort out the early ones in her head . . . Aethelwulf, Aethelbald, Aethelbert . . . 'Well?' Miss Monk demanded, when she finally returned.

'I've been studying as you asked.'

'You've been studying as you asked, *Miss Monk*.'

Did the woman think she was some sort of queen herself? Queen of Briar Lodge?

She snatched the book. 'Henry the First?'

'King from 1100 to 1135.'

10

'Queen Anne?'

'1702 to 1714.'

Miss Monk looked peeved when all of her questions were answered correctly. Her expression turned cunning. 'Who became king in 1553?'

'Mary the First became *queen* in 1553.'

Frustrated, Miss Monk returned the history book to its shelf and brought out an atlas. 'Learn the names of every country in Europe.'

With that she returned to the door but paused and looked back. 'I'm making changes from tomorrow,' she warned, gloating. 'Lots of changes.'

It was obviously Miss Monk's way to torment her victims.

★ ★ ★

More chimes from the grandfather clock . . . Eight, nine, ten o'clock. It was rare for Papa and Miss Monk to retire for the night this early but, still determined to take no unnecessary chances, Lizzie took her coat off, bundled it under her bed and lay down, ready to feign sleep.

★ ★ ★

Lizzie had got her dinner that first night. She was secretly enraged to see Miss Monk sitting in Mama's place but kept her anger to herself, heading for her usual seat and deciding to say nothing unless invited.

Miss Monk served the soup into bowls, took a sip from her bowl and grimaced. 'Hmm.'

The soup was tasty in Lizzie's opinion. Cook's food was always tasty.

A joint of beef followed. Miss Monk poked it with a fork. 'I need to have words with the butcher,' she told Papa. 'According to the household accounts, he's charging for the best cuts but this meat is inferior. Either he's imposing on Cook or she's making money out of the arrangement.'

How dared this woman accuse Cook of stealing? Lizzie seethed quietly.

Betty brought in treacle tart for pudding. 'Stodgy,' Miss Monk declared, though it was delicious.

There was little conversation during the meal. The silence hung heavily and Lizzie felt herself to be very much in the way.

As soon as the meal was over Miss Monk rose to her feet. 'We shall leave your papa to his port,' she told Lizzie, who got up too.

Reaching the door, Miss Monk turned back to him. 'Elizabeth damaged a book today. I think it fitting that she goes straight to her room to reflect on her behaviour rather than enjoy the indulgence of tea.'

'Oh, certainly,' Papa said. 'I defer to your judgement on all things domestic, Susan.'

A triumphant glow lit Miss Monk's mean eyes. It occurred to Lizzie then that this woman had been testing Papa to see how far she could go with chastising his daughter. The answer seemed to be pretty far — which didn't bode well for the future.

Glad to be spared Miss Monk's company, Lizzie read a book until Betty came to see her into bed, a task Mama had always undertaken. 'You and Cook are my only friends now,' Lizzie said.

Betty looked troubled instead of flattered. 'Get some sleep, because heaven alone knows what the morning will bring.'

It brought a new schoolroom for Lizzie . . . a table and chair in the icy attic room that overlooked the front of the house. There was a second table and chair, presumably for Miss Monk but apparently just for show, as she showed no inclination to sit. Instead, she instructed Lizzie to copy out several pages from the history book and calculate a few basic sums. Having got Lizzie out of her way, she swept downstairs again, doubtless to upset Betty and Cook with more criticisms and orders.

Lizzie managed the work easily. Miss Monk looked disappointed but Lizzie was thrilled to be told that exercise was next on the agenda. A long tramp was just what her body needed. Miss Monk had other ideas. 'Six turns around the garden only. I won't have you letting your papa down by behaving like a hoyden.'

Lunch was taken with Miss Monk in the dining-room as Papa was at the glassworks that Mama had inherited. Lizzie had long known that her father had married her mother for money. 'Of course, it's *her* money as bought this house,' she'd heard Cook telling Betty. 'The glassworks belonged to *her* family too. I suppose he saw his chance when her parents died so quickly. They should have tied her money up tighter. Then he might have looked elsewhere for a wife.'

'I understand why he married her, but why did she marry him?' Betty had asked.

'There's them that turn two faces to the world and he's one of them. When he had her money in his sights I'm sure he made himself agreeable . . . charming, even . . . and she was too innocent to realise he had another side to him. Until it was too late.'

Lunch was a silent meal. 'May I play the piano

now?' Lizzie asked afterwards.

'Certainly not. I can't have you thumping the keys and bringing on one of my headaches.'

'I don't thump. Mama taught me well and we played together every day.' Music had given them joy, but realising it only made Miss Monk look even more determined to thwart Lizzie's wishes.

Within a week, the true purpose behind Miss Monk's constant complaints about Betty and Cook was revealed when she dismissed them both. Some of Betty's work was given to the regular cleaning lady, who had a sick husband at home and wouldn't cross Miss Monk in anything. Mrs Clegg arrived too.

* * *

... Nine, ten, eleven o'clock. Lizzie heard Mrs Clegg huffing and puffing as she made her way to her room. Not Cook's old attic room. Only a room on the middle floor was good enough for Miss Monk's crony.

A few minutes later, Papa and Miss Monk retired. Lizzie stayed in bed. Waiting.

* * *

Miss Monk met Mrs Clegg in the hall the day she arrived at Briar Lodge. 'It's good to see you, Hilda. Things are falling into place nicely.'

'I can see that.' Mrs Clegg looked around the hall with eyes that appeared to be putting a price on everything they saw. 'Yours at last, eh?'

'Of course, things aren't *quite* perfect.' Miss Monk nodded towards Lizzie who was standing inside the dining room where they'd just eaten breakfast.

The women exchanged looks which suggested they'd talked about her before, and not in flattering terms.

'Mrs Clegg is our new cook, Elizabeth,' Miss Monk said.

Lizzie came forward. 'I'm pleased to meet you, Mrs Clegg.'

'It's a pleasure, I'm sure.' The words were polite but the accompanying look was insolent.

'Go to the school room and learn the capital cities of Europe, Elizabeth,' Miss Monk instructed.

Lizzie walked upstairs but lingered on the landing. The women must have moved into the drawing-room because their voices grew fainter.

'So that's *her*,' Mrs Clegg said.

'A sly, scowling sort of a girl. Very different from that lily-livered fool of a mother. But if she thinks she's a match for me, she'll soon discover her mistake. I've spent the best years of my life waiting for this triumph, and I'm not going to let a chit of a girl spoil it for me.'

'Edward had to marry money, but it's a pity the wife lasted so long.'

'All those years I had to sit in that mean little house on Canal Street waiting for him to visit! But it's my turn now, and once I've broken the brat's spirit, she'll be no bother to me.'

'Trust you to have it all worked out, Susan.'

Lizzie had never suspected that her father was involved with another woman but perhaps it explained his lack of interest in Mama. Pondering the matter kept Lizzie awake after everyone had gone to bed that night, and when she heard the rustle of movement out on the landing, she got up and opened her door

15

the merest crack to see Miss Monk in her nightclothes, tapping on the door that led to Papa's room. The room he'd shared with Mama.

Papa opened it and Miss Monk began to move inside. But then she whirled around as though instinct had warned her she was being watched. Her harsh gaze pinned Lizzie to the spot. 'What are you doing?' she demanded.

Lizzie thought rapidly. 'I heard a noise. I thought it might be a burglar. Did you think it was a burglar?'

Miss Monk looked ready to shout at Lizzie for lying. Then her expression changed. Clearly, it had occurred to her that the lie could work to her advantage. 'That's why I'm here. I came to warn your father.'

She looked at him expectantly. For a moment he did nothing. Then he sighed and headed for the stairs as though to investigate.

'Go back to bed,' Miss Monk ordered Lizzie, who duly obliged.

A murmur of voices signalled Papa's return but Miss Monk swept away to her own room, her footsteps no longer furtive but brisk and angry.

The next day Betty's old iron bed was carried into the attic schoolroom. 'You'll be sleeping in here from now on,' Miss Monk announced. 'It makes sense for you to occupy one room instead of two.'

No, it didn't. She simply wanted the freedom to visit the room of a man who wasn't her husband.

Did Papa know how spartan Lizzie's accommodation was now? Perhaps it suited him not to ask about it.

There was more to come. One day Lizzie returned from her six turns around the garden to hear Miss Monk and her crony laughing in one of the bedrooms.

Papa's bedroom.

'Look at this, Sue. Does it suit me?' That was Mrs Clegg.

'You look grand, Hilda. I like these earrings. Real pearls. Good quality too.'

'Take 'em. You've earned 'em, biding your time all those years.'

Mama had looked exquisite in her pearl earrings. The thought of Miss Monk taking them was too much. Lizzie raced along to the room to see Miss Monk studying her reflection in the dressing-table mirror as she held the pearls to her ears while Mrs Clegg rifled through Mama's wardrobe. 'Why are you touching my mother's things?'

Miss Monk's eyes flashed annoyance. She didn't like being caught out. 'We're following your father's instructions to pack them away. What are *you* doing here?'

'They're my things now. Mama wanted me to have them.'

'Your mama isn't here,' Mrs Clegg said.

Miss Monk sent her friend a warning frown then turned back to Lizzie. 'It isn't for you to question your father's instructions.'

'It isn't for you to steal my mother's earrings.'

The hand lifted threateningly and would have struck at Lizzie's head had she not darted back. 'You were going to hit me!' An angry slap across the face was very different from a smack across the hand with a ruler.

'Did you think I was going to hit her, Hilda?'

'Not me.'

Miss Monk bent forward and hissed into Lizzie's face. 'If I take anything, it's only what I'm due. Not that I'm actually taking anything. But don't cross me again. Get upstairs this minute.'

Straightening, Miss Monk returned the earrings to the jewellery box and signalled to Mrs Clegg to pack up a dress she'd taken from the wardrobe.

Lizzie ran back upstairs. What vile people those women were. After a while they came up to the attic floor. They didn't enter Lizzie's schoolroom, but heaving and shuffling sounds indicated that they were putting Mama's things in the storage room.

At dinner that night Miss Monk turned to Papa and said, 'Mrs Clegg was helpful when I was packing up Grace's things. I take it you were satisfied with how we left the room?'

Papa sipped his wine and grunted an assent. Miss Monk didn't look at Lizzie but this conversation was obviously intended to make her squirm.

'It occurred to me that the most valuable jewellery — the pearl earrings, for example — shouldn't be left in an attic,' Miss Monk continued. 'I've put them on your desk in case you'd prefer to keep them at the bank.'

'I'll take them tomorrow,' Papa said.

Miss Monk stood and Lizzie followed her into the drawing-room. Instantly, Miss Monk turned with menace flashing in her eyes. 'I'm here to stay and it'll make life easier for both of us if you accept it sooner rather than later. The more you fight me, the more I'll make you suffer. Now go to your room and stay there.'

Soon Lizzie was eating her meals alone after she knocked over a glass of water at dinner, creating a small puddle that Miss Monk chose to treat as a major flood. 'It's such a pity to have your peace disturbed,' she told Papa. 'It would be no trouble for Elizabeth to

18

eat her dinner earlier.'

'Just as you like, Susan.'

Clearly, Papa wasn't going to defend his daughter and it became apparent that neither was anyone else after Mrs Chant, one of Witherton's wealthier residents, called. Lizzie stole down to the middle floor to listen in on the conversation. 'I haven't called before because I wanted to give you a chance to settle in,' Mrs Chant told Miss Monk. 'Now I feel it's time to welcome you to Witherton.'

'How kind.'

Miss Monk was putting on a show of friendliness as well as putting on airs, as though her upbringing had been more genteel than had actually been the case. She spoke the same way to Papa, though she dropped the pretence of refinement with Hilda Clegg.

Miss Monk must have pulled the bell because Mrs Clegg bustled out of the kitchen to be asked to provide tea. 'Yes, Miss Monk,' she said, and Lizzie imagined the cronies swapping secret winks.

'So very sad,' she heard Miss Monk say next. 'I feel for poor Elizabeth, but I believe it would be a mistake to let her throw herself into her grief completely. The child has a taste for drama and an inclination to consider herself a victim of all sorts of imaginary offences. It isn't the child's fault that she's been so indulged, of course, but it wouldn't be kind of me to let the mistakes of the past continue. Discipline and routine are what Elizabeth needs now if she's to take her proper place in the world. I consider it to be my duty to provide them.'

It was clever of Miss Monk to cast Lizzie as the sort of child who made up stories. No one would believe her now if she complained of Miss Monk's ill treatment.

Little by little Susan Monk was digging herself into the household while pushing Lizzie out, testing Edward Maudsley's tolerance along the way.

It comforted Lizzie to have Mama's things close by in the neighbouring attic, especially after she found two slender diaries among them in which Mama had written of her time at school. Reading those diaries gave Lizzie a chance to escape her woes temporarily. So did watching the fair-haired girl pass by on Amesbury Lane, presumably on her way to and from school. When she sang the girl's voice was sweet and silvery. Utterly charming.

But Lizzie needed to be more than just an observer of life. She grew ever more desperate for simple human contact, and in time she had an idea for making her life just a little more tolerable.

* * *

That plan had been risky in its way but it had succeeded and, as a result, Lizzie had survived a whole year since Mama's death, even finding moments of happiness. Circumstances had changed again, though.

Now Lizzie had another, infinitely more desperate plan in mind. Only one other person in the world knew of it, and that person was full of fear for her.

. . . Ten, eleven, twelve o'clock. Midnight. It was time.

2

For a moment the enormity of what she was doing paralysed Lizzie with terror. Then she reminded herself that she was thirteen years-old now — almost an adult — and deeply desperate. Pushing through the panic, she dressed quickly, thankful for the moonlight that bathed the room in a silvery glow.

Unwilling to risk the clatter of boots on bare floorboards, she moved on silent, stockinged feet to her door and listened. Hearing no one stirring, she opened it carefully then glided into the attic which was used for storage. Here she'd left a bag packed with what she considered to be essentials — a spare set of clothes, her toothbrush, her hairbrush and a selection of her mother's most precious things.

Choosing which of those things to take had been agonising, as she'd wanted to take them all. She'd settled on a trinket box, a sewing set with a silver thimble and silver scissors, a silver-framed photograph of Mama in evening dress before her marriage, another silver-framed photograph of Mama cradling Lizzie as a baby, and the diaries from Mama's time at school in London.

Retrieving the bag, Lizzie collected her boots then crept downstairs to the kitchen. There she took a hessian bag from a hook and filled it with bread, cheese, a pork pie, apples, cake and a bottle of lemonade. The house keys were kept in a dresser drawer. Lizzie used one of them to unlock the back door then lock it behind her after she'd stepped outside. Much as she

21

disliked the people inside the house, she wouldn't be responsible for letting a murderer walk in to slay them in their beds.

She tiptoed around the house to post the key through the letter box then made her way to the gateposts, keeping to the frosty lawn as much as possible to avoid crunching the gravel. Pausing, she looked back at the house. She'd had happy times there with her mother but those days were over and Lizzie needed to carve a future elsewhere — unless her departure changed the way her father felt about her and made him want her back. Unlikely, perhaps, but time would doubtless tell.

Lizzie saw not a single soul as she walked through Witherton. Houses were dark and all was quiet on this wintry night. She kept her footsteps soft and moved in shadow where possible, just in case anyone happened to look out of a window.

Witherton had a train station but concern over being recognised had made Lizzie decide to catch a train further down the line where no one would know her, finding her way by a map in a traveller's guide she'd taken from Papa's study a few nights previously.

Soon she reached the very edge of town and all that lay before her were fields. Dark, isolated fields. Lizzie swallowed and kept on walking, with only the sound of her own footsteps for company. Fear danced inside her and, knowing she had to keep it at bay, she thought back to that other plan of almost a year ago, the plan that had brought her moments of joy in dark times.

* * *

It started as a modest ambition to make contact. When the poor children passed the following morning, Lizzie waved from the window. She was disappointed when neither of them appeared to see her. Clearly a mere wave wasn't enough to attract their attention so when they returned in the afternoon she also called out, 'Hello!'

It still wasn't enough, and she didn't dare to shout louder in case Miss Monk or her crony came to investigate. Lizzie gave the matter more thought, and as she waited for the children to draw near the following afternoon, she had a message ready. It was tied to a stone with bright red ribbon to make it visible. *Look up at the window, it read. My name is Lizzie.*

She chose her moment then threw the message as far as she could. It landed in a bush. 'What was that?' the girl said.

'A bird?' the boy suggested, but the girl moved towards the bush.

Moments later she emerged again only to walk on. Lizzie thought she must have given up searching for the source of the noise but the girl reached the place where the sycamore had stood, looked up at Lizzie's window and waved.

She waved every time she passed after that. Sometimes her friend waved too. Lizzie was thrilled, but soon she wanted more.

★ ★ ★

Trudging along the road to Witherlee — the first hamlet she'd reach on her journey — a horrifying sight suddenly jolted Lizzie from her memories and stopped her in her tracks. Eyes were glowing in the

23

darkness ahead. Belatedly, she realised they belonged to a fox rather than a spectre. Sure enough, the creature loped away, and, after lingering a moment to let her heartbeat steady, Lizzie walked on.

She reached Witherlee and, having partly memorised the map, knew she'd walked two miles, leaving five miles to go before she reached the village of Witherwast. The town of Streeforth was three miles further on, making a total walk of ten miles.

From Streeforth she could catch a train, but Lizzie wanted to try to beg free rides on carts before she spent money on tickets. The closer she got to London, the cheaper the ticket would be. Or so she hoped, as she was by no means sure she had enough money to pay for such a long journey.

Ten miles hadn't looked far on the map. But the bags were heavy and Lizzie's pace was slow. She stopped to drink some lemonade then trudged on again, drifting back into her memories.

★ ★ ★

It hadn't taken long to think of a plan to see more of the fair-haired girl, but worry over the risks held Lizzie back for more than a week until the loneliness bit deep and she knew she had to take a chance. She threw another note out of the window: *I'm coming down to see you tomorrow.*

The plan involved stealing down to her old bedroom and climbing out of the window into the tree that grew nearby, then making her way down to the ground. In theory it was simple. In practice it wasn't simple at all. The distance to the ground was dizzying and the tree was too far away to step into with ease.

24

The thought of jumping into it was frightening but giving up was bleaker. Lizzie took a deep breath and launched herself at the tree, catching hold of a branch and clinging to it until she felt a little steadier. Studying the branches below her, she plotted a way down and finally stood at the bottom.

There was no cry of outrage from Miss Monk or anyone else to suggest that Lizzie had been seen, but she glanced up at the open window uneasily. If Miss Monk noticed it, she might assume the cleaning woman had opened it, but then she'd close it and how would Lizzie get back in? Deciding to worry about that later, Lizzie crouched low and ran towards Amesbury Lane, squeezing through the hedgerow as the children drew near. Now she was close to them she could see they were around her own age, though perhaps the girl was a little younger.

'Hello.' Lizzie stepped in front of them. 'I'm the girl from the attic. Lizzie Maudsley. What are your names?'

'Polly Meadows,' the girl said. The name suited her, as she was pretty and graceful.

'Davie Perkin.' Brown-haired and solid, he suited his name too.

'Have you been to school?' Lizzie asked.

Both children nodded.

'It must be nice going to school.'

'It must be nice living in a big house like that!' Davie flicked a hand towards Briar Lodge. It wasn't a mansion, but it was one of Witherton's better houses, a substantial Victorian property, set on three floors and surrounded by gardens. 'What does a rich girl want with the likes of us?'

Lizzie supposed he meant poor children. She'd been careful not to stare, but couldn't help noticing

25

that the sole of one of his boots was separating from the upper part, while his shirt was frayed and his jacket was too small. Polly's clothes looked equally worn. Her boots were too big, her dress was darned, and her shawl was an old sack.

None of that stopped Lizzie from wanting to befriend them. 'I just wanted to say hello.'

Davie still looked wary but Polly smiled and said, 'I'm glad.'

How pretty she was with that silvery hair and those soft blue eyes. She reminded Lizzie of Mama, though Mama's hair had been golden rather than silvery. Lizzie much preferred fairness to her own heavy chestnut hair and brown eyes, though Mama had insisted that they were lovely, adding that Lizzie's pink cheeks made her a picture of health and freshness too. Lizzie hadn't believed a word of it. Mama was always kind.

'May I walk with you?' Lizzie asked.

'I'd like that,' Polly told her.

'It's got to be a secret, though. You mustn't tell anyone.'

'Why not?' Davie looked more interested at the mention of a secret.

'I'm not allowed out alone.'

'Did you sneak out?'

'Climbed out. From that window there.' Lizzie pointed. 'I had to jump into the tree.'

Davie looked impressed. 'What will happen if you're caught?'

'I'll be punished.'

'How?'

'With a ruler. Or something worse, knowing Miss Monk.'

'Who's she?' Polly asked.

'The woman who's come to keep house for my father now my mother . . . isn't here.'

'My dad uses the flat of his hand on me,' Davie said. 'Once he used his belt.'

'I've never been beaten,' Polly said.

Davie smiled at her. 'I'm glad, Poll. Anyone who tried beating you would have me to answer to.'

Lizzie realised then that Davie was sweet on Polly.

They walked a little way along the lane. 'Did you have a nice time at school?' Lizzie asked.

Davie pulled a face but Polly smiled again. 'I did.'

Lizzie would have liked to ask more but she was nervous about staying out for more than a few minutes, especially as she wasn't sure she could get back in by climbing the tree.

She turned to Polly. 'I have to return home. I know I've only just met you, but can I ask for a favour?'

'What sort of favour?'

'Could you put some flowers on my mother's grave? Wild flowers will do. Like those.' Lizzie pointed to some primroses.

'I can do that.'

'Thank you. She's buried in —'

'I know where she's buried. She was a very pretty lady.'

Lizzie nodded. Her throat felt tight all of a sudden.

'I'll tell her you'd have taken the flowers yourself, if you could,' Polly added kindly.

'I'll try to come out another day,' Lizzie said. 'If you don't mind?'

'Of course we don't mind,' Polly assured her.

★ ★ ★

27

Lizzie was jolted from her memories again as clouds swept in and trapped the moonlight behind them. She looked into the blackness of the road ahead and apprehension inched along her spine like an icy finger.

Fighting it down, she continued onwards, burrowing back into her memories in search of solace.

★　★　★

The first time she'd climbed out, Lizzie had returned to find the window still open and, with some difficulty, had managed to climb back in. Worried that she might not be as lucky a second time, she tied a ribbon to the window's handle then pushed the window shut after her, using a ruler. Hopefully, it would open again when she pulled on the ribbon.

'Why don't you come to the den?' Polly asked that day.

'Den?' It sounded exciting.

'It isn't far.'

'Won't there be other children there?'

'Davie, will you go and look?' Polly smiled at him and he visibly softened before running down the lane, disappearing into trees then reappearing to beckon them forward.

The den was a small space surrounded by bushes and containing a fallen log on one side that made a convenient seat. In summer the bushes would be green. At this time their branches were bare.

'I like this place,' Lizzie declared.

She sat on the log and Polly sat beside her. Davie leant against a tree trunk.

'I haven't put the flowers on your mother's grave

28

yet, but I haven't forgotten,' Polly said.

Lizzie smiled gratefully. 'How was school?'

'A waste of time,' Davie said. 'I know how to read and write, and I can reckon numbers too, so I'd be more use helping my dad.'

'Helping to do what?'

'Look after Mr Anstey's cows.' Mr Anstey was a local farmer.

'I help at home too,' Polly said. 'My job is to look after the little ones. I've three younger sisters.'

'I have two,' Davie said.

'Do you have brothers or sisters, Lizzie?' Polly asked.

'Not one.'

'Your house must be quiet. You go to school, though?'

'I'm being educated at home.' Not that she was getting much of an education from Miss Monk. All Lizzie did was copy out of books, study the atlas and whizz through simple sums. 'School must be fun.'

'I like it,' Polly told her, 'but I'm leaving soon now I'm twelve. My favourite thing is singing.'

'I've heard you singing in the lane. You have a beautiful voice.'

Polly blushed. 'Do you like singing?'

'Yes, though my voice is deeper than yours. I like playing the piano too.' Sadness washed over Lizzie as she realised weeks had passed since she'd sung or played the piano. But she wasn't here to mope. 'Do you like music, Davie?'

'Can't say as I bother with it. I prefer to be outside.'

'I like reading, writing and sewing too,' Polly said. 'I'm not so good with numbers.'

'That's because you're a girl,' Davie told her.

'What difference does that make?' Lizzie demanded.

29

'There's men's work and there's women's work,' Davie offered.

It wasn't a good explanation as far as Lizzie was concerned, but she didn't want to argue.

Davie pushed away from the tree. 'I have to get home.'

'So have I.' Lizzie got to her feet. 'I'll meet you another day.'

★ ★ ★

An icy sleet began to fall as Lizzie reached Witherwast at last. She comforted herself with the thought that she only had three miles left to walk before she arrived at Streeforth. Only! Hauling her bags along had exhausted her already, and she had a blister on one of her heels.

She was tempted to find shelter and rest for a while, but she needed to reach Streeforth before the town stirred so no one would see her enter and wonder why a child was emerging from the countryside bedraggled and alone. She had no idea of the time but suspected several hours had passed since she'd set out from Briar Lodge.

Leaving Witherwast meant being sucked back into the isolation of fields, so Lizzie burrowed back into her memories.

★ ★ ★

'Thank you for putting flowers on my mother's grave,' she told Polly, the third time they met. Lizzie had seen the jar of primroses on Mama's grave when she'd gone to church with Papa and Miss Monk.

30

This time Davie didn't linger but Polly looked happy to stay for a while. 'I'll put different flowers in the jar when the primroses die.'

'Will you tell me about your family?'

Lizzie learnt that Polly's parents were Bill and Janet. Bill laboured on a farm and Janet kept house. Polly's sisters were Marjorie, Mary and Ruth.

'It must be wonderful to be part of a large family,' Lizzie said.

'It's annoying sometimes, but mostly I like it.' Polly paused then added, 'Is it lonely being the only child?'

'I wasn't lonely when I had Mama. Since then . . . But, I have you for a friend now, haven't I?'

'You have,' Polly said, smiling.

Lizzie met Polly often after that. Sometimes Davie joined them, looking hopeful of food to eat after the time Lizzie smuggled cake out of the house in return for the pheasant's feather Polly gave her as a gift. The sponge cake had been part of Lizzie's lunch but it was worth going without it to see the happy looks on her friends' faces.

'Do you have food like this every day?' Davie asked, chomping enthusiastically.

Lizzie had never given much thought to her meals. But as she answered questions about them, she saw his eyes widening. Polly's too. Lizzie already knew they were poor, but now she realised that at times they actually went hungry. It must be awful to go to bed with an empty stomach, but perhaps it was better to be hungry occasionally and live surrounded by love than to have a full stomach and no love at all.

Lizzie smuggled food out as often as she could after that first time, wrapping it in a handkerchief so she could carry it in her pocket. Polly gave more gifts too — flowers, pretty pebbles and, once, the blue egg-shell in which a robin had grown.

Most times Davie didn't stay long. Probably, he only came at all so he could spend time with his beloved Polly and eat Lizzie's food. Not that Lizzie minded. She liked having Polly to herself because it gave them a chance to talk about other things.

'What will you do when you leave school?' Lizzie asked once.

'Go into service, I suppose.'

'Is that what you want?'

'I don't much care. It'll only be for a few years until I'm sixteen or so. Then I'll be able to do what I really want.'

'Which is?'

'Marry Davie, of course, and settle down with a family of our own. What do you want for your future, Lizzie?'

'To earn a living so I can escape from Miss Monk. I've no idea what sort of job I'll be able to get, though.'

She'd thought of teaching, but perhaps she'd be considered unsuitable as her own education had ground to a virtual halt. Shop work was another possibility, but might mean serving people like Miss Monk.

At least Lizzie wasn't expected to work from the age of twelve. She had years in which to decide on a direction.

Sometimes Lizzie told Polly about her mother's diaries. 'It's like hearing about a princess in a fairy story,' Polly said.

There hadn't been a happy ever after following Mama's wedding but Lizzie still understood what Polly meant. To a girl like Polly who'd never been further from home than she could walk, Mama's life at a smart school in London must feel like a different world entirely.

'Maybe you'll get to see London one day,' Lizzie suggested.

Polly laughed. 'London isn't for girls like me.'

'Don't you want an adventure before you settle down?'

Polly only smiled as though Lizzie couldn't understand what life was like for poor girls.

'I'd like an adventure,' Lizzie said.

'I'm sure you'll have one, because you're different from me. You're brave and full of spirit. But what sort of adventure would you like?'

'I don't know yet,' Lizzie admitted, though perhaps leaving Briar Lodge would be an adventure in itself.

When the girls weren't talking, they were singing, keeping their voices quiet so no one would overhear. Polly taught Lizzie songs she'd learnt in school, including a song about a bee buzzing around a garden, which made Lizzie smile.

In return Lizzie taught Polly songs she'd learnt from Mama. One of Polly's favourites became 'Scarborough Fair'. Lizzie would begin with the melody: *Are you going to Scarborough Fair? Parsley, sage, rosemary and thyme . . .*

Then Polly would chime in with a descant.

'Greensleeves' became another favourite.

Even after Polly went into service in the house of a Miss Hepple, the girls continued to meet on Sundays and Wednesday afternoons when Polly only worked a half-day. Polly was cheerful about working and Lizzie wondered if she too might be happier if she could work and begin to save for a future away from Briar

Lodge. Papa and Miss Monk would be too concerned with appearances to allow it, though.

It still upset Lizzie to see Miss Monk in Mama's place, flaunting the finery that Papa must have bought her . . . pearl earrings that were bigger than Mama's, a gold bracelet, a fur coat, a hat from London . . . But Lizzie took pleasure in knowing she was leading a secret life behind Miss Monk's back.

Of course, she didn't know then that things were about to change. With hindsight Lizzie supposed she should have foreseen the announcement, because there was always a look in Miss Monk's eye that said, 'Just you wait!'

But it still came as a shock.

'It's a year since your mother died and that means the mourning period is over,' Miss Monk told her triumphantly, 'Your father and I are getting married.'

There'd be no end to her cruelty then, and the hand she'd once raised to strike Lizzie wouldn't be held back again.

'I can't stay,' Lizzie told Polly the next time they met.

'Where can you go? I don't think your father would like you to live in my little house even if we could fit you in. He'd think it a disgrace.'

'I wasn't hinting at you to take me in, but it's kind of you to think of me.' Lizzie paused then added, 'I may not have any family, but I do have a godmother.' Reading her mother's diaries had reminded her of that. Mama and Miss Penrose had met at school.

'I thought you hadn't heard from her in years?'

'I haven't. She had some sort of argument with my father. But she was fond of my mother once, and she might come to be fond of me.'

'Will you write to ask her for help?'

'Writing might make it too easy for her to say no.'

'You can't just turn up on her doorstep!'

Lizzie didn't answer.

Polly's eyes grew wide. 'Are you even sure you know where she lives?'

'I know she was living in London thirteen years ago.' Lizzie had found the address in Mama's address book.

'London is miles away.'

'Nearly two hundred miles.'

'She might have moved. Heavens, Lizzie, she might not even be alive. Promise you won't do anything stupid.'

'I can't promise anything, but I *can* say that I've no way of getting to London at the moment.' Lizzie had only four shillings and sixpence, left over from the time Mama had given her pocket money for small treats.

'The train would cost a lot of money, I suppose, but Miss Penrose might send you the fare if you write to her.'

That was true — *if* Miss Penrose agreed to give Lizzie a home. But it would be all too easy to refuse a plea from a girl she'd only seen as a baby. A baby, moreover, who had the hated Edward Maudsley as a father. Lizzie felt strongly that only by seeing Miss Penrose face to face would she have a chance of talking her round.

'She might even come to collect you,' Polly continued. 'That would be better than travelling all that distance on your own. You could be kidnapped or —'

'I don't think people are kidnapped off trains in broad daylight, Poll. Trains are full of passengers.'

'You might be kidnapped when you get off the train.'

'I won't be going on a train at all unless I can find some money.'

The problem vexed Lizzie for a week before she remembered the secret compartment in Mama's trinket box and found ten shillings in there. Had Mama left it there especially so her daughter could find it one day? Lizzie liked to think so. It meant she now had fourteen shillings and sixpence in total. Enough to get her to London? Lizzie could only hope so.

'I'm leaving tonight,' she told a worried Polly, when they met in the den the following afternoon.

'Lizzie, I'm scared for you.'

Lizzie was scared for herself. Terrified, in fact. But the idea of Miss Monk as her stepmother was unthinkable. 'I'm going to be careful.'

'You don't know who you might meet. Bad people. And don't tell me you'll avoid bad people because you won't know that they're bad. Not at first. What if you need help?'

'I'll ask a nice motherly lady. Or a policeman.'

Polly shook her head then burst out with, 'I'm going to miss you so much!'

There were tears in her eyes and Lizzie felt tears springing up in her eyes also. 'I'm going to miss you too, Poll. You've been the most amazing friend.'

'You'll write to tell me you're safe?'

'Of course. I'll try to send paper and stamps as well, so you can write back.'

Polly gave most of her wages to her family so hadn't the money for such things.

'You won't tell anyone where I've gone?' Lizzie pleaded. 'If my father finds out I'm going to my godmother's house, he might speak to her on the telephone, if she has one, and I won't have a chance to persuade her to take me in.'

'I'll keep your secret, Lizzie, even though I think you're mad.'

The girls hugged, then Lizzie sped off down the lane to spend her last few hours in Briar Lodge.

★ ★ ★

Now she was tired, wet and bitterly cold. Frightened too. When a face suddenly loomed out of the field next to her, she screamed, dropped her bags and began to flee, before her mind made sense of what she'd seen and she realised the face belonged to a cow. Halting, she turned around and walked back. 'Bad cow,' she called, but the pale ghost had wandered away.

She found the bag containing her clothes and mother's things easily, but the bag of food must have slipped into the ditch at the side of the road. Tentatively, she began to climb down, but it was a foolish endeavour in the darkness. Lizzie slipped and fell, landing with her feet in the water that had accumulated at the bottom of the ditch. Bitter coldness seeped into her stockings and Lizzie knew the rest of her must be covered in mud. She felt around for the bag but found only what felt like sharp, rusted metal. Her food and drink were lost to her.

When she finally reached Streeforth, Lizzie felt more tired than ever before. A cart rattling with milk churns came along the road. Unwilling to attract attention at this early hour, she ducked behind a wall until the cart had passed. It would probably be a while before the town was fully stirring. Until then Lizzie needed somewhere dry to hide.

Dawn was suffusing the sky with feeble grey light as she looked around the town. She saw a shed in the garden of a house, but the moment she set foot on the drive a dog began barking. The door to the church was locked.

Turning, she noticed a motor van parked in a nearby yard. The words *Kitson & Co, Deliveries Undertaken with Speed and Courtesy* were painted on the side. Lizzie tried the van's rear doors with no expectation of finding them unlocked. But unlocked they were.

There were boxes inside but plenty of space for Lizzie too. She climbed in, closed the door and made a hiding place behind one of the larger boxes. Seeing a pile of sacks, she fashioned them into a cushion and sat down on them. Hunger echoed inside her. There was sure to be a shop in the town that sold buns and bottled drinks but that would have to wait for another hour or two. In the meantime, she'd rest, get dry and warm up.

To pass the time she began to sing one of the songs Polly had taught her, but in her head rather than out loud.

The little bee knew what to do,
So twice around the garden flew,
Then slipped into his favourite bower,
To drink of nectar, flower by flower . . .

What came next? Lizzie couldn't remember. She was so very tired.

3

Lizzie surfaced from sleep to an awareness of movement. For a moment it felt rather pleasant, but then memories of her flight from home rushed in on her and, realising what had happened, she sat bolt upright. Like a fool she'd fallen asleep, and now someone was driving the van to goodness-knew-where.

Grabbing her bag, she scrambled to the van doors to take a peek outside and assess when it would be safe to leap out. The doors were locked.

Fighting down panic, Lizzie tried to console herself with the thought that the van might be taking her closer to London. On the other hand it might be returning her to Witherton, or heading in a different direction entirely.

Time passed. At least an hour. More time passed. Two hours? Three? Lizzie's hunger wore off but she was horribly thirsty.

At least she was warm now. Too warm actually, but that was preferable to feeling cold and wet.

The van stopped at last. Hearing the driver get out, Lizzie tensed. The doors were thrown open and light flooded in.

More footsteps approached. 'You found us then,' a man's voice said.

'I did.'

'Let's get everything unloaded, then you can come in for a cuppa. Wife's got the kettle on and, unless I'm much mistaken, she'll have a nice fruit-cake too.'

'I like the sound of that. Let's start with the big box.'

Oh, no. Lizzie looked around for another hiding place but it was too late. The men tugged the box towards the door and Lizzie was exposed. The driver sprang back in surprise. 'What on earth —'

Lizzie didn't stay to hear the rest of his words. She leapt out, broke into a run and kept running, heedless of the shouts of the men behind her. She was in a farmyard. Running through the open gate, her bag banging painfully against her side, she found herself on a country lane.

'Stop!' one of the men called.

Lizzie heard them come after her but kept going until she was sure she'd outrun them. Chest heaving, she slowed to a walk — until it occurred to her that the driver might come after her in the van. She climbed into a field and took care to stay hidden from the lane until she came to a crossroads.

A signpost pointed to four different places, none of which Lizzie recognised. She chose the road leading to the nearest place, but it proved only to be a small hamlet so she walked on, hot and bothered now despite the frosty day. She was hugely relieved when she saw the chimneys of what looked to be a town to her left. Crossing fields, she made towards it, a head-ache settling over her eyebrows. She was desperate for water.

Despite her thirst, Lizzie was careful to enter the town unobserved. Luckily, it was market day and the town was bustling with farmers selling vegetables, fruit and livestock. She spent precious pennies on a bottle of lemonade and a bun, and sat on a step to consume them. The drink was welcome but, oddly,

Lizzie's appetite had gone. She wrapped the bun in a handkerchief, hoping she'd fancy it once her headache had worn off.

Her next task was to find out where she was. Walking through the market, Lizzie came to a large building with a sign outside announcing that it was Stropley Town Hall. She'd never heard of Stropley, but she sat on another step and studied the traveller's guide. The headache made the words and lines swim in a sickly fashion, but she discovered that the town was to the north-west of Stafford, a place she knew was celebrated for its pottery.

Fortune had smiled on her in taking her closer to London. If only fortune would rid her of this headache and the hot sensation that was making her feel stifled and fretful.

There was a train station in Stafford. If Lizzie could get there, she could ask about the fare to London. The thought of walking there was daunting, but perhaps she could beg a ride from someone.

She wandered through the market again. One stall belonged to a butcher, a stout, middle-aged man who wore a straw hat and a white apron over his swollen belly. His business appeared to be doing well, perhaps because he constantly called out to passing housewives and housekeepers, 'You'll find no finer pork anywhere . . . Try these sausages and I promise you won't be disappointed . . . They say the way to a man's heart is through his stomach, and your man's heart will beat with joy at the taste of these chops . . . '

Lizzie felt queasy at the sight and smell of meat but there were two reasons she lingered near the stall. Firstly, Amos Bradley was a butcher in Stafford according to the sign above his stall. Secondly, he had a woman helping whom he called Ada and whom Lizzie took to be Mrs Bradley. Surely there was safety in a married couple?

She lingered at a distance as the afternoon wore on then sagged with relief when the stallholders began to pack up. Eventually Mr Bradley walked off, presumably to fetch his van or cart. Lizzie moved towards Mrs Bradley but at that moment an acquaintance of hers came up and stopped to chat. Frustrated, Lizzie stepped back again. The moment the acquaintance moved on, Lizzie hastened onwards. She wanted to appeal to Mrs Bradley's sympathies and had no trouble in bringing tears to her eyes. The lemonade had done little good and Lizzie felt dreadful.

'Excuse me, but I wonder if you might help me?' Lizzie said. 'I was supposed to get a ride back to Stafford on my cousin's cart but he left without me. It was my fault because he warned me he'd leave if I didn't meet him on time, but —'

'What's all this?' Amos Bradley returned, leading a horse and cart.

'Girl wants a ride to Stafford,' Ada told him.

'Does she indeed? Well, I see no reason for refusing a damsel in distress. Especially a pretty one.' He laughed heartily then reached out for Lizzie's bag and put it in the back of the cart.

Lizzie helped Amos and Ada to load the market stall boxes though her body ached all over. 'Up you get,' Amos said then, and surprised her by lifting her into the cart, his hands around her waist.

Lizzie didn't like being touched by a stranger. Not even a friendly one. She slid along the seat, hoping Ada would sit in the middle.

Amos dug in his pocket and brought out a handful

of coins. 'Next time, next week?' he said to Ada, handing the coins over.

'Right you are, Amos.' Ada pocketed the money
and walked away. Not Mrs Bradley after all.

Lizzie was aghast. 'Actually,' she began as Amos
climbed into the cart, 'I think my cousin is only hiding from me to teach me a lesson. I'd better go and
find him.'

'You should teach *him* a lesson by getting home
under your own steam.' With that Amos jiggled the
reins and the cart lurched forward.

'I might get into trouble. My cousin might get into
trouble too. Please, Mr Bradley, I need to get down.'

'Nonsense. Just sit back and enjoy the ride. Bates
may be an old horse but he's steady. He'll soon have
us in Stafford.'

Bates wasn't all that steady, because Amos urged
him into a fast trot as though to leave Stropley behind
as soon as possible. Lizzie's heartbeat quickened
again. She wasn't comfortable being alone with Amos
Bradley, especially when she noticed him watching
her with something hot and unpleasant in his eyes.

Deciding to jump down at the earliest opportunity,
Lizzie turned to locate her bag. She was dismayed to
see that Amos had placed it well out of her reach. She
couldn't run away without it, as it held her money as
well as her godmother's address, the traveller's guide
and the precious items that had belonged to Mama.
Lizzie would have to bide her time until they reached
Stafford.

'What's your name?' Amos asked.

'Jane,' Lizzie lied.

'A pretty name for a pretty girl.' He patted her knee
and kept it there until a motor car approached from

the opposite direction and required him to use both hands on the reins.

Lizzie seized the chance to ease further away until she was squashed against the wooden side of the cart.

'Whereabouts in Stafford to do you live?' he asked next.

'Rosalie Street,' Lizzie invented, 'but you can set me down on the High Street, if that's convenient?'

Amos smiled but didn't answer. Lizzie's unease grew.

Not having been to Stafford before, she had no idea if they were heading for the High Street as they made their way through the outskirts but her heart jumped when Amos drew Bates to a halt at the back of a terrace. 'Help me with the gates, Jane,' he said.

He got down but Lizzie hadn't time to jump into the back for her bag because he took her around the waist again and lifted her to the ground, rather more slowly than was necessary.

'Thank you for the lift. I can walk to the High Street,' Lizzie said.

'I'll take you there, but let's have a drink first. I'm parched and you must be too. I've a nice bottle of lemonade indoors.'

He steered her towards the gates as he spoke. Lizzie helped him to open them and saw that they led to a yard and what might be the back of a shop. 'I really have to —'

Lizzie's words were cut off as Amos picked her up and put her back on the cart. He got up beside her and drove Bates inside. Leaving her in the cart, he swung down to close the gates by himself. Lizzie scrambled for her bag, jumped down to the ground and ran to the gates. 'I can't stay. I'm expected at home.'

Amos had already closed one gate. Now he closed the other. 'A few minutes for a glass of lemonade won't hurt.'

Why was he bolting the gates if he only meant to delay her for a few minutes? Possibly he intended to let her out through the front door, but all of Lizzie's instincts were screaming at her to get away now because Amos Bradley wasn't a nice man.

She swung her bag and brought it crashing into him just below his overhanging belly. He let out a gasp and doubled over in pain.

Wasting not a single second, Lizzie climbed up onto a water trough and swung herself over the wall. She landed heavily on the cobbles, overbalancing onto her knees and hands, but she scrambled up again and fled, hearing curses on the other side of the gates followed by the sound of the bolts being opened. He was coming after her.

She reached the end of the row of shops and cut down another alley, hoping to find people at the end but finding herself opposite a copse of trees instead. Glancing over her shoulder, Lizzie saw Amos enter the alley, his face red and murderous. She ran into the copse, only to realise that running through undergrowth with twigs snapping and branches swishing would soon give her position away. She ducked behind a bush instead.

She trembled when she heard Amos crash into the copse. He came so close that she could hear him breathing and muttering irate curses. Halting nearby, he tried a different approach. 'Come out, Jane. I only want to help. You'll find yourself lost soon, and what will you do when it's dark?'

Lizzie huddled in silence.

Cursing, Amos walked deeper into the copse.

Lizzie backed out of the bush and stood. She tried to be careful but a twig snapped loudly. Amos turned, saw her and broke into a bulky run.

Lizzie ran in the opposite direction.

'Hey!' a voice called, but it wasn't Amos's voice.

To her horror, Lizzie realised Amos wasn't alone. He had an accomplice. A much younger, faster accomplice judging from the glance Lizzie gave him.

He was coming at her almost head-on. With Amos coming at her from behind she was in danger of being caught between them.

Lizzie veered off sideways, slipping when the ground dipped suddenly into a slope. She managed to stay on her feet but the men had to know the lie of the land better than she did. Suspecting she couldn't outrun them, she tried to outwit them instead by squeezing into another bush and throwing a large stone so it would crash through the undergrowth far ahead of her and make them think it was Lizzie doing the crashing.

The stone duly crashed and one man blundered past her. Amos, judging from the laboured breathing. Where was the younger man? Lizzie waited for a moment then eased tentatively from her hiding place.

Arms closed around her. 'Got you.'

4

Lizzie tried to swing the bag back at him but it was hopeless. 'I only want —' he began, but broke off, wincing, as she kicked his shin with her heel.

'I only want to know if that man is troubling you,' he said, releasing her.

'What?' Lizzie searched his face. Did he really have nothing to do with Amos, or was this just a trick to win her confidence?

'I saw him chasing after you. That's what it looked like anyway. If I'm wrong, I'm sorry.'

Lizzie whirled around as Amos came thundering towards them. 'There you are, Jane,' he said, eyeing the younger, taller man warily.

So the men really didn't know each other. Lizzie moved closer to the younger one, though perhaps he didn't yet qualify as a man, as he was no more than seventeen or eighteen.

His hair was the colour of bronze, his eyes green and surprisingly penetrating for someone so young. 'Why were you chasing this child?' he demanded of Amos, his voice hard.

'You misunderstand,' Amos blustered, red-faced. 'I was concerned for her. She ran off and I wanted to be sure she was safe.'

'She's certainly safe now, Mr —?'

'Bradley,' Lizzie supplied. 'Amos Bradley. He's a butcher.'

'I wonder if the police might be interested in a chat with you, Mr Bradley?'

Lizzie was horrified at the thought of the police. They'd discover she was a runaway and drag her back to Witherton. 'I don't think we need to bother the police,' she said quickly.

Her rescuer looked at her with those all-seeing green eyes but Lizzie's gaze shied away from them.

'The girl is right.' Amos was happier now. 'There's no need for the police because there's nothing amiss.'

'I hope not, Mr Bradley,' the younger man said. 'And I hope I won't see you chasing after any other young girls next time I happen to be passing. Which is often. At all hours of the day, and sometimes the evening too.'

Amos's happiness dimmed a little. 'I'll bid you good day, Jane.'

Lizzie didn't reply but stood with her rescuer as Amos walked away. 'Thank you,' she said then.

'I'm curious about why you didn't want to go to the police,' he answered. 'I'm curious about your name too. If I were a betting man, I'd wager it isn't Jane.'

'It was kind of you to help, but I won't keep you any longer.'

'You're not from these parts, are you?'

'No, but I'm staying with relatives nearby. They're expecting me home so —'

'They're expecting you to turn up looking like a scarecrow from one of my fields? With a muddy bag packed with what I'll hazard are all your worldly goods?'

'I'm a little untidy but —'

'I've never run away from home, but I know a runaway when I see one.'

'You're mistaken. It isn't your business anyway. Just because you helped me, it doesn't mean . . . It doesn't

48

mean . . . '

Something strange was happening. The world seemed to be moving dizzily. Lizzie took a step forward only to sway and put a hand to a tree trunk to steady herself. Instantly the young man moved closer. 'You're ill.'

'No,' Lizzie denied, but he put a hand to her forehead.

'You're burning up. You need a doctor.'

'No doctor!'

'Then it looks as though I have no choice but to abduct you, doesn't it?'

Lizzie wanted to run again but hadn't the strength. Overwhelmed by weakness, she slumped to the ground.

5

'She's waking up.' The voice was female. Young too.

Who was waking up? Surfacing from what felt like the bottom of the ocean, Lizzie realised the person must be her.

She opened her eyes, squinting against the light and feeling confused by the unfamiliar ceiling that sloped above her head. Then memories of Amos Bradley rushed in on her and she fought to sit up.

Firm hands pushed her down again. 'Steady on, young lady,' another voice said, this one male. 'You've had a fever and you need to rest.'

Lizzie turned to the speaker, a middle-aged, kindly-looking gentleman. 'Are you a doctor?'

'I am. Your cousins called me in.'

'My cousins?' Lizzie glanced around the room and saw a young woman.

This must be her rescuer's sister. She was a year or two older than him, her hair honey-coloured rather than bronze and her eyes a lighter shade of green, but there was still a resemblance. She sent Lizzie a conspiratorial look that prompted Lizzie to say, 'Yes, of course.'

'My prescription is rest. Plenty of it. I don't wish to see a relapse. Goodbye, Jane.'

Jane? Oh, yes. 'Thank you, doctor.'

The young woman accompanied him out of the room. Lizzie heard their feet on what sounded like the uncovered treads of a staircase. Alone, she took in more details of her surroundings. She was in a small room tucked into the eaves of what she supposed must be a cottage. There was a single casement window with a climbing plant growing around the outside.

In addition to the narrow bed in which Lizzie lay, there was a second bed, a chest of drawers, a washstand and a tall cupboard. All was clean and neat, but Lizzie could see that this was a modest household. The curtains were faded, the sheets had been mended carefully and the only fripperies were Mother Nature's bounty — fir cones, a jug of winter greenery, a piece of wood whittled into the shape of a hedgehog . . .

Lizzie's conscience suddenly stirred as she realised someone must have paid the doctor's fee on her behalf. She hoped she had enough money to repay it, though heaven knew if it would also cover her train fare to London.

Footsteps sounded on the stairs again. Brisk and too heavy to be female. A tap on the door followed then her rescuer appeared. 'Welcome back to the world,' he said, sitting in the chair the doctor had vacated and stretching his long, rangy legs.

Now she was no longer fleeing from Amos Bradley, Lizzie noticed that her rescuer's voice was low and pleasant. It had dry humour in its depths that matched the glint in his eyes, as though he enjoyed life but also liked to tease it.

There was something fresh, outdoorsy and strong about him that suggested he worked hard at some sort of manual labour, though probably for little money. Rolled to the elbows despite the January weather, his shirt sleeves showed darns. There was no collar on his shirt and his trousers were almost worn through at the knees.

'Do you remember what happened?' he asked.

'I think so.' Lizzie's throat was dry.

He took a glass of water from the chest of drawers and passed it to her.

'Thank you.' Lizzie drank some down then asked, 'Where have you brought me?'

'I didn't know where else to take you, so I brought you home to be looked after while we work out what comes next.'

'Your family . . .'

' . . . Is glad to help because it's made up of good people. All of my brothers and sisters are good people.'

She wondered about his parents.

'We lost our father a year ago and our mother two years before,' he explained, as though he'd read the question in her face. 'Now there's just the five of us.'

So many!

'We're the Warrens. Edith is the eldest. She's been nursing you. I'm Matthew — Matt — next in line to Edith. Then there's Joe, Mikey and Molly. They're our real names, by the way.'

The green eyes gleamed again and she remembered that he hadn't believed her name was Jane. Lizzie blushed but, despite being grateful for the care she was receiving, she was still wary of sharing her true identity.

Matt didn't push her to reveal it.

'I hope I'm not in the way,' Lizzie said, concerned that she was occupying one of his sister's beds. She was wearing one of their nightdresses too.

'You're welcome here,' he said, 'but does anyone need to know where you are? We don't have a telephone, but I can go into the village to make a call or post a letter.'

Lizzie shook her head, lowering her gaze to the cotton counterpane and expecting him to insist that there must be someone who had an interest in her whereabouts.

She sensed him watching her, but then he got to his feet. 'Edith will be up with some broth and I need to get back to work. We're farmers. Arable, mostly. That means we grow crops. We have a few animals, though. A horse to pull the plough. A pony. Two cows for milk, and several dozen chickens for eggs. We have house animals too. A dog and a cat.'

Lizzie looked up, which had probably been his intention. 'It sounds wonderful.'

'It is, though it's also hard work. Try not to fret.' He left her with a smile that told her he understood that not fretting would be easier said than done.

Edith came up soon afterwards carrying a tray. 'You must be hungry.'

'I am,' Lizzie admitted. 'I haven't eaten in hours.'

'At least twenty-four of them,' Edith said. 'It was yesterday when Matt brought you here.'

Goodness!

Lizzie's absence from Briar Lodge would have been discovered long ago. Was it too much to hope that her father might actually be concerned for her? Probably. It was more likely that he and Miss Monk were simply furious at her for running away and making them look bad. Appearances were important to Edward Maudsley.

What were they doing about it, though? Would they think of Margaret Penrose and get to her before Lizzie had a chance to plead her case?

'Eat,' Edith urged. 'You need to build your strength before you tackle whatever's worrying you.'

53

'I'm sorry I'm being a burden.'

'Hardly a burden.'What a kind young woman Edith was.

'Whose bed is this?'

'My sister, Molly's, but she's perfectly happy sharing my bed. She often creeps in with me anyway.'

'This is your nightdress?'

Edith nodded. 'We didn't like to look to see if there was one in your bag. Not without your permission.'

Honourable, as well as kind. 'The doctor's fee,' Lizzie began.

'We don't begrudge a penny.'

'I can repay you.'

'You need to talk to Matt about that, but for now I know he wants you to concentrate on getting stronger. I'll return for the tray later.'

Lizzie did need to get stronger. Clearer-minded too.

The broth was delicious and Lizzie finished all of it along with the bread, cheese and apple Edith had provided. She placed the tray on the chest of drawers and lay back against the pillows to think.

She didn't intend to sleep but she slept anyway, waking to find that Edith must have crept in to remove the tray. Fed and rested, Lizzie tried again to think of a solution to the problem of getting to London and persuading Miss Penrose to take her in, but fear licked her stomach like a flame. It was frustrating to think that even now Edward Maudsley might be in contact with her godmother and insisting that, if Lizzie turned up, she should be sent straight home. Not because he wanted her, but because people might talk. The slight hope that he might actually want her back resurfaced, but it still felt unlikely.

Lizzie became aware of whispers outside her door. 'What can you hear?' a girl's voice said.

'Nothing. Stop talking and I might —'

'You two! Downstairs. Now!'

That was Matt's voice. Not shouting, but forceful enough to make the eavesdroppers gasp and scurry back downstairs, still whispering and giggling.

Firmer footsteps sounded and, after a rap on the door, Matt entered, bringing fresh air and energy with him. 'You're looking better,' he observed.

'I'm feeling better, thanks to you and your sister.'

'Edith will be making supper in a while. Would you prefer yours on a tray or would you like to come downstairs?'

'I'd like to come down, if I won't be in the way?'

Matt smiled. 'You'll be doing Edith and me a favour. The children are curious, and if they see you for themselves, they might stop nagging us with questions.'

Matt returned with Edith when supper was ready. Lizzie was glad of their help because she wobbled when she got out of bed and might never have got down the stairs if Matt hadn't scooped her up and carried her, depositing her in a chair at a large farmhouse table. Wide eyes stared at her and Matt made the introductions as Edith placed a hand-knitted blanket around Lizzie's shoulders.

'Joe, Mikey and Molly.'

They all smiled a welcome. A year or two older than Lizzie, Joe was tall and rangy like Matt, though with Edith's colouring. Mikey was younger — eleven or twelve — with darker hair and an air of thoughtfulness, even as he smiled. Molly was the baby of the family, a pretty bundle of mischief of around five.

'Thank you for letting me stay,' Lizzie said.

'We're glad you're out of bed because now we can see what you look like,' Molly said. 'You're pretty.'

Lizzie laughed. 'Not really,' she said. 'But it's kind of you to say so.'

Edith brought two serving bowls to the table. One held potatoes. The other held some sort of stew that smelt delicious. As the guest Lizzie was offered the bowls first but was careful to take only modest portions, as this family was clearly far from rich. The kitchen was homely, though, with a warm fire, colourful hand-made rugs, flowered cushions and more of Mother Nature's bounty in the form of fir cones, dried flowers and a ceiling rack with herbs hanging from it in bunches.

'I hear you have animals,' Lizzie said, and the children launched into a clamorous account of their names and personalities.

The dog, Crocker, was a black and white collie who lay curled up in front of the fire. The cat, Sally, lay beside him, purring. The plough horse was Herbert, the pony was Prince, and the cows were Mabel and Matilda. There were too many chickens for Lizzie to remember all of their names.

'Do you have any animals?' Mikey asked, then looked guiltily at Matt as though remembering he'd been told to ask Lizzie no questions.

'I'd have liked a dog, but it wasn't to be,' Lizzie said. Papa hadn't allowed it, which was probably just as well, as it would have been difficult to run away with a dog and she couldn't have left it to the unkindness of Miss Monk.

Apple pie and custard followed the stew. 'This is a delicious dinner,' Lizzie declared.

'Edith's a great cook,' Matt said, and the others

nodded enthusiastically.

There were no awkward silences because the family was full of chatter and affection. It made Lizzie all too aware of what she'd missed in having no brothers and sisters, but she was glad to be here now.

When the meal was over, all the Warrens went about the business of clearing up. Lizzie made to get up too, not wanting to leave the work to others.

'Tonight you should rest,' Matt told her.

Did that mean she could help to clear up another time because he expected her to stay for at least a day longer? Lizzie's anxiety must have shown on her face because he added, 'Tomorrow's soon enough for talking too.'

He unhooked a jacket from a row of pegs near the door and went out, Joe and Mikey following. 'There's always work to be done on a farm,' Edith explained.

She had a big pot of tea waiting when they returned. Everyone received a cup except for Molly, who had milk. 'Are you going to play tonight?' Molly asked Matt. She turned to Lizzie, adding proudly, 'Matt can play the piano.'

'Maybe Jane needs an early night,' he said.

'I'd like to hear you play,' Lizzie told him.

'All right. Just for a little while.'

Matt helped Lizzie into another room which the family called the parlour. There was a small sofa, some chairs and a piano. Lizzie was steered to the sofa then Matt settled at the piano, running his fingers over the keys with unexpected assurance. 'Any requests?' he asked, as the others gathered around him.

''Lazy Maisie'!' Molly cried.

'What does Jane think?'

''Lazy Maisie' sounds fun,' Lizzie said, earning a

57

beaming smile from Molly.

Matt began to play, and to sing too.

There once was a donkey named Maisie,
Whose farmer thought she was lazy . . .

His singing voice was low and pleasant, like his speaking voice. When he reached the chorus all the Warrens joined in.

Maisie, Maisie, get up off that bed,
Lazy Maisie, that's what the farmer said,
You can't sleep all day,
Just snoozing in the hay,
There's no time for you to tarry,
When these baskets you must carry.

Lizzie applauded when the song finished.

'Would you like 'The Rustling Grasses', Edith?' Matt asked then.

'Yes, please.'

This song was soft and dreamy. Perfect for Matt's voice.

Mikey's choice was a song about a river. Matt sang alone but with the others swaying beside him. Joe wanted a jolly farming song, and the chorus had all of the Warrens singing again.

Hey, ho, and drink your ale down!

It was impossible to picture Mama singing, *Hey, ho, and drink your ale down* but Lizzie was still reminded of the happy times she'd spent singing with Mama. With Polly too. Her throat tightened on a wave of emotion just as Matt turned to her. She guessed he was going to ask if she had a request, but he stared for

58

a moment then said, 'That's enough for tonight.'

No one argued. Matt had a quiet air of authority.

'That was terrific,' Lizzie said, not wanting him to think she hadn't taken pleasure in his playing.

'Do you play?' he asked, as he helped her back into the kitchen and placed her in one of the armchairs beside the hearth.

'I did. Not for a long time, though.'

'A little rustiness among friends doesn't matter. Perhaps you'll play for us tomorrow? If you're well enough.'

'I'd like that. Don't expect me to be as good as you, though. Where did you learn to play so well?'

'Our mother taught me.'

Edith protested at that. 'Our mother knew only a few simple tunes. Mostly Matt taught himself. By ear too, as our mother never learnt to read music.'

How talented Matt was to have taught himself simply by listening. Clearly, he felt the music deeply.

'I can't read music either,' he said, as though praise embarrassed him, then he changed the subject. 'Up to bed, you younger ones.'

Mikey and Molly pouted but didn't argue, and Lizzie was struck again by the love and respect that existed in this small farmhouse. It gave her a warm feeling all over.

Edith laid the table for the morning's breakfast while Joe polished shoes and Matt went out for a final circuit of the farm. They were all early to bed and Lizzie was glad, because tiredness was overwhelming her.

Molly was asleep when Lizzie and Edith entered the girls' bedroom. It felt strange to share a room but Molly's snuffles were comforting and it was good to have Edith close by. Not that Lizzie had long to reflect on this stage in her fortunes, as exhaustion soon swept her into sleep.

6

Lizzie was the last to wake in the morning but was determined that none of the Warrens should have to take time out of their busy lives to wait on her like a princess. Alone in the room, she noticed that her bag had been placed on the chair with her clothes — now laundered — folded neatly on top.

Hot water, soap and a towel had been left out for her, so Lizzie washed and dressed. She paused for a moment to look out of the window, seeing that the bedroom overlooked the front of the farmhouse with a lane beyond the pretty garden and gently-rolling fields stretching into the distance. Idyllic.

Downstairs, Edith was cooking breakfast. Only Matt was absent. Doubtless he'd been hard at work for hours. The other Warrens all smiled and Edith invited Lizzie to sit. 'You've more colour in your cheeks today, but you needn't have come down. I was planning to bring you a tray.'

'I'm well enough to help out now.'

Edith looked sceptical. 'We'll see about that.'

Joe went to the kitchen door to call Matt in. He arrived a moment later, washing at the sink then sitting at the table. There were scrambled eggs and bacon but once again Lizzie took only modest portions.

It was Saturday so there was no school for Molly and Mikey but all of the Warrens still helped out, whether sweeping floors, collecting eggs, feeding livestock or ploughing a field. Edith planned on baking.

'I've never baked before, but I'll gladly help,' Lizzie

offered.

'You still need to rest.'

'Edith's right,' Matt agreed. 'If you push yourself too quickly, you'll be ill again. Rest this morning and I'll take you for a look around the farm this afternoon.'

It would give her the chance to talk about money and what needed to happen next. No one seemed to think that Lizzie should leave today and for that she was grateful. Much as she disliked being a burden, she was by no means fully recovered.

In fact she dozed off in one of the armchairs by the fire as she stroked Sally the tortoiseshell cat and watched Edith go about her business, waking only when the others came in for lunch. They brought wafts of coldness with them but the kitchen soon warmed up again, the air fragrant with Edith's bread, pastry and cake.

Edith made tea then cut slices of still-warm bread, spreading them with butter. 'This is the nicest bread I've ever tasted,' Lizzie said.

There was soup too — very tasty — followed by stewed pears and custard.

'Are you ready for a tour of the farm?' Matt asked, after they'd eaten.

'I am,' Lizzie said, though the thought of talking about her situation made her nervous.

Running away had been the only option in Lizzie's eyes, but Matt might feel differently. He valued his own family highly and perhaps that would blind him to the fact that her family was different, her father being cold while Miss Monk was cruel.

Lizzie put on her coat and scarf — sponged clean by Edith — then followed Matt outside. The kitchen door opened onto a yard and Lizzie was pleasantly surprised to see that, not only was it clean despite the muds of winter, it was also made charming by tubs of greenery. Edith's work, Lizzie guessed, imagining that the tubs would be filled with flowers in spring and summer.

'This place is small as farms go,' Matt told her, 'but we consider ourselves lucky to own it. We're not yet lucky enough to afford a tractor or other modern equipment, but we manage with a lot of hard work.'

There was a barn across the yard with what looked to be stables and outhouses to Lizzie's left. To her right was a chicken coop. Matt led her in that direction and she saw that the hens were allowed to wander at will during the daytime. One of them stared at her before continuing its stilt-legged walk to who-knew-where. Behind the chicken coop the land opened into an orchard that Lizzie guessed must front onto the lane she'd seen from her window.

'We grow apples, pears, cherries and plums,' Matt told her. 'We sell some and keep the rest. Edith is amazing at storing, bottling and jam making.'

Next to the orchard and behind the barn were two large growing beds. 'This is where we grow delicate foods like lettuces and raspberries,' Matt said. 'Also beans and peas.'

Canes were already in place for the climbing plants to use.

'These are the main fields.' Matt's arm swept round to take in the rest of the land. 'We grow oats, barley and wheat, but we don't have the acreage for a lot of them so we concentrate on root vegetables like potatoes, carrots and turnips.'

Joe and Mikey were mending a distant fence. 'We

do as much maintenance in winter as possible,' Matt explained. 'We're still growing winter crops but even so there isn't quite as much work as in the rest of the year, so we have to make the most of our time.'

'It all looks very tidy,' Lizzie observed.

'We do our best.'

They walked along the back of the barn and Lizzie saw that, behind the stables and outbuildings she'd seen from the yard, there were two paddocks. One was occupied by a strong-looking horse and a small pony that she guessed was the children's pet. 'Hector and Prince,' Matt told her.

The other held the cows. 'Mabel and Matilda.'

It was cold and Lizzie could see that Matt was keeping a careful eye on her. He took her back to the yard and into the barn where he made two seats from bales of hay. 'Warm enough?'

Lizzie nodded, but nerves were tight inside her. 'I have money to pay you back for the doctor,' she began.

'We'll see.'

Clearly, Matt wasn't prepared to agree to anything until he'd heard more about the circumstances that had led her into Amos Bradley's clutches.

'My name isn't Jane, as you've already guessed. It's Lizzie M —' A thought struck her and she changed direction. 'Lizzie Kellaway,' she said. 'My father's name is Maudsley, but I don't want to bear his name anymore. I want to bear my mother's maiden name.'

'I'm sure you have your reasons.'

Lizzie told him everything that had happened.

'I'm sorry,' he said, watching as she sat breathless and upset from the telling.

But would he help her?

'This Miss Penrose,' he said. 'Your mother lost

touch with her years ago?'

'Just after I was christened.'

'You're not sure you have her current address, and you've no idea if she'll welcome you?'

Lizzie winced. He made her idea of throwing herself on her godmother's mercy sound ludicrous, and he was probably right. Even so . . . 'She's my only chance of escape,' Lizzie pleaded.

'What if you can't find her? Or she refuses to help?'

Lizzie had no answer.

'I can't let you go to London on that basis,' Matt said firmly.

'But —'

'Alone, I mean. I'm coming with you.'

'What about the farm and your family?'

'They'll manage without me for one day.'

There was the train fare to think about too, though. 'I only have fourteen shillings and a few coppers. I have to pay the doctor's fee out of it so —'

'We have money put by for emergencies,' Matt said. 'I think this qualifies as one.'

'You can't spend your family's money on me!'

'Either I take you to London or I return you to your father and that awful woman he plans to marry.'

Lizzie was silenced. 'Perhaps my godmother will repay the expenses,' she suggested then.

'Let's wait and see. When would you like to set off? Certainly not before you're well again. You won't make a good impression if you arrive weak and emotional. Would Friday suit?'

Every day that passed gave her father another chance to reach Miss Penrose first, but what Matt said made sense. Lizzie needed to be strong in order to make her plea for help as persuasive as possible.

'Friday will be perfect, as long as I'm not in the way here?'

'We're glad to have you.'

Lizzie could only hope that was true. 'Thank you,' she said. 'You're all so kind.' And it was such a relief to know that Matt would accompany her to London.

Despite her uncertain future, Lizzie enjoyed the days that followed. Recovering quickly, she was able to help a little, learning to collect warm eggs, wash laundry, feed the animals and especially, to cook.

Bread, pies, cakes and stews . . . Edith showed Lizzie how to make all of them, and took her into the front garden to see the herbs she used to add flavour to her stews and roasts. It was a pretty garden, though the only flowers in bloom at this time of year were snowdrops and primroses. 'It's full of colour in the summer,' Edith told her.

'Full of bees too?' Lizzie guessed, pointing to a sign that peeped out from between the lavender bushes near the front door. It was a wooden sign with *Bee Corner* carved into it. A lovely name for a farm.

'The bees and butterflies love this garden.'

Lizzie liked all of the Warrens. Admired them too. They pulled together as a family, but each of them valued the personalities and talents of the others — Edith's cooking, Matt's music, Joe's farming skills and Mikey's love of books. They were all proud of how well Mikey was doing at school and keen for him to stay on until he reached fourteen, though Edith, Matt and Joe had worked since the age of twelve. It was too soon to know where Molly's talents lay, but she was loved by all of them.

Two particular times of day became Lizzie's favourites. The first was her daily walk with Matt. Lizzie had always admired nature but Matt taught her to see beauty in everything — the patterns of frost on windows, the delicate veins of leaves left skeletal by winter, a kestrel hovering above fields . . .

Sometimes he probed her with questions. At other times he teased her. Often he was content to let quietness settle between them. A comfortable quietness.

Lizzie knew what it was to be loved. Mama had adored her and Polly loved her too. But Lizzie had never met anyone who made her feel quite so safe and quite as understood as Matt. Was this what it was like to have a brother who cared for you despite your flaws? Who'd always look out for you? Lucky, lucky Warrens! Matt's kindness warmed her inside even when her body shivered from the January chill.

Her second favourite time was evening when they gathered around the piano to play and sing. Lizzie played sometimes but mostly Matt did, never ceasing to amaze her with his natural feel for the music.

In turn, he encouraged her to sing. 'You have the perfect voice for my ballads,' he told her.

Probably, he was just being kind, but the praise gladdened her anyway.

'Are you happy to be a farmer?' Lizzie asked him on one of their walks. 'It's just that you obviously love music.'

'Farming puts food on the table for all the family.'

He was sacrificing his dreams for the sake of his brothers and sisters. Doing it uncomplainingly, too. Matt's selflessness made Lizzie question her own behaviour in seeking to impose herself on her godmother — a virtual stranger — but the thought of returning to Witherton filled her with dread.

'What do you know about your godmother?' he

asked one day.

'She didn't like my father.'

'So far, she sounds like a sensible woman,' Matt said, smiling. 'What else?'

Lizzie fetched her mother's diaries, explained how Mama's shyness had made her nervous of going to a boarding school in London at the age of sixteen, then read out loud from some of the entries.

'*There are twenty girls in the Academy and I share a bedroom with three others. A girl called Margaret Penrose is our bedroom monitor. She's an upright, efficient and rather brusque sort of person, and I'm a little in awe of her.* That's the first mention of my godmother.'

'Go on.'

Lizzie found the next mention. '*I'm still a little afraid of Margaret but I think it's only her efficient manner that makes her intimidating.*'

'Encouraging,' Matt said.

Lizzie turned the page and read more. '*Margaret invited me to learn a duet with her this evening. It was such an honour as she's so proficient on the piano. My playing was nowhere near as good as hers but she told me I'd done well and I couldn't stop smiling.* Most of the other entries are about the music they played together. My godmother took a lot of trouble with my mother and cared enough about her to travel to Witherton for my christening.'

'So she's crusty on the outside but soft on the inside, like one of Edith's loaves,' Matt suggested.

Lizzie could only hope so, but much might have changed over the last thirteen years.

It gave Lizzie pain to part from the Warrens when Friday came. Hugging Edith, Joe and the children, she was touched by how generously they hugged her back and told her they'd miss her. 'You must come and stay again,' Edith said. 'We can meet you off the train.'

The others nodded enthusiastically.

'I'd love to come back and the sooner the better,' Lizzie said. 'In the meantime, I'll write to let you know how I'm getting on.'

She patted the pocket of her dress. It was here that she'd tucked the envelope Matt had given her with the address of the farm inside. Lizzie hoped to be able to send money for the doctor's fee and Matt's train fare, as well as a report on her progress.

Joe drove them to the station in the cart. It was a long journey of an hour or so but Matt kept her entertained with funny stories, probably because he knew she was feeling sick with nerves over what might await her in London, particularly if her father had reached Miss Penrose before her.

Matt refused to let her pay when he bought their train tickets though she hated draining the family of money they needed for tools or seeds or boots. Settling on the train, they ate some of the hard-boiled eggs, pork pie, apples and cake Edith had packed for them, though Lizzie made sure she left plenty for Matt's journey home.

He kept her entertained again as the train chugged southwards but eventually said, 'This is it, I think. The outskirts of London.'

7

Lizzie had expected the capital city to be bigger and busier than Witherton, but she was still taken aback by just how bustling a place it was. The station was loud with shouts, whistles and hisses of steam. Outside, the street was packed with vehicles of every description — omnibuses, vans, carts, motor cars and bicycles — while people rushed here, there and everywhere.

'Rather different from home,' Matt commented, but he didn't look intimidated.

Calmly, he enquired of a newspaper seller about the best way to get to Highbury where Margaret Penrose lived — or had lived, all those years ago. Then he guided Lizzie onto an omnibus. She would have liked to climb the spiral staircase to the top deck but it had begun to rain so they sat inside with Lizzie peering out of the window in the hope of seeing some of London's landmarks. Buckingham Palace, Hyde Park, the Houses of Parliament, St Paul's cathedral . . .

Unfortunately, their route took in none of them, but she'd have plenty of time to get to see London properly, if she settled here. *If.* Lizzie's stomach cramped with tension.

To take her mind off it, she looked out at the advertisements on billboards and on the sides of buses. Anderson's Waterproofs, Fry's Cocoa, Borwick's Baking Powder, Paton's Knitting Wool, Rexine Leather Cloths, Poulton & Noel's Potted Meats, Valet Autostrop Safety Razors . . .

In time they left the bus to walk the rest of the way. Nothing could distract Lizzie from her anxiety now they were so close to their destination. She touched a hand to her middle, wondering if she might disgrace herself by being sick.

'Take courage,' Matt said, but at that moment a passing van drove into a large puddle and threw up a tidal wave of water that drenched them both from head to toe.

They stared at each other in shock, then Matt laughed. 'That was unlucky, but it means you're due some good luck now.'

Lizzie wished she could believe that luck took turns like that. It dismayed her to know she was going to arrive at her godmother's house looking like a sodden urchin from the slums.

Matt finally paused outside a narrow, terraced house that was four storeys high and made from red bricks that appeared to be crumbling with age. An iron gate led into a tiny front garden with two stone steps at the end rising to a green-painted front door. Panels of stained glass were set into its upper half. In between them were a brass door knocker and numbers announcing that this was indeed 11 Marchmont Row.

Matt used the knocker to rap loudly on the door then turned to Lizzie. 'Do you want me to do the talking or would you prefer to plead your own case?'

'I think I should plead my case,' Lizzie said, though her heart beat *rat-a-tat-tat* as she looked through the glass panels and saw someone approaching.

The door was opened by a woman who was tall and thin like the house, but much more severe. She had greying hair swept back off her face and pinned to her head with no apparent thought for softening the effect of a hawk-like nose, downturned mouth and sharp grey eyes. Her blouse and cardigan were no-nonsense grey. So was the skirt that reached to the floor.

If this was Miss Penrose, she was only a year or two older than Mama, so had to be less than forty, but she looked much older. And distinctly unwelcoming. 'Yes?' she demanded.

Oh, heavens. Mama had been in awe of Margaret Penrose when they'd first met, but Lizzie still hadn't expected quite such a terrifying personage as this. But perhaps this woman was someone else and Margaret Penrose had mellowed into a cosy creature who was somewhere inside the house? 'Miss Penrose?' Lizzie enquired, hoping the answer would be no. 'Miss Margaret Penrose?'

'What of it?'

Lizzie's hopes were crushed. She tried to draw comfort from the reflection that her father couldn't have been in touch or Miss Penrose would surely have guessed her identity. Even so, it was hard to believe that being the first to talk to her would make any difference to this frosty woman.

Lizzie reminded herself of Matt's suggestion that her godmother might be crusty on the outside and soft in the middle, but crusty all the way through was looking more likely.

'Be quick, child. State your business or move along,' Miss Penrose snapped.

The razor eyes turned to Matt and the downturned mouth tightened. 'If you're begging, let me tell you now that you'll get no money out of me.'

Lizzie was mortified on Matt's behalf. 'It's nothing like that,' she said, though she supposed she *was* begging after a fashion. 'I'm Lizzie Kellaway. I used to be Lizzie Maudsley but I've taken my mother's name. You knew her as Grace Kellaway and she chose you to be my godmother.'

Surprise and something else — regret? — rippled across the granite face. 'Did Grace send you?'

Lizzie swallowed. 'My mother died last year. But you were fond of her once, and I need your help. My father isn't a nice man and he's going to marry a woman who's even worse than him.'

'You want me to intercede on your behalf?'

'Not exactly.'

'Then what?'

'I've run away,' Lizzie said. 'I need somewhere to stay.'

Miss Penrose looked startled. She turned to Matt again. 'Did you put her up to this?' She made it sound as though Matt had an ulterior motive. A reward, perhaps.

'Matt *helped* me!' Lizzie cried.

The rain worsened suddenly and a cold wind whipped it towards Lizzie and Matt.

Miss Penrose clucked annoyance. 'I suppose you'd better come in. Don't think you're staying, mind.' She stepped back to let them enter. 'Wipe your feet and don't leave drips.'

It was impossible to avoid dripping. Frowning, Miss Penrose led them downstairs to a basement kitchen. It was fitted out with a stove and cupboards but appeared to be little used.

She pointed to the chairs that surrounded a table. 'Hang your coats over the backs.'

They did as instructed but still dripped from their wet hair. Lizzie's stockings and the hem of her dress were sodden and muddy too. So were Matt's trousers.

'Who are you, young man?' Miss Penrose barked.

Was she looking down her nose at Matt because his clothes were limp with wear? Lizzie thought he carried his modest circumstances with dignity.

'I'm Matthew Warren, a farmer from Staffordshire. As Lizzie said —'

Matt's casual use of Lizzie's name hadn't met with approval.

'Miss Kellaway, if you prefer,' he corrected.

'I do prefer.'

'Miss Kellaway found herself in a spot of bother. My family helped her.'

'You're expecting a reward, I suppose.'

'You suppose wrong.'

The denial caused Miss Penrose's chin to come up. Clearly, she wasn't used to being contradicted.

Matt met her glare with steadiness.

'You're forthright for someone so young and . . . modestly circumstanced,' she accused.

'I'm honest.'

'Humph. As you're unrelated to Miss Kellaway, I suggest you remain here while I speak to her upstairs.'

'As you wish.' He gave Lizzie an encouraging nod.

'You may sit,' Miss Penrose told him, but her expression warned him against touching anything.

Back upstairs, Lizzie was taken into a room at the front of the house. It was a dull room with faded flowered paper on the walls and a meagre fire in the hearth, though there were signs of activity in the form of a piano, two music stands and a tall cabinet with shallow drawers designed to hold sheet music. Miss Penrose hadn't been playing the piano, however. An upright armchair stood to one side of the fire and beside it was a small table on which a pair of spectacles rested alongside a book. Miss Penrose had been reading about the life of the composer Handel.

She pointed to another, smaller chair. 'Sit there and tell me why you've come all the way from Witherton. If Witherton is still your home?'

Lizzie nodded and sat. Miss Penrose sat too and looked at Lizzie impatiently. 'Well, child?'

Could a girl have two more miserable alternatives? Life with Susan Monk or life with this hard-edged woman? At least Lizzie had no reason to suspect Miss Penrose of actual cruelty.

'My father is a horrible man,' she finally began, and soon the words were tumbling out.

'I warned your mother against marrying him,' Miss Penrose said, when Lizzie reached the end of her story. 'She wouldn't listen.'

'She made a mistake and I'm sure she regretted it every single day. Except that she always said she was glad to have me. She said I brought her joy.'

'Hmm.' Miss Penrose's tone suggested it was beyond her imagination to comprehend how Lizzie could bring joy to anyone, let alone a spinster like her.

'You thought well enough of my mother to travel to Witherton to be my godmother,' Lizzie pointed out.

'That was years ago. Your mother and I argued because I stood up to your father and told him what I thought of him. He ordered me from the house and your mother urged me to go without a fuss. I thought she might write afterwards to apologise but she never did.'

Once again Lizzie saw something in her godmother's face — a fleeting glimpse into private hurt?

'My mother was afraid of my father and did

75

everything she could to protect me from his anger,' Lizzie explained. 'I'm sure she missed your friendship terribly. Why else would she have spoken to me so fondly about you?'

Another 'Hmm.'

'She wrote of you affectionately in her diaries too.'

Growing desperate, Lizzie took one of the diaries from her bag and began to read aloud from it. '*Dear Margaret taught me a new duet today. How kind and patient she is!*'

Had Miss Penrose's face softened a little just then?

Lizzie ploughed on. '*Margaret gave me a silver pen for my birthday. It's beautiful.* Mama kept that pen. I have it here in my bag.'

'I'm sure it was useful.'

'Mama didn't keep it because it was useful. She treasured it because you gave it to her. Have you kept anything she gave to you?'

Another flicker passed across Miss Penrose's face.

'You have kept something!'

'What of it? This is a large house and I've lived here all my life. I've kept a lot of things because I've never needed to throw them away.'

'You've kept everything anyone ever gave you? Of course you haven't!'

'Upon my word, you're as forthright as that farmer downstairs. I'm surprised your mother didn't teach you how to behave more respectfully to your elders.'

'I do respect you, Miss Penrose. But we all tell ourselves things that aren't true in the hope of feeling more comfortable.'

'Forthright indeed!' Miss Penrose retorted, but Lizzie saw the bony hands thresh together as if their owner was troubled. 'Even if I do have fond memo-

76

ries of your mother, you've wasted your time in coming here. You're a child under your father's authority. I have no right to keep you from him. You're more your father's child than your mother's anyway. You don't look anything like her.'

'My character comes from my mother.'

'It doesn't appear so to me.'

'I'm more . . . forthright as you put it. But my mother loved me dearly, while my father dislikes me and Susan Monk hates me.'

'Your father might still have reasons for wanting your return.'

'Pride, do you mean?' Edward Maudsley did care about appearances. 'I'm sure we could suggest a story to save him from looking bad. Something about my education and your loneliness, perhaps.'

'My loneliness?' Miss Penrose was affronted.

'I don't mean that you're actually lonely,' Lizzie said, though now she came to think about it, she wondered just how many friends the abrasive Miss Penrose had. 'It would only be a story. No one knows you in Witherton, so what would it matter?'

'I have no room for a child.'

'This house is big! You just said so.'

'I wasn't referring to the house. I was referring to my life. I live alone and know nothing of children. I also have a living to earn. I teach piano. It isn't as though I have staff to look after you. I only have a cleaning woman who comes twice a week.'

'I wouldn't be any trouble.'

'That, I find hard to believe.'

'I've spent months banished to an attic. I know how to keep quiet and how to entertain myself. If you're worried about the money side of things —'

'Must you be so uncouth?'

'I'm sorry. But money matters, doesn't it? Especially when it's in short supply.' Lizzie knew that from Polly and Davie. 'My father might be willing to pay you for my keep.'

'Edward Maudsley wouldn't spend a farthing more than he needed.'

'To save face, he might. I could be useful too. I could run errands and fetch the coal in. I could learn to dust and polish too.'

'No, it won't do. And before you attempt to stir my conscience by saying your mother would have expected better from the woman she chose to be your godmother, let me tell you that I can't abide emotional blackmail.'

So there it was. Rejection. Lizzie got to her feet, blinking back tears. Her mission had come to nothing and she dreaded the vengeance Miss Monk would inflict when Lizzie was in her power again. 'I'm sorry I disturbed you. I won't take up any more of your time.'

'Will that farmer take you home if I pay him for his trouble?'

'Please don't concern yourself, Miss Penrose.'

Lizzie returned to the basement where Matt was waiting. He raised an eyebrow in enquiry but one look at her face must have told him what had happened. He helped her into her coat, patted her shoulder sympathetically then ushered her back upstairs and out onto the street. Shoulders hunched against the rain, they walked away.

8

'Wait!'

They were halfway down the street when they heard the voice. Turning, they saw that Miss Penrose had come out behind them. She glanced up at the falling rain and grimaced. 'Come back inside, for goodness' sake!'

Matt looked at Lizzie. She'd had enough of her godmother's abrasiveness for one day, but she finally nodded.

Miss Penrose allowed them into the hall. 'I just want to be sure you're going straight home, Elizabeth, and that this young man is taking you.'

'*I* shan't be abandoning Lizzie,' Matt said, and Miss Penrose flushed as though he'd accused her of abandoning her goddaughter. 'But I shan't be returning her to Witherton today.'

'If it's a question of money, I —'

'It's a question of time. I'm responsible for a farm as well as my family.'

'You'll take her soon?'

'I'll take her when it's convenient, but I shan't hand her over to a pair of tyrants without making it clear that there'll be trouble if they treat her unkindly.'

'What sort of trouble?'

'I'll expose their cruelty to their neighbours.'

'You've never even met Edward Maudsley.'

'He won't scare me no matter how much he rants and raves. Lizzie was brave to run away, but she's only thirteen and needs friends to stand up for her. It looks as though I'm her only friend.'

'I find your tone offensive, young man.'

'I expect you do. It doesn't trouble me.'

'Bad manners are —'

'Of no consequence compared to standing up for someone in need.'

Miss Penrose looked furious. But she also looked frustrated and full of doubt. 'All right,' she finally said. '*I'll* see the child is restored to her father, and *I'll* have the strongest possible words with him. He doesn't scare me either.'

Matt smiled and his green eyes glinted. 'You're a formidable person, Miss Penrose.'

'You're a shocking manipulator.'

Matt only smiled again then looked down at Lizzie. 'Is that acceptable?' he asked gently.

'I think so.' It wasn't fair to expect Matt to do more for her but Lizzie felt horribly reluctant to part from him. In fact, the pang of loss she felt was immense and she found she was blinking back tears again. Stepping forward, she wrapped her arms around his middle, wishing she could keep them there forever.

Miss Penrose humphed and moved further down the hall as though distancing herself from what she considered to be an unbecoming exhibition of sentiment.

'Thank you, Matt,' Lizzie said. 'For everything. You'll give my love to Edith and the others?'

'I certainly will. You'll write to let us know you're well? Happy too, I hope?'

'I'll write,' she promised, then added in a whisper, 'I'd like you to have my money.' She didn't want Miss Penrose to hear in case she thought Matt's motive in helping had been money all along.

'Keep it for the moment. You should have a small emergency fund so you won't be tempted to cross paths with the Amos Bradleys of this world again.' He bent to kiss her cheek. 'Farewell, little Lizzie. I have a train to catch so I mustn't linger.'

She wanted to say, 'Farewell, big brother,' but her throat was too tight.

'Miss Penrose.' He nodded at her godmother, who nodded back but didn't speak. Probably, she hadn't bothered to remember his name.

Lizzie watched him walk down the street. Reaching the end of the road, he turned, waved, then disappeared from sight. Desolation washed over her at the loss of her friend.

'Close the door, for goodness' sake!' Miss Penrose called.

Lizzie closed it.

'Take your coat off downstairs then come back into the music room. Change your boots as well.'

'I have no other shoes. I could only pack what I could carry.'

'Then wipe your boots thoroughly.'

Lizzie did as instructed, returning to find Miss Penrose sitting in her armchair and frowning. 'Staying here is a temporary arrangement. I trust you understand that?'

'I do, and I'm grateful for your help.'

'I don't have a telephone but I shall go out to make a call shortly.'

Lizzie felt worry slither in her stomach as she guessed the call would be to her father.

'Don't stand there idling, Elizabeth. Go to the bookcase. Choose a book to read.'

Lizzie found a whole shelf of books about music.

81

There were history books too, as well as books about travels, philosophy and science. Moving down a shelf, Lizzie saw —

Goodness, what were these? Pamphlets about women and the fight for the vote? Did Miss Penrose support the suffragettes?

Lizzie was impressed. She'd hated growing up in the shadow of a bully like her father, who'd taken Mama's inheritance. Allowing women to vote for the people who sat in Parliament and made all the laws was surely a perfectly reasonable step towards a fairer world. After all, females were just as clever as men, as far as Lizzie could see, and the work they did in or out of the home was just as valuable.

Of course, not all men were bullies. Lizzie thought of Matt and realised he treated the females in his family with respect as well as love.

'May I read one of these pamphlets?' she asked.

'Are you interested in women's suffrage?'

'I can't say I know much about it, but I'd like to learn more. Perhaps my father would benefit from reading about it too.' It was a joke and it wasn't lost on Miss Penrose.

The arctic eyes gleamed in momentary appreciation then resumed their glacial state. 'You're not like your mother at all.'

More was the pity. 'Most people call me Lizzie.'

'I can't abide diminutives.'

Lizzie wasn't sure what a diminutive was, but supposed it was a shortened name.

Miss Penrose's next words confirmed it. 'My name is Margaret but you shall call me Miss Penrose. Not Maggie, Meg or Peg, and definitely not Peggy. Is that understood?'

'Perfectly, Miss Penrose.'

'Then sit down and read.'

Miss Penrose stared into space for a while — deciding what to say to Edward Maudsley? — then got to her feet. 'Behave yourself while I'm gone.'

She hadn't been out for long when she burst back in, breathing outrage like a dragon breathed fire. 'The cheek of the man, expecting me to go to Witherton to spare him the trouble of collecting his own daughter!'

She threw herself into her chair.

Lizzie's absence from home had changed nothing, it seemed. She felt a pang of hurt but swallowed it down and asked, 'Are you taking me to Witherton?'

'I most certainly am not! That brute is coming here tomorrow. To London, I mean. I won't have him in this house.'

Sensing that Miss Penrose was in no mood to entertain further questions, Lizzie lowered her gaze to the pamphlet, but for a while she could think only of Edward Maudsley and how livid he might be when she saw him.

'Do you play?' Miss Penrose finally asked.

'The piano?'

'Of course the piano. It was your mother's favourite instrument.'

'She taught me.'

'Then play something.'

Lizzie went to the piano. 'I haven't played much since Mama died.' She didn't want Miss Penrose to have high expectations.

'Just do your best.'

Lizzie chose a minuet by Bach, hoping to make a decent performance of it, but realising she wasn't playing well at all.

'Hmm,' Miss Penrose said. 'Perhaps you take after your mother in singing?'

Lizzie sang 'Greensleeves' as she was familiar with both the words and the music.

'Your mother had a different sort of voice,' Miss Penrose remarked, crushing Lizzie even more. 'I have pupils now. Take your reading down to the kitchen.'

For the next three hours Lizzie sat at the kitchen table hearing pupils arrive and leave above her. Between times the piano tinkled or thumped according to the talents or incompetence of the pupils. More than once Miss Penrose's voice cried out, 'No, no, no!'

When she descended to the kitchen at last, she looked fraught. Lizzie suspected she was a brilliant pianist but an impatient teacher.

'I expect you're hungry,' Miss Penrose said. 'I know nothing of children, but I believe they're always hungry.'

'Aren't your pupils children?' Lizzie asked.

'Certainly. But I only teach them piano. Their other needs are no business of mine. I don't keep a cook and I don't cook for myself beyond warming soup or boiling eggs. I haven't the interest.'

She opened the pantry door and Lizzie saw that it was almost empty. A covered plate, the end of a loaf, something wrapped in greaseproof paper and a butter dish were taken out and placed on the table. There was ham under the plate and cheese in the grease-proof wrapping.

Lizzie would have preferred one of Edith's heartening stews but hoped she kept her longing hidden. Miss Penrose prepared two plates and carried them back to the music room where she pulled out a small table.

84

Seeing her godmother pick up her book and read as she ate, Lizzie did so too, supposing she wasn't good enough company to warrant a conversation.

Afterwards Miss Penrose washed the dishes. Drying them, Lizzie was left in no doubt that her godmother regarded domestic tasks as nuisances. An even bigger nuisance loomed when, as though it had only just occurred to her, Miss Penrose said, 'I suppose you need somewhere to sleep.'

Lizzie was shown to a bedroom at the back of the house. Like the rest of 11 Marchmont Row, it appeared to have been frozen in time many years ago. The wallpaper was faded, the curtains looked brittle with age and the furniture had probably been undisturbed since before her godmother's birth. Miss Penrose took sheets and blankets from a cupboard and made the bed inexpertly. 'The bathroom is across the landing.'

'A bathroom?' What an unexpected luxury.

'It was installed when my father became infirm,' Miss Penrose explained.

Lizzie wondered if she should go to bed now, to give Miss Penrose some time to herself.

'I'm tired after the journey. Would you mind if —'

'Goodnight, Elizabeth.'

'Goodnight, Miss Penrose. And thank you.'

Lizzie's room was cold. She remade the bed but the sheets felt chilly when she slipped between them. It had been an emotional day, though, and despite the discomfort, Lizzie slept.

She woke with a sense that the morning was already well underway and hoped her sleepiness hadn't inconvenienced her hostess. The linoleum felt icy beneath her feet as Lizzie got out of bed. She put on her boots for the trip to the bathroom, a space that she guessed must have been made out of the third bedroom on this floor. She'd noticed another staircase leading to what must be attics, but she hadn't dared to investigate.

Only when Lizzie returned to her room did she realise her yesterday's clothes were no longer on the chair. Miss Penrose must have taken them last night or earlier this morning. Dressing in the spare clothes she'd brought with her, Lizzie brushed her hair and ventured downstairs.

Miss Penrose was in the kitchen, her sleeves rolled up to the elbows and her face flustered.

'Good morning,' Lizzie said.

'That brute is going to have no chance to complain that you're being sent home dirty.'

Irons were warming in the fire and Lizzie recognised her underwear in the small pile of linen on the table. A glance out of the back window into a small rear garden established that her dress was hanging on the washing line.

Lizzie was thinking that it would take an age to dry when a cold fear rushed into her mind. 'Did you take the envelope from my pocket, Miss Penrose?'

'What envelope?'

The one which contained Matt's address, of course.

Lizzie rushed outside and pulled the envelope from her dress pocket. It was sodden and breaking into pieces. Oh no . . .

Carrying it carefully, she took it inside and set it on the table. The envelope itself was ruined but perhaps the paper inside was —

No such luck. The paper was sodden too, the writing reduced to a few streaks of ink, washed pale and utterly illegible.

9

'What's that?' Miss Penrose demanded, when she noticed the wet remains of paper on the table.

'It was a note.'

'It isn't much of a note now. Throw it away.'

Might the words become more readable once the paper had dried? Not a chance. Lizzie tidied the mess into the bin.

She must have looked dejected because Miss Penrose's manner changed to guilty awkwardness. 'Was the note important?'

Lizzie was near to tears but she didn't want her godmother to feel bad about an accident. 'Matt had written his address down for me but I may be able to remember it.' Lizzie couldn't actually remember anything more than Bee Corner Farm but it occurred to her that she might be able to locate it on a map and that gave her hope.

They breakfasted on a boiled egg and slice of bread and butter each. The eggs were hard but Miss Penrose appeared not to notice. Lizzie helped to clear up then escaped to her room to pull the traveller's guide from her bag. She studied the map which featured Stafford but where on earth was Bee Corner Farm?

Quelling her rising panic, Lizzie tried to think logically. She'd met Amos Bradley in Stropley and there it was, to the north-east. He hadn't taken her through the middle of Stafford so maybe he lived on the north-east outskirts. Perhaps Bee Corner was to the north-east too.

Lizzie could still find no mention of it and none of the villages or hamlets in the area triggered any memories. Of course, Amos might have gone round the outskirts of Stafford to the north, south or even the west of the town. Bee Corner Farm could be in any direction too.

Why, oh why hadn't she paid more attention to the route when Joe had driven her to the station?

It occurred to her that Miss Penrose might have a more detailed map but when Lizzie returned to the kitchen her godmother was looking harassed. She'd brought Lizzie's still-soaking dress off the line and was attempting to iron it. 'Can I help?' Lizzie asked, grimacing at the smell of scorched wool.

'Are you packed? We leave at twelve.'

'I can be ready in five minutes.'

'Then please tidy the music room. I have pupils later.'

Miss Penrose's routine had been interrupted and she wasn't happy about it. Lizzie tidied the music room and looked in the bookcase but couldn't see a larger map.

Just before twelve Lizzie packed the clothes Miss Penrose had laundered — still damp and horribly creased — then put her coat on. A frowning Miss Penrose joined her in the hall and they hastened to a bus stop, Lizzie's bag banging against her legs, though she didn't complain.

She felt sick at the thought of seeing her father. Miss Penrose was a worthy match for him, but after crossing swords with him today would she bother checking on Lizzie by writing for reports and perhaps even visiting? Maybe for a little while. But as time passed and Miss Penrose was caught up by the demands of her own life, Lizzie might be forgotten.

A walk followed the bus ride. Miss Penrose strode out purposefully and Lizzie hastened after her, trying not to wince as the bag bruised her legs. They turned into a side street and Lizzie came to an abrupt halt.

A man had turned into the street from the other end. A man with a bad-tempered mouth showing beneath his hat, and resentment coming off him like steam.

'Come along!' Miss Penrose urged, glancing round, but something in Lizzie's face caused her to turn back again. Her shoulders stiffened as she too saw Edward Maudsley.

He disappeared into a building. Drawing nearer, Lizzie saw that it was the Mostyn Hotel. Miss Penrose swept in and Lizzie followed.

The reception area was large and gloomy. 'Sit over there and don't move.' Miss Penrose pointed to some armchairs.

Lizzie sat in a chair, half-hidden by an aspidistra in a brass pot. Miss Penrose spoke to the receptionist then swept through another door.

It was one o'clock according to an ornate clock on the fireplace. At five past one Miss Penrose surged back into the reception area. 'Come,' she commanded, continuing towards the outer door.

Confused, Lizzie scrambled up, grabbed her bag and followed. She had to run to catch up with Miss Penrose then half-walked, half-ran to stop herself from falling behind again. Only after they'd rounded several corners did Miss Penrose spit out, 'That brute is insufferable!'

'Where are you taking me?' Lizzie asked, but Miss Penrose was marching ahead again.

Eventually Lizzie realised they were returning to Highbury. Miss Penrose headed straight for her armchair when they arrived at the house. Lizzie hovered at the music room door. Had her father foisted her onto her godmother for another night?

Long minutes passed before Miss Penrose looked at Lizzie. 'What am I going to do with you now?' she asked despairingly.

'I'm not returning to Witherton today?'

'You're not returning to Witherton at all. Unless there's someone there who might look after you?' Miss Penrose suddenly looked hopeful.

'No,' Lizzie said, and her godmother's face slumped.

'What happened?' Lizzie asked. 'At the hotel?'

'That brute said I should stay out of his business and either leave your upbringing to him or keep you myself. I told him that I was in no position to keep you, but then he insulted your mother. After that . . .' Clearly, Miss Penrose had let her temper get the better of her.

So Edward Maudsley really didn't care if he never saw his daughter again. Lizzie hadn't expected to be wanted, but even so . . .

'Heaven knows what I'm going to do with you,' her godmother continued. 'I could send you to school, but the fees would be beyond anything I could afford and I can't imagine that brute paying.'

Lizzie surfaced out of her thoughts. 'Are you going to put me in an orphanage?' That was what happened to unwanted children in the books she'd read.

'Don't be ridiculous. You're not an orphan as long as that brute lives.'

So . . .

'We'll have to muddle along here until I can find a

'better solution.'

No one wanted Lizzie, it seemed. It stung her to think she was regarded as a burden. 'I'll make myself useful,' she promised. 'I'll start now by making you a cup of tea. Something to eat as well, perhaps.'

'Be quick. My first pupil arrives shortly.'

Lizzie went down to the kitchen, set the kettle to boil on the stove and scraped together a meal of bread, cheese and sliced apple, not finding much else in the larder. She left her plate on the kitchen table then carried a tray up for Miss Penrose. 'Would you like me to go to the shops while you're teaching?'

'The shops?'

'For food.' Lizzie could see no other way of providing supper. 'I have fourteen shillings so—'

Miss Penrose put up a hand to demand silence. She reached for her bag, took out her purse and passed over a pound note. 'I'm not taking money from a child. Buy eggs and cheese and . . . Oh, I don't know. I've never seen the value in spending long hours cooking.'

'I'll see what I can find.'

Miss Penrose picked up some sheet music and studied it. Lizzie was loath to interrupt her but the loss of Matt's address was preying on her mind. 'Might I borrow a map of England if you have one?' she asked.

'In the dining-room,' her godmother told her.

Lizzie discovered the dining room behind the music room. It contained a formal table and eight chairs as well as a chiffonier and bookcase, but none looked as though they'd been used for years. The bookcase yielded a promising-looking atlas of Britain, however. Lizzie was taking it downstairs when Miss Penrose called, 'Don't spend my money on sweets!'

91

Eating her own meal, Lizzie found Stafford in the atlas and studied the area around it. Some farms were named but she couldn't find Bee Corner among them. She wasn't giving up, though. She'd look further afield once she returned from the shops.

She took a basket from the pantry and, not liking to interrupt her godmother to ask for a key for the front door, she left through the kitchen door, locking it behind her and taking the key. She found the shops by asking a passer-by. There was a row of them — butcher, grocer, cobbler, greengrocer, tailor, baker, haberdasher . . .

Lizzie had never shopped for food in all her life, except for buying the bun and drink in Stropley, but she was determined to make a good job of it. She visited several shops as she tried to work out the best way of spending Miss Penrose's money.

She finally bought a loaf from the baker, a small piece of mutton from the butcher, vegetables from the greengrocer, and several items from the grocer — eggs, cheese, meat paste, tinned soup and corned beef, as Edith had told her that corned beef mashed into potato made for a cheap and filling supper. There wasn't a great deal of change from the pound note, but Lizzie hoped she'd bought enough food for several days.

When she returned to the house a pupil was banging heavily on the piano upstairs. Lizzie pictured Miss Penrose gritting her teeth at the awfulness of it. The noisy pupil departed as Lizzie put the shopping away, and a gentler pupil arrived. Half an hour later the lesson finished and Miss Penrose came downstairs.

'Oh,' she said, as though she'd forgotten her god-daughter's existence, then she frowned when she heard what Lizzie had bought. 'Doesn't mutton need to be cooked?'

'I plan to make a stew. Matt's sister taught me.'

'Hmm.'

At that moment the door knocker sounded. Miss Penrose took a glass of water upstairs and answered the door to her next pupil.

By the time she returned after another two lessons Lizzie had the stew simmering on the stove. It didn't smell as delicious as Edith's stews, but with luck it would be edible.

Worryingly, Lizzie had still found no mention of Bee Corner Farm on the map and none of the village names had stirred her memory. The thought that she might never be able to get in touch with the Warrens seared her with distress, but surely there was more she could do to locate them? Lizzie wouldn't give up yet. In the meantime, she wouldn't bother her godmother with her troubles.

Miss Penrose looked tired, in fact.

'Would you like me to make you a cup of tea?' Lizzie offered.

'Thank you, I would.' Sitting at the table Miss Penrose stared abstractedly into space. 'You need an education,' she said. 'I told you before that I haven't the funds for a decent school.'

'Can't I go to the local school?' Polly and Davie hadn't had to pay to go to school. They'd both left at twelve but some children stayed on until fourteen. Like Mikey Warren hoped to do.

'And learn what?' Miss Penrose asked.

Clearly Miss Penrose's opinion of the local school wasn't high. 'I can teach myself,' Lizzie said after a while. 'I like to read, and you have a lot of books here.'

'I'll teach you,' Miss Penrose decided, though without enthusiasm. 'We'll have lessons in the mornings, but only until I can make other arrangements.'

Lizzie couldn't blame her for wanting her goddaughter gone. Clearly, Miss Penrose valued her solitude and it hadn't been fair of Lizzie to descend on her uninvited.

Fortunately, the stew was edible even if it wasn't up to Edith's standards. Lizzie supposed it was Edith's herbs that made the difference but Lizzie hadn't seen any herbs on sale.

'You haven't played today,' Miss Penrose said, after they'd eaten. 'You'll never become an accomplished pianist unless you practice diligently. Go upstairs and play now. You'll find music in the drawers if you need it. The easier pieces are at the top.'

Lizzie went upstairs and investigated the drawers. Miss Penrose had indeed arranged the contents so that the beginners' music was in the top drawers with the pieces becoming more advanced the further down she explored. The music in the lower drawers was too advanced for Lizzie but she continued working her way down just to see what sort of pieces Miss Penrose liked. All were classical.

Reaching the bottom drawer, Lizzie was surprised to find that it contained just one piece of music, wrapped in tissue paper. She drew it out carefully and eased the tissue aside. The music was handwritten and titled 'The Girl with Grey Eyes' by George Gilbert Grafton.

'What are you doing?' Miss Penrose's voice sliced into the quietness like a blade, icy with anger.

Startled, Lizzie dropped the music, just managing to catch it again before it hit the floor.

94

She placed it in the hand her godmother held out. 'I was looking for music. I thought —'

'Does this look like the sort of music a child would play?' Miss Penrose's fury made Lizzie tremble.

'I don't know. I only —'

'Find something else.' The handwritten piece was returned to the drawer, and the drawer was slammed shut.

Lizzie opened a middle drawer and took out the first piece that came to hand.

'Play!' Miss Penrose barked.

Lizzie did so. Badly, because her fingers were trembling.

'Concentrate, child!'

Heaving breath into her lungs, Lizzie played as well as she could. Miss Penrose's comments were scathing but the shouting gradually diminished and no more was said about 'The Girl with Grey Eyes'.

But in bed that night Lizzie's mind wouldn't rest as three questions bounced around inside it. Was Miss Penrose the girl with grey eyes? Had she once been in love with George Gilbert Grafton, only to be disappointed for some reason? And had Lizzie's intrusion into her godmother's private affairs hastened her departure from the house?

10

Nothing was said over the following days about Lizzie leaving. She tried to make herself useful in the kitchen as Miss Penrose had little interest in food and Lizzie rather liked to eat. She also took her godmother's shoes to the cobbler, opened the door to her pupils and took her tea as well as fresh water in the lull between pupils.

When she wasn't being useful, Lizzie tried to keep quiet. She studied the atlas again and was sorely disappointed to find no mention of Bee Corner Farm anywhere near Stafford. When they received no letter from her would Matt and the other Warrens think she'd taken advantage of their hospitality — not to mention their meagre savings — only to forget about them because she had brighter excitements in her life? It was vexing in the extreme.

A week passed and still nothing was said about Lizzie leaving. One week became two, and then three, and a routine gradually took shape. Mornings were for lessons. Miss Penrose was an exacting taskmaster and Lizzie had never been gladder that her own brain worked swiftly. The lessons weren't always interesting, but Lizzie gave her godmother credit for the effort she put in to planning a decent grounding in English, Mathematics, History, Geography, Science and French.

In the afternoons, Lizzie shopped, tidied the house and cooked, helped by finding a recipe book on Miss Penrose's shelves. *The Housewife's Encyclopaedia of*

Cookery had looked unopened, as though it had been a somewhat puzzling gift from a friend.

Not that Miss Penrose had a large number of friends, but she certainly had some. Lizzie met them in her second week when Miss Penrose attended a meeting of her women's group. Miss Penrose had considered missing the meeting because she wasn't sure if it was appropriate to leave a child alone in the house but, after making a telephone call to a Mrs Bishop, had decided to take Lizzie along.

'I'll sit quietly,' Lizzie promised.

The meeting was held a fifteen-minute walk away in a much grander house than Miss Penrose's. This house was painted pristine white and had sturdy pillars supporting a porch under which were imposing black doors.

A maid showed them into a large drawing room that was sumptuously fitted out with chandeliers, gold-coloured silk furnishings and numerous silver-framed photographs. 'This is the child?' a woman asked, getting to her feet and coming to greet them. She was handsome and richly dressed in dark satin relieved by lace and sparkling jewels.

To Lizzie's relief, she looked kind.

'Elizabeth, isn't it? Or do you prefer to be called Lizzie?'

'Actually I do,' Lizzie said.

'We're glad to have you with us, Lizzie. I'm Cordelia Bishop. Please sit wherever you like.'

A benign-looking gentleman got up from a sofa. 'I'll leave you ladies to your meeting,' he said, and winked at Lizzie as he left.

Mr Bishop, Lizzie assumed. Clearly a decent man, like Matt, for welcoming a group of suffragettes to his home.

Biscuits, cakes, sherry and wine were handed around, with lemonade for Lizzie. Sipping it appreciatively, she listened to the meeting with interest. As well as Mrs Bishop the group comprised Mrs Caroline Hopkins, Miss Emma Caswell, Mrs Ida Trumpington, the Misses Eve and Evangeline Pirrow, Mrs Clarice Osborne, and a Miss Sparkes who seemed not to use her Christian name.

They were all members of the NUWSS, which Lizzie learnt stood for the National Union of Women's Suffrage Societies, and a few years earlier they'd joined three thousand other women in marching from Hyde Park to Exeter Hall in support of votes for women. They'd also been members of the WSPU — the Women's Social and Political Union — but had declined to continue, for reasons Mrs Bishop explained to Lizzie. 'Mrs Pankhurst wants to run the organisation free from challenge by anyone else. We believe all women should have a voice. We're also worried about their tactics. Window-smashing, for one. Our aim is to present ourselves as responsible, reasonable women who deserve the vote. Vandalism rather undermines that in our view.'

'What tactics do you use?' Lizzie asked.

'We've all joined the WFL — the Women's Freedom League — to use political influence and persuasion to win the day.'

All of the women in the group spoke passionately and intelligently, not just about the fight for the right to vote, but about women's opportunities in general. 'What do you think of us, Lizzie?' Cordelia Bishop asked as the meeting ended.

'I think you're amazing,' Lizzie said. 'Justice is on

your side and I hope the world sees sense soon, because if God didn't mean women to help to run the country, he wouldn't have given us brains.'

'Spoken like a true suffragette,' Miss Bishop approved, to murmurs of, 'Here, here.'

Lizzie's cheeks warmed with pleasure but mostly she was relieved she hadn't disgraced her godmother.

Three weeks became four and it was Miss Penrose's turn to host a meeting. 'I suppose I'd better buy sherry,' she said, but made no mention of biscuits or cakes.

Lizzie set to work with the cookery book, baking biscuits *and* cakes.

'I say,' the Misses Pirrow commented, eyeing the plates in pleased surprise.

'Your work, Lizzie?' Mrs Bishop's eyes twinkled. 'Your godmother is an admirable woman but disinclined to consider the needs of the stomach.'

So true!

As Lizzie settled into her fifth week she began to hope that maybe — just maybe — she might be allowed to stay. She hadn't written to Polly before as she'd been hoping to share a permanent address and, until her future was more certain, she'd been wary of spending precious money on buying paper and stamps.

Polly would be worried, though, so Lizzie finally broke into her funds and wrote to tell her friend about everything that had happened. She enclosed paper and a stamped envelope so Polly could write back.

Lizzie had still been unable to find the Warrens' farm on any map and had come to the reluctant conclusion that it was just too small to warrant a mention. The thought of never being with that welcoming, jolly family again — of never feeling the warm safety of Matt's regard, let alone repaying the money she owed — filled her with distress, so she wrote to Matt at Bee Corner Farm, near Stafford without mentioning a village name and prayed the letter would reach him somehow. She decided she wouldn't send any money until she was sure he'd receive it, though.

Polly wrote back straight away. She'd been appalled to hear about Amos Bradley. *You must have been so scared*, she wrote, *and so relieved to find yourself among friends with the Warrens. What a pity you don't have their address.*

Polly's family didn't move in the same circles as Edward Maudsley but Polly had seen Miss Monk talking to Mrs Chant in the street and slowed down to eavesdrop on their conversation. *Mrs Chant asked about you and Miss Monk told her you were extending your stay with your godmother for educational reasons as Miss Penrose is a teacher and London has galleries and museums for you to visit. I don't think Mrs Chant believed her because there was something knowing in her eyes that made Miss Monk walk off with a face like thunder. The wedding is still going ahead, though. She was wearing a very grand fur jacket, by the way, and a large hat which looked horribly expensive.*

I do miss you, Lizzie! Please write again soon. Your loving friend, Polly (Davie says hello too) x

No letter came from Matt so Lizzie drew up a list of villages around Stafford. Choosing two of them — Furzeley and Cottam — she wrote one letter addressed to Bee Corner Farm, Furzeley and another to Bee Corner Farm, Cottam.

Still no letter came in reply. After three months she'd written twenty-five letters but none appeared to have found him. She had enough money to continue writing for a while but not enough to replace her shoes which were pinching badly as Lizzie was growing. She also had several darns in her stockings.

When she could bear the pinching no longer, she spoke to Miss Penrose. 'I'd like to earn a little money of my own and I wonder if you have any ideas for how I might go about it?'

'Money for what?'

'New shoes, stockings, and eventually —'

'For goodness' sake, Elizabeth! Why didn't you say you needed new clothes? How am I to know these things if you don't speak up?'

Perhaps because it was the way of the world for children to outgrow their clothes? But that was unfair. Miss Penrose couldn't have made it plainer that she had no experience of children and had only taken Lizzie on because she'd felt she had no choice.

'I'd like to pay for my own things, if possible,' Lizzie said. She also wanted to put money aside for repaying Matt if she ever located him.

'It isn't possible, is it?' Miss Penrose snapped. Then she sighed. 'We'll go shopping tomorrow.'

'I'm sorry to be a trouble.'

'Hmm.'

Shopping for clothes clearly gave Miss Penrose as much satisfaction as cooking. Urged to say what she needed, Lizzie did so quickly, not wanting to incur her godmother's wrath by requiring another clothes-buying expedition in the near future. In addition to shoes and stockings, Lizzie came away with a new dress and underwear.

'I'm truly grateful,' Lizzie said on the way home. 'But if you can think of a way I might earn a few shillings, I'll be even more grateful.'

Lizzie suspected that Miss Penrose earned little enough herself, possibly because she was too strict a teacher to suit all but the most talented or robust children. It seemed likely that she'd dipped into savings to make the purchases. After all, Edward Maudsley hadn't sent any money as far as Lizzie knew. He hadn't written a single letter.

No answer came and Lizzie supposed her godmother's thoughts were tuned to an imaginary orchestra in her head. But then she said suddenly, 'Practice.'

Lizzie didn't understand. Was this another criticism of her piano playing?

'I mean you might earn a little money supervising the younger pupils when they practice. I often receive requests for that sort of service. It wouldn't pay as much as a proper lesson, of course, but if women want the right to influence the political landscape, they shouldn't shy away from earning for themselves.'

'How would it work?'

'You could hear the pupils play on the old piano in the attic. You wouldn't interfere with my teaching up there. You might also be asked to attend pupils' homes.'

'It sounds ideal.'

'Tiresome, actually. You'd only be helping the youngest pupils. But I'll let it be known that you're available and we'll see if any families respond.'

A number of families did respond and Lizzie began supervising practices up in one of the two attic rooms, a small oil stove taking some of the bite out of the chill. The pupils weren't afraid of Lizzie in the way they feared Miss Penrose. Some of them preferred chatting to playing but Lizzie made sure the chatter didn't get out of hand. Occasionally she got a headache from a pupil thumping down on the piano keys but mostly Lizzie enjoyed being useful, and it was gratifying to see her modest savings build.

Earning money meant Lizzie could continue writing to Polly — and attempting to write to Matt — without worrying about the price of paper and stamps. She could also venture into London on the bus on Saturday afternoons. Not just to visit the galleries and museums Miss Penrose insisted were a part of a civilised education, but also to see other places of interest, particularly those Polly would love to hear about — Buckingham Palace, Westminster Abbey, the Houses of Parliament, the Tower of London — Lizzie bought postcards to send to Polly when she had a spare penny or two.

Working gave Lizzie a sense of comradeship with her friend, though Polly's job had to be harder. Not that she ever complained. *Mrs Hepple is old and doesn't entertain so I'm hardly worked into the ground as some maids are*, she wrote.

She also informed Lizzie that Edward Maudsley and Susan Monk had married. *I was in the grocers buying sweets for the little ones at home when Miss Monk came in. Mrs Maudsley, I should say. The shop was busy and some of the women congratulated her on her marriage. One of them suggested that it must have been a quiet sort of wedding and Miss Monk said she'd preferred quietness. But that mean mouth of hers was all pinched up so I knew she was lying. After she'd gone, the women exchanged the sort of satisfied looks that made me think they knew she was lying too.*

So Edward Maudsley hadn't seen fit to inform his daughter that he'd remarried. What had Lizzie expected? Nothing, really, but still . . . Would he ever realise what he was missing and want to see her?

When her birthday came, he either forgot it or chose to ignore it. Polly remembered, though, and Lizzie was delighted by the small parcel she received from her containing a hand-drawn greetings card and a bright red satin ribbon. *For your hair*, Polly wrote. *The red should look lovely in all that silky darkness.*

Lizzie was touched. Not only because Polly had gone to the trouble of choosing a ribbon that would indeed look lovely, but also because Polly had sacrificed hard-earned money to pay for something long and wide and luscious.

Polly also sent a funny drawing of Miss Monk, emphasising the woman's mean eyes and narrow lips. She had more gossip to report too. *People are saying the first Mrs Maudsley might not have thrown herself into Witherton society but at least she was a lady. Which was more than could be said for her successor.*

Lizzie was delighted all over again when Miss Penrose gave her a new coat and hat in bottle green that would look very well indeed with Polly's red ribbon. Miss Penrose also produced a cake. Not home-baked — obviously — but she'd gone to some trouble to buy it from a bakery.

'It has a candle . . . ' Miss Penrose waved a hand as though she couldn't bring herself to mention something as foolish as making a wish but by now Lizzie knew her godmother for a kind woman beneath the brusque manner and tactlessness.

'I love it all,' Lizzie said. 'The coat, the hat, the cake . . . Thank you so much.'

When Miss Penrose's birthday came, Lizzie's little job meant that she was able to return the kindness by buying her godmother some new sheet music, placing it on the table beside her as they ate breakfast.

'What's this?'

'A birthday gift.'

'It isn't your birthday again already?'

'No, it's yours.'

Miss Penrose looked surprised. 'I haven't celebrated my birthdays in years.'

'Then a celebration is long overdue.'

'Goodness.'

It was unusual for her godmother to be flustered. Lizzie found it endearing. 'I know you don't normally bother with cake but a birthday cake is different, so I'm going to bake one.'

Mindful that the household budget was modest, Lizzie made a simple sponge, decorating it in pale yellow icing as she couldn't see Miss Penrose taking kindly to pink.

'Well, really!' Miss Penrose said, as though Lizzie was being nonsensical in making a fuss of an ageing spinster, but Lizzie knew her godmother was secretly pleased. Touched, even.

'You have to make a wish then blow the candle out,' Lizzie said.

An eye-roll followed but Miss Penrose did as asked. There was more colour in her cheeks than usual and Lizzie wondered what she'd been like as a younger woman. Never pretty, but perhaps softer. Had George Gilbert Grafton been responsible for turning her starchy and severe? Had he stirred her hopes of romance only to let her down because he wasn't serious? Or had *she* rejected *him* for some reason?

The fact that she'd kept his music and tucked it carefully into tissue paper suggested he still held a place in her heart. But perhaps the reason for keeping the music was nothing to do with romance.

Lizzie peeped at the tissue-wrapped music several times before she found the nerve to take it out and carry it to the piano one day when her godmother was out. Lizzie wasn't driven by curiosity alone — she would never have invaded Miss Penrose's privacy for something so disrespectful — but by a desire to understand the woman who'd taken her in.

She studied the music then played it through experimentally. By the time she'd played it three times she was in no doubt that this music had been written with love. It was a soft and dreamy tribute. Beautiful.

Something must have happened to separate these star-crossed lovers. But what?

*　*　*

When Christmas came, Lizzie bought sprigs of holly and fir from the greengrocer and arranged them on the mantelpiece. There were no other decorations because Miss Penrose never bothered. The mantelpiece arrangement appeared to strike her favourably, however. 'Perhaps next year we'll have a Christmas tree,' she said.

Lizzie was thrilled, not only because she wanted a tree, but also because the comment suggested she'd been accepted as a permanent addition to her godmother's life. The thought of it made Lizzie glow warmly.

The glow dimmed a little when she thought of Matt and the other Warrens. She'd sent dozens of letters all over Staffordshire to no effect. It was hard to accept that they were lost to her and might be thinking badly of her, but she wouldn't stop hoping that she'd find them again one day and had two pounds set aside to repay them if — or preferably when — that day arrived.

Perhaps her father might come to miss her too.

Within days 1909 had eased into 1910. It was the year in which Miss Penrose first let the name Lizzie slip from her lips. It was also the year Lizzie turned fourteen and assured her godmother that she'd happily take on the house cleaning when their cleaning lady left to live with her sister. It made Lizzie feel better to know that Miss Penrose could use the money she no longer had to pay to replenish her depleted savings.

Lizzie's life was busy. Taking lessons from her godmother, supervising piano practices and looking after the house and small garden left little leisure time during the day, while evenings were taken up with improving her own piano playing, dinner, exchanging letters with Polly — still such a good friend even over a distance — and involvement in the women's group.

After a lot of reading, listening and thinking, Lizzie had decided that she too preferred Cordelia Bishop's approach to winning suffrage, though she admired the courage of the women who went to prison for breaking the law in protest at the refusal to allow women to vote. Some went on hunger strike and braved brutal force-feeding.

Along with the other members of the women's group, Lizzie was thrilled when the Conciliation Bill was passed by the House of Commons. It only gave votes to women with property worth more than ten pounds and, as Mrs Bishop said, 'We want all women to have the right to vote.' But it was a start. Unfortunately, the Bill failed to become law and they were outraged. 'But we won't give up,' Mrs Bishop said, expressing the mood of all of them.

1910 rolled into 1911 and Lizzie went on her first suffragette march, the Women's Coronation Procession on the eve of the coronation of King George V.

Afterwards Mrs Bishop announced, 'I think you're old enough to call me Cordelia, my dear. I assume that's acceptable to you, Margaret?'

'Oh, certainly. If that's what you'd prefer.'

Cordelia sighed and Margaret frowned. 'What is it?' she asked, then the penny dropped. 'Oh! Yes, Lizzie must call me Margaret if she wishes.'

'Thank you,' Lizzie said.

It was a step too far for both of them, though, and they settled on Miss Margaret instead. That lasted for a year until Lizzie turned sixteen and they felt comfortable enough to take that final step with Miss Margaret becoming simply Margaret.

It also felt the right time for Lizzie to say, 'I'm so grateful for the education you've given me over the past few years, but now I'd like to start working properly.'

Margaret frowned. 'I attended school until I was eighteen. So did your mother.'

'That was an academy for young ladies. It was more about learning social graces than anything I'm likely to need.'

Margaret couldn't deny it, and it wasn't as though she was qualified to teach social graces, not having absorbed many herself.

'I'd like to start teaching piano lessons instead of just helping with practices,' Lizzie continued. She already taught to some extent as even supervising practices meant demonstrating how to play and correcting the children's playing. 'It'll mean we can take on more pupils.'

And that would help Margaret in two ways. It would enable Lizzie to contribute to household expenses, and increasing the number of pupils would give Margaret more choice over those she taught. Margaret was a wonderful woman, but patience didn't loom large in her store of personal qualities. It tortured her to teach the slow and less talented pupils, and some of them were too afraid of her to stay with her teaching for long. If Lizzie took over their lessons, Margaret could focus on the talented pupils to whom her teaching was invaluable.

Lizzie got her way and gradually built a following of pupils, seeing her reward not only in the money she earned, but also in the happy faces of the pupils she taught and the more satisfied demeanour of her godmother.

Life became even busier, but Lizzie still made time for the women's group, attending meetings and joining her fellow members in handing out leaflets on women's suffrage outside the Houses of Parliament.

'You need to get yourself a decent chap,' one young man told her cheekily. 'You wouldn't need to make a show of yourself with all this protesting then.'

An older man said he'd take her over his knee and tan her hide if she were his daughter.

'Luckily, I'm not,' Lizzie told him sweetly, moving on to offer a leaflet to another gentleman. 'Give it to your wife if you can't bring yourself to read it,' she suggested.

'My wife knows her place and I won't have such unnatural nonsense in my house.'

'I'm sorry you feel threatened by independent-thinking women,' Lizzie told him. 'It must be awful to be so insecure.'

1912 slid into 1913 and Lizzie took part in another march, this time the Pilgrimage for Women's Suffrage which ended with a rally in Hyde Park.

It sounds exciting, Polly wrote.

I have exciting news of my own, though you might think it rather tame after all your protesting. I'm engaged to be married! Davie proposed last night with an adorable ring that used to be his grandmother's.

We're going to wait a couple of years before we actually get married so we can save some of our wages. We're lucky in that we're going to have a home with his family for a while, but we still need some things of our own — linen and such — so I'm starting to put things aside in a bottom drawer.

Lizzie was delighted for her. She wrote to say it was exciting news indeed and sent a pair of embroidered pillow cases to help the bottom drawer along.

Her thoughts turned to Polly the following year when Cordelia invited Lizzie to write an article for a magazine produced by the NUWSS. 'You're eighteen now, and I think readers will be interested in a young woman's view of a fair world,' Cordelia said.

Keen for her article to reflect Polly's world as well as her own, Lizzie sought for a word that would best express what she most wanted. After thinking of Matt and the rest of the Warrens, she settled on respect. Matt not only loved his brothers and sisters, he also respected each of them and listened to their views.

The article flowed easily once she'd decided on her approach. In Lizzie's ideal world, all women — whether domestic servants, factory workers, shop assistants, wives, mothers, single women or anything else — would be valued and their wishes, needs and opinions recognised as being of equal worth to men's, even if they were sometimes different.

'Excellent!' Cordelia declared, and Lizzie was thrilled when readers praised the article too.

Matt would be proud of her. Or so she liked to think. Years had passed since she'd spent those few days on Bee Corner Farm, but he'd made himself the brother of her heart and that wasn't to be forgotten.

The weather was glorious over that summer of 1914. Basking in the sunshine and the chance it gave her to wear lighter dresses, it felt unreal to realise that storm clouds of conflict were gathering across Europe.

But so they were. And they threatened a war that could turn all of their lives upside down.

11

The idea that Germany was spoiling for a fight was nothing new. Lizzie had been hearing it for years, but never quite believed anything would come of it. Even when she read in the newspaper that the heir to the throne of Austria-Hungary had been assassinated alongside his wife in distant Serbia, it felt too remote to have repercussions on British soil. But it began to appear as though Germany was using the tragedy to launch a quest for domination by encouraging Austria-Hungary to threaten Serbia in retaliation. Soon old alliances were stirring other countries into possible action. France. Russia . . .

But would Britain stay out of it? Discussions at the women's group gave Lizzie little confidence in British neutrality. Certainly, some people expected it, but others feared the worse, Cordelia Bishop among them. Cordelia was both level-headed and well-connected to the armed forces as well as the government, so her opinion counted most with Lizzie.

On 28th July, with Germany promising support, Austria-Hungary declared war on Serbia. Days later, Germany declared war on Russia and soon afterwards on France. Then Germany invaded Belgium and refused British demands to withdraw.

On 4th August, as people strolled leisurely in Highbury Fields, watched cricket and played games with carefree children, Britain went to war with Germany too. Gradually more countries entered the war on one side or the other.

'We're luckier than many,' Margaret told Lizzie. 'We have no husbands, brothers, sons, or anyone else close to us in the conflict.'

That was true. Lizzie felt deeply for those who had loved ones in the armed forces, including Cordelia and other friends. Soon more people they knew had menfolk involved because the call had gone out for volunteers to enlist to serve King and country.

'I hope I love my country as much as anyone,' Lizzie told Margaret on returning from the shops one day. 'If I were a man, I might well volunteer, but only with a heavy heart. I saw a group of young men while I was out and they were urging each other on to enlist as though signing on for a game. One started making chicken noises when a friend hesitated. Another said enlisting would be a lark, especially as it wouldn't be for long.'

'Over by Christmas, many people are saying,' Margaret commented. 'The war may well be over by then for some of these young men, but not in the way they expect.'

'A woman in the grocers boasted that both of her sons had volunteered, as though it were some sort of competition. It just can't have occurred to her that they might be injured or killed. Another woman crowed that her sweetheart had enlisted and any young man who didn't join him should be labelled a coward. She didn't stop crowing even when a third woman pointed out that some young men were also husbands and fathers with families that might struggle to get by on the separation allowance. Seventeen shillings and sixpence a week for a wife and two children doesn't go far.'

'Let's hope it doesn't take a tragedy to wake them

up to their foolishness.'

Tragedy called early for some regular soldiers, including the son of one of Cordelia's cousins. He was in the British Expeditionary Force that sailed to France in the middle of August and fell in the Battle of the Marne less than a month later.

Fortunately, Polly had written to say Davie was safe because he was needed on the farm. Lizzie was pleased to think that the same must be true of Matt and the other Warren boys.

At the women's group they all agreed that it was a good thing the more militant suffragettes had decided to stop using force. 'The focus is on supporting the country through the war now,' Cordelia observed.

With so many men enlisting, there was a labour shortage, so women were beginning to take on work that had traditionally been done by men, from selling tickets on buses and delivering post to producing munitions.

'I'd like to do something to help,' Lizzie confided to Cordelia.

'You already have a job.'

And it wasn't a job Lizzie could easily abandon, even for other paid work, without making Margaret suffer financially and in her enjoyment of her teaching.

'I'd do volunteer work if I could find something to fit around the time I have available,' Lizzie said.

Cordelia's niece was a volunteer ambulance driver and Ida Trumpington's granddaughter was helping in a hospital, but they weren't juggling paid work or looking after a house as Lizzie was doing.

'Some of us are going to take First Aid and Home Nursing classes from the Red Cross,' Cordelia told her. 'I'm hoping you and Margaret will join us. We may not plan on becoming nurses, but who knows when the skills might be useful? I'm also organising a knitting initiative. Now it appears that the troops will be spending the winter in cold, muddy trenches, they'll be glad of warm socks and scarves.'

Margaret and Lizzie joined in both the Red Cross classes and the knitting evenings. Lizzie enjoyed them but, while she was clearly making an effort, Margaret's talents lay in neither direction. She was awkward with first aid and her attempt to knit socks was a disaster. How fingers that could coax magic from a piano could produce only misshapen knitted items was a mystery.

'I'm not sure they're quite perfect,' Margaret said, holding up some socks.

'Perhaps you could try knitting a scarf,' Cordelia suggested, sending Lizzie a grimace.

Margaret tried a scarf but produced a sorry length of dropped and wobbly stiches. 'I'm sure it'll keep someone warm,' Cordelia soothed.

Ida Trumpington piped up then. 'I'm not sure why we're bothering with knitting if the war's going to be over soon.'

But they were already in December and there was no sign of peace. 'Whatever we knit won't be wasted,' Cordelia pointed out. 'Even if the war ends, London has plenty of poor people who'll be glad of what we produce.'

At their last meeting before Christmas, they gathered around the piano for carol singing. After being the dunce of the knitting and first aid sessions, Margaret became the star. From 'Silent Night' to 'Oh Come, all ye Faithful', her gifted fingers never faltered.

'Thank you, Margaret,' Cordelia said sincerely. 'That was perfection. And thank you, Lizzie, for leading the singing.'

'We all sang,' Lizzie pointed out.

'But you have the strongest voice. The loveliest voice too. Full of emotion.'

The others agreed.

Embarrassed, Lizzie steered the conversation towards the weather, wondering if they'd have a white Christmas.

They had rain instead. 'I wonder if the men in the trenches are having rain?' Lizzie said to Margaret.

'They'll be having a miserable Christmas if so.'

As usual, they were spending Christmas Day quietly. Lizzie had bought Margaret a new blouse and Margaret had bought Lizzie a new case in which to store sheet music. Both of them had received gifts from pupils. Lizzie's were varied — a china cat, chocolates, a notebook, perfume, a small framed print of Highbury Fields, a trinket box, a brooch . . .

Margaret's were handkerchiefs and soap. Lots of soap. Mostly lavender-scented with two bars of lemon verbena. Lizzie guessed that her godmother's pupils just didn't know what else to buy their formidable piano teacher. Fortunately, Margaret had little patience for fripperies and was glad to have the household supplied with enough handkerchiefs and soap to last the year.

From Polly, Lizzie received a jaunty scarf. Lizzie had sent Polly new stockings, knowing they were useful to a girl who was still giving some of her wage to her mother.

There was no card or gift from Lizzie's father. There never was. Lizzie dismissed him from her mind, though not before three words crept into her mind. *Maybe one day*.

The horrible sherry came out on New Year's Eve so she and Margaret could toast in 1915 with a single glass each. 'Let's hope it'll be a peaceful year,' Lizzie said.

'The sooner peace comes, the better,' Margaret agreed.

The Red Cross classes and knitting evenings resumed in January, the women hastening through the frigid January air and icy rain to get into the warmth of each other's houses.

There was hope that a springtime push might bring victory but Cordelia confided her fear that this wasn't going to be an easy war to win. 'It isn't like battles of old when soldiers fought out in the open and cannon-balls caused damage only where they fell. In this war the men are hunkered into trenches and the weapons can do terrible damage. Modern shells can travel over long distances and a single machine gun can kill a dozen men in seconds.'

Lizzie shuddered. 'Are you suggesting there's likely to be a stalemate?'

'One side or the other will have to push forward eventually, but perhaps there'll be more casualties and less chance of decisive victory.'

Lizzie's wish to do more for the war effort grew, though she still couldn't see a clear path to helping while juggling her other commitments.

January gave way to February and the war made itself increasingly felt on the home front. Food was in short supply and prices were rising. German U-boats were destroying ships bringing supplies to Britain, and many of the country's young farmworkers had enlisted. *Farmers are struggling to find workers to tend their animals or bring the crops in*, Polly wrote. *Davie did the right thing in staying. The responsible thing.*

But the next letter Lizzie received from Polly told a different story.

I hardly know how to begin because I'm in such a tizzy. I thought Davie was safe on the farm, and Heaven knows the country needs farmworkers. I suppose he's been a little distracted recently, but I never suspected . . .

Lizzie, he's enlisted. I never got a chance to try to talk him out of it because he joined up with two friends without telling me his plans. I cried when he told me what he'd done and then I grew angry. Davie said I should understand that he isn't a boy anymore but a man who needs to act like one so I should be proud of him for joining up. Well, of course I'm proud of him, but I'm terrified for him too. He leaves for training camp soon, so between his work and mine we'll have little chance to see each other.

Am I wrong in wishing he was staying safe on the farm? Selfish and unpatriotic? Please don't judge me too harshly.

Poor Polly! Lizzie lost no time in writing back.

Of course you're worried and upset. I wish we lived closer to each other so I could hug you. As it is, I can only tell you I'm thinking of you and of Davie too.

Davie will be at training camp for two or three months so let's hope peace comes before he has to join in the fighting . . .

118

A few days later Polly replied.

Thank you for not thinking too badly of me. I know thousands of other girls are going through the same upset, and many have gone through the worse agony of losing their loved ones or seeing them suffer terrible wounds. I may be spared that.

Davie's mother was in tears when I saw her last night and his father was furious with him. All the opposition made Davie quite churlish. He said there was nothing wrong in wanting a bit of adventure before he settled down and his father called him a fool because there was no adventure in dying. The bad atmosphere spoilt the evening and Davie's mood lasted even when he walked me home. I hope I see him again before he leaves for camp. Whatever happens, I have to make the best of it.

Two days later another letter arrived.

He's gone!
I'm sick with worry, but at least we parted with words of love. I'm living for his letters and for your letters too. You're always such a comfort, Lizzie, and I so enjoy hearing about your life in London.

Lizzie did her best to entertain Polly through her letters, describing London, her pupils, her Red Cross lessons and her knitting. Time never hung heavily for Lizzie but she still hungered to do more for the war effort than knit socks, useful as they were.

Out shopping one morning — the queues at the food shops growing ever longer — Lizzie winced as the winter chill pinched her fingers. The weather felt mean and spiteful, with spring seeming far away and the jollity of Christmas fading into the past. Christmas had made the dark, chilly days and nights more bearable with festive decorations, pupils chattering about Father Christmas, carols around the piano . . .

An idea struck Lizzie suddenly. It took shape in her mind as she walked towards home. On impulse, she turned and hastened in the opposite direction.

12

'I know you aren't expecting me so if this isn't a convenient time . . . ' Lizzie began.

'I have half an hour before I need to go out,' Cordelia assured her. 'What is it, Lizzie? You look excited.'

'Please say if you think this is a bad idea.' Lizzie took a deep breath, told Cordelia of her plan and was glad to see a smile grow on her friend's face.

'I think it's an excellent idea,' Cordelia said.

'Really? Then my next challenge will be to persuade Margaret.'

'I'm sure she'll be only too glad to do something more suited to her talents than knitting or nursing. Let's face it, Lizzie. Margaret's creations are suitable only for dog beds. As for her nursing . . . It's lucky you were a healthy child.'

Lizzie smiled, knowing it was true.

'You'll give Margaret my regards?' Cordelia asked, because for all the gentle mockery she held Margaret in high regard.

'Of course.'

'And do let me know if I can be of any help in your venture.'

Encouraged, Lizzie headed home to find Margaret playing the piano. How beautiful it sounded.

'Exquisite,' Lizzie said as Margaret finished.

'I was a little stiff.'

'No one would have noticed.' Lizzie drew a chair near to her godmother and sat down. 'I think we should offer music as our war effort.'

Margaret looked puzzled.

'Concerts for sick and injured servicemen,' Lizzie explained. 'Music might lift their spirits a little.'

'You're not suggesting a music hall style of entertainment?' Margaret's distasteful expression showed her opinion of music halls.

'Nothing like that.' Though Lizzie wouldn't mind any style of musical entertainment if it gave the audience pleasure. 'I thought you might play a solo or two, and then we could play some duets together. I can also sing if you'll accompany me.'

'Are you sure we'll be wanted?'

'I think the servicemen will want us. Whether the hospitals and convalescent homes will allow us to give concerts on their premises remains to be seen. I'll ask them. Cordelia will know the best people to contact as she's so well connected.'

'They'll need to make a piano available.'

Lizzie smiled, pleased that Margaret was going along with the idea. 'You're right. We can hardly make our way through London pushing your piano, though it might make for an interesting spectacle. I'll talk to Cordelia and see what she suggests.'

Lizzie returned to Cordelia's the following morning. 'We've agreed we want to offer concerts but we're not sure how to set about making arrangements.'

'You can leave that to me. I suspect a lot of buildings and even private homes are going to be used to accommodate the sick and wounded before this war is over. There'll be no shortage of places for you to perform.'

'Thank you, Cordelia. Perhaps we should commit to only one small concert for the moment. Just so we can be sure it's the sort of thing servicemen want.'

'I understand. We have a women's group meeting on Wednesday. Hopefully, I'll have news for you then.'

Cordelia did have news. She had a date for a concert at a small convalescent home in Hampstead, if they wanted it. 'You'll have three weeks to prepare and you'll perform to about twenty patients. How does that sound?'

Lizzie looked at Margaret who turned slightly pale but raised no objection. 'It sounds perfect,' Lizzie said, though her stomach felt unsteady too.

It was one thing to imagine performing to an audience. Now it was becoming a reality, stage fright was stirring.

Fortunately, the performance would be short. 'The men are injured and exhausted,' Cordelia explained. 'They won't be able to concentrate for long, but even a short event should cheer them.'

It would also take place late on a Sunday afternoon when neither Lizzie nor Margaret were due to teach so no lessons — and no income — would be missed.

They settled on a programme and practised it often over the weeks that followed. Was it the right programme for their audience, though? Lizzie hoped they hadn't chosen badly.

13

The convalescent home was a red brick building that had probably started life as a handsome family house early in Queen Victoria's time. Three storeys high, it had stone steps leading to a central porch built around a sturdy black door. Lizzie used the brass knocker gently, hoping she wasn't disturbing any of the sicker patients.

A porter answered and showed them to a large room which might have hosted dancing in its heyday. A piano stood at one end and several rows of chairs had been placed to face it. 'I'll fetch Matron,' he said.

Margaret walked towards the piano. 'I suppose we'd better prepare ourselves.'

She lifted the lid and ran her fingers along some keys.

'I hope it's satisfactory,' someone said.

Lizzie turned to see the matron.

'It needs tuning,' Margaret told her, doubtless stating a simple fact rather than criticising, but the bluntness still made the matron blink.

Lizzie swooped in with a peace-making smile to make introductions. 'I hope your patients will enjoy what we offer,' she said then. 'This will be our first performance.'

'The patients who are well enough to attend are looking forward to it. The staff too. I'm afraid I must leave you now, but I hope to catch at least some of your performance. Thank you so much for coming.'

Margaret settled down to familiarise herself with

the piano. Lizzie attempted to sing scales but her throat was hoarse with tension. She begged glasses of water from the porter which helped her voice but did nothing to stop her stage fright.

Soon the audience began to arrive. Some men were walking wounded with bandages identifying lost arms, head wounds or injuries to chests and abdomens. Others hobbled in on crutches, while three men needed wheelchairs, one poor soul having lost both legs above the knee. There were several nurses among them.

'Are you nervous?' Lizzie asked Margaret.

'We're doing our duty,' her godmother answered, affronted. 'Nerves would be self-indulgent.'

Lizzie only smiled, knowing the sharpness arose from the very thing Margaret was denying. Nervousness.

Eventually it appeared that all of the audience members had arrived and were sitting waiting. Oh, heavens. Should Lizzie say a few words of introduction or simply begin the programme?

She was relieved when the matron returned to address the audience. 'I'm delighted to welcome Miss Penrose and Miss Kellaway to Upton House,' she began. 'Together they form . . . ?'

She looked at Lizzie, an eyebrow raised in enquiry. Were they supposed to have a special name? Panicked, Lizzie glanced at Margaret who simply studied her music. 'The Penrose . . . Players,' Lizzie said.

The matron turned back to the audience. 'Please join me in giving an Upton House welcome to the Penrose Players.'

The audience clapped politely.

Swallowing, Lizzie joined Margaret at the piano,

though she had nothing to do for this opening piece except to turn the pages of her godmother's music.

Margaret began with Beethoven's 'Moonlight Sonata'. She was too proficient a pianist to let nerves affect her beyond a certain stiffness but Lizzie could have cheered when the stiffness melted away because what followed was lovely.

The music ended. Lizzie turned to gauge how the audience had received it . . . and was appalled to see a wheelchair patient in tears. Oh, no! The music had been too mournful. Far from raising his spirits, it had brought them low.

But then the audience broke into applause and the wheelchair patient wiped his eyes to smile. The music hadn't brought him low. It had simply moved him— beauty in the face of the horror he must have experienced at the front.

Margaret acknowledged the applause with the merest nod but her cheeks were pink. After another solo and a duet, it was time for Lizzie to sing. Standing in front of the expectant patients, she felt her confidence drain away, but she couldn't turn tail and run. She closed her eyes to steady herself, swallowed hard and began, her voice gradually loosening as she sang the old folk song, '*Where are you going? To Scarborough Fair* . . .'

Eager applause broke out as she finished. 'More!' someone shouted.

Relieved, and beginning to relish the performance, Lizzie obliged and the rest of the concert passed amazingly quickly.

'Well,' the matron said, inviting the audience to thank the Penrose Players at the end. 'Wasn't that a treat?'

'A corker of a show!' one patient called.

'Come back soon!' yelled another.

More patients sent grins and approving nods.

'I think we can call that a successful afternoon,' Lizzie said to Margaret, as they made their way outside.

'Music soothes the soul.'

It certainly did.

The women's group met at Cordelia's house the following week. Cordelia had champagne and glasses ready. 'To toast the Penrose Players,' she explained. 'I heard how popular you were.'

'Just doing our duty,' Margaret snapped, but her cheeks were pink again.

Cordelia exchanged smiles with Lizzie, then said, 'Oh, of course, Margaret! I imagine your sense of duty means you're willing to perform for more sick and injured servicemen now.'

'Certainly. If they want us.'

'I've drawn up a list of hospitals and convalescent homes you might approach. Shall I pass it over to you to make arrangements, Lizzie?'

'Yes, please.'

'Excellent. Now, who wants more champagne?'

Lizzie wrote to all of the places on Cordelia's list. It was time-consuming to put together a timetable without a telephone, but over the weeks that followed a schedule of performances took shape. 'I'm not sure we'll be able to keep to Sunday afternoons,' Lizzie had warned Margaret when requests came in for weekday concerts.

'We'll rearrange our lessons as best we can, even if it means teaching at less convenient times. We all have to make sacrifices in times of war. Besides, with prices going up, some families may not be able to afford to pay for lessons anyway.'

That was true. Lizzie's household budget was already being squeezed. Some foods such as sugar, butter and meat were difficult and sometimes impossible to come by, and the queues at the shops remained long. Prices were continuing to rise too. Eggs that had once cost one penny each had already risen to three pennies and bacon that had once cost ten pence now cost double that amount.

'I should tell you that Brian Herbert's mother informed me she couldn't afford to continue paying,' Margaret continued. 'Her husband was killed at Ypres, if you remember? I said we'd teach Brian for free. We shouldn't let a talent like his go to waste.'

Lizzie had overheard the conversation with Mrs Herbert. In a rare moment of tact, Margaret had pretended the offer of free lessons was a regular scholarship. Lizzie couldn't have been prouder of her. Margaret's heart was tender even if her manner could be flinty.

May brought the first Zeppelin raid on London and three pupils left in the hope of finding safety in the countryside with their grandparents. Lizzie bought long strips of paper and pasted them to the windows in criss-cross fashion to stop glass from flying about in the event a bomb fell nearby.

She also made sure the curtains were closed tightly each night as the Defence of the Realm Act — DORA as it was known — made it unlawful to show light outside in case it guided Zeppelin crews to built-up areas.

Despite the anxiety and sadness of the war, Lizzie took pleasure in the concerts, especially when the audiences let it be known how cheered they felt. The concerts also gave Lizzie plenty to say in her letters to Polly.

One of the men asked if we took requests for songs and asked for 'When Father Papered the Parlour', she wrote one day.

I had to tell him we didn't have the music for that song or for 'Boiled Beef and Carrots' which he requested next. As a tease I offered him 'The Girls Know as Much as You' then we settled on 'If You Were the Only Girl in the World' though I changed girl to boy.
Other men began to request songs too, and many wanted lively tunes. I was worried that Margaret might not like the direction the concerts were taking but she agreed I should buy the sort of music the men seem to want. 'We're performing for their benefit, after all,' she told me.

Margaret was adjusting, not only to the lively music, but also to the lively atmosphere. *An older soldier — a Sergeant Major — called Margaret his darling today,* Lizzie wrote another time. *She looked shocked at first, and I thought she might take offence, but she only rolled her eyes and told him to stop talking nonsense.*
Mindful that Davie would soon be going off to fight, Lizzie took care never to write about the terrible injuries she saw at the concerts — missing limbs, disfigurements, burns, and also blindness caused by the enemy's new weapon: poisonous gas.
Neither did she mention the poor young man who collapsed in a fit brought on by a head injury, or the man with a shattered jaw who sobbed during one of Margaret's heart-stirring piano solos and had to be

helped from the room.

Instead she wrote about lighter incidents — the men who flirted or sent her cheeky winks, the doctor who forgot himself during one of Margaret's piano pieces and began to accompany her on an imaginary violin, and the piano with a broken key that made every piece sound like a comedy act. *You know how much Margaret loathes music hall vulgarity, but she took it well and even gave a little bow when the audience applauded her.*

Polly was devastated when Davie was finally ordered to France. *But I know I mustn't be feeble about it,* she wrote. *After all, Davie's the one who's in danger while I'm safe in Witherton. I've wanted this war to be over from the day it started but it feels different now. Having a fiancé involved in the fighting gives me more of a stake in the war and I'm desperate for peace.*

Even Lizzie felt more closely connected to the war now someone she'd once known was involved in the fighting, especially as she had a dear friend whose happiness depended on his survival.

Keep sending me letters, Lizzie, Polly urged. *I'm depending on you to help me stay cheerful.*

Lizzie was happy to oblige and Polly never failed to write back about life in Witherton.

Occasionally she mentioned Lizzie's family, enclosing funny sketches of the new Mrs Maudsley with her nose in the air. *I never knew a person could have so many hats and furs. She shows them off all over Witherton but people dislike her for it. I've heard that she's persuaded your father to buy a motor car so she can show off even more.*

When he paid for all these luxuries, did Edward Maudsley ever spare a thought for the daughter he'd left to be brought up at someone else's expense? Not that Lizzie wanted money from him these days, as she preferred to earn her own. But a thought now and then . . . At least Lizzie was sure her mother would be proud of her, and she had friends who loved her too.

Your sketches made me laugh, she wrote to Polly.

A few days later she wrote again. *A man came up to us after today's concert and said, 'That were grand, lasses,' in a broad Yorkshire accent. I know you're in Cheshire rather than Yorkshire, Poll, but it was good to hear a northern voice. I miss your voice, and hope it won't be too long before we meet again.*

Polly replied with, *We'll meet again when you're bridesmaid at my wedding. I hope that won't be too far away though I don't know when my Davie will be home again . . .*

But the summer wore on and, as the war approached its second year, there was still no sign of peace. *So much for all that boasting about how soon we'd stampede to victory,* Polly wrote. *Let's not wait any longer before we meet. Let's meet this summer when some of your pupils take a break and you're not so busy.*

Lizzie was thrilled by the idea. *Yes, let's!* she wrote back.

14

They met in Birmingham, which was roughly midway between Witherton and London. Lizzie's train arrived first, but she soon noticed a fair-haired girl looking around uncertainly. 'Poll!'

Polly saw her, smiled and waved back.

They hugged when they reached each other. 'You're so pretty!' Lizzie cried, at the same time as Polly cried, 'You're so pretty!'

They laughed. 'It's true,' Lizzie said, and Polly said, 'I mean it.'

With her silvery hair, blue eyes and slender figure, Polly was a dainty fairy. Lizzie was slender too, but not as slight as her friend, and far less fairy-like with her dark eyes and heavy, glossy hair.

'Good journey?' Lizzie asked.

'I've only been on a train once before, when Davie and I went to Southport for the day, so I was nervous travelling alone,' Polly admitted. 'I expect you think I'm silly, but I've never been brave like you, Lizzie.'

'Next time you'll be more confident. Shall we find somewhere to eat lunch and settle down for a long chat?'

'Sounds perfect.'

They looked in shop windows as they walked, admiring hats and dresses and shoes, though neither of them bought anything because money was tight. They saw several places where they could buy lunch, but finally chose a small tea shop in a side street because the menu displayed in the window looked both appealing and cheap.

'How's Davie?' Lizzie asked, once they'd ordered soup and bread.

'He doesn't say much about the war itself, but he likes the men in his platoon. I hope that means they look out for each other.' Polly's expression faltered a little.

'It's natural to worry,' Lizzie told her, 'but there are nice things to think about too. Like that pretty engagement ring you're wearing.'

'Oh! You haven't seen it before, have you?'

Polly held out her hand so Lizzie could admire the ring, a slim gold band supporting an oval sapphire.

'It's perfect,' Lizzie declared. 'The sapphire matches your eyes. Tell me what sort of wedding you're planning.'

'It's hard to make plans with Davie away but we'd like something simple. To be honest, we haven't the money for anything else. But I'm determined it's going to be beautiful. I'm saving up to have as many flowers as possible — in the church, in our bouquets and even in my hair.'

'It sounds utterly charming. What will you wear?'

'A white dress, of course, though I'll have to make it myself.'

'What would you like me to wear?' There was no question of a special dress for Lizzie.

'Just whichever of your dresses you feel is prettiest. Hopefully, we'll be able to book the Sunday School hall for the reception, as my family's cottage is tiny and Davie's home isn't much bigger. Both families will provide sandwiches and cakes. I wonder if you might play the piano and sing? You must be used to performing now.'

133

'I'll do whatever you like,' Lizzie promised.

Polly paused then said, 'I'm so happy with my Davie. I hope you'll find someone special soon.'

'I'm in no hurry.'

Lizzie had been invited to walk out by several young men — the brothers of pupils, a neighbour's son, and a doctor at one of the hospitals — but none had sparked her interest.

Was she destined to remain a spinster? There was nothing wrong with remaining unmarried if that was what a person wanted. Miss Sparkes from the women's group was one of them. She shuddered at the mere mention of men. But Lizzie rather liked the idea of a husband and children eventually.

Not that there was always a choice. Lizzie still didn't know what had happened between Margaret and George Gilbert Grafton, but if Margaret had rejected him, she'd long regretted it. Or so Lizzie suspected.

After lunch, the girls lingered over a cup of tea before taking another look at the shops. 'I hope you can have your wedding soon,' Lizzie said, folding her friend into a hug when the time came to part. 'Whatever happens, we must meet up again. Perhaps you might come to London for a few days. Margaret won't mind putting you up, and I can show you the sights.'

'That would be lovely,' Polly agreed.

With a final wave they went their separate ways.

Thoughts of romance lingered in Lizzie's thoughts over the following days. She was in their local music shop collecting an order for Margaret when an impulse prompted her to ask, 'I wonder if you have any music by George Gilbert Grafton?'

'The Girl with Grey Eyes' was a wonderful song. He might have written more and had them published.

'I'm afraid I'm unfamiliar with the name. Is he a classical composer? We only supply classical music, of course. If he writes popular music . . . ' The shop assistant made it sound like a disease.

'You wouldn't stock it, I suppose.'

'Not at Millerfield's.'

What a snob he was. Lizzie liked classical *and* popular music. In their different ways they both gave joy.

But perhaps it was just as well that she'd found no music by Mr Grafton, because what would she have done with it? Even if he had shared a romance with Margaret, many years must have passed since then. Mr Grafton might be married to someone else and have forgotten all about poor Margaret. Perhaps he'd been married all along and she'd never been more than a passing fancy to him.

Whatever had happened, Lizzie was fairly sure that Margaret knew what it was to pine for a sweetheart. She had a way of saying, 'Poor girl,' when letters from Polly arrived.

Then there was the time when Lizzie, wanting a book to read, chose *Persuasion* by Jane Austen. 'I haven't read this in a while,' she told Margaret.

'Humph.'

'Not your favourite?'

'It's a good enough book if you like that sort of thing.'

Clearly Margaret didn't. Did she dislike the book because its heroine had been reunited with the sweetheart she'd been persuaded to reject in her youth but there'd been no such happy outcome for Margaret's own romance?

If anyone had persuaded her godmother against Mr Grafton, Lizzie imagined it had been Margaret's

135

father. He'd brought her up alone after his wife died young, yet appeared to stir no affectionate memories in his daughter. Margaret mentioned him rarely and displayed not a single photograph of him.

Lizzie had Mr Grafton in mind when she travelled to a music shop near Waterloo station a few weeks later in search of the ragtime music one of her pupils had requested. 'My cousin gets to play ragtime at his piano lessons,' the pupil had added.

Lizzie didn't want to lose the pupil to another teacher when money was increasingly tight so she promised to see what she could do about acquiring the sort of music he wanted. She rather liked the jollity of ragtime anyway.

She chose two pieces that were suitable for learners then asked about Mr Grafton's music.

'We have several of his pieces in stock,' the sales assistant told her.

Lizzie gaped at him. So Mr Grafton really was a professional composer. She snapped her jaw up again. 'Might I see them, please?'

There were five pieces and Lizzie chose two — 'In the Park', which looked to be a lively song, and 'Twilight Serenade', which looked to be slower. She left the shop feeling pleased and a little stunned by her purchases.

She had no suspicion that she was about to receive a second surprise.

15

The streets around Waterloo were busy but Lizzie's thoughts were on Margaret and Mr Grafton, so she took little notice of her fellow pedestrians as she navigated her way around them. It was only when she paused to give space to an elderly woman that her eye was caught by a man in khaki uniform on the other side of the street. His face was mostly obscured beneath his cap, but being tall, upright and rangy, he put her in mind of Matt. His way of walking reminded her of him too. It was confident. Elastic.

Good grief. It couldn't actually *be* Matt. Could it?

Frustratingly, the passing traffic and pedestrians allowed only brief glimpses of the man. Lizzie moved to the kerb for a clearer view but a bus halted beside her. By the time she'd hastened around it, the soldier had already passed by.

Dodging traffic, she darted across the road in pursuit, earning an irritated toot from a car driver and a raised fist from a man in a cart. 'Sorry!' she called.

The soldier's height put him several inches above most people and made him easy to spot, but his long strides were taking him onwards at speed and the pavement was too busy for Lizzie to break into a run. She dipped this way and that instead, apologising when she got in people's way.

The soldier turned into Waterloo station. Lizzie followed, but it was even busier in the station concourse, not only with servicemen but also with families there to greet them or send them on their way. Where was

Lizzie's soldier?

There! She squeezed through the throng but realised she wouldn't be quick enough to reach him before he arrived at a platform where a train stood waiting, presumably to take soldiers to the boats that would transport them to France.

'Matt!' she called, but the soldier simply eased through the families that had gathered around the barrier and set off down the platform.

Lizzie arrived at the barrier to see him stop by a train door. 'Matt!' she called again, and felt a thrill of excitement as he paused and turned.

It was him! Surely it was him? But he'd looked around only to speak to another soldier who'd come up behind him. Both men boarded the train and, while some soldiers leant out of windows, this man wasn't one of them.

Or was he? Yes, there he was.

Lizzie stood on tiptoes and waved. 'Over here, Matt!'

Had he seen her? He was looking in her direction but perhaps he was merely looking at the crowd. A whistle blew, steam hissed and the train lurched away, picking up speed until it disappeared from sight.

Lizzie's heels slumped back to the ground and she trailed out of the station, trying to talk herself out of her disappointment. Much as the man had reminded her of Matt, it made no sense that he'd be here in London in army uniform. He'd be hard at work on the farm instead. Unless . . .

Of course! All three Warren brothers must be old enough to serve their country now, and perhaps the farm couldn't justify them all staying at home. If one brother had to join the fighting and risk death or injury, Matt would have insisted on that brother being him.

Lizzie still wasn't entirely sure that the soldier had been Matt, but it was certainly possible, and she knew she'd worry about him for as long as the war endured. Her personal stake in the war — begun with Polly's Davie — had deepened.

* * *

The moment Lizzie reached home, she took Mr Grafton's music up to her room and hid it under the lining of a drawer. Not for anything would she risk upsetting Margaret with a reminder of the man she might once have loved. Lizzie would have to wait until her godmother was out of the house before she played the songs.

The opportunity didn't come for more than a week. Margaret walked out each morning on what she called her constitutional, but it was difficult to predict how long she'd be away. Only when Margaret went to a pupil's home to teach did Lizzie feel safe enough to take the music from its hiding place.

She played 'In the Park' first. It was the sort of catchy tune that people would hum under their breath for days.

'Twilight Serenade' was different. A love song. Lizzie wondered if it had been written with Margaret in mind. For all its beauty, it was still what would be termed a popular song rather than a classical one. Had highbrow Margaret caused the split in their relationship by looking down on Mr Grafton's music? Possibly, though opposition from Margaret's father continued to be the more likely cause in Lizzie's mind.

139

She was glad she'd spent precious pennies on buying the music. It helped her to feel closer to her godmother.

Lizzie was returning the music to the drawer in her room when she noticed the publisher's name on the cover — Williams Landish — with addresses in London and New York. She stared at the London address for several seconds as it occurred to her that she might be able to write to Mr Grafton through his publisher. But then she made an impatient sound and closed the drawer. What had she been thinking? That she might somehow reunite him with Margaret?

Even if she composed a letter that simply gave news of an old friend rather than a romance, he might consider the approach to be impudent, intrusive and embarrassing, especially if he happened to be married. Margaret might feel the same if he got in touch. No, Lizzie didn't know enough about their relationship to risk it.

Dismissing the idea, she turned her thoughts back to the man who might have been Matt. Several years had passed since she'd last looked for Bee Corner Farm in the atlas.

She looked again now, and even went to the library to study a larger reference map. Frustratingly, she could still find no mention of it.

★ ★ ★

Summer slipped into autumn. Every morning Lizzie bought a newspaper and read the casualty lists, feeling relieved when neither Matt's name nor Davie's were mentioned. Then she'd turn her attention to her teaching and the concerts, which were growing increasingly popular. Many hospitals and convalescent homes were inviting the Penrose Players back for second or even third concerts.

Most satisfying of all was the reaction of the men they entertained. 'First rate . . . '

'A corker, Miss . . . '

'You can come and kiss me better anytime, me darlin' . . . '

October came and towards the end of the month one member of their women's group, Miss Sparkes, broke an ankle and went to stay with her sister in Pimlico in order to recuperate. When the mother of Lizzie's two last pupils of the day — twins — cancelled their lessons because she thought they might be coming down with measles, Lizzie fitted in a visit to the invalid.

'It was the darkness that did it,' Miss Sparkes said, explaining how her ankle had come to be broken. 'Don't misunderstand me. I know we need to keep lights hidden to keep us safe from those dreadful Zeppelins, and I've no sympathy for the people who are fined for letting their lights show. But the darkness does make it harder for a person to see steps and kerbs and slippery patches.'

This was true. Lizzie had even heard of one poor soul being killed by a car because the driver had been unable to see him.

'I misjudged the edge of a kerb and now look at me,' Miss Sparkes said.

Lizzie duly sympathised.

War talk occupied the rest of Lizzie's visit. 'Terrible as this war is, it's at least showing what women are made of,' Miss Sparkes said. 'Women are doing all sorts of jobs these days, not least making munitions, and that's horribly dangerous work. If the contribution women are making to the war effort doesn't result in the right to vote, there's even less justice in the world than I thought.'

It was very dark outside when Lizzie took her leave. Not wanting to follow her friend's example in breaking an ankle, Lizzie walked carefully.

She was nearing Victoria train station when she saw an elderly lady stagger and clutch a lamppost. Hastening over, Lizzie touched the woman's arm. 'Excuse me, are you unwell?'

'Bless you, dearie. I don't feel quite myself.'

'May I fetch someone? A relative? A doctor?'

'What I need most is to get off these feet.'

'Take my arm. There's bound to be a seat in the station.'

Lizzie helped the woman inside and found a seat for her. 'That's better,' the woman said. 'I'm Ida Braithwaite, by the way.'

'Lizzie Kellaway. Would a cup of tea be welcome?'

'It would, dearie.'

Lizzie bought tea from a mobile canteen and was pleased to watch it bring colour to Mrs Braithwaite's cheeks.

'That did me a world of good,' she said. 'I'll sit here a while longer, but don't let me keep you from going about your business.'

'I'm not going to leave you. Rest for as long as you like and then I'll see you home.'

It was half an hour before Mrs Braithwaite felt able to move. Luckily, she didn't live far away and insisted there was no need for a cab.

Her home was in Masons Buildings, a tenement that looked run-down from the outside but was clean and comfortable on the inside. 'I always try to keep things nice,' Mrs Braithwaite said.

'I can see that. Do you live alone?' Lizzie had been hoping there'd be someone here to help.

'I've been a widow for twenty years, and my Sal left to get married almost as long ago. You've done me a kindness in seeing me home, but you needn't linger any longer.'

'At least let me make you something to eat.'

There was soup in a pan so Lizzie warmed it on the stove.

'You're welcome to share it,' Mrs Braithwaite offered.

'Thank you, but I've already eaten.' It wasn't true but Lizzie wouldn't take food from a woman whose budget was obviously tight.

She sat with Mrs Braithwaite while she ate, noticing that a jaunty little black hat decorated with green feathers sat beside a sewing box on the table. 'Are you a milliner?' Lizzie asked.

'I trim hats for the shop my daughter runs with her husband.'

'This hat is delightful.'

'It's kind of you to say so. How do you make your living, dearie? If you don't mind me asking?'

Lizzie told her about piano teaching and the concerts too.

'The poor soldiers deserve a sing-song after all they've been through. My Sal's Frank had consumption as a child, so his wind isn't good enough for fighting, thank goodness. The hat shop suits him. Suits my Sal too. Quiet, you see?'

'I'm glad he's safe. Let me wash these dishes then I'll be on my way.' Margaret would be worried and

Ida was looking much better now. 'Are you sure there's no one I can fetch to help you?'

'I don't want to impose, but could you get a message to my Sal? She's in Exeter Street near Covent Garden. Lives above the shop. Don't worry if it's out of your way, though.'

'I can take a message.' Lizzie imagined it would take half an hour to walk there, but at least it was in the right direction for Highbury. 'What would you like me to tell her?'

'Could you say I've had one of my turns? She shouldn't worry because I'm all right now. But I'm behind on a couple of hats.'

'I'm sure she'll be more concerned about you than the hats.'

'She's a good girl, my Sal. But I don't want her wondering why I haven't got over there. Tell her I'll try again tomorrow.'

Lizzie bade Mrs Braithwaite goodbye and set out, hurrying now despite the darkness in case Margaret was imagining her in an accident. After racing down Buckingham Palace Road, Lizzie passed the Palace and continued along The Mall towards Trafalgar Square. Skirting it, she hastened along the Strand and finally reached Exeter Street. The subdued lighting made it difficult to read the numbers above the doors but Lizzie finally found a window in which she could make out hats on stands.

A knock on the door brought a woman downstairs.

'Sally?' Lizzie realised she didn't know the woman's surname.

'Yes.' The answer sounded suspicious.

Lizzie explained what had happened and passed on Mrs Braithwaite's message. Sally's manner changed to gratitude. 'I'm obliged to you! Mum suffers with her heart sometimes, but she won't come to live with us. We haven't really got room, but we'd make do. Mum likes her independence, though. Come in for a minute. Catch your breath. I've got a bottle of stout in the cupboard.'

'I really must be going,' Lizzie said.

She continued onwards, passing behind the Lyceum theatre as she tried to work out the best place to pick up an omnibus or train.

The sudden explosion lifted Lizzie off her feet and slammed her into a wall, driving all the air from her lungs. A painful, high-pitched ringing assaulted her ears. Then chaos rained down on her, along with what felt like the wall itself.

16

Lizzie curled up instinctively, covering her head with her hands and bracing herself for death. Eventually the wall stopped falling and, amid the chaos and awful ringing noise, she became aware of more sounds — screams, wails, cries for help . . .

Then other voices. 'Someone fetch a doctor . . . '

'Careful where you tread . . . '

'Watch out for fire . . . '

'Can anyone smell gas?'

'Has the Zeppelin gone?'

Zeppelin? Of course! Lizzie must have been caught in an attack.

Still more sounds. Running footsteps. New voices . . .

'My God!'

'Holy Mary!'

'Pass the rubble along . . . '

'Where's that doctor?'

'This poor lad's a goner . . . '

'Must be lots of goners in that pub . . . '

Gradually it dawned on Lizzie that she was alive. She stretched her fingers, moving slowly for fear of bringing more debris down. They encountered only empty space. How was that possible when she was surely buried in rubble? She reached out further and her fingers connected with something that felt like a flat sheet of wood sloping above her head. It rose to a peak where it met another sheet of wood angling downwards.

She realised then that it was a sign from a building, a two-sided sign that must have stuck out from the wall so it could be seen by people approaching from several directions. In falling over her like a tent, it had protected her from harm. From serious harm, that was. Lizzie's head was wet with blood and she could feel the sting of cuts and bruises elsewhere on her body.

She took a deep breath so she could call for help but her lungs filled with choking dust. She tried again and the same thing happened. Panic closed around her. She could barely breathe and her body was cramped . . .

Lizzie fought through to self-control. Clearly, others were much worse off than her. If she was patient, help would come eventually.

But it was hard to wait. Horribly hard.

'Hello?' a voice called eventually. A male voice, close by.

Thank God! Lizzie breathed in dust and coughed again, hoping the cough would be enough to communicate her presence.

'I'm coming for you,' the voice promised. It was a warm voice, a giver of confidence.

Hands burrowed beside her, tugging out debris and tossing it elsewhere. Lizzie tried not to think that the movement might bring more of the wall cascading down, then gasped as something hard and heavy hit the sign above her and knocked it lower onto her head. Once again, she braced herself for death but the sign had come to a halt before it could crush her into the rubble. She was horribly claustrophobic, though.

'Nearly there,' the voice called.

Someone else must have come to help because the

first man began to shout instructions, insisting his fellow rescuer take every care to avoid any more debris falls. Would they manage it, though? Lizzie's heart beat fast with sickly dread.

But then she felt the load above her easing. She caught the gleam of a lantern or torch. Wasn't it against the law to be showing light out of doors when it might guide Zeppelins to —

What a ridiculous thought! A Zeppelin had already struck. Was panic getting the better of Lizzie again? She forced herself to stay calm.

The gleam brightened as more rubble was cleared then the sign was lifted away. Lizzie's relief was profound. She was pushing herself up when a hand reached out to stop her. 'Don't rush. You might do yourself harm.'

Lizzie saw the sense in taking her time though her cramped muscles were screaming for relief. She eased her arms and legs a little. Blood flowing through the tortured limbs brought pain but soon gave way to more normal sensations. She could breathe more easily too.

She turned her head to her rescuer. Dust swirled in the lantern light but she could see that he was a young man in army uniform. A filthy uniform after helping her. 'Thank you,' she said, 'but I don't think I'm seriously hurt.'

At that moment blood trickled down her face from a wound somewhere on her scalp. Her rescuer produced a handkerchief and applied it to her face.

After a moment he drew back and waited to see if the bleeding continued. Lizzie felt another trickle but this one was slower. He wiped it gently away.

'Hardly a gush,' Lizzie pointed out.

Her rescuer smiled. 'Are you always this brave?'

Another small fall of debris rattled to the ground around her. 'I'm not brave enough to stay here when this entire wall might come down on me,' she said.

'Time to move,' he agreed.

He helped her to her feet, guided her over the rubble, and steadied her when she stumbled. Reaching safety, she turned and looked up at the building whose bricks had rained down on her. Only the corner had been blasted away, but even so Lizzie could have been killed if the sign hadn't fallen over her like a guardian angel. *McCalls for fine cigars*, she read. 'I don't like the smell of cigars but I'll never complain about them again. That sign saved my life.'

Turning back, she looked at the scene in front of her and felt weak at the sight of so much destruction. People were sitting or lying on the ground, some injured, some past all human help. Other people wept or comforted as best they could. The Bell public house had been hit badly, and from the looks on the faces of the people who were attempting to reach those inside it, the situation was grave indeed.

Lizzie started forward to offer help but her rescuer touched her arm. 'There's nothing you can do that isn't already being done.'

He was right. Numerous people were already helping and more were arriving, including an ambulance and a doctor who'd been watching a performance in the Lyceum when the bomb struck.

'But you should let the doctor check you over before you leave,' Lizzie's rescuer said. 'You may not consider yourself a priority, but it's better to be safe than sorry.'

'It'll be hours before I can be seen, and I need to

get home.' Poor Margaret would be frantic. 'Did I have a second rescuer? I'd like to thank him.'

'He's over there but has other things on his mind just now.'

'Of course.' Lizzie's second rescuer was helping to reach people trapped in The Bell. It wouldn't be right to distract him.

It occurred to her then that she'd lost her bag with her purse and keys inside.

She stepped back towards the cigar sign and spotted a strap under some debris. 'Let me,' her rescuer said.

He pulled on the strap. The pile of rubble shifted slightly, but the bag came free. He shook the worst of the dust off and passed it to her.

'Thank you,' Lizzie said again. 'For everything.'

'I have a car nearby. Let me take you home.'

'Thank you, but I won't take up any more of your time.'

'I came to London to visit an old school friend who was invalided out of the army last year but I've already seen him. And, if you'll forgive the insult, I doubt any conductors are going to want you on their buses or trains.'

She was a filthy mess, of course, and her hair was askew.

'Unless you live more than a hundred miles away, it'll be no trouble to drive you,' he continued. 'The car is going to get dirty anyway with me driving it. I'm Harry Benedict, by the way.'

Lieutenant Harry Benedict, she realised, noting the insignia on his uniform. 'Lizzie Kellaway. I live in Highbury. If it isn't too far out of your way, a lift will be welcome as there's someone there who'll be worrying about me.'

'Oh?'

'My godmother.'

'Ah.' He looked pleased to hear it, which puzzled Lizzie until she noticed the admiring glow in his eyes and realised he was relieved she hadn't mentioned a husband or sweetheart.

She was flattered. Yet it felt uncomfortable for attraction to flourish in a scene of tragedy.

Harry appeared to feel the same way because he suddenly turned brisk. 'Let's get you home,' he said, though he softened the suggestion with a smile.

His car was parked just a few yards away. 'I saw the blast and came running,' he explained, holding the passenger door open for her.

Lizzie hesitated to get in with so much dirt covering her, but Harry really was almost as grubby. She climbed inside and he walked around to the driver's seat. 'How are you feeling?' he asked, as they set off.

'A little shaky,' Lizzie admitted. 'In urgent need of a bath.'

'Only to be expected.'

Even in the limited light she could see him more clearly, away from the dust that was swirling in the air. She'd already realised that he was a little above average height and trim. Now she registered the fact that his hair and eyes were dark, his forehead wide and smooth, his smile warm. An attractive man indeed.

The journey to Highbury didn't take long as the evening traffic was light. Lizzie directed him to the house and he eased the car to the kerb. 'May I call on you tomorrow to be sure you're recovering?' he asked.

'I wouldn't like to inconvenience you.'

'I'm home on leave with time on my hands.'

'Then a visit will be welcome. Perhaps in the morning? I work in the afternoons, teaching piano.'

'You're not planning to rest after tonight's trauma?'

The idea shocked her. 'I'm sure I'm well enough to sit at a piano.'

Harry laughed. 'Brave,' he repeated.

He got out of the car and walked around to help Lizzie get out. He offered his arm on the short walk to Margaret's door but once there he said, 'I shan't impose at this hour,' and retreated back to the car.

Lizzie knocked on the door because she didn't trust her trembling fingers to manage her key. Margaret's tall, thin shape appeared through the stained-glass door panels. Glancing back, Lizzie waved to Harry, then the door opened and she was tugged roughly into Margaret's bony arms.

'Thank God!' Margaret murmured. 'Thank God!'

Thrusting Lizzie away again, Margaret looked her up and down. 'Where on earth have you been? What happened? You look . . . ' Unable to say any more, she trailed off, swallowing.

Lizzie placed a hand on Margaret's shoulder. 'I'm sorry I made you anxious. Let's go inside and I'll explain.'

A glance behind her showed that Harry was already driving off. Lizzie suggested going down to the kitchen so she wouldn't tread dirt into the carpets. 'It was a Zeppelin bomb,' she said when they reached it.

Margaret clutched the back of a chair.

'I was passing the Lyceum theatre and got caught on the edge of the blast. I know I look as though I've been dragged through a building site, but I'm fine. A few cuts and bruises only. I'm one of the lucky ones.'

'Oh?'

'Not everyone will be going home tonight.'

Margaret nodded gravely, then, as though needing to anchor her emotions in activity, she pulled off her spectacles, wiped them and put them back on. 'Tea,' she declared. 'Sweet tea for shock. Toast too.'

She busied herself with the kettle and a loaf while Lizzie sat at the table, feeling cold and weak. She thought of the poor people who'd been killed or seriously injured, and wanted to weep for them.

'Here,' Margaret said, setting a cup and saucer in front of her.

Tea had spilt into the saucer because Margaret's hands were shaking too, but there was plenty left in the cup. Lizzie sipped it, grimacing at the sweetness and realising Margaret must have used their precious sugar instead of the honey they'd begun to use due to the shortages. The toast was burnt in one corner but not for anything would Lizzie show ingratitude by pointing it out.

'Were you . . . trapped?' Margaret asked, strain showing in her lined face.

'Not for long. Help came soon.'

'The Lyceum theatre, you say?' Clearly, Margaret was puzzled about what had taken her goddaughter there.

Lizzie told her about Ida Braithwaite.

When the clock upstairs struck eleven Margaret's thoughts moved into another direction. 'You should be having supper instead of toast but I didn't cook.'

It wouldn't have occurred to her.

'I don't need more food, but I do need a bath.' Lizzie was stiffening-up. Feeling sore and fragile.

Luckily, there was enough hot water for a deep bath. Lizzie winced as her cuts and scratches began

153

stinging in the heat but they soon grew used to it. Lying back, she let the warmth envelop her battered body. She tried to relax by closing her eyes and breathing deeply, but images, sounds and remembered sensations kept snapping into her memory.

The bang of the tobacconist's sign falling onto her head . . .

Screams and terror . . .

Wails of despair . . .

'This poor lad's a goner . . .'

'Must be lots of goners in that pub . . .'

Sitting up again, she washed and rinsed her hair then dried herself and dressed in her nightclothes. She was touched to discover that Margaret, who usually had no instinct for nurturing, had placed a stone hot water bottle in Lizzie's bed. Margaret appeared a moment later. 'Hot milk,' she said, setting the cup and saucer on the chest of drawers next to the bed.

The milk was scorched but it was the thought that counted. 'Thank you.'

'I'm glad you're safe, Lizzie.'

With that, the emotion became too much for Margaret and she left the room.

Despite the assault her body had taken, sleep proved elusive to Lizzie. Time and again, she felt herself drifting off only to be jolted back into wakefulness.

'This poor lad's a goner . . .'

'Must be lots of goners in that pub . . .'

The grief of the victims' families must be terrible. Even survivors might face disability for the rest of their lives. Poverty too, if unable to work.

Lizzie slept eventually, waking to daylight around the edges of her curtains. She groaned as her movements set up aches as she got out of bed, then groaned again when her mirror showed a ghost-white face, bruises and the red tracks of cuts and scrapes. It could have been much worse, though.

She washed, dressed and suppressed grimaces as the bristles of her hairbrush met the wounds in her scalp. She could only hope her appearance didn't frighten her pupils that afternoon. Lizzie didn't want to let them down, and heaven knew she needed both the distraction of teaching and the money.

'I look worse than I feel,' she insisted, joining Margaret in the kitchen.

'You should eat some breakfast. I could scramble an egg . . .'

'No!' Lizzie couldn't face a burnt egg this morning. 'I'll do it. My muscles are stiff so I need to keep moving.'

She scrambled an egg for each of them. 'I was brought home last night by the person who helped me,' Lizzie said. 'A lieutenant in the army. He asked if he might call this morning to see how I am.'

'How kind,' Margaret said, though a moment's hesitation suggested she was wondering if there were more to the visit than kindness.

She'd never had to think about Lizzie and romance before. Was Margaret remembering the heartache she'd endured over George Gilbert Grafton and feeling wary in case her goddaughter suffered a similar experience?

If so she was premature. Much too premature. Lizzie might meet Harry today and realise that last night's frisson of attraction owed more to the heightened emotions of the bombing than to any real spark. Besides, he'd soon be returning to the front.

Margaret had nothing to worry about. Not yet, anyway.

17

Lieutenant Benedict arrived at eleven. Opening the door to him, Lizzie wondered if her battered appearance would disappoint him, but his smile held just as much warmth as last night. 'Good morning, Miss Kellaway. I'm glad to see you're well enough to be out of bed.'

There was certainly nothing to disappoint in his appearance. He was a handful of years older than Lizzie and even more attractive in daylight, the face in which those dark eyes were set being fresh and open, while the teeth behind the kind smile were white and even. He was in uniform again, but it had been sponged and pressed since last night, and his shirt was fresh.

'Please come in. My godmother wishes to thank you for helping me.' Lizzie raised her voice, hoping Margaret would take the hint as she sometimes forgot the niceties of polite behaviour.

Margaret was keen to thank him, however. 'Terrible things, those Zeppelins,' she commented, shaking his hand.

'Indeed,' Harry agreed. 'Have you seen the newspaper reports?'

They hadn't.

'Last night's Zeppelin went on to bomb elsewhere. Lincoln's Inn and Farringdon, among other places.'

Lizzie suppressed a shudder. 'Tea?' she suggested, looking meaningfully at her godmother, who finally realised she was being asked to make it.

'Oh! Yes. Tea.'

'I'd welcome a cup,' Harry said. His manners were as relaxed and charming as Margaret's were stiff and awkward.

He waited until Margaret left the room then turned to Lizzie with concern cutting a small frown into the smooth forehead. 'How are you really feeling?'

It was sensitive of him to guess that she didn't wish to worry her godmother more than necessary. 'Shaky,' she admitted. 'But there's nothing seriously wrong. I don't like the thought of the enemy vanquishing me, so I plan to carry on as normal.'

He nodded as though she'd given further proof of her courage. 'I think I mentioned that I'm home on leave?'

'From France?'

'Belgium, actually. Near Ypres. A week's leave is precious and I'm determined to enjoy it. Would you help by having dinner with me?'

Lizzie hadn't been out to dinner with a young man before. She hadn't been *anywhere* with a young man. But she'd never met one who attracted her like Harry Benedict. 'I'd like that,' she said, hoping she wasn't blushing.

'Tomorrow evening?'

'As long as you can wait until after I've finished teaching?'

He smiled. 'I'll wait as long as necessary.'

Margaret's tea wasn't the best, even allowing for the fact that they were drinking it weak these days because it was expensive and not always available to buy. Harry drank it manfully, though, and thanked Margaret graciously when he got up to leave.

'Hmm,' Margaret said, after he'd gone. 'That young

man has manners.'

He certainly did. And Lizzie's excitement stirred at the thought of seeing him again.

★ ★ ★

Harry came in the car to collect her the following evening. Unused to restaurants, Lizzie opened the door to him feeling self-conscious, though she'd done her best with her appearance, choosing what she considered to be the nicest dress from her limited collection. It was a royal blue crepe dress that had drawn compliments from members of the women's group because the strong colour brought out the gloss of her dark hair and the healthy glow of her cheeks.

She'd made the dress herself, using fabric bought before the war had put material in short supply. The bodice was fitted while the sleeves finished at the elbows and the skirt swept almost to the floor. Gold braid around the square neckline was the only embellishment. Lizzie hoped it was enough to make the dress suitable for a dinner engagement, though it could hardly be described as a typical evening dress, most of which were delicate confections of silk chiffon, lace and beads, judging by those she'd seen in shop windows. She hoped Harry didn't have a particularly smart restaurant in mind.

'Thank you for collecting me.'

'It's my pleasure,' Harry told her, and if he thought her unsuitably dressed, the glow in his dark eyes masked any sign of it.

Harry himself looked pristine and handsome.

Margaret came into the hall. 'Good evening, Lieutenant.'

'Miss Penrose. Thank you for sparing Miss Kellaway this evening. I'll bring her back safely.'

He didn't add, 'If I can,' though the possibility of another Zeppelin attack was clearly in the thoughts of all of them.

Lizzie had expected to have to wear her ordinary coat, but Margaret had surprised her by saying, 'I have a cloak you can borrow.' It was a black velvet cloak. 'I had it when I was a girl. It hasn't been worn in twenty years, but you're welcome to borrow it.'

Lizzie was grateful. Being plain, the cloak wasn't unduly old-fashioned, and it looked much more appropriate than an everyday coat. 'I'll take care of it,' she promised, wondering if Margaret had worn it when she'd seen George Gilbert Grafton.

There was just a hint of wistfulness in Margaret's grey eyes as she waved Lizzie off.

'Feeling better?' Harry asked, as they settled in the car.

'I think so.'

Lizzie's limbs had loosened over the day, but memories of that dreadful scene kept flashing up in her mind. Those poor people! Even as she'd walked to the car, she'd glanced up at the sky apprehensively, though it was much too dark to see if one of those cigar-shaped monsters of death was flying above them, ready to hurl down more death and destruction.

She supposed Harry must have seen many scenes of horror at the front. No wonder he wanted to make the most of his leave before he returned. Pushing her own dark memories aside, Lizzie smiled across at him.

'I booked a table at the Savoy,' he said. 'I hope that's acceptable?'

The Savoy sounded grand. 'I've never been to a

fashionable hotel before,' Lizzie admitted. 'My idea of a treat is an egg on toast in a Lyon's Corner House.'

Much as she wanted Harry to enjoy the evening, she wouldn't put on an act and pretend to be wealthy. She wasn't ashamed of her modest circumstances and believed qualities such as kindness were more important anyway. Did Harry feel the same, though? Or would he spend the evening wishing he'd never invited her?

'There are times when an egg in a Lyon's is exactly what we need,' he said, grinning.

It was the perfect answer, but Lizzie's self-consciousness returned as she entered the restaurant to see other women in frothy, glittery dresses and blazingly bright diamonds. Thrusting the feeling aside, she looked at her surroundings instead. 'This place is beautiful.'

'It was designed by the impresario of the Savoy Theatre, so it's certainly flamboyant.'

A waiter settled them at a table and they studied their menus. 'I'm going to eat as much food as I can manage,' Harry told her. 'I want to remember this meal when I'm back at the front eating cold beef stew out of tins, with biscuits hard enough to break teeth.'

'It sounds grim.'

'The food is terrible, but we try to make up for it in our rest periods. Some of us go to hotels for decent food if we can get to them. Decent baths too. You can't imagine the bliss of a hot bath and clean clothes when you've lived in mud day after day.'

'Lice-free clothes?'

'You've heard about the lice? Awful little blighters, and hard to get rid of, even with fumigation.'

'They lay eggs in the seams of uniforms, I believe.'

160

'Yes, and when they hatch out, they make a chap itch like crazy. They can cause sickness too. Trench fever. But there's nothing more we can do except endure them. Unless we want to lose the war.'

'I have it easier, being a woman. In wartime anyway.' Not in other ways.

'You must have suffered food shortages,' Harry pointed out.

'Yes, and high prices too, but we haven't come close to starving and we can make hot food and drinks anytime we like.'

'Talking of food and drink . . . ' Harry smiled as the waiter returned to take their orders: soup to be followed by fish and then cutlets. Harry also ordered wine.

'Have you lived with your godmother for long?' he asked when the waiter left them.

'Six years. My mother died when I was twelve. My father remarried and . . . Well, I decided I'd be happier with my godmother.'

'Second marriages can be tricky,' Harry agreed. 'I'm lucky in still having both of my parents. They're jolly decent people too. I also have three elder sisters, so I was thoroughly spoilt growing up. All three sisters are married with children of their own now.'

'Were you in the army before the war?'

Harry shook his head. 'I worked with my father in a small merchant bank in London. But I felt someone from the family should volunteer, and as the only son . . . I'd been a member of the OTC — the Officers' Training Corps — at school, so I was given a commission straight away.'

'Perhaps women will be allowed to fight one day. Not that they're sitting idle even now. Many women are doing work that used to be done by men. They're mechanics, ambulance drivers, munitions workers . . .'

'I admire them for it.'

'Really?' Lizzie was delighted.

'Of course. They're helping the country in a time of emergency.'

'Your sisters are looking after their families, I suppose.'

'Yes, but all of them — my mother too — knit for the troops and organise Christmas parcels. Have you had the chance to get involved in that sort of thing?'

'I have. My godmother has no talent for knitting, though, so she and I give concerts to sick and injured servicemen.'

'How splendid!' It was Harry's turn to look delighted. 'I wish I could see one of your performances.'

'Perhaps you will one day. But not because you're injured,' she added quickly.

She'd heard that some soldiers were actually glad of what they called a Blighty one — an injury that was severe enough to merit being brought back to Britain to recover or, better still, to put a permanent end to their military service. She'd even heard that some men inflicted Blighty wounds on themselves. Not that she could imagine Harry doing such a thing. Lizzie guessed that Harry's sense of honour and duty ran deep.

'Please call me Lizzie,' she said. 'Calling me Miss Kellaway puts me in mind of my pupils.'

Harry laughed. 'I'll be happy to call you Lizzie if you call me Harry. Tell me about your teaching. Are your pupils talented and attentive?'

'Some of them are talented. Some of them are attentive. Some are both, and —'

'Some are neither?' Harry suggested, brown eyes glinting humour.

'Don't tell anyone I said so.'

It was a lovely evening. Harry was kind, considerate and fun. 'I've had a wonderful time,' Lizzie told him, as he drove her back to Highbury.

'I have too, and I'd like to repeat it. Soon.'

Lizzie's cheeks grew warm with pleasure. 'That would be nice, but I mustn't keep you from your family.'

'I shan't neglect them. I'm actually staying with my parents down in Surrey, but they don't begrudge me time away from them. In fact, they're encouraging me to make the most of my leave by lending me this car. It belongs to my father.'

'And very comfortable it is. I'm used to trains, omnibuses, and my own two feet.'

'So . . . Dinner tomorrow?'

Keen as she was to see him again, Lizzie hesitated. Was it fair to let Harry pay for another meal? Tonight's dinner must have cost him dearly. 'The Savoy was magnificent but I don't need luxury all of the time,' she said. 'Perhaps we could go somewhere more modest. Or perhaps I could treat us.'

Harry looked horrified at the thought of Lizzie paying. 'I'm grateful for the offer but . . . No, Lizzie. A chap likes to do the treating.'

It was also a sad fact of life that men earned more than women. Another injustice for women to fight. 'I should tell you that I'm a suffragette. I campaign for women to have rights, so shouldn't they have responsibilities too?'

Harry opened his mouth to argue then narrowed his eyes. 'Are you teasing me?'

'I really am a suffragette, though not a window-smashing one. But perhaps I am teasing you a little.'

'Meaning you think I'm hopelessly old-fashioned about these things, but you'll let me have my way because you know it's important to me?'

'A compromise,' Lizzie suggested. 'Your treat, but a modest one.'

'Agreed.'

He walked her to the door when they arrived at Margaret's house. 'Thank you again for your company,' Harry said.

'Thank you for yours. And for the delicious meal, of course.' She kept her smile in place, but awkwardness settled over her as Harry looked down with glowing eyes.

Did he want to kiss her? The thought was exciting but unnerving. Lizzie had no idea how a young lady should behave when she said goodnight to a man. A handshake would feel too formal. Perhaps a kiss on the cheek . . .

She never got the chance to allow any sort of kiss. Margaret must have been listening out for Lizzie's return because she opened the door looking embarrassed, as though she felt obliged to protect her goddaughter's reputation but was just as unsure as Lizzie about what was and wasn't proper.

'Home safe and sound, Miss Penrose,' Harry said. 'I hope you had a pleasant evening?'

'Thank you, I did. Miss Kellaway too, I think.'

'Indeed,' Lizzie said.

Margaret showed no sign of going back inside so

Harry wished them both goodnight, sent Lizzie a secret wink and headed back to the car.

Lizzie and Margaret waved him off them moved inside to the music room. 'We went to the Savoy,' Lizzie said.

'Goodness.'

'He's invited me out again tomorrow.' It occurred to Lizzie that she was being selfish in abandoning Margaret for two evenings in a row. 'But perhaps I shouldn't go.'

'Please don't stay home on my account,' Margaret said.

Lizzie waited, sensing that her godmother had more to say. Her fingers were plucking the back of a chair in obvious awkwardness.

'It isn't my way to offer advice on matters of a . . . romantic nature,' Margaret finally got out. 'As a spinster I don't consider myself qualified to offer an opinion on romantic happiness. But I wouldn't want you to think I've never known . . . That I've . . . ' She took a deep breath. 'What I'm trying to suggest — rather clumsily, I'm afraid — is that you should follow the dictates of your heart and not let yourself be swayed by obligation or the expectations of others. Don't assume that the consequences of a wrong decision now will be of short duration and soon remedied by other opportunities. Happiness may be offered to us only once in our lives, Lizzie, and I'd hate to see you throw it away.'

As Margaret had thrown away her chance of happiness with George Gilbert Grafton?

'Now I'm going to add something that might seem to contradict everything I've just said. Which is that I hope you'll take care. Follow your heart but take care

165

not to . . . rush. Lieutenant Benedict will be returning to the front soon, and we live in uncertain times.'

Harry might be killed or simply forget all about the girl he'd rescued from a bomb site.

Lizzie walked over to kiss her godmother's cheek. 'You're very wise, Margaret, but you've no need to worry. I've only met the man three times.'

'Even so.'

'I'd like to enjoy Harry's company while I can, but I won't let myself be swept away. There. Does that reassure you?'

Margaret smiled but it was a tight smile. Was she thinking that a person could be swept away whether she chose it or not?

18

Lizzie decided to wear an emerald-green dress for her second dinner with Harry. It had been her best outfit before she'd made the blue dress she'd worn last night and, even if it was a little shabby now, the colour suited her. Which was just as well as she had nothing better to wear.

The thought of seeing Harry again filled Lizzie with pleasant anticipation. Mostly, she was simply looking forward to spending time in his company, but it had also occurred to her that he might be able to help her with something. Not that she planned to ask him necessarily, as she didn't want him to think she was taking a liberty, but the opportunity might still arise.

Collecting her later, Harry gave no sign of noticing that her dress was a little old. His smile was as warm as before.

They drove to a restaurant in Mayfair. 'Modest?' Lizzie chided, glancing round at plush red furnishings, crisp white tablecloths and sparkling silverware.

'Compared to the Savoy, it is.'

'Compared to a Lyon's Corner House, it isn't.'

'You're not cross, I hope? I'm glad to spend money having a marvellous time now because I want to store up happy memories to look back on when I'm far from home.'

When he put it like that, Lizzie hadn't the heart to protest further.

The evening was just as entertaining as the previous one. Harry spoke about growing up in Surrey and she soon learnt that his childhood had been almost idyllic. Tennis and croquet in the garden of the family home, long walks with pet retrievers, charades at Christmas, summer holidays on the south coast . . .

He'd attended a boarding school and enjoyed it, winning trophies for rugby and cricket, and getting up to mischief too, playing tricks on the masters, staying up for midnight feasts, and sneaking out to the local pub to drink beer for a dare.

He also spoke more about his sisters, Eleanor, Alicia and Charlotte. Lizzie formed the impression that Eleanor led with energy while the others were a little more relaxed, Charlotte especially.

'Are their husbands involved in the war?' Lizzie asked.

'Eleanor's Frank is a staff officer, currently based in London. Alicia's Paul was invalided out due to a foot injury, and Charlotte's Jonathan can't serve because he has a heart murmur. He isn't sickly. Nothing like that. But the rigours of battle would be too much for him.'

'Of course.'

'He's still contributing to the war effort, though. He's taken leave of absence from his stockbroking work to join the War Office. It frustrates him that he can't fight — it makes him feel cowardly — but I keep telling him that all war work is valuable, whether it's ensuring the supply of weapons and uniforms, doctoring, nursing, or performing concerts for the sick and injured as you do, Lizzie. Your concerts are important for keeping up morale as well as giving comfort.'

'We like to think so.' Lizzie told him about the concert she and Margaret had given that afternoon. 'The audience was on the lively side. Cheeky.'

'Not offensively so?' Harry was concerned.

'Oh, no! Nothing like that. The patients just wanted a little fun. Which is understandable.'

'Indeed. Wartime makes us more aware of the fragility of life and the importance of treasuring every moment.'

The comment reminded Lizzie that Harry's leave would be over soon, so she set about trying to entertain him with tales of Witherton and her own childhood, though she was selective in what she told him. She spoke affectionately of her mother, but skittered away from saying much about her father, not wishing to depress the mood. She talked of her friendship with Polly and Davie instead. 'I used to climb out of my bedroom window to meet them,' she confided.

'Heavens, Lizzie. That was dangerous. Were you never hurt?'

'I twisted an ankle once.' She'd slipped when climbing back up the tree. 'Not seriously, though.' It had been extremely painful but she didn't want Harry to feel sorry for her. 'I was a little wild at times,' she admitted with a smile.

'You were a child. You wouldn't climb out of a window now.'

'Not unless I had no other choice. Are your nieces and nephews well behaved?'

'They can be.' He paused then grinned. 'They can also be quite spirited.'

'You sound as though you like being an uncle.'

'I do. Very much. Though my sisters say I spoil the children horribly.'

Lizzie could imagine him being their favourite uncle. Thoughts of Harry's happy family put her in mind of the Warrens.

Should she ask Harry the question that had been hovering in her mind?

'What is it, Lizzie?'

'I have a friend and I'm wondering if you know a way of finding out which regiment he's serving in?'

'A friend?' Lizzie saw a touch of dismay flicker over Harry's face at the thought of a rival. It was flattering. Exhilarating too.

'I met Matt when I was a child of thirteen and haven't seen him since,' she explained, and Harry's expression turned rueful. Embarrassed, even.

'Sorry. It's just . . . Well, I like you, Lizzie. Very much.'

Goodness. He was only confirming something she'd already guessed, but it was still quite a step forward for him to put it into words. Lizzie was beginning to see that it would be easy indeed to be swept away by romantic feelings despite the war. In fact, far from holding them back, the war might push those feelings forward on a tide of tender-hearted urgency, because who knew what the future might hold? Or even if there'd be a future?

'I'm rushing you,' Harry said.

'A little.'

'Then I'll slow things down, because I don't want you running away from me.' There was understanding in his eyes. 'What's the name of this old friend?'

'Matthew Warren from Staffordshire. I don't have an address.'

'You're sure he's in the army, rather than the navy or Royal Flying Corps?'

'I thought I saw him in army uniform a few weeks ago but I'm not completely sure. He lent me some money once, but I lost his address and I've never been able to repay it. I'd like to find out how he is, too. Him and his family.'

Harry took a small notebook from his pocket and wrote the name down. 'I can't promise success, but I'll do my best.'

'Thank you.'

Harry grew thoughtful on the drive back to Highbury. He caught her glancing at him and sighed. 'I'm thinking about what I said earlier. I really don't want to rush you, but having only three more days of leave makes it difficult to go slowly. May I see you again?'

Lizzie hesitated. Tomorrow was Sunday and she wouldn't leave Margaret alone for a third time no matter how much she wanted to say yes to Harry. Perhaps it would be sensible to spend a little time apart from him anyway. 'I have to stay with my godmother tomorrow.'

'The following day?'

'I already have a commitment for Monday evening.' Lizzie and Margaret were hosting a meeting of the women's group. 'But if you'd like to go for a walk in the morning . . .'

'A walk will be terrific,' Harry said, smiling.

The smile turned a little rueful when he realised Margaret was observing them from behind the curtain of the music room. He walked Lizzie to the door and left her with a bow rather than a kiss, calling, 'Safely home again, Miss Penrose!' as Margaret opened the door.

Lizzie was glad to be able to tell Margaret that she wouldn't be seeing Harry again until Monday. Margaret nodded and looked relieved.

Out of sight didn't mean out of mind, however, and

Lizzie's thoughts turned to Harry often. There was so much more to him than dashing good looks. He was kind, generous, thoughtful, and fun. Thoroughly decent, in fact, based on what she'd seen of him so far. Who wouldn't take pleasure in his company and the admiring glow in those dark eyes?

But their circumstances were different. While Lizzie would remain here in London Harry would soon be gone, and an attraction of just a few days' duration — however promising it appeared now — might wither and be all-but forgotten once he was submerged back into fighting a war. This was especially the case if the attraction owed some of its intensity to a soldier's need to seize every possible moment of joy from life while he could.

Lizzie liked Harry Benedict a lot. She could see how easy it would be to feel even more for him. But it would be sensible to proceed with caution, enjoying his company while remembering that nothing might come of it.

He duly called for her on Monday morning and they spent an hour walking in Highbury Fields. Lizzie saw nothing to change her opinion of him. In fact, her liking only grew when he chased after a puppy that had slipped its lead then restored the dog to its owner with a good-humoured smile and the comment, 'Jolly little creature, isn't he?'

When Harry seemed unaware of the admiring glances that were sent his way by two young women who were walking arm in arm, Lizzie added modest to her list of his personal qualities and her liking for him deepened still further.

They moved into a tea room to warm themselves, as the day was cold. Harry didn't mention Matt and, not wanting him to feel bad if he'd forgotten all about her favour, Lizzie kept quiet too. She wouldn't see Harry again before he left for the front and, though he was as charming as ever, she noticed signs of strain in his eyes.

'I hope you won't mind if I write to you?' he said.

'Not at all. I might even reply.'

Harry smiled at the joke but his smile bore a wisp of sadness. 'You've made the last few days special, Lizzie. In other circumstances, we'd have time to get to know each other properly. Unfortunately, we don't have time, but I hope we can pick up where we're leaving off one day, and keep in touch in the meantime.'

He took the notebook from his pocket and tore out a sheet of paper on which he'd already written an address. 'This is where you can write to me. And this,' he tore out another sheet, 'is where you can reach a corporal called Matthew Warren who's serving with the West Staffordshire Regiment.'

Lizzie was thrilled. 'I'm so grateful,' she told him, tucking the notes into her bag.

They returned to Marchmont Row slowly as though to spin out their time together. Harry stopped her with a touch on her arm while the house was still some yards away. 'I'll walk you to your door but I'll say goodbye here.'

Lizzie felt herself blush as he bent to kiss her. It was a chaste kiss ... on her cheek instead of her mouth ... but it was delivered with a sigh that suggested Harry would have much preferred to kiss her lips. Rather thoroughly.

Lizzie wouldn't have been ready for that sort of kiss, so this was perfect, full of affection without being

173

full of rushed commitment.

'I hope I wasn't taking a liberty?' Harry asked afterwards.

'Not at all.'

'One day I'll kiss you properly,' he said, smiling, and Lizzie hid a blush by continuing towards the house.

Once there Harry called in to bid goodbye to Margaret then left again. Lizzie saw him to the door and watched him walk away. He reached the corner and looked back, his expression wistful.

'Please write!' he called.

'I will!'

With that he was gone.

Davie, Matt and now Harry. Lizzie's stake in the war had deepened further. She'd be scouring the casualty lists with even more sick dread from now on, searching for three names and praying she wouldn't find any of them.

19

I hope you're the Matt Warren who helped a girl called Lizzie Kellaway in 1909 when she needed rescuing from an awful man called Amos Bradley, Lizzie wrote that night.

If you're not that man, I apologise for troubling you. But if you are him, I'd like to explain why, despite all your kindness in taking me to your farm to recover then accompanying me to my godmother's house in London, you're only hearing from me years later. There was an unfortunate accident, I'm afraid. With the best of intentions my godmother washed my dress while your address was in the pocket and the ink on your note ran so badly that I couldn't read it.

I've spent many hours since then poring over maps in the hope of locating Bee Corner Farm but I've never found a mention of it. I even wrote to you at what must have been a hundred villages around Staffordshire in the hope that I'd hit upon the right one, but either none of the letters reached you or you were too disgusted by my behaviour to write back.

I'm very sorry for losing your address, even though it was unintentional. I hope you'll forgive me and write back now you know what happened as I want so much to know how you are. Edith and the others too. How is Bee Corner?

I haven't forgotten that I owe you money. I'd have sent it with this letter but thought it best to wait until

175

you confirm you're the Matt Warren I once called my friend.

In the meantime, I send my best wishes to you and the family.

Lizzie Kellaway.

PS If you're wondering how I know you're in the army, it's because I saw you catching a train at Waterloo station. At least I think I did. A friend gave me your service address.

★   ★   ★

She posted the letter the following morning. Returning home, she found to her surprise that a letter had already come from Harry.

Dear Lizzie,

For someone who said he wouldn't push, I'm afraid I'm pushing again. Perhaps not pushing exactly, as by the time you receive this, I'll be on my way overseas. I just want to say again how much I appreciated your company during my leave. You've given me lovely memories to treasure.

Please write soon.

Fond regards, Harry.

The letter bore the address of his parents' house in Surrey — Ashlyn, Beechfield Green. Lizzie supposed he must have written it soon after parting from her yesterday. She glowed warmly at the thought of him taking the trouble to write when he must have been preparing to leave as well as spending precious time with his family.

But perhaps his imminent departure had made the

need to grab every moment of joy from life feel even more urgent. Happy as she was to receive it, Lizzie wouldn't read too much significance into the letter. In fact, she decided to wait several days before replying, thinking that slowing things down might spare them both from awkwardness if time and distance made Harry feel that their time together had been a pleasant interlude but not something that had a future.

Much as Lizzie liked Harry, Margaret was right. It would be unwise for Lizzie to let her feelings run away with her.

Four days passed before she allowed herself to write, and she took care to couch the letter in friendly rather than romantic terms.

Dear Harry,

I hope your journey was safe and as comfortable as it could be on a troop ship.

I too enjoyed the time we spent together, and it was touching to hear from you so quickly. I imagine you want letters from home to be entertaining so I'll do my best to oblige, but please bear in mind that the life of a piano teacher tends to lack both glamour and adventure. Luckily, there was an incident yesterday that ruffled the sedateness of lesson time slightly — just in time for me to write about it. One of my pupils, Percy, smuggled his pet mouse into his lesson by hiding him in a pocket. Unfortunately, Albert Mouse grew bored with his owner's heavy-fingered rendition of Twinkle, Twinkle Little Star and escaped.

Percy panicked when he realised what had happened. By then Albert was long gone and I was beginning to fear my godmother's house would suffer a mouse infestation when in she marched, holding

the mouse and demanding to know if Percy had any
knowledge of the creature. I'm not sure what overset
Percy more — horror at almost losing his pet, or awe
that my godmother should have scooped the creature
up so calmly. He told me his female relations would
have screamed and fled at the sight of a mouse . . .

Lizzie wrote a little more then signed off by writing,
Fond regards as he'd done.

It was a nice way of ending a letter. Friendly without being intimate.

Two weeks passed and brought another lovely letter from Harry. If his feelings had cooled, it wasn't apparent from his letter, which told her how much he missed her.

Once again Lizzie wrote back in friendly terms that still kept the door open for him to withdraw from the correspondence without embarrassment.

No letter came from Matt. Perhaps she'd written to the wrong Matthew Warren, or perhaps he'd decided not to forgive her. Either of those options was better than a third possibility — that he'd fallen in battle.

But there were other alternatives. Matt might have lacked the time to write or his letter might have been caught up in the postal system. Post from the front could be erratic. Lizzie wouldn't give up hope.

Three weeks after she'd first written to him, she had her reward when a letter finally arrived. Lizzie tore into the envelope where she stood in the hall.

Dear Lizzie,
How surprised I was to receive your letter but how
delighted too.

178

And how happy Lizzie was to know that she'd made contact at last and Matt was well disposed towards her.

I never thought badly of you and neither did the others. We took it as a sign that you were busy with your new life and were glad for you.

I'm sorry you spent so much time — and so many stamps — on writing to us at Bee Corner Farm. I was puzzled when I read that — until I remembered that Edith gave that name to a section of garden where lavender attracted whole hosts of bees. Perhaps you saw the sign I made for her birthday one year. The farm is actually called Sorrel's Patch but I suppose we never mentioned the name in your hearing. There's a sign on one of the gateposts but it's often overgrown by bushes so is easily missed.

Please don't worry about the money you feel you owe. It was a pleasure to help you and we don't begrudge a penny.

You don't mention how you are, but I can assure you that we're all well. Edith is married now and her husband, Peter, is helping to run the farm alongside Joe and Mikey. Molly is still at home, of course, and Edith has a child of her own to add to the liveliness, a little boy called Thomas.

It was the knowledge that I was leaving Sorrel's Patch in excellent hands that enabled me to enlist. I've fared pretty well and have an advantage over many chaps as I've always lived an outdoor life. Wind, rain, snow, ice, mud . . . they don't trouble me unduly, though I'm as grateful as the next man for a bath and a hot meal. Apart from a small shrapnel scar (and I've had worse

179

injuries on the farm), I've stayed whole as well as healthy.

I'm sure Edith would be happy indeed to receive a letter from you if you have time to write to her so I'm adding her address to the bottom of this letter. She's Mrs Foster now. I'd love to hear more about you and your new life too.

With fond memories of a spirited little girl who's doubtless become a spirited young woman.

Matt Warren

The letter thrilled Lizzie — warmed her through and through, in fact — though she was sure Matt must be suffering more than he was admitting, and missing the farm too. She read it several times, lingering on his description of her as a spirited little girl. Lizzie supposed she had been spirited, but she'd also been afraid. Meeting Matt all those years ago had made her feel she'd reached safe harbour. Even the memory of the time she'd spent with him wrapped her in softness. Matt had not only been kind to her. He'd understood her.

Lizzie wrote back and told Matt all about her early life with Margaret, being careful to paint Margaret's eccentricities in a generous light. She also told him about how she was living now . . . teaching piano, attending the women's group and, of course, performing as one half of the Penrose Players. Her pen flew over several pages before it occurred to her that she might be overwhelming him. She finished by urging him to write again.

She also wrote to Edith, explaining her silence over the last years, congratulating Edith on her marriage and family, and begging for more news of all the Warrens. Edith wrote back to say she was delighted to hear from Lizzie and assured her that everyone on the farm was well. *We're all so proud of Matt*, she added, *but worried for him too. He enlisted as a private but has already been promoted to corporal. I hope his promotion doesn't mean he takes more risks . . .*

Exchanging letters with Harry, Polly, Matt and Edith kept Lizzie busy over the last months of 1915. She had much to report about life in London, her teaching, the concerts and the characters she met at them.

She also made a special effort to note funny incidents when she was out and about or reading newspapers. The dressing-down a rather hoity-toity woman gave to a carter when his horse snatched her handbag went into Lizzie's letters. So did the gentleman who embraced a stranger in the street in the mistaken belief that she was his wife after his spectacles broke and he could barely see. Then there was the newspaper report of a fight between two drunk men who were arguing about the best beer in London, another report on a woman who'd reached the age of one hundred and put her longevity down to eating mint imperials, and the time a pupil confided that a chimney sweep had accidentally caught his mother in her underwear.

To Matt's letters she added the sort of observations of nature she thought would appeal to him. The dazzle of winter sun as it set behind leafless trees, the jewelled appearance of a spider's web after rain, clouds surging across the sky like mighty galleons . . .

To Harry's letters she added comments about the London bustle and mood. She also began throwing caution to the wind by telling him that she missed

181

him. It was true, and he said it to her every time he wrote, his letters suggesting his interest in her hadn't cooled at all.

Not that Lizzie was in love with Harry. Not yet, though perhaps the wind was set fair for it. After all, it wasn't only his handsomeness she remembered whenever she thought of him. There was something open, honest and eager about him. Caring and generous too. And it was those qualities that warmed her affection for him. But they'd met in person only five times in total, and love . . . It was just too soon.

* * *

Christmas approached and Lizzie sent parcels for Harry and Matt containing warm socks, soap, tinned ham, sardines, cocoa, and — partly as a joke — packets of lice killer. To Edith she sent a basket of nuts and also a jacket and bonnet she'd knitted for Edith's new baby, a little girl called Rose.

To Polly, Lizzie sent a pretty enamel brooch with a set of teaspoons for her bottom drawer, while for Margaret she bought another blouse. Just a new grey blouse to replace an old grey blouse, but at least this one had a white collar and thin white stripes to liven it up.

Lizzie was thrilled with the gifts she received in return. Harry arranged for delivery of a hamper from Fortnum and Mason and, among other treats, it boasted cake, shortbread, tea and sherry. Delicious.

Edith sent a box of produce from the farm, explaining that it was also from Matt. She included several small plants for Lizzie to start her own herb garden. Polly sent a little hat she'd trimmed for Lizzie and

Margaret gave her a diary with an exquisite design of wildflowers on the cover.

From her father Lizzie received nothing at all. Unsurprisingly. Time wasn't changing Edward Maudsley, it seemed, but the New Year wasn't slow to usher in other unexpected developments.

20

One bleak Sunday afternoon in January, Lizzie and Margaret were sitting reading by a small fire in the music room when a knock sounded at the front door. They looked up at each other. 'Are you expecting someone?' Margaret said.

'No.' Lizzie got up anyway, shrugging off the blanket she'd wrapped around her shoulders in an effort to save money on coal.

As soon as the door was opened, the visitor launched herself into Lizzie's arms.

'Polly!' Lizzie cried. 'How lovely to see you.'

But Polly was in tears. Oh, no. Had something happened to Davie?

Lizzie drew Polly inside, closed the door and steered Polly into a chair in the dining room. It was icy in there but Polly would have some privacy. She sobbed for a while then raised her gaze to Lizzie. 'Davie's broken off our engagement. He's broken off everything.'

Lizzie was stunned. 'Why? I mean, what happened?' Surely this was a hiccup rather than a permanent breech?

'His letters have been rather short recently. I thought . . . I thought . . . ' Polly's face puckered under the threat of more tears but she blinked them away. 'I thought he was just too busy or too cold to sit writing for long, but then he wrote to say he thought we'd made a mistake in getting engaged so young. He said he still loved me in a way, but he wasn't sure it was the right way for marriage. In fact, he was sure it wasn't because he was craving his freedom.'

'Perhaps he said that because he doesn't want you to feel bound to him while he's away at the war,' Lizzie suggested. 'He must know he could be injured, and he might not want to tie you down as nursemaid.'

Polly shook her head. 'I don't think so. He mentioned his two closest army friends and how they'd made him come to see that a man shouldn't be tied down until he's tasted something of the world.'

'That might have been an excuse.'

'The thought of being free excited him. I could tell.'

'Then I'm sorry. Terribly sorry.'

Polly nodded, her pretty face wan and tear-stained. 'He said I should keep the ring but I couldn't do that. I gave it to his mother to look after.'

Lizzie was glad. The ring would have been a permanent reminder of what Polly had lost.

'Davie breaking off the engagement isn't the only thing that's happened. Mrs Hepple's daughter scolded me for not paying attention, and when I explained that my engagement had been broken off, she told me it was no concern of hers and I should do the job properly or find a different job. I told her I'd find a different job. I'm sorry to arrive uninvited, but I couldn't stay in Witherton where I'd been so happy with Davie. I'd like to find work here in London, but first I need a place to stay. Do you know of any cheap —'

'You'll stay here tonight.'

'I can't. It's your godmother's house, and I know she's—'

'A kind woman. When did you last eat?'

Polly looked puzzled as though food hadn't featured in her thoughts. 'I don't actually remember.

Yesterday, I suppose.'

'Then you must eat something now. Wait here while I tell Margaret what's happened, then we'll go down to the kitchen. It's warmer there.'

Margaret was as sympathetic as Lizzie had expected. 'I'll stay here for a while to give your friend time to collect herself,' she said, not being comfortable with excesses of emotion.

Polly was looking troubled when Lizzie returned to the dining room. 'I don't want to be a burden. Really, Lizzie. I have the money I'd been saving for when Davie and I . . . ' Polly faltered then steadied herself. 'What I mean is that I have enough to pay for a lodging.'

'Tomorrow, perhaps, but a Sunday afternoon is no time to be looking for somewhere to stay.'

They moved down to the kitchen where Lizzie warmed soup. 'You need to eat,' she insisted.

Margaret appeared as Lizzie was pouring tea a little later. Lizzie wasn't surprised to see wariness enter Polly's face. Margaret's flinty features always looked formidable. 'Thank you for allowing me to stay,' Polly said.

'You're welcome. I expect you're exhausted after your long journey.'

'I intend to look for work and a place to live straight away.'

'Commendable. What work have you done?'

'I was a housemaid, but became a sort of companion to an elderly lady.'

'You have references?'

'From both employers.'

'There must be many opportunities here in London. Domestic work especially, as so many young girls are filling men's jobs or working in munitions.'

'That's what I'm hoping.'

Silence descended, Margaret's stock of social conversation being limited and Polly still being in awe of her hostess.

'Perhaps Polly could sing for you while she's here,' Lizzie suggested, hoping to create common ground between them.

'Yes, I hear you can sing,' Margaret told Polly.

'Only a little.' Polly looked even more nervous now. 'I've never had lessons or anything like that.'

'I'd like to hear you anyway. It's no bother if you need to stay a few nights more.'

'Thank you.'

They drank the tea then Lizzie said, 'Come upstairs and get settled, Polly.'

Polly collected her bag from the hall and followed Lizzie up to one of the two attic rooms. 'It isn't very homely,' Lizzie apologised.

'I'm just grateful for somewhere to stay.'

They made the bed up together. 'I hope you didn't mind me suggesting you sing for my godmother. I'm sure singing is the last thing you feel like doing, but she'll appreciate listening to you.'

'I just hope she isn't disappointed.'

'I doubt it. Oh, Polly!'

She'd begun to cry again. Lizzie held her close then insisted she should get into bed for a sleep. 'Rest now. This house hasn't many creature comforts but it does have indoor plumbing. The bathroom is next to my bedroom one floor down at the back. I'll wake you for supper.'

Polly insisted on getting up early the following morning to look for work.

187

'We have the women's group coming tonight and it would be nice if you could join us,' Lizzie told her.

'Must I? I don't mean to be rude but —'

'You needn't join us for long.' And it would do her good.

Lizzie gave Polly a spare key. 'Margaret and I are teaching today so just let yourself in when you get back from your job hunting. Good luck!'

Polly was obviously tired when she returned but, as Lizzie had expected of her hardworking friend, she'd left no stone unturned in her search for work. 'I had interviews at three employment agencies, made enquiries at several shops and bought two newspapers for the Situations Vacant pages.'

'You've made an excellent beginning,' Lizzie said.

'I didn't look for anywhere to stay. A live-in job might suit me best, but I can move into lodgings temporarily if I'm in the way here.'

'You're not. I've made stew for supper so I hope you're hungry. We need to eat soon as our friends are coming. You're going to join us?'

Margaret swept into the kitchen. 'Of course, she's going to join us.'

Outnumbered, Polly nodded and after supper changed into her Sunday Best dress, a simple pale blue dress that looked extremely pretty on her dainty frame.

Her nervousness still showed when the guests began to arrive. 'I'm a farm labourer's daughter,' she whispered to Lizzie. 'I don't fit in with grand people like these.'

'Both Margaret and I have to work for our livings,' Lizzie pointed out. 'These people aren't snobs. They're friendly. Just be yourself, Polly. You have lovely manners.'

Polly was unconvinced but Lizzie was proud of her friend as she talked to the guests. Polly was sweet by nature and far too modest to put on airs. She answered the questions that came her way with simple honesty.

'Yes, I knew Lizzie when we were children in Witherton . . . '

'No, we weren't at school together. I went to the town school while Lizzie was educated at home . . . '

'I left school at twelve to help to support my family . . . '

'I'm in London to look for work . . . '

'What sort of work?' Cordelia asked, and Polly told her about being both a housemaid and a companion.

All of the guests promised to look out for opportunities and Polly thanked them with touching charm.

'All we need to round this evening off nicely is some music,' Cordelia declared later. Over the years they'd got into the habit of finishing with music.

Lizzie and Margaret moved towards the piano. 'Do you play?' Cordelia asked Polly.

'I never had the chance to learn.'

'Polly sings,' Margaret said.

'Not properly. I've never been trained,' Polly said hastily.

'It would be nice to hear you anyway,' Cordelia told her.

Thinking Polly's confidence would be boosted by the praise her voice was sure to win, Lizzie joined in the encouragement. 'Remember how we used to sing '*Greensleeves*' together?'

'That was years ago.'

'I haven't forgotten the words and I can't believe you've forgotten them either. I'll start, and you join in when you're ready.'

Lizzie began to sing and after a moment of obvious terror Polly began to sing too, her voice gradually gaining strength until its silvery tone could be heard by all.

'Why, that was delightful!' Cordelia said. 'Do favour us with another song.'

This time Lizzie and Polly sang 'Scarborough Fair', Lizzie being content to let Polly take the lead.

'Thank you, my dears,' Cordelia said when they'd finished. 'I hope we'll have a chance to hear you sing again, Polly.'

The guests began to leave but Cordelia held back. 'I was struck by what you said about keeping an old lady company, Polly. My mother-in-law is becoming frail, and she's unable to go out as much as she'd like. I know some people don't warm to their mothers-in-law but I'm fond of mine. Not that she's an easy woman, because she doesn't suffer fools, especially now she's riddled with arthritis and losing her sight. You might be just what she needs — someone to talk to her, read to her, take her out in her wheelchair, and write letters for her so she can stay in touch with old friends. But perhaps you'd prefer different work?'

'No, the job sounds appealing,' Polly said.

'I can't make any promises. I must speak to my husband and the old lady herself. You'll need to meet her too. But I think you have the sort of sweet temper that would help you to cope with her peccadilloes. The pain gets too much for her, you see? So does the frustration.'

'I understand.'

Cordelia patted Polly's arm. 'Don't let what I've said stop you from exploring other possibilities.'

'You see, Poll?' Lizzie said, after Cordelia had left. 'Everyone liked you.'

'They were kind.'

'They liked you! Cordelia even wants you for a job.'

'I shan't depend on her making me an offer. I'll go out job hunting again tomorrow.'

'Don't get up too early, though.'

Polly was looking tired again and doubtless there'd be more tears shed over Davie before she slept. Lizzie ordered her to go straight to bed. 'I'll wash the glasses and plates. It's no more than I usually do.'

Polly was still pale the following morning but insisted on washing the breakfast dishes before she left to look for work.

'Nicely-behaved sort of girl,' Margaret said, after Polly had left. 'Excellent voice.'

From Margaret those were compliments indeed.

Polly had news when she returned later. She'd just left the house that morning when Cordelia pulled up in her chauffeured car. 'She was hoping to catch me before I set out,' Polly explained. 'She'd spoken to her husband and he agreed that a companion was just what his mother needed. Old Mrs Bishop herself wasn't convinced, but Cordelia took me to meet her.'

'She liked you?' Lizzie asked.

'I'm not sure she liked me exactly. She just sniffed and said, 'Hmm,' a lot.'

'It sounds as though she and Margaret would get on a treat. But I'm interrupting.'

'Mrs Bishop didn't appear to *dislike* me either because she agreed I should work for her on a trial.'

'Polly, that's wonderful! Assuming you want the job?'

'Certainly, I do. It's a live-in position not far from

191

here so I won't have to look for lodgings. I'll have Saturday afternoons and Sundays off so I hope to spend some of that time with you, Lizzie.'

'Of course. I'm glad you found work so quickly.'

'I was lucky.' Lucky in employment, even if unlucky in love.

'When do you start?'

'Cordelia suggested I spend a week with you first, but if that isn't convenient . . .'

'It's more than convenient. It's welcome.'

'But Miss Penrose? Margaret, I mean?'

'She'll be glad of your company. Especially if you sing to her.'

Lizzie showed Polly some of the London landmarks over the days that followed. When Lizzie was working Polly cooked and cleaned because she was keen to repay Margaret's hospitality. Knowing Polly needed to keep busy, Lizzie didn't argue.

Polly also sang.

'You should join us on Saturday,' Margaret said.

'Saturday?'

'We're singing at a convalescent home,' Lizzie explained.

'You're not suggesting I should sing in public?' Polly looked appalled.

Margaret opened her mouth — probably to talk of duty — but Lizzie cut her off before she could speak. 'I know you wouldn't like that, Poll, but you could cheer us on.'

Getting Polly there was the first step. Once she saw for herself how much the men appreciated the concerts, she might feel more comfortable about taking part. That was the explanation Lizzie gave later when she apologised to Margaret for cutting across her.

'That sounds subtle, Lizzie. I prefer plain speaking but I daresay you're right.'

Lizzie hoped so. Polly certainly needed *something* to help her through her sadness over Davie.

21

They travelled to the convalescent home by under-
ground railway. Polly's eyes widened and her slim
shoulders shuddered as they made their way along
the tunnels. 'You'll soon grow used to it,' Lizzie told
her.

Polly looked doubtful and was clearly glad to get
back in the fresh air. The convalescent home was in a
former school. The administrator showed them into a
large room which had a piano at the far end. 'No
stage, I'm afraid.'

'We're used to making do,' Lizzie assured him.

Margaret played a few notes and grimaced. 'When
was this instrument last tuned?'

'Some time ago, I imagine,' he said. 'I hope it isn't
going to be a problem?'

'We're used to working with less-than-perfect
pianos too,' Lizzie assured him, and the administrator
looked relieved.

'Is there anything I can bring you?'

'Glasses of water, if it isn't too much trouble?'

He went off to fetch them while Margaret and Lizzie settled down to practice with Polly looking on.
Soon the wounded soldiers began to arrive and Polly's expression softened with sympathy as she saw
their bandages, empty sleeves and wheelchairs.

Some men grinned with cheerful enthusiasm. 'They
really are looking forward to hearing you,' Polly whispered to Lizzie.

'Let's hope they enjoy it.'

They did enjoy it, listening enraptured to Margaret's classical piano solos then livening up as the programme progressed to popular songs sung by Lizzie who encouraged the men to join in with the more rousing ones such as 'Tipperary'. They did so vigorously, clapping their hands and even stamping their feet.

Polly clapped and stamped with them. 'They loved every moment,' she told Lizzie, when the men were leaving at the end.

'That's why we do this. The men are having a terrible time at the front and you can see that some have suffered awful injuries. We see our job as lifting their spirits.'

Polly nodded, looking thoughtful.

Monday came and Polly moved to old Mrs Bishop's house. She called in on Lizzie on Thursday evening to let her know all was well. 'I wouldn't call Mrs Bishop an easy person, but she told me I was a good girl yesterday.'

'You're patient and gentle. She must know she's lucky to have you.'

Polly was far too modest to agree.

'Yesterday's concert went well,' Lizzie told her. 'We have another on Saturday. Would you like to come along?'

'Yes, please.'

This time they took the omnibus to a small cottage hospital where they were welcomed warmly. Margaret's piano playing went well and so did Lizzie's, but when the time came for her to sing, she took a sip of water and choked on it. Several coughs didn't help. Eyes watering, she looked at Polly whose face drained of colour as she realised what Lizzie was asking.

Lizzie beckoned Polly closer. 'The men are waiting,' she got out hoarsely. 'It would be a shame to disappoint them. Please, Poll. You can shut your eyes, if it helps. I shut mine the first time I sang in public.'

''Golden Barley'?' suggested Margaret, knowing that Polly was familiar with the words.

Polly glanced at the audience and visibly quaked but she took some timid steps forward. Margaret played the introduction and Lizzie willed Polly to do justice to herself.

Polly's voice faltered as she began and was so quiet it had no chance of reaching the back of the room but, just as had happened when she'd sung to the women's group, it grew in confidence as well as volume.

I look over fields and see barley so fair,
A sweet, luscious gold like my dear lover's hair . . .

Pure, silvery beauty soared through the room. When the song finished, the applause was so loud that Polly took a startled step backwards.

Lizzie got up to join her and they sang 'Scarborough Fair' together before Lizzie took over for the more rousing songs.

When the concert ended, Lizzie stood back so Polly could receive a share of the praise that came their way.

'A real treat, that was . . .'

'Voices of angels . . .'

'Better than medicine . . .'

The men left and Polly turned to Lizzie suspiciously. 'Did you cough on purpose?'

'The choking was genuine, but I admit to exaggerating the coughing to persuade you to sing.'

'That was sly. I'm not sure I can forgive you.'

She was teasing, of course, and Lizzie was pleased to see that singing had been good for her friend. It was going to take a long time for Polly to come to terms with her broken engagement, but a boost to her confidence in the meantime could only help.

'You're one of the Penrose Players now, and there's no going back,' Lizzie said.

'I don't play,' Polly pointed out.

'Then we'll change our name to the Penrose Players and Singers.'

Polly came often to the house after that so they could work out a programme of songs that suited both of their voices. They added simple dance steps too. 'What do you think?' Lizzie asked Margaret.

'I think you'll please the patients,' Margaret said, though doubtless she was thinking that there was no way such a performance would ever sully the stage at Covent Garden.

The new programme did indeed please the patients.

Polly had expected her work commitments to limit her performances to Saturday afternoons and Sundays, but old Mrs Bishop proved to be an unexpected ally. Hearing how Polly was spending her free time, she insisted that Cordelia should bring her to a rehearsal at Margaret's house.

She was a fierce woman who barked orders at Cordelia's chauffeur as he helped her inside then poked Cordelia with her walking stick when she wanted a cushion adjusted. She watched the rehearsal with hawk-like eyes, as though keen to find fault.

'Well!' she said at the end, but no one knew what that meant.

She turned to Margaret. 'Congratulations, Miss

197

Penrose. You play superbly. As for you younger girls . . . '

Lizzie held her breath, waiting for the verdict.

'Highly entertaining.'

Phew!

'I've been looking for a way to support the war effort but I'm not interested in all that knitting nonsense Cordelia organises. I wouldn't knit socks even if my arthritic fingers were up to it. But concerts . . . Yes, I think they're just the thing I've been waiting for.'

Oh, no. She wasn't thinking of performing, was she?

'Don't look so horrified, you silly girls. I'm not proposing to join you on stage. Who wants to watch a wrinkled old crone who can't sing? That wouldn't entertain the audiences. It would torture them. My contribution to the war effort will be to give you time off for concerts, Polly. I'll expect you to make up for it, though.'

'Oh, I will!' Polly cried, delighted.

All through spring and into summer of 1916 the Penrose Players and Singers performed to grateful audiences. Polly's confidence grew, though she was still desperately unhappy about Davie. Not that she ever complained or moped. On the contrary, she made a heroic effort to be cheerful. But it was clear that her tender heart wouldn't heal quickly.

Lizzie wrote to both Harry and Matt, praising Polly's voice and the difference she made to the concerts. *Singing duets, a little dancing . . . Thanks to Polly we have a more varied programme now and the patients appear to love it.*

Both replied with words of praise. *Polly sounds a*

lovely person, Harry wrote, and Matt wrote, *All those singing sessions in your little den in Witherton are paying off.*

'I enjoy our concerts but wouldn't it be wonderful if they weren't needed anymore?' Lizzie said to Margaret one day.

'Because the war would have ended?'

'Exactly.'

'Maybe this latest push will be the turning point,' Margaret suggested.

Cordelia had spoken of a big campaign by the allies. It started at the beginning of July after enemy trenches near the river Somme had been bombarded for several days with a view to destroying barbed wire and enemy positions before the foot soldiers went on the attack. Lizzie was torn between hope of a successful outcome and dread in case Harry or Matt fell in action. Davie too, because Polly still loved him and Lizzie couldn't hate him.

She rushed out for a newspaper every morning and it soon became apparent that the attack was proving disastrous in terms of casualties with thousands of men being killed or injured. She felt limp with relief whenever letters came from Harry and Matt, though the relief was always short-lived because the letters took time to arrive and who knew what had happened after they'd been written?

One day Polly arrived looking grave. 'Davie's been captured. He's in a prisoner of war camp. His sister got my address from my mother and wrote to tell me.'

'He's alive, Poll. He's safe.'

'For the moment. I can't help wondering if he'll have enough to eat and be given medical attention if he needs it.'

'He's safe,' Lizzie repeated. 'Don't go looking for worries.'

'You're right,' Polly finally agreed. 'Shall we practise for a while? I'm not sure about that new song . . . '

★ ★ ★

August came and moved towards September. Lizzie was showing a pupil out one afternoon when a telegram boy came along the street on his red bicycle. Dismay swelled inside her as she watched him skid to a halt in front of her. 'Miss Kellaway?' he asked.

Lizzie nodded and took the telegram with trembling fingers. A moment later she slumped against the door in relief.

The telegram was from Matt. He was on leave and would be in London tonight! He suggested she leave a message at the hostel where he'd be staying if she was free to see him.

Hastening inside, Lizzie told Margaret about the telegram then rushed to the Post Office to telephone the hostel. Matt hadn't arrived yet, but he was expected soon. Lizzie left a message to say she'd meet him outside the hostel at seven o'clock.

She walked home again, remembering the warm glow of comfort she'd felt in his presence and fizzing with excitement at the thought of seeing him again.

'I'm sorry I won't be cooking dinner tonight,' she told Margaret.

'I'm glad you have a pleasant evening ahead of you. But take care being out alone at night, Lizzie. The nights are drawing in again, and with the streetlights dimmed . . . I've heard that some criminals are taking advantage of it to steal people's belongings.'

'I'll be careful.'

It was only as she sat on the omnibus that doubts crept in. Memory might have exaggerated how comfortable she'd felt with Matt as a child and perhaps she'd feel differently now she was an adult. Or Matt might have changed. There'd been no hint of change in his letters but anyone could put on a cheerful act for the time it took to write a letter. And war could break the strongest person. Lizzie's nerves began to flutter.

22

The hostel was near Kings Cross. Lizzie waited outside, trying to avoid the eyes of the men who passed by. Not that any of them were offensive.

She recognised Matt as soon as he stepped out of the hostel. There was something imposing about such a tall, upright man, especially in uniform. He glanced around, saw her and for a moment stood simply looking at her.

Lizzie swallowed. Was he the Matt of old? Or was he a different sort of man these days?

The familiar smile spread across his face and Lizzie felt a surge of emotion — relief dancing alongside joy. She breathed out slowly and smiled back.

Matt walked towards her, green eyes gleaming. 'Edith was right.'

'About what?'

'She said you'd been a strikingly pretty child who'd have grown into a strikingly beautiful woman.'

Lizzie pulled a face at such nonsense.

'Can an old friend take a liberty?' he asked, then bent to kiss her cheek. 'It's good to see you, Lizzie.'

'It's good to see you.'

'I didn't intend for you to wait here, though. This isn't the pleasantest of places.' Doubtless the hostel was cheap. 'Unfortunately, it was too late to send another telegram by the time I received your message.'

'I've been fine.'

'Hungry? I asked in the hostel about where we

might get a decent dinner and I've been given the name of a place not far from here. You won't mind walking?'

'Of course not.'

Matt offered his arm. Lizzie took it, glad to feel the old warmth returning as they set off for the restaurant. 'How was your journey?' she asked.

'Eventful.'

'Oh?'

He grinned and told her about a poor chap who'd got to the port late and tried to jump into the boat as it was beginning to move off only to fall in the water. Another chap had spent the entire crossing being sick over the side. Two men playing cards had got into a fight about cheating, and another man had made a fuss about cheese having been stolen from his pack before realising he'd been looking for it in someone else's pack.

'This place isn't fancy but I'm told the food is good and hot,' Matt said, as they reached the restaurant.

'Suits me.'

Inside they ordered meat pies with gravy to be followed by treacle tart, then Lizzie sat back to study her friend properly. His face was thinner and there were fine lines at the corners of those shrewd green eyes. She imagined they'd been put there by the war instead of the passage of time, and wondered what horrors he'd experienced. Not that she intended to ask about those experiences. It was for Matt to decide what he felt able to share with her.

She realised he'd begun to study her in return and some sort of private thought had brought a smile to his lips.

'What?' she asked.

'I'm remembering the little Lizzie. Now you're all grown up,' he said.

'Twenty years old. Thanks to you.'

'Oh?'

'Amos Bradley wished me harm. I might never have got past thirteen if you hadn't rescued me.'

'You were an enterprising child. You might have escaped his clutches some other way if I hadn't happened along.'

'I doubt it. I was unwell.'

'Well, who knows?' he said. 'But I've always been glad I helped you, Lizzie.'

'I've never stopped being grateful.'

Smiles passed between them and for a moment neither of them spoke.

'Tell me about everyone at the farm,' Lizzie suggested then.

Matt's face softened with affection for his family, just as she'd expected. 'You've been writing to Edith, I hear.'

'Regularly. She sounds happy with Peter.'

'Very much so. I couldn't wish for a better brother-in-law. Peter's hardworking, kind, and an excellent father.'

'And he's working at Sorrel's Patch.'

'Making a success of it too. He used to work for another farmer but never had the chance to influence how the farm was run. Now he has that chance alongside Joe. Mikey's working on the farm too just now. He was a clerk in a pottery for a while and hopes to return to that sort of work eventually.'

'After the war, you mean. Meanwhile he's safer on the farm.'

Matt sent her a speculative look.

'You enlisted to save your brothers and brother-in-law.' Lizzie wasn't asking a question. She was stating what she believed to be a fact.

Matt would have foreseen that there wouldn't be enough volunteers to sustain the fighting indefinitely so men would be called up to fight whether they liked it or not. Conscription had been introduced earlier in the year but farming was essential work so its workers could apply for exemption. Sorrel's Patch wouldn't have justified four exempt workers, though.

Matt didn't answer but Lizzie hadn't expected him to. She simply wanted him to know that she understood his decision and admired him for it.

'How's Molly?' she asked.

Relaxing, Matt told her how Molly loved life on the farm too. 'She's only twelve but she's taken over from Edith in looking after the chickens and the cows. She has a third cow now. Maude injured her leg as a calf and her owner was going to put her down. Molly persuaded him to let her nurse Maude back to health instead. These days Molly is even better than Edith at making butter and cheese.'

The food arrived. 'This looks good,' Matt said. 'Smells good too.'

'I hear army food is grim.'

'It's terrible!'

He talked about the food and other day-to-day challenges such as having to strip off boots and socks in cold, wet trenches to dry the feet and smear them with whale fat to stop trench foot from developing. 'Awful thing, trench foot. Men lose toes and other parts of their feet to it and, once the rot sets in, it can spread.'

He talked about the camaraderie too — games of

cards, shared parcels, teasing, banter and Foxworth, the terrier the battalion had unofficially adopted to catch trench rats.

Mostly Matt was interested in hearing about Lizzie's life in London, particularly the concerts. 'What you're doing is wonderful,' he said.

'Sometimes I think I should be nursing or driving an ambulance. Not that I can drive, but I could learn. Singing feels . . . easy, I suppose. Too comfortable.'

'Nursing and ambulance driving are important jobs, but so is raising the spirits of men who are injured or sick,' Matt insisted. 'Your concerts are about more than an hour or two of entertainment. They remind the men that there's life beyond their suffering. A life they're fighting to protect and which they'll enjoy again when the war finally ends. They also give them happy memories to look back on while they're away.'

These were arguments that had been put to Lizzie before but, coming from a serving soldier as wise and thoughtful as Matt, they were doubly reassuring.

A waiter took their empty plates and returned with the treacle tart. 'Delicious,' Lizzie declared.

Matt nodded, eating hungrily. 'Tell me what happened after I left you with Miss Penrose.'

Lizzie had summarised events in her letters but now she told him more.

Matt listened intently. 'I'm glad you found a home with your godmother but I'm sorry your father has never seen sense about you,' he finally said. 'The loss is his.' Reaching out, Matt touched her hand. Gently, and just for a moment, but it was enough to make her feel better.

It was getting late. Matt had to be tired after his journey and Margaret would worry if Lizzie wasn't home soon. 'Time to go?' Matt questioned.

'Unfortunately it is.'

He called for the bill.

'I'd like to pay,' Lizzie said, but Matt wouldn't hear of it and had an ally in the waiter who gave her no chance even to see the bill.

'At least let me repay the money I owe you from when we first met,' Lizzie pleaded.

'Certainly not. I've said it before and I'll say it again. Think of it as paying for all the stamps you bought trying to get in touch with me. I could have saved you the cost — and the trouble — if I'd written to you because I knew your godmother's address.'

But he'd wanted to free her to get on with her new life instead of reminding her of a debt she might not have had the funds to repay.

'Don't try sending the money to Edith either,' he added. 'She'd be offended because her hospitality comes from a generous nature rather than a hope of repayment.'

With that Matt insisted the subject was closed. 'I'll see you home,' he said, when they got outside.

'You can see me to the bus stop but you can't take me all the way to Highbury. You need to rest.'

'I need good company and quietness more than rest.'

Quietness? Lizzie had heard how the relentless noise of shellfire could rip men's nerves to shreds.

The walk to Highbury was long but Matt preferred it to an omnibus and Lizzie felt no fear of the dark with him at her side. They walked in companionable ease, pausing only now and then for Matt to point out the constellations in the sky or for Lizzie to comment on the fragrance of a late-flowering rose that lingered in the night time air.

'I feel we could have talked for longer,' Matt said, after a while.

'We barely got started,' Lizzie agreed.

'Please say if this isn't convenient, but would you be free to meet me again if I came back from the farm early?'

'That would be lovely! But won't Edith and the others want to keep you with them for as long as possible?'

'I'm catching the boat back to France on Friday but I could spend Thursday evening in London.'

'If you're sure . . .'

Matt grinned. 'We didn't even touch on your votes-for-women work. How can I return to the front without hearing all about it?'

'How indeed? You approve of votes for women, I hope?'

'Do you need to ask? Of course I approve of it.'

'Good.'

They reached Margaret's house and Matt kissed her cheek again. 'I won't disturb your godmother as it's late, but please give her my regards.'

'Would you like to come here on Thursday? For a meal?'

'Thank you, but I may be late getting into London. Would you mind meeting me there again?'

'Of course not.'

They agreed a time and place then Lizzie opened the door and watched Matt set off down the street. He walked a few yards then turned and waved. He paused to look up at the sky and draw air deep into his lungs. Then he continued on his way unhurriedly, as though this taste of England was to be savoured.

It warmed her over the following days to imagine the welcome Matt would be receiving at home — hugs, kisses, his favourite foods, chatter around the big farmhouse table, singing around the piano in the parlour . . . Doubtless his family was spoiling him. Equally doubtless, Matt was insisting on pitching in with the work.

He'd be taking walks around the farm's acres too, examining crops here, soothing animals there . . . In the daytimes he'd watch the clouds passing overhead in an ever-changing pattern of whites, pearls, pinks and greys. He'd follow the paths taken by birds and take pleasure in the supple sway of grasses in the breeze. In the evenings he'd feel the cooling air on his cheeks — velvety soft with damp or crisp with hints of autumn. He'd listen for the hoot of a distant owl and the rustle of leaves in the trees.

She wished she could be there with him instead of waiting to see him, because his return to London would also mean his return to the war. But Lizzie still felt a burst of joy when she saw him walking towards her on Thursday evening. He bent to kiss her cheek and she smiled up at him. 'I've been imagining your family spoiling you and I see I was right,' she said.

The few days with his family had done him good. There was more of the old colour back in his cheeks, though strain still cut lines around his eyes. Of course it did. He was going back to face hell.

He was calm, though. Smiling. And an image burst into Lizzie's mind of how he'd be in the trenches. A steadying influence. Unflinching and unflustered no matter how much fear and dread tortured him inside.

'The uniform spruce-up is courtesy of Edith,' he said. It was immaculate. 'Molly polished my buttons and buckles. Mikey and Joe cleaned my pack and boots. And everyone contributed to the parcels of food and drink I'm lugging around.'

The pack was bulging.

'Can I carry anything for you?'

'Thanks, but I've got everything tucked in neat and tight. Shall we go for some food? I asked a chap on the train for a recommendation and he's given me the name of a place.' Matt's green eyes glinted. 'Usual criteria. Decent food at decent prices. Unless you already have somewhere different in mind?'

'I don't. Let's see if the chap on the train can be trusted.'

It appeared that he could. 'Shepherd's pie for me,' Matt said. 'I may not be a shepherd, but I'm a farmer and that's close enough.'

'I'm sitting opposite a farmer and that's close enough for me too,' Lizzie said, ordering the same.

'Before I forget . . . ' Matt dug into his pack and took out two parcels. 'Dried herbs from Edith, and a small cheese from Molly.'

'How kind! I grow herbs at home now, but the garden is small and shaded so the plants don't grow quite as well as Edith's. I remember hers growing abundantly.'

'Edith has a magical touch with herbs. And also with the lavender in Bee Corner.' Matt's eyes danced and Lizzie groaned, remembering the foolish mistake she'd made all those years ago.

'I can't believe I was such a fool! But tell me how everyone is.'

'All well. All delighted to know I've seen you again. All wishing they could see you again too.'

Pleasure wrapped itself around Lizzie like a blanket. 'I'd love to see them again one day.'

Matt talked about his family until the food arrived. 'So,' he said then, 'votes for women.'

'It was my godmother who got me interested, though perhaps I might have leant towards the cause sooner or later anyway, because I don't see it as being about voting rights only. I see it as being about respect for women.'

'Your father isn't a respectful man.'

'He was horribly controlling when I was a child and my poor, gentle mother was afraid of him. Not that he ever hit her or anything like that. But he intimidated her. He didn't value her.'

'Was your godmother's father like that too?'

'I think so. She doesn't talk about him, but I suspect he stopped her from living the sort of life she might have chosen for herself.' A life with Gilbert George Grafton. 'Anyway, she introduced me to her women's group. It's an informal group with no official leader but Cordelia Bishop is the woman who does most of the organisation. She'd make a wonderful Member of Parliament though I think she prefers organising people and bringing them together with other people of influence. She's incredibly well connected.'

'So you have meetings?'

'We do. Sometimes just for ourselves, sometimes with guests such as Members of Parliament. We've been on marches too, and handed out leaflets.'

'I imagine that's an . . . interesting experience,' Matt said, eyes gleaming humour again.

'Oh, yes. Abuse is common. Mostly from men, but sometimes from women who think we should leave it to men to get on with running the world while we stay at home.'

'There's nothing wrong with a domestic life, if that's what a woman wants. Edith loves a domestic life. But it doesn't make her a fool, and neither should it stop her from having a say in how the country is run.'

'That's what I think.'

'I expect no less of the girl who ran away from home, then ran from Amos Bradley too.'

Lizzie smiled, then said, 'Of course, the suffragette cause is taking second place to the war effort just now, but it hasn't been forgotten. If anything, the work women are doing should show the country that females can contribute in all sorts of ways.'

'It'll be outrageous if it doesn't,' Matt said.

The evening passed too quickly again but, as before, Matt walked Lizzie home despite her protests.

'I don't want to say goodbye now,' Lizzie said, when they reached the house. 'May I come to the station tomorrow to wave you off?'

Matt looked pleased. Lizzie supposed that, with his family so far away, no one had ever waved him off on the boat train before. 'I'd like that.'

They met near Waterloo station and had a quick cup of tea, smiling over the drawings Edith's little boy had given Matt to keep him cheerful on the journey. But soon it was time to head for the train.

'You'll write?' he said. 'I look forward to your letters.'

'Of course I'll write.'

Lizzie looked around the station concourse. 'This is where I saw you in the distance that time. I waved but you didn't see me.'

'You managed to get in touch eventually. I'll always be glad of that. And this time I'll wave back.'

'Stay safe,' she urged, when they reached his platform and he dug in his pocket for his travel warrant. 'Please stay safe.'

'I'll try.'

He kissed her cheek, then, obeying a mutual impulse, they hugged. 'Write,' he urged again, and walked onto the platform.

He boarded the train without looking back but reappeared moments later, leaning out of a window to wave as the train pulled away.

Lizzie kept waving until all that remained of the train was a faint cloud of steam. She realised she was crying . . . for Matt, for Harry, and for all the young men who were risking life and limb to serve their country. 'Dratted war!' she muttered.

'You're right there,' a man said, presumably a father who'd been waving off a much-loved son. 'Dratted war indeed.'

23

It was hard to think that a year was likely to pass before she saw Matt again, but Lizzie would simply have to put one foot in front of the other and go about her life. After all, she'd been doing exactly that since had Harry left eleven months ago, and surely he was due to be granted leave again soon?

She returned home after seeing Matt off on his journey to find a letter from Harry had arrived. Opening it down in the kitchen, her heart beat fast in hopeful anticipation but, while he wrote as affectionately as ever, he had no news of any leave.

Sighing, Lizzie reached for the second of the three letters that had come for her. She hadn't paid much attention to the envelope in her eagerness to read what Harry had to say, but when she drew the letter out and saw the address at the top, her stomach clenched in troubled surprise.

'Is everything all right?' Margaret asked, looking up from her lunch.

'This letter is from Miss Monk. Mrs Maudsley, I should say.'

Lizzie read it quickly.

Dear Elizabeth,

I hope this letter finds you well and that I can prevail upon you to return to Witherton on a visit. It's been a long time since we saw you so a visit is long overdue. Your father hasn't been well recently, so the sooner you come the better. I'll keep a bed made up

*for you in the hope that only a day or two need to
pass before you're with us.*

   Your loving stepmother,
   Susan.

Loving stepmother? Lizzie almost choked. 'She asks me to visit. Apparently, my father is unwell.'

'Is his condition serious?'

'She doesn't say. I suppose it's possible that illness has given him a change of heart about me, but after all these years of silence I find it hard to believe.' Yet Lizzie was aware of a feeling of hope creeping up on her. It was a ridiculous hope, but it wouldn't be dismissed.

'Will you go?'

'I'm not sure.' Even if Edward Maudsley had thawed towards his daughter, Lizzie couldn't believe that Susan Monk had undergone a change of heart. Was something going on?

It all became clear when Lizzie opened the third letter. 'This is from the family solicitor,' Lizzie told Margaret. 'My father has suffered a stroke and isn't expected to recover.'

'I won't make a hypocrite of myself by saying I'm sorry.'

'Apparently my father's estate will come to me, but the business is in trouble and there are debts. He warns me to moderate my expectations.'

'Did you expect to inherit?'

'I can't say I've given it a moment's thought. I always assumed my father had complete power over my mother's money, but it seems the terms on which he got it mean it comes to me after his death whether he likes it or not.' Doubtless Susan Monk was currying favour with a view to getting her hands on it. 'The solicitor is some sort of trustee and wants me to go and see him.'

'So you're returning to Witherton come what may.'

'Mmm.'

'Do you wish me to accompany you?'

'Thank you, Margaret, but I'd prefer you to cover as many of my lessons as possible. I may ask Polly to come, though. Her mother has been clamouring for her to visit, so we could travel together.'

Lizzie spoke to Polly later that day. 'I'll only stay one night, but you could stay longer if Mrs Bishop will give you the time off.'

Polly chewed on her lip and Lizzie guessed she was balancing the pleasure of seeing her family against the distress of returning to the place where she'd been so happy with Davie. 'All right,' Polly said. 'If Mrs Bishop gives permission, I'll come. I'll just have to hope I don't see any of Davie's family.'

They took the train to Witherton the following afternoon. Lizzie had telephoned to the solicitor to make an appointment for the morning after her arrival but she hadn't contacted Susan Monk, wanting to catch the woman unawares if possible. 'I'll call on her, but I've no intention of staying at the house,' Lizzie told Polly. She'd booked a room in a small lodging house instead.

Arriving at Witherton station, Polly wished Lizzie luck then set off for her family home. Lizzie headed for the lodging house of a Mrs Burrows, who offered plain but adequate rooms and plain but adequate breakfasts at reasonable rates.

Dinner wasn't included but Lizzie ordered ham and an egg — a real egg instead of the powdered stuff! — at a nearby tea shop just before it closed. She spent the next couple of hours wandering the streets of Witherton and finding it little changed, though here, as everywhere, there were reminders of the war — a tattered recruiting poster attached to a noticeboard, a soldier in khaki and, further on, a sea-man in navy blue.

Advertisements in shops urged families to buy sup-plies, from boot laces to cigarettes, to send to the boys serving overseas. Some houses boasted patriotic flags in their windows. One sad window displayed black mourning crepe around a photograph of a young man in army uniform. Lizzie pitied his poor family.

Only towards the end of her walk did she approach her childhood home. Even then she kept a distance. Happy memories came to her first — walking in the garden with her mother and learning the names of flowers, playing piano in the drawing room, being tucked into bed in her pretty bedroom . . .

Unhappy memories followed — her father's cold-ness, Susan Monk's cruelty, the insolence of Mrs Clegg . . .

Lizzie looked up at the attic window behind which she'd been virtually imprisoned. Below it was the win-dow of her old bedroom, with the tree beside it, a little taller now. It made her shudder to think of the risks she'd taken in climbing out into that tree — so high above the ground! — but misery had made her desperate, and she'd had her reward in Polly's friend-ship.

Edward Maudsley lay behind one of the other win-dows, perhaps in the room he'd once shared with Mama. Was it possible that he wished to see his daugh-ter at last? To tell her he'd been wrong to neglect her

217

and that he loved her? For years Lizzie had told herself, *Maybe one day*. Perhaps that day would be tomorrow.

She slept only fitfully that night, but felt determined as she walked to the solicitor's office the following morning. Mr Patchett was tall and stooped, with hair that had whitened with age, but his eyes were both shrewd and kind as he shook her hand. 'Thank you for calling, Miss Maudsley.'

'Actually, I've taken my mother's maiden name. Kellaway.'

'I see,' he said, and Lizzie thought that he really did understand.

He gestured her to a seat then moved behind the old mahogany desk to a chair of his own. 'I'm sorry I don't have better news.'

Half an hour later Lizzie knew the worst. Her father had let the business run down, failing to invest in modern machinery or replace staff who'd left for the war. 'Other businesses are coping using female labour,' Mr Patchett had explained, 'but Mr Maudsley . . . I warned him, but he wasn't inclined to listen.'

'No.'

'The more unreliable the business became, the more contracts it lost. It was a downward spiral, I'm afraid.'

'Yes,' Lizzie said, to reassure him he was neither shocking nor upsetting her.

'Regretfully the debts are substantial, both for the business and Mr Maudsley personally. The second Mrs Maudsley has a taste for extravagance and turned deaf ears to my pleas for economy. It appeared to be beyond the scope of her imagination to believe that she and Mr Maudsley might face ruin, but now that

218

it's happening, she's a frightened woman.' The curl of Mr Patchett's lip suggested he considered her to be an unpleasant woman too.

He rallied himself. 'It may be that some debts will die with him so it might be possible to salvage something of your inheritance, Miss Kellaway.'

'If there are debts, they need to be repaid,' Lizzie said. 'I won't have the livelihoods of creditors threatened by my father's incompetence.'

'That will mean selling the house.'

'I'll behave honourably even if my father wouldn't.'

'In that case your inheritance is likely to be small indeed.'

'So be it.'

An offer had already been made for the business and Mr Patchett agreed to see to the sale of the house too. 'I suggest an inventory of the house contents be made sooner rather than later,' he added. 'It would be a pity if some of those contents went missing.' In other words, it would be a pity if Susan Monk made off with them.

'I agree.'

'I'll send someone today.' He promised to keep her informed of developments and Lizzie got up to leave. 'You must miss your mother,' he said. 'She was a lady through and through.'

Whereas Susan Monk was no lady at all.

24

Lizzie headed next to Briar Lodge. She passed between the gateposts into the garden, but instead of knocking on the front door she walked around to the rear door and stepped into the passage through which she'd fled all those years ago. Voices reached her from the kitchen. The bitter, grumbling voices of Susan Monk and Mrs Clegg. Their easy lives were coming to an ignominious end and they were livid.

Lizzie opened the kitchen door and both women turned, their faces registering so much shock that neither could speak for several moments. Mrs Clegg recovered first. 'Well, haven't you turned out a beauty, Miss Elizabeth? We always said you would. Didn't we, Susan?'

Susan's tongue appeared to be stuck inside her mouth, probably because Lizzie was sending her a contemptuous look that made it clear that she wasn't going to fall for flattery.

'It's good to see you've turned out so well,' Mrs Clegg continued, oblivious. 'You're quite the young lady and so gracious-looking. There's no trace of the rebellious child in you now. When you were little . . . Why, I remember how you took against poor Susan for no reason at all. Still, that's ancient history now, isn't it?'

Lizzie sighed irritably. 'I know what you're trying to do, Mrs Clegg, and it won't work. The past may be history but I won't allow you to rewrite it to cast yourselves in kinder roles. Both of you were cruel to me

220

and disrespectful about my mother. You'll leave now, Mrs Clegg.'

The older woman looked scared. So did Susan.

'There's a month's wages in here.' Lizzie handed over an envelope. 'Not as much as you'd like, I'm sure, but then the pair of you have been squandering my family money for years. Which brings me to a warning, Susan. My solicitor is sending someone to make an inventory of this house's contents. I suggest you also draw up an inventory of any items you consider to be your personal property so I can compare the two. If you attempt to cheat by claiming things which aren't your own, you'll leave with nothing.'

Susan paled. 'You can't leave me with nothing. It wouldn't be right.'

'Please don't attempt to tell me what's right. There are debts, so the business and this house will be sold to pay them. I'll consider making a payment to you from any money that remains, but not if you cheat me of a single penny or a single item. Neither will I tolerate any spiteful damage to this house or its contents. Is that clear?'

Hatred burnt in Susan's eyes but so did fear for her future. She nodded.

'I'm glad we understand each other.'

The doorbell rang. 'I expect this is the solicitor's clerk, come to make the inventory.'

Lizzie let him in. Leaving him to his task, she went upstairs to her father's room, nervousness stirring as she wondered again if the day had finally come . . .

Edward Maudsley lay in bed. Lizzie felt pity to see his lopsided mouth and helplessness, but as she looked into his face her last hope of achieving any sort of closeness to him withered and died.

There was no pleasure in his eyes as he looked back at her. No regret for his past coldness, and no yearning for the relationship they might have enjoyed, had he wished it. He didn't want her here even now.

Sadness washed over her. All those years of hoping . . . For a moment Lizzie blinked back tears but then she squared her shoulders.

'I'm sorry to see you brought so low,' she told him. 'I hope the doctor will keep you comfortable.'

With that she left the room because there was nothing more to be said. Out on the landing, emotion ambushed her again and her shoulders slumped. But the doctor arrived and she steadied herself to greet him as he came upstairs.

Doctor Moore remembered her. 'I'm glad to see you looking so well, Miss Lizzie.'

'Thank you. My father . . .'

'Isn't much longer for this world.'

'I want him to have all the care and medicine he needs.' Edward Maudsley might be going to his grave as a cold, unfeeling man but Lizzie wouldn't let him drag her principles down to his level.

'Of course.'

'You'll let me know when . . . When the time comes? A message through Mr Patchett will reach me.'

Doctor Moore bowed his agreement and, parting from him, Lizzie moved along the landing to the bedroom of her childhood.

It was a neglected room now, its former prettiness a ghostly echo from the past, but still reminding her of happy times with her mother, as it was Mama who'd chosen the pretty things for her. Lizzie put a few of the smaller items into her bag — books, a china bird, a tray cloth her mother had embroidered . . .

Continuing up to the attics she looked out of the window of the room in which she'd been imprisoned. How heartless Susan Monk had been to trap her in loneliness in this cold, bare place.

She moved into the room that had been used for storage, expecting to find that her mother's things had been looted by Susan and her crony over the years. She was right. Boxes had been opened and some of the contents taken but other things remained. Lizzie packed a selection into her bag. Silver-backed brushes and a matching mirror, sadly tarnished now but likely to improve on re-acquaintance with polish. More framed photographs. Several cut-glass perfume bottles. A silver inkwell . . .

There was no point in voicing farewell to Susan and her crony, who were doubtless cursing Lizzie down in the kitchen. She descended the main staircase and left through the front door.

For old times' sake she walked down Amesbury Lane where she'd met Polly all those years ago. She passed the ruined trunk of the lightning-struck sycamore from where Polly had waved to her, then rediscovered the den amid the trees. The ground showed signs of being trampled by small feet and the log remained. Doubtless the den was used by other children now.

Lizzie lingered long enough to visualise herself sitting here as a child with Polly and Davie, and to remember the songs they'd sung. Who'd have guessed then that Lizzie and Polly would be singing some of those songs even now and entertaining servicemen with them? Or that Davie would become a soldier, and then a prisoner? But then who'd have guessed that war would be raging across the world and destroying so many hopeful lives?

Turning around, Lizzie walked into town and had tea and a bun in a café. The bun was coarse, probably because wheat was in short supply and some other grain had been mixed into the flour. Lizzie ate it anyway. Wasting food was bad at the best of times. In wartime it was criminal.

Afterwards she bought flowers then headed for St Paul's churchyard where she laid them on her mother's grave.

'I'm sorry I haven't visited for so long, Mama. I'm unlikely to visit again, but I know you won't mind because you want the best for me. Thank you for all the love you gave me. I'll never stop loving you. Neither will Margaret.'

She touched a fingertip to her mother's name on the headstone. 'Goodbye, dearest Mama.'

Straightening, Lizzie blew a kiss towards the grave then walked away to meet Polly at the station. Not wanting to impose on Mrs Bishop's goodwill after being given time off for the concerts, Polly had decided to follow Lizzie's example in staying in Witherton for only one night so the girls were to travel back together.

Lizzie arrived first and sat on a bench to wait for her friend. But several minutes ticked by and there was no sign of Polly. Beginning to worry, Lizzie got up and paced the platform. 'You need to board, Miss,' a guard warned, as the train shuffled into the station and pulled up alongside her.

At that moment Polly ran up, holding onto her hat as hair flew around her face like silvery thistledown. Despite her exertion, Polly's face was pale. Had something — or someone — upset her?

They settled in an empty carriage. 'Your family is

well, I hope?' Lizzie asked, concerned.

'All well.'

But?

'I crossed paths with Davie's mother as I was walking to the station,' Polly explained. 'That's why I was late.'

'Is Davie . . .?'

'He's well enough, it seems. But his mother said I shouldn't give up hope of him wanting to take up with me again. She thinks the war has addled people's brains and that Davie will soon realise he was a fool to let me go. She was actually quite insistent that I shouldn't let my head be turned by anyone else because Davie and I are meant for each other. What do you think, Lizzie?'

'I think Davie's mother loves you and wants you to be part of her family. Whether she's right about Davie I can't say. But I'd hate to see you wasting your life waiting for something that might never happen. If the war has taught us nothing else, it's shown us that life is precious and we shouldn't waste a second of it.'

Polly nodded, but as the train left the station she leant towards the window and looked back at Witherton as though at least a part of her wished to stay. Lizzie, on the other hand, had finally come to terms with being unloved by her father. Yes, there was sadness and always would be. But other people cared for her and her future lay with them — if they came through the war, of course.

Despite that uncertainty, this trip to Witherton had done Lizzie good. But had it done Polly harm by stirring up hopes that could come to nothing and hurt her all over again?

25

Mr Patchett's letter came one week later. Edward Maudsley was dead. Lizzie sat quietly after she read it. She felt an echo of sadness for what might have been, but she couldn't grieve for a man who'd chosen to be an unpleasant stranger to her.

Mr Patchett had also sent the inventory. It included some lovely things — furniture, pictures and china — but few held sentimental value for Lizzie. Besides, it would be expensive to have them transported to London and kept in storage. She chose to keep only her mother's graceful writing desk, a mirror, some porcelain items that were family heirlooms, and what remained of her mother's jewellery — the pearl earrings, a gold bracelet, an emerald and diamond ring, and two necklaces. One was a simple silver chain. The other was a heart-shaped gold locket which was another relic from her mother's youth. No other jewellery was listed in the inventory. Doubtless it had been plundered by Susan Monk over the years.

Mr Patchett had received a private offer for the house and recommended acceptance. He'd drawn up an estimate of how much he expected to be raised by the sale of the properties and how much was owed to creditors. *This is just a provisional account*, he cautioned, *though I expect it to prove fairly accurate. As you will see, I anticipate that there will be no more than one hundred pounds remaining after the funeral expenses and the costs of the sales.*

'One hundred pounds must be only a small fraction of the sum your mother inherited, but it could still be useful,' Margaret said.

She was right, but Lizzie wrote to Mr Patchett to instruct him to use some of the money to ensure the upkeep of her mother's grave and to pay the rest to Susan Monk.

'You don't owe that woman a penny!' Margaret protested.

'She's a dreadful person,' Lizzie agreed. 'But I won't let her make me a dreadful person too. I saw real fear in her eyes when I was in Witherton. The money I give her won't keep her in luxury but it should help her to make a start somewhere. And it's subject to two conditions. The first is that she takes nothing that doesn't belong to her or damage anything she leaves behind.'

'And the second?'

'That she doesn't contact me. Ever.'

'I suppose that's a good use of the money,' Margaret conceded.

Lizzie was still glad to receive the items she'd selected from the inventory. The writing desk, mirror and porcelain fitted in her bedroom. She hung the emerald ring on the silver chain and fastened it round her neck. It felt good to have something of her mother's close to her heart.

She wrote to both Harry and Matt to tell them of her father's death.

Unfortunately, I wasn't close to him so it isn't as big a blow as it might have been, she assured Harry.

Close or not, it must still be upsetting and I wish I were there to comfort you, my darling, Harry wrote back.

My darling? Lizzie was touched. Thrilled, in fact. Harry was unaware of the full history of her family

227

situation, but Lizzie would tell him one day. Hopefully, that day would come soon.

Matt was long familiar with the sorry story, of course. *It's natural to regret what might have been*, he counselled, *but don't waste much time or thought on it. Edward Maudsley didn't deserve you. It's as simple as that. Close the door on him, Lizzie. Move forward.*

Sound advice. There was too much to concern Lizzie in the present to waste time on a past she had no power to change.

* ★ *

As autumn progressed it became clear that there was going to be particular demand for Christmas concerts. Lizzie was glad to be busy. So much of her life had become an ordeal of waiting. Waiting for letters from Harry and Matt to reassure her they were well. Waiting for the casualty lists to appear in the newspaper and hoping fervently that their names wouldn't be included. Waiting to see if Polly heard from Davie. Waiting for the war to end . . .

Worry was a constant companion, but keeping busy — and feeling useful — helped Lizzie to fight it. Margaret's no-nonsense attitude to self-pity made her a valuable ally. Polly too was making a valiant effort to get on with things. She'd said no more about Davie, though Lizzie knew her friend well enough to be sure that hope was beating fervently in Polly's gentle heart.

Amid the approaching winter chill, a letter from Harry made Lizzie feel the sun had suddenly burst into the room. He'd been granted leave at last. He was coming home.

I can't wait to see you! he wrote.

Lizzie couldn't wait to see him either, though she told herself to be cautious. A year had passed since they'd last been together. Absence could build false expectations. Reality could bring them crashing down with disappointment.

Harry spent a night with his parents before coming to London. *They must be desperate to see you and I don't want them to think I'm stopping that from happening*, Lizzie had written, and Harry had appreciated her consideration. *Though I'm torn*, he told her.

The moment Lizzie opened the door to him tenderness swelled inside her. He looked so handsome, so kind — and so very tired. She wanted to reach out and touch his cheek but hesitated. They'd known each other for only a few days before they'd parted last year, and while their letters had brought them closer — much closer — Lizzie still had no experience of what was — and wasn't — appropriate in such a new romance. And though her heart was urging her to reach out, her head was urging caution.

Harry cut through the dilemma by stepping forward to fold her into his arms. 'I keep saying I don't want to rush you, but oh, my goodness, Lizzie, it's wonderful to see you.'

It was lovely to be held so close but then Harry laughed and drew back, looking over her shoulder guiltily as though worried that Margaret might have seen him and be snorting outrage like fire.

Seeing no sign of her, he sent Lizzie a conspiratorial grimace and this time they both laughed.

Lizzie's laughter had a mix of emotions behind it — not only amusement, but also joy and relief, because she was realising the year of separation hadn't painted a false picture of Harry or her liking for him.

On the contrary, he was everything she remembered — open, eager, fun — Seeing him now and feeling such warmth towards him, Lizzie thought that, if this wasn't yet love, it was surely very close to it.

'Come in and say a quick hello,' she said.

Harry was as charming as ever to Margaret, and Lizzie was pleased to see that Margaret's expression was approving. Why not? There was nothing false or self-serving about Harry's manners. They were natural and sincere.

'I'm pleased to see you safely back in England,' Margaret told him. 'Did you find your parents well?'

'Thank you, I did.'

'You have plans for this evening?'

'I have a table booked for dinner.'

'Then I expect you wish to be on your way. But first let me congratulate you on your promotion, *Captain* Benedict.'

Harry's nod was embarrassed. He was a modest man. 'I hope I can live up to it.'

'Oh, I think you will,' Margaret said.

Harry had brought his father's car again. He helped Lizzie into the passenger seat then got into the driver's seat and turned towards her. 'I hated being apart from you, Lizzie. Separation is terrible when a man wants to court a girl.'

'The war won't last forever,' Lizzie told him, but she'd said it often over the past two years and peace felt as far away as ever.

'It won't,' he agreed, though his voice was full of doubt and Lizzie was struck again by how tired he looked.

But then he shook himself and rallied. 'Of course it won't. Let's not think about the war tonight. Let's enjoy ourselves.'

'I've no fault to find with that plan,' Lizzie said, smiling.

He took her to a restaurant on Piccadilly and talked enthusiastically about their surroundings, the menu, the wine list and how much he was looking forward to spending time with her. He was heroic in his attempts to entertain her, but he was clearly battling exhaustion. 'It's all right to be quiet for a moment,' Lizzie said, softly.

'Oh, dear. I'm being dull, aren't I? Sorry. And I wanted so badly to make a good impression.'

'You're not being dull, Harry. You're just tired, and with good reason. I may be living a sheltered life as a piano teacher, but I'm often in hospitals and convalescent homes. I see the impact of war.'

He reached for her hand. 'Kind, considerate Lizzie! You're right, of course. I *am* feeling jaded. This Somme campaign has been grim. I've lost men — good men — from my company. And that's hard.'

'Appalling, I imagine.'

'The past few days have been particularly difficult. I had to sit up most of one night with a chap who'd just received news that his wife had died and so had the child she'd been bringing into the world. Some people think bad news runs in only one direction in wartime. From the front to home, I mean. But men at the front live in fear of receiving bad news too — a loved one's illness, a broken engagement, a faithless wife . . .'

'It must be terrible to receive news like that and be unable to do anything about it.'

'It is. And an upset soldier is a vulnerable soldier. A moment of distraction is all it takes to fall victim to a sniper. It's my job to support the chaps I command when they're suffering. Not just because it's the decent thing to do, but also to try to keep them safe. It's my job to write to the families of some of the fallen too. That's what I was doing last night after spending the evening with my parents — worrying about whether my letters were the best they could be kept me awake even after I'd gone to bed.'

'It's to your credit that you care so much, Harry. I know that war takes a toll so please don't feel you have to pretend that all's well when it isn't. You're not an actor in a play, and I'm not a member of the audience.'

He smiled at her. 'It was a lucky day for me when I met you, Lizzie.'

'It was lucky for me too, despite the bombing. We live in a strange world, with triumph and tragedy all mixed up together, but perhaps the tragedy helps us to treasure the triumph. Now, let's treasure this wonderful food by eating it before it gets cold.'

They didn't linger late. Harry was staying at the club rather than driving home to Surrey and Lizzie was glad of it as he clearly needed to sleep.

He called the next morning and Lizzie was pleased to see that the overnight rest had done him good. 'What would you like to do today?' he asked.

'Might we go for a walk? It needn't be a long one.'

'I don't mind if it is a long one. Hyde Park? I haven't been there for years.'

He parked the car in a Bayswater side street and they entered the park from the north side, Harry offering his arm to Lizzie who took it willingly, savouring the closeness. 'Thank you for last night,' Harry said. 'Your understanding, I mean.'

They came to a halt as they saw soldiers practising a drill on the grass. Lizzie groaned. 'And we came to escape the war for a while!'

'It's fine,' Harry insisted. 'I may dislike war, but I've never gone into a blue funk or anything like that. I'm coping, and I'd hate you to think otherwise.'

'I don't think otherwise. Courage isn't being unafraid. Only a fool would be unafraid at the front. Courage is being afraid and carrying on despite it.'

Harry smiled down at her. 'That's what I say to the chaps in my company.'

They walked for a while longer then went in search of a tea shop. Finding one called The Copper Kettle not far from where they'd parked the car, they went in for lunch. 'Did I mention in my letters that I met with Matthew Warren, the soldier whose address you found for me?' Lizzie asked, picking up a menu card.

'You touched on it, yes.'

'He's a very steady sort of man but he looked tired when he first came home on leave. He looked a lot better after a few days with his family.'

'Good food and rest work wonders?'

'They certainly do no harm.'

'Then I'll eat the biggest lunch I can manage.'

Lizzie had to teach in the afternoon and Harry returned to Surrey to spend more time with his family but they went out for dinner the following evening. Harry was looking well and Lizzie was delighted.

He drove her home afterwards and kissed her for the first time. A proper kiss, that was. There'd been plenty of pecks on the cheek. He drew her into his arms, looked down at her and lowered his mouth to hers. It was delicious.

They had another two days together, meeting for a

walk, a tea and a third dinner, but then the time came for them to part. Harry held her tightly, kissed her, then said, 'I love you, Lizzie Kellaway.'

The declaration caused her heart to leap and dance with joy. She looked up into his face and felt a burst of tenderness for him. Such an honest, eager, caring man. 'I love you too,' she told him, and was promptly kissed again.

'You'll take care?' she asked, stroking his dear face with her finger.

'I've everything to live for with you, my darling, and the war shouldn't be quite so busy now we're moving towards winter.'

The war wouldn't actually stop, though. Shelling, trench raids and sniper fire would continue. But hope was her lifebelt in a stormy sea, and Lizzie intended to cling to it.

Meanwhile, there were Christmas concerts to organise.

26

Lizzie looked at the audience, as usual before a performance, and was pleased to see that this appeared to be a jolly crowd of men. One particularly wide grin stood out for her. It belonged to a trimly-built young soldier who carried his arm in a sling. He had a thick thatch of fair hair, twinkling eyes that she guessed were blue, and white, straight teeth that looked designed for smiles. From somewhere — probably charmed from one of the nurses — he'd acquired a red hat onto which he'd pinned a bobble of cotton wool so that it resembled a Father Christmas hat.

He applauded enthusiastically, particularly after Polly had sung 'Silent Night' in the sweetest, clearest of voices.

'It's been a pleasure to be with you today,' Lizzie said at the end. 'We'd like to finish with 'The Twelve Days of Christmas' but we're tired and need your help.' She was teasing, of course. 'Will anyone join in?'

Hands went up, the fair-haired man's among them. He wasn't a big man by any means, but his voice was a powerful tenor and Lizzie was delighted when he reached the final line and belted out, *'And a partridge in a pear tree!'*

This time a doctor thanked the Penrose Players and Singers for the concert. 'That was splendid. Just the tonic we needed,' he said, then invited the audience to show their appreciation in the traditional way by putting their hands together.

Cheers, whistles and applause followed, then the men began to file out. Except for the fair-haired man. He moved forward instead, aiming for Lizzie though she didn't miss the admiring glance he sent in Polly's direction.

'Are you in charge?' His voice held a faint Scottish burr.

'We work as equals, but I tend to look after the bookings, if that's what you mean?'

'I suppose it is.' His gaze strayed to Polly again then, realising Lizzie had noticed, he laughed. 'Sorry. I'm making a hash of this. Let me start again by introducing myself. I'm Jack Lomax.'

'Lizzie Kellaway.'

'I'm happy to meet you, Miss Kellaway. Congratulations on a first-rate performance.'

'Thank you.'

'I sing too. Professionally. Or rather I sang professionally before the war, and I hope to return to it now I'm out of the war.' He gestured to his arm. 'The doctors saved it but I won't have enough strength for active service.'

'I'm sorry.'

'Better to have lost the strength of an arm than my life. Anyway, I have to earn a living and I'd like to earn it by singing again. But I'd also like to raise funds for the men who won't be able to work anymore, and the men who've left widows and orphans behind. The pensions they receive don't amount to much, and some families are struggling.'

'That's a fine ambition.'

Jack Lomax pulled a face. 'I don't know if I'll be able to achieve it, but I want to try. I have a concert in mind. Rather like the one you've just put on here, but with a paying audience. I wonder if the Penrose Singers might be willing to take part? There won't be a fee as all the profits will go to the families.'

'Do you think we're good enough for a paying audience?'

'Without a doubt. The lady who plays the piano is superb, while you and your friend . . . ' He sent another admiring look in Polly's direction, ' . . . have the most beautiful voices.'

'When will this concert take place?'

'I've no idea yet. I've another week or so here then I'm returning to Scotland to see my family and get a little fitter. Only then can I look into the possibilities. Might you give me your address so I can write to let you know if my plans make any progress? I promise I won't make a nuisance of myself.' He nodded towards Polly sheepishly.

'I think you can be trusted,' Lizzie said, smiling.

He wrote her address into a notebook. 'Luckily I'm right-handed and it was my left side that was hurt. Thank you, Miss Kellaway. I hope to be in touch. In the meantime, I wish you and your friends a happy and healthy Christmas.'

'The same to you, Mr Lomax.'

He cast one more glance in Polly's direction then left.

Polly hadn't noticed him at all as far as Lizzie could judge. She'd simply helped Margaret to pack away the music then fetched their coats and hats from behind the makeshift stage. Lizzie walked over and took her coat. 'The man I was talking to asked if we'd be interested in taking part in a concert to raise funds for servicemen's families.'

'What sort of concert?' Margaret wanted to know.

'Similar to the one we performed here, but it's just an idea at present.'

With that Margaret appeared to decide that, like many an idea, it could come to nothing, so excitement was a waste of time.

Lizzie knew it could come to nothing too, but still felt disappointed when January and February brought no word from Jack Lomax. It would have been rewarding to raise much-needed funds. A show would also have helped Lizzie to cope with the long wait for the war to end. And Jack Lomax might have been good for Polly.

A year had passed since her broken engagement. Polly never complained of feeling unhappy and made every effort to present a cheerful face to the world, but it was clear to Lizzie that her friend was still pining for Davie, even though nothing had come of his mother's prediction.

Davie might not have Polly's present address but he could have reached her easily through her mother. The fact that he hadn't written suggested to Lizzie that his feelings for Polly were unchanged — he was fond of her, but he didn't love her.

Polly deserved better. She deserved a man who loved her as much as Harry loved Lizzie. His letters were full of affection and hopes for their future.

Typically, Polly had been generous with her goodwill when she'd heard about Harry's declaration of love. 'I'm so pleased for you!' she'd said, but her own hopes of happiness still appeared to depend on Davie.

If she'd been thrown into company with Jack, Polly would have had a chance to get to know him. Not only might he have helped her to see that there were other attractive men in the world besides Davie Perkin, Jack might also have boosted her confidence by helping her to realise that she was admired and valued by them.

Ah well, it wasn't to be. Lizzie just hoped her friend wouldn't fall into the same groove of long-lasting disappointment as her godmother. Like Polly, Margaret had been pleased to learn of Harry's love, though it was clear that the uncertainties of the future still troubled her even if she said nothing about them. They troubled Lizzie too, and because of them she'd decided to say nothing about Harry to anyone else yet.

But she wished she could do something about Margaret's heartache. What, though? Lizzie's thoughts returned to a letter but so did her doubts about the wisdom of stirring up the past. It was frustrating.

'Easter bonnets,' Lizzie said suddenly.

Margaret and Polly looked up from the newspapers they were reading down in the kitchen and exchanged puzzled glances.

'It just occurred to me that wearing Easter bonnets for our next concerts might help to cheer the men,' Lizzie explained.

'That's a wonderful idea,' Polly agreed.

Margaret's expression bordered on horror but she wasn't the woman to spoil the men's fun just because her taste was different. 'What do you have in mind?'

'We haven't the money for shop-bought bonnets but we might be able to put something together from things we already have.'

'I have dozens of fabric scraps in my sewing box,' Polly said. 'We could use them to make flowers.'

'You want us to make flowers?' Margaret's tone was even more dubious now. Doubtless the memory of her disastrous attempts at knitting loomed large in her mind.

'Lizzie and I will be happy to trim your bonnet,' Polly assured her.

'Just as long as it isn't gaudy.'

They agreed to search their possessions for anything that might be useful.

Two days later, they came together to share their treasures. 'I'm afraid I found little,' Margaret said, producing two old hats. Both were small and dull, one being faded black and the other a tired grey. Margaret had never followed the Edwardian fashion for extravagant hats.

Lizzie had only one old hat to offer, but it was a straw boater and therefore promising as an Easter bonnet. She'd also found an ancient green skirt with a tear in the back. 'I thought we could cut it up to make leaves. What have you found, Polly? That's an awfully large bag you're holding.'

Polly pulled out a hat, an enormous Edwardian confection in cream.

'Goodness! Where did you get that?' Lizzie asked.

'I told old Mrs Bishop about our plans and she had her maid look out this hat for us. It isn't the only one.'

She brought out another two enormous hats. 'There's one for each of us.'

'Good heavens,' Margaret muttered faintly.

One of the hats sported feathers, another wax fruit and the third a posy of silk flowers. 'Mrs Bishop doesn't want the hats returned so we can chop them about as much as we like. We can use Lizzie's dress for leaves then add to these silk flowers with some of our own.'

Polly showed them a rose she'd made out of red fabric scraps. 'I can make more red roses and I've fabric for pink and yellow ones too. I think we should look as bright and cheerful as possible.'

'I agree,' Lizzie said.

Margaret merely swallowed.

The hats took shape over the days that followed. Trying them on in the music room, Lizzie and Polly were delighted with the results. 'They're so bright and cheerful,' Lizzie declared.

Margaret shuddered when she looked in the mirror but stayed stoic and even managed a weak smile. 'The

241

men will like them, no doubt.'

'We should get used to wearing them while singing,' Polly suggested.

They were due to practice anyway, especially as they had a new song in their repertoire called 'The Gardens of England', chosen by Lizzie with Easter bonnets in mind.

They ran through the song several times, making the chorus particularly rousing:

So when I'm called to roam,
Many miles from home,
This will I know,
Wherever I go,
That in hedgerow and woodland glade,
In flowerbed, in sun and shade,
It's springtime in the gardens of England!

'Excellent!' Lizzie declared. 'I hope the men will join in.'

There was a knock on the door.

'I'll go,' Polly said, being nearest to the hall.

Lizzie followed her out. 'Polly, you've still got—'

But Polly had already opened the door in her big flowery hat.

A young man stood on the step. Lizzie knew him immediately. 'Mr Lomax! How nice to see you.'

'I hope this isn't an inconvenient time to call?'

'Not at all.' Lizzie pitied him because he obviously thought Polly looked adorable in her colourful hat but she'd shown no sign of even recognising him. 'Please come in.'

'Mr Lomax is the gentleman who had the idea for a fundraising show,' Lizzie said, leading him into the music room.

Having whipped her hat off, Margaret shook his hand. Polly took her hat off too and did likewise. She was as friendly as ever but the special spark in Jack's eye appeared not to register with her.

'Would you like tea?' Lizzie offered. 'We were going to have some soon anyway.'

'Tea would be welcome. Thank you.'

Lizzie hoped to leave Polly and Jack together but Polly returned to the door. 'I'll make it.'

'I'm sorry I haven't been in touch before,' Jack said. 'I spent longer at home than anticipated because my grandmother was ill and I didn't like to leave before she was better. I'm very fond of Granny Lomax and I owe her a lot. My interest in music, for one. That was a rousing song I heard you singing as I reached the house.'

'We're practising for our spring concerts, hence the Easter bonnets,' Lizzie explained.

He grinned. 'I'm sure they'll cheer your audiences.'

Margaret cleared her throat. 'I recall your voice from the concert we gave. You're a tenor, if memory serves me correctly. Are you classically trained?'

'I have a little training. I began singing as a boy when Granny Lomax encouraged me to join the church choir. I had a different sort of voice then. High and clear. The choirmaster took an interest and gave me some coaching. We all thought my singing might come to an end when my voice broke, but I was lucky to find myself a tenor. I continued singing in the church choir and joined another local choir as well, singing the sort of classical music I believe would please you, Miss Penrose.'

'Bach?' she asked naming one of her favourite composers. 'Brahms? Grieg?'

'All of those. Again, I was fortunate. The classical choirmaster took an interest and coached me too. I haven't had any other training. My family has never been wealthy, you see. In fact, Granny Lomax and my grandfather lived in a one-room croft for several years after they married. Neither of them had much education, but Granny Lomax in particular wanted her boys to do better.'

'She sounds wise.'

'She's canny, all right. Like both of his brothers, my father became a clerk. We led a respectable life as I was growing up, but I'm one of four children so there wasn't money for luxuries such as singing lessons. Not that I'm complaining. I may never sing at the Royal Opera House but I've managed to make a good living by singing in theatres, including London theatres.'

Lizzie liked Jack's openness. From the look of approval on Margaret's face, so did she.

He stood when Polly returned with the tea tray. 'Let me help,' he said, taking it from her. His gaze was tender again though Polly still appeared unaware of his interest.

'Thank you. If you could put it on the table . . .'

He did so and Polly poured tea for all of them.

'About the fundraising concert,' Jack said then. 'I've been in touch with the manager of a theatre on Drury Lane. I've worked with Charlie Sparrow before and he's willing to help.'

'Which theatre?' Margaret enquired.

'The Merriment.'

Margaret paled. The Merriment sounded like a music hall.

The reaction wasn't lost on Jack. 'I'm trying to put

together a musical programme that's entertaining and rousing, as the aim is to raise funds. But I also want it to be tasteful.'

'Tasteful,' Margaret repeated, as though finding comfort in the word.

'I don't have a date yet, but I'm here to ask if you're agreeable in principle to taking part?'

Lizzie looked at Margaret and Polly then nodded. 'We'll take part if we possibly can.'

'Splendid.'

He really did have the most engaging grin. Lizzie glanced at Polly again and saw that she was smiling too. It wasn't the sort of smile that suggested he'd made an impression on her as a man, but it was a small step forward.

'What sort of music would you like from us?' Lizzie asked.

'Perhaps a piano solo, a duet and some singing?'

'We can wait to choose our songs until you're sure of your other performers,' Lizzie suggested. 'That way you can ensure the programme is balanced.'

'How considerate of you, Miss Kellaway. Naturally I'll give you as much notice as possible.'

He didn't stay much longer. 'Thank you for the tea, and thank you even more for agreeing to help my little venture. I hope to be in touch soon. In the meantime, let me give you my address in case you need to contact me.'

He passed over a card.

Goodbyes were said but, despite the wistful look he sent in her direction, Polly left it to Lizzie to show Jack to the door. Lizzie didn't mind too much. If the show went ahead, there'd be plenty of chances for Polly and Jack to be together.

The Easter bonnets were a great success. Audiences began smiling as soon as they saw them and appeared thoroughly to enjoy the new springtime programme. One song was called 'Piccadilly Promenade'. Lizzie and Polly sang it together and danced together too though, not wanting to shock Margaret, they kept the steps modest. The audience still clapped loudly. 'The Gardens of England' was just as successful and Lizzie had no problem persuading the audience to join in the chorus.

'I wish we had a camera so I could take photographs of our bonnets to send to Harry and Matt,' Lizzie said. Cameras were expensive, though. An idea struck her. 'Polly, would you draw the bonnets for me?'

Polly was a talented artist but lacked confidence in her talent as in so much else. 'I don't mind drawing things for you to see, Lizzie, but my sketches aren't good enough for anyone else.'

'Your sketches are wonderful, Poll. I'm sure they'd amuse Harry and Matt.'

It was the right thing to say because Polly could never hold out against an appeal to her kindness. The sketches were as terrific as Lizzie hoped and both Harry and Matt wrote to say they thought so too.

Polly smiled when Lizzie told her what they'd said but it was the sort of smile that implied she thought the men were simply being kind. Lizzie wished she knew how to make Polly value herself more.

* * *

Three weeks after his first visit Jack called again. Lizzie and Polly were practising dance steps while Margaret played piano. 'I have a date!' he said, grin in place. 'Monday, 18th of June. I hope that's convenient?'

'I'm sure we'll be able to rearrange any lessons that clash with it,' Lizzie assured him. 'Have any other performers committed to the show?'

'Happily, yes, so I've been working on a programme.' He pulled a folded sheet of paper from his jacket pocket. 'It's just a scribble at this stage, but tell me what you think.'

The paper was handwritten in spiky black writing with many of the entries crossed out and rewritten elsewhere.

'I'd like Miss Penrose to begin with a piano solo to settle everyone down, then move onto a lively piano duet with you, Lizzie, to start lifting the mood.'

Jack proposed to sing a solo next. His name was down for another song later, this one to be sung with someone called Amy. 'A friend,' he said.

Just a friend? Or something more? Lizzie hoped not.

'As you can see, I've put you down for four songs — two in the first half and two after the interval. How does that sound?'

Lizzie pulled her thoughts to attention. 'It sounds fine. Doesn't it, Polly?'

Polly nodded but looked at the programme instead of at Jack.

'You have ballet dancers coming?' Lizzie asked, interpreting a line of scrawl as *Galina and Alexei, ballet*.

'You don't object to ballet, Miss Penrose?'

'Not at all.'

'Excellent. I also have a quartet of male singers, a violinist and a pair of opera singers.'

'Opera singers?' Polly looked concerned. 'Won't our singing seem a little frivolous in comparison?'

'Trust me, Miss Meadows. Your singing will be different from opera but equally enjoyable. More enjoyable, I suspect.' He glanced towards Margaret as though concerned she might rebuke him for slighting opera, then sent Polly a smile that combined humour with softness.

Lizzie wouldn't give up hope of him helping to restore Polly's happiness just yet.

'I believe I interrupted another practice,' Jack said then. 'I seem to be timing my visits badly.'

'We're running through a few songs for our concert on Saturday,' Lizzie told him. 'You could act as our audience if you don't have to rush away?'

'I'll be honoured to be your audience.'

They sang 'The Gardens of England' and 'Piccadilly Promenade'. Jack applauded warmly. 'Where are you performing on Saturday?'

'A place called Brookville. It's a small auxiliary hospital for injured seamen in Clapham.'

'I wonder if I might come along? I'd love to see you perform again. But perhaps I can't just walk into a hospital . . .'

Lizzie thought for a moment. 'There won't be a problem if you're a temporary member of our group.'

'I could perform with you?'

'If you like.'

Jack expressed himself to be even more honoured and neither Margaret nor Polly objected. He stayed to practice with them then left, promising to see them on Saturday.

They travelled down to Clapham together, arriving in time for a short rehearsal before the performance

began. Lizzie and Polly performed 'Piccadilly Promenade' with Jack linking arms with both of them then
gliding to the side with each of them in turn before
spinning them together again. His voice made a rich
addition to the singing and he danced well too, his
movements light and fluid. Certainly, the audience
appeared to appreciate him.

Moving on to 'The Gardens of England', Jack
helped to rouse the audience into joining in with the
chorus. Loud applause followed then one man shouted
out, 'That's lovely, mate, but it's only about England.
What about Scotland?' His accent was strong.

'I'm from Scotland too, as you can probably tell,'
Jack called back. 'Though I'm from Edinburgh while
I suspect you're from Glasgow?'

'Aye,' the man confirmed. 'How about, *Speed Bonny
Boat*?'

'*Like a bird on the wing*?'

'Aye.'

Jack looked at Lizzie who smiled encouragement.
With that Jack launched into the 'Skye Boat Song'
unaccompanied. His voice was rich and warm, and
even Margaret joined in with the clapping when he'd
finished.

'I'm from Wales,' another man called.

'Then a Welsh song you shall have,' Jack told him.
''Men of Harlech'?'

'That'll do nicely.'

Again, Jack sang with gusto. '*Men of Harlech, march
to glory . . .*'

'Is anyone from Ireland?' he asked at the end.

A man at the back put his hand up. ''Danny Boy'
would be grand, so it would.'

Jack began to sing. '*Oh, Danny boy, the pipes, the*

pipes are calling . . .'

Men swayed along and a few joined in.

'Enough of me,' Jack declared then. 'I'm going to step aside for these three wonderfully talented young ladies.'

Margaret rolled her eyes but Lizzie thought she was secretly pleased.

There was no doubt that the concert was enjoyed by its audience. 'I hope you don't feel I took over,' Jack said afterwards.

'Of course not,' Lizzie told him. 'The men loved what you did.'

'You sang well, young man,' Margaret added.

Jack smiled. 'High praise indeed.'

He had an appointment elsewhere so couldn't see them home. 'Jack is fun, isn't he?' Lizzie commented to Polly as they settled on the train.

'Yes,' Polly agreed.

Lizzie waited, but it seemed Polly had nothing more to say. Still, they'd see Jack again soon. He'd suggested a visit to the Merriment so they could familiarise themselves with the stage before finalising their song choices.

Lizzie hadn't given much thought to being inside a theatre, but now she found memories of the night she'd passed by the Lyceum theatre rushing in on her again, squeezing her with anxiety. But the Zeppelins hadn't raided in months as the British had become better at shooting them down. Besides, the men who were serving their country faced death and danger daily but still fought on. Lizzie wouldn't let what had happened that night hold her back either. At least . . . she hoped not.

28

They met at the Merriment early one Tuesday morning. Zeppelins didn't raid during daylight hours so Lizzie felt safe. Jack let them in through a side door then led them along corridors to the front entrance so they could see the theatre as the audience would see it. 'Rather lovely, isn't it?'

There was plush red carpet underfoot and above them an ornate ceiling decorated with gold plasterwork. Framed mirrors and theatre posters boasted gilding too while the dark wood of the box office and doors gleamed with care.

Jack pushed through a pair of doors that opened into another large space which appeared to be where the audience would gather in the interval to meet friends and chat over drinks. There were graceful sofas and chairs upholstered in red, more gilding, and stairs sweeping up towards the dress circle and balcony.

'This way.' Jack opened a second set of doors into the auditorium itself where the theme of decorative red and gold continued.

'It's spectacular,' Lizzie said.

She was pleased to see Margaret looking equally impressed but Polly's eyes had widened in dismay. 'What is it, Poll?'

She turned to Lizzie as though surfacing from a nightmare. 'I can't sing here. It's too big. Too grand. And my voice is so small.'

Momentarily distracted by the beauty of the place, Lizzie hadn't yet thought about how it would feel to stand on the stage and perform in here. Now she too felt somewhat weak about the knees. She took a deep breath and said, 'It's natural to be nervous, but Mr Lomax wouldn't have asked you to sing if he didn't think you could do it. Would you, Mr Lomax?'

'Please call me Jack. Trust me, Miss Meadows — Polly — I know you can make a success of this.'

Polly shook her head.

'And just think of how good you'll feel knowing you've helped to raise much-needed funds for injured servicemen and their families,' Jack continued.

Poor Polly was no match against that sort of appeal. She was silent for a moment then nodded. 'All right, I'll try.'

'Thank you.' Jack patted her arm though Lizzie suspected he really wanted to draw Polly into his arms and kiss her.

They walked down the aisle and mounted side steps to the stage. Margaret looked to be struggling with nerves too as they stared out at all the seats. Lizzie forced herself to speak reassuringly. 'We might not actually be able to see many people in the audience because the stage will be lit up and they'll be in darkness.'

'That's right,' Jack confirmed. 'You can pretend no one's there, if it helps.'

He turned to Margaret. 'I hope you feel able to begin the programme with your piano solo?'

Margaret squared her bony shoulders. 'I'll do my duty, Mr Lomax. You can be sure of that.'

Feeling another burst of pride in her godmother, Lizzie grinned.

Jack treated them to a cup of tea in a tea room on

the Strand after they left the theatre. 'The show is called *Midsummer Melodies* and I'm arranging for leaflets to be printed to advertise it,' he told them. 'Selling tickets isn't your job, but do let me know if you'd like any leaflets.'

'Certainly we would,' Margaret said. 'We can give them to our pupils' families and our women's group.'

'We can also take some along to our concerts in case any of the hospital staff are interested,' Lizzie suggested.

Jack looked pleased. 'The Merriment will be promoting the show too and I'm hoping to get at least one of the London newspapers to advertise it for free. I've been touched by the generosity of people so far. Not just the performers like you, but also the Merriment staff. From booking clerks to cleaners, they'll be working unpaid.'

'None of it would be possible without your own generosity,' Lizzie pointed out.

Jack shrugged but the truth was that he'd done an immense amount of work. The thought reminded Lizzie that he'd once told them he had a living to earn. 'Are you waiting until the show is over before resuming your own singing career?' she asked.

'Actually, no. I've secured a singing engagement for the next few weeks. It's in an established show called *Blossom Town*.'

'I've heard of it,' Lizzie said.

'I'm replacing a man who's developed a problem with his vocal cords, poor chap. His understudy was fired due to a scandal with a chorus girl so I've been engaged to finish the run. It isn't the leading role, but I still have a solo and a duet.'

They were delighted for him.

Jack organised the rehearsal for early in June. 'I'm sorry it has to be on a Sunday,' he said. 'The theatre is busy on other days and we couldn't fit an entire rehearsal into an early morning visit.'

In addition to the performers who'd appear on stage Jack had recruited a small orchestra which was already hard at work practising. He gathered everyone else backstage and introduced them all.

Lizzie was particularly curious about Amy, the girl who'd sing with Jack, so it was frustrating to be told a previous commitment had prevented her from rehearsing today. Lizzie still enjoyed meeting the other performers, all of whom were friendly, though one of them — Galina, the ballet dancer — seemed particularly highly-strung. 'Artistic temperament,' Jack told them, winking.

He allocated dressing rooms. 'I'm afraid we'll have to look after our own costumes and make-up. Not that make-up is essential,' he added, after a look at Margaret's face.

Lizzie, Polly and Margaret were in a small room together. 'We'll be quite comfortable here,' Lizzie said.

They gathered again in the wings of the stage. 'I'll try to arrange a dress rehearsal for next Sunday, but I can't promise anything so let's make the most of the time we have today,' Jack said. 'Would you begin, please, Miss Penrose?'

She tilted her chin bravely and headed for the piano that had been wheeled onto the stage. Back ramrod straight, she launched into 'Arabesque' by Claude Debussy and gave a faultless performance which everyone cheered enthusiastically.

Polly was obviously terrified when the time came for her to sing with Lizzie but Jack sent her the warmest smile and Lizzie whispered, 'Remember to close your eyes if it helps. As long as you don't fall off the stage.'

Polly looked horror-struck at the thought of falling but she saw that Lizzie was joking and relaxed a little. As always when she was nervous, Polly's voice began softly but grew with her confidence.

'Beautiful!' one of the Tierney Tenors declared.

'You see?' Jack asked Polly.

If only it would occur to her that he could be more than just a friend.

They all worked hard for the rest of the day. Lizzie was impressed by the talents of the others, though she supposed it was only to be expected as they were professionals. Jack produced a box of leaflets before they all went home. Margaret took a large stack of them. 'There are hundreds of seats in this theatre and we need posteriors on all of them,' she said, and Lizzie was pleased to see that all of the performers followed her lead.

* * *

'I certainly do want some leaflets,' Cordelia told them a few days later. 'I'll be buying tickets for my own party of twelve — which includes my mother-in-law, who wouldn't miss it for the world — and I'll be urging others to buy tickets too.'

Cordelia was an unstoppable force when it mattered, and this cause was dear to her heart. Not that she'd urge anyone who couldn't afford a ticket to buy one. Cordelia was sensitive to such things.

Lizzie was touched by the number of pupil's families who wanted to buy tickets too. 'Such a worthy venture,' one mother said.

Everyone appeared to know someone who'd lost a family member or friend to the war.

'I'm fortunate that my husband left us well provided for,' another pupil's mother said. Her husband had been killed after a German U-boat torpedoed his ship. 'It must be dreadful for families in less comfortable circumstances. We owe it to their menfolk to help them.'

Harry and Matt both wrote to say that they were proud of Lizzie and wished they could be there to see the show. Lizzie wished they could be there too, though she'd be happy to see them anywhere as she missed them so much. She wasn't going to complain, though. The most important thing was that they were safe.

Not that London was all that safe anymore. The Zeppelin attacks might have stopped but a new menace arrived a week before the show in the form of Gotha aeroplanes, faster and deadlier than the airships. Bombing raids were back and Lizzie had to work hard to keep memories of the bombing near the Lyceum at bay. She reminded herself that she'd visited Central London restaurants with Harry and been fine. And just because the Lyceum had been caught on the edge of a blast there was no reason to suspect that another theatre would be unlucky. Even so . . .

The week before the show Jack called to confirm there was to be a dress rehearsal.

'We'll be there,' Lizzie promised, hoping it might settle them because all three of them were jumpy with stage fright, even if they were trying to hide it. 'Have many tickets been sold?'

'Lots.' Jack looked thrilled. 'We might even sell out.'

'That's wonderful! Is your singing engagement going well too?'

'That's partly why I'm here.' He brought an envelope from his jacket pocket. 'I'm sorry for the short notice, but I have three complimentary tickets for Tuesday's performance if you can make it?'

'How lovely!'

'I've never been to the theatre before,' Polly told him. 'I can't wait.'

They both looked at Margaret, suspecting that *Blossom Town* wouldn't be to her taste, but she looked gratified by the invitation. 'How kind, Mr Lomax. I've been broadening my horizons all through this war and I'll be glad to broaden them a little further.'

Lizzie smiled, feeling a rush of affection for her godmother, and glad to have the chance to enter a theatre at night before their own show. Hopefully, it would help her to lay the worst of her anxieties over bombings to rest.

Blossom Town was running at Fordham's Theatre on St Martin's Lane. Lizzie paused outside it then took a deep breath and followed the others inside. It was another exquisitely appointed theatre and considerably bigger than the Merriment. 'Our audience will be much smaller than this,' she whispered, hoping to reassure Polly. Hoping to reassure Margaret and herself as well.

'Everyone's smiling too,' she observed. 'People come to the theatre to be entertained so they're full of goodwill.'

'That could change if the performance is bad,' Polly

said.

'Let's put all of our worries aside and enjoy the evening.'

Polly nodded, though she still looked afraid.

Blossom Town told the story of Cherry and Augustus. Their path to romance was difficult due to a number of misunderstandings, not least because Cherry's friend, Sybil, also loved Augustus, and his friend, Max — played by Jack — also loved Cherry. All was well in the end, as not only did Cherry and Augustus become a couple but so did Sybil and Max.

'Wasn't that wonderful?' Lizzie asked at the end, applauding loudly and realising she'd been so engrossed that she'd barely given a thought to bombs.

'Just perfect,' Polly agreed, her eyes shining now.

Jack had invited them backstage so they walked around to the stage door where the doorman had been told to expect them. It was *Blossom Town*'s last night and a party was being held in the dressing rooms.

Jack grinned broadly as he greeted them. 'What did you think?'

'We loved it,' Lizzie told him.

He looked at Polly and her smiling nod of agreement clearly pleased him deeply.

Turning to Margaret, he raised an eyebrow.

'Congratulations, Mr Lomax,' she said. 'I may be advanced in years but it appears I can still be pleasantly surprised.'

'I'm honoured,' he told her, then signalled to someone to bring glasses of sparkling liquid that Lizzie guessed was champagne or something like it.

He introduced them to some of the other cast members. All were friendly. Lizzie was given a second glass of champagne and her head began to buzz rather pleasantly. But then a low, drawling voice reached her ears. 'Jack, darling. How delicious of you to invite me to the party!'

Lizzie turned to see a young woman standing in the doorway. She wore a black dress that fitted rather daringly to her slender figure. Her hair was dark and so were her glittering eyes, while her pouting mouth was red with lipstick. She'd arrived as Jack was talking to Polly, and Lizzie didn't miss the jealous glare that was directed at her friend.

'Amy!' Jack moved forward to welcome her with a kiss on her cheek.' He looked around and said, 'Amy's performing in *Sweet Kisses.*'

Lizzie saw little sweetness in Amy but smiled politely when Jack introduced her.

'Delighted,' Amy said insincerely, then her gaze flickered over Polly who greeted her with gentle charm.

How pretty and fresh Polly looked compared to this lizard-like creature. Lizzie moved to Polly's side protectively but Amy simply linked arms with Jack and drew him away to talk to another performer she appeared to know.

Jack brought her back eventually to talk about the fundraising show. There was nothing wrong with Amy's words, but Lizzie knew instinctively that the last thing this girl wanted was to be working with Polly.

'My goodness, isn't Amy attractive?' Polly remarked to Lizzie as they made their way home.

'I suppose she is. In a brittle sort of way.'

'I hope she doesn't think we're horribly amateur.'

'Jack doesn't think so. He's heard us sing and it's his opinion that matters.'

Polly looked unconvinced but said no more.

Lizzie was more than a little frustrated as she prepared for bed that evening. Polly and Jack couldn't be better suited in Lizzie's opinion, but Polly's disappointment over Davie and lingering hope of a reconciliation with him were blinding her to other routes to happiness.

Should Lizzie talk to Polly about it? Suggest that she should open her eyes to Jack's admiration and give him a chance? Explain that it needn't mean more than taking pleasure in each other's company in an open-minded sort of way while they saw what, if anything, came of it?

Intuition warned Lizzie against anything of the sort. The mere mention of Jack's interest was likely to make shy Polly clam up in his presence and avoid him as much as possible.

Patience was needed instead, but, without some sort of answering spark of interest from Polly, Jack's patience might run out, especially as Amy and doubtless other girls would be only too pleased to walk out with him.

Margaret's comment on her advancing years was on Lizzie's mind too. Margaret wasn't old. She had years ahead of her and Lizzie wanted them to be happy years. Maybe it wouldn't harm to write to Mr Grafton. He could simply throw the letter away if it didn't interest him. She made several beginnings but finally settled on something short.

Dear Mr Grafton,
I have had the pleasure of playing a number of your songs and would like to thank you for the enjoyment they've given me.

Although my name is unknown to you, I believe you may once have known my godmother, Margaret

260

Penrose. I live with Miss Penrose in the house which has been her home for all her life and I'm pleased to report that she's well. She teaches piano to children but also helps to entertain convalescent soldiers with musical concerts. Miss Penrose plays the piano while my friend Polly and I sing. We call ourselves The Penrose Singers and Players.

Please forgive me if this letter is unwelcome. I simply wish to thank you for your music and give you news of someone I believe may have once been a friend.

Yours sincerely,
Lizzie Kellaway.

Surely he couldn't take offence at that? She wrote out an envelope, stamped it and took it to the pillar box the next day. But doubts ambushed her again, surrounding her like spectres warning her to leave well alone. Sighing, Lizzie dropped the envelope back into her bag and walked away. She wouldn't send it until she was confident it was the right thing to do.

It wasn't until she went to bed that Lizzie had a chance to hide the letter in the drawer with Mr Grafton's music. But the letter wasn't in her bag. Panic swept over her as she wondered if she'd lost the letter in the house and Margaret had found it. But, no. Margaret had behaved normally all evening.

Lizzie remembered then that she'd been walking home from the pillar box, huddled beneath an umbrella because it had started to rain, when she'd collided with a man who was huddled beneath another umbrella. The impact had caused her bag to fall to the ground. They'd both picked up the contents and stuffed them hastily back into the bag but the letter must have been missed, caught on a gust of wind perhaps and blown into the road where it would have been crushed to a wet pulp by the passing traffic.

Lizzie's first feeling was relief but soon she was thinking of writing a substitute letter. She even reached for paper and a pen only for the doubts to flood back. If Margaret wanted to see him again, wouldn't she have tracked down his publisher's address as Lizzie had done?

Maybe. Maybe not. She might have been too hurt, or too afraid of a second rejection, or . . . There was a whole world of possibilities.

Sighing, Lizzie returned the paper and pen to their drawer. She wouldn't write again today. She might never write.

29

Sunday's dress rehearsal was a disaster. Before anyone had even set foot on the stage the Tierney Tenors reported that they'd left their music behind, Galina's Sugar Plum Fairy costume tore and the violinist fell over his own feet, twisting his ankle. Amy stroked Jack's arm sympathetically. 'Poor Jack.'

'Terrible dress rehearsal, excellent performance when it counts,' Jack said gamely.

Margaret was the first to walk onto the stage and she did so like a warrior determined to preserve her dignity, even if she couldn't win the battle. 'When you're ready,' Jack said.

Her playing was faultless in terms of hitting the right notes but Lizzie could tell that her fingering was awkward. 'Well done, Miss Penrose,' Jack said when she'd finished. 'That was marvellous.'

Vowing not to let him down, Lizzie concentrated hard as she played her piano duet. Again, it was competent, if uninspiring, and Jack looked relieved, as though he hoped things would improve from now on.

But they didn't. A Tierney Tenor dropped his hat, opera singer Eduardo accidentally smacked fellow opera singer Estella in the face, and Galina complained that she couldn't dance with pins in her dress. Lizzie caught Amy smirking at Jack. 'Let's show them how it's done,' she said, getting up like a snake unfurling its long, sinuous body.

Her singing was good — she was a professional, after all — but there was something arch about the performance that Lizzie didn't like, though perhaps she was confusing dislike of the performance with dislike of the girl who might wean Jack's attention from darling Polly.

Walking offstage, Amy aimed another smirk at Polly. 'Good luck,' she said, but her tone suggested that all the luck in the world wouldn't help Polly to deliver a performance half as good as her own.

Lizzie touched Polly's arm reassuringly then realised the smirk had actually stiffened Polly's backbone. She began her duet with Lizzie timidly but soon she was singing her kind and generous heart out. Lizzie couldn't resist casting a smirk in Amy's direction.

'Oh, first rate!' Jack declared.

'Sweet,' Amy corrected. In other words, amateur.

But she was wrong. Polly's soaring, silvery voice drew praise from everyone and Jack's eyes glowed as he looked at her.

Unfortunately, the rehearsal deteriorated into more mishaps. Forgotten lyrics, a wrong turn in a dance, an argument between the opera singers . . .

Jack looked drained by the time the rehearsal limped to an end. But he rallied to thank them all for coming and repeat the comforting theory that a bad rehearsal could be followed by a breath-taking performance. 'The important thing to remember is the reason we're doing this. Every penny we raise will help servicemen, widows and orphans in need. That thought should inspire all of us.'

Lizzie sat next to Polly on their return to Highbury. 'I can't say that I warmed to Amy,' Lizzie said.

'I can't say I did either.'

'I think she's setting her cap at Jack. He deserves someone nicer.'

'Yes,' Polly agreed, but it didn't seem to occur to her that the someone nicer might be her.

Lizzie's nudges weren't working. The rut into which Polly's spirits and confidence had fallen was deep but Lizzie didn't know how to help.

★ ★ ★

'Goodness,' Margaret said when Lizzie walked into the music room bearing an armful of yellow roses.

'They're from Cordelia to wish us luck tonight.'

'How kind.'

More flowers, cards and notes had come from other members of the women's group and the families of pupils. Most precious of all were the letters Lizzie had received from Harry and Matt. Both men wished her luck and seemed to have every faith in her.

The girl who stepped out of the rubble of a bomb site with such self-possession has deep reserve of courage, Harry wrote. *A show can't be more frightening than that.*

Matt wrote in a similar vein. *The girl who ran away from home all alone on a dark winter's night can manage a theatre performance with aplomb, especially when she's doing it to help people in need.*

Lizzie hoped desperately that she wouldn't let everyone down.

The day dragged slowly despite teaching and a visit to the shops. Each time Lizzie glanced at the clock her stomach clenched as she calculated how many hours remained before the show would begin. Ten hours, nine hours . . .

Polly joined them for an early supper though none of them ate much. Lizzie supposed Margaret and Polly were trying to hide their nerves just as Lizzie was trying to hide hers.

Arriving at the theatre — Lizzie resolutely thrusting all thoughts of bombs from her mind — they found more flowers in the dressing room. These flowers bore a card from Jack which said, *Thank you for giving your time and talent tonight. I won't say good luck as that's actually an unlucky thing to say in a theatre so I'll say break a leg instead. I don't mean it literally, of course. Jack x*

When the performance began Lizzie had a heart-in-mouth moment as Margaret walked onto the stage only to sit at the piano as though frozen with terror. But she was only steadying herself. Soon her fingers were flying over the keys and sending notes of pure beauty into the air. She'd never played better and it set the tone for the evening with everyone rising to the occasion to perform very well indeed.

'Each and every one of you is the star of this show so we'll take our bows in the order of the programme then we'll all bow together,' Jack had said.

It meant Margaret went on first and Lizzie was thrilled to see that rare flush of pleasure rise to her godmother's cheeks at the reception she was given. Lizzie was also delighted when the audience clapped and cheered Polly at least as much — probably more — than Amy. Polly was overcome. 'The audience is so kind!' she said.

'They know good singing when they hear it,' Lizzie told her.

Backstage, it was time to celebrate in the dressing rooms and the corridor that connected them. Cordelia had sent champagne and old Mrs Bishop had sent a bottle of gin with a note saying, *Enjoy a proper drink instead of that fizzy nonsense.* More drinks had been provided by Jack and the theatre manager, Charlie Sparrow.

He was a round but sleek man in his forties, smartly dressed in black evening wear and holding a cigar in a way that suggested he was rarely without a cigar, even if it wasn't always lit. 'I reckon you can say I'm pleased,' he said. 'We've raised more than three hundred pounds for the people we want to help. The theatre hasn't done badly either, as we've sold tickets for our regular shows and had a decent amount of publicity. If young Jack here wants to put on another charity night, I reckon I'm agreeable.'

Jack took Lizzie, Polly and Margaret aside before they left for home. 'I have a singing engagement in Brighton coming up, so I'll be away from London for a while. Might I take you all to dinner before I leave? As a thank you for tonight?'

'You've thanked us enough,' Lizzie told him. 'Why don't you come to us for a home-cooked dinner instead?'

Lizzie was concerned he might spend more than he could afford after being so generous with the flowers and drinks. It also occurred to her that there might be more chance to throw him together with Polly at home.

'I won't be any trouble?' he asked.

'None at all.'

'Jack!' It was Amy, thin lips pouting but eyes suspicious.

'Coming!' Jack settled on a date for the dinner then went to her.

★ ★ ★

Lizzie managed to give Jack ten minutes alone with Polly in the music room when he came to dinner, but it did no good. Lizzie returned from the kitchen after checking on the food she was cooking to find Polly talking to Jack as though he was her brother instead of a handsome young man who was clearly sweet on her.

'Dinner's ready,' Lizzie announced.

They moved into the dining-room where Margaret was trying to open a bottle of wine. Lizzie took it from her before disaster struck. It had been a dangerous move to ask Margaret to open wine, but Lizzie had needed an excuse to draw her away.

'Are you looking forward to your Brighton engagement?' Lizzie asked as they ate the chicken pie she'd made, stuffed full of vegetables to make it go further.

'I am,' Jack said. He went on to tell them about the show. It was called *A Rhapsody of Roses* and Jack was taking the lead role of Valentine Jones. 'We'll be running for eight weeks.'

'It must feel good to be settled for a while,' Polly said.

Jack looked at her as though searching for a sign that his absence would cost her a pang.

'I'll miss London,' he said. 'I'll miss all of you.'

'We'll miss you too,' Polly said, but once again he could have been her brother.

'Have the other performers from our show got work?' Lizzie wondered then. She was thinking of Amy and hoping the lizard-like girl wouldn't be joining Jack in Brighton.

They all had work and Lizzie was pleased to hear that Amy would be continuing with her current show, fifty miles away from Jack. Lizzie would have preferred her to be a hundred and fifty miles from him, but fifty miles were better than nothing.

'You'll write to let us know how you're getting on?' Lizzie said.

'Of course.'

'Perhaps you could send us a postcard?' Polly asked. 'I've never had a postcard from the seaside.'

'Certainly.' Jack looked at her with a tenderness that suggested he'd give her the world if she wanted it.

Polly gave no sign of noticing.

Open your eyes, Lizzie wanted to shout. Instead she asked Jack, 'Are you still hoping to organise another charity concert?'

'I am. I've spoken to Charlie Sparrow and we're thinking of November or December. It won't be possible before then because of my Brighton engagement. I hope you're not having second thoughts about taking part?'

'Not at all,' Polly assured him. 'The money we raise will make such a difference to people's lives and it'll be fun too. Terrifying, but fun.'

At the end of the evening Jack cast a wistful look at Polly, but how long would it be before he gave up on her? Amy might be working in London, but she could travel to Brighton by train and be back in time for an evening performance. Or Jack's eye might be caught by a girl in his new show.

Several days passed before Lizzie saw Polly again. 'Life feels quiet now the fundraiser is over,' Lizzie said.

'Mmm,' Polly agreed.

Her mood seemed flat today. Was she feeling Jack's absence? Lizzie could only hope so.

The next time they met Polly asked if they'd received

a postcard from Jack.

'We have indeed.' Lizzie produced a card which showed a photograph of Brighton pier.

'Maybe we could go to the seaside one day,' Polly said.

'Maybe.'

But for now they were busy. Conscious of being the only amateurs in the show, they'd invested a lot of time in practising, which meant they'd fallen behind with other things. For Lizzie, that meant giving the house a thorough clean, weeding the garden, catching up with sewing and darning, and arranging concerts. For Polly, it meant making up to old Mrs Bishop for all the time spent rehearsing.

More postcards came from Jack as the weeks passed. Polly always looked pleased to see the pictures — the seafront, the clock on Marine Parade and the wonderfully exotic Royal Pavilion with its domes and minarets — but also seemed keen to read the messages Jack had written on the back. 'It's nice that Jack's show is doing so well,' she said, more than once.

Encouraged, Lizzie thought that the sooner he returned to London, the better. But just before the Brighton show finished its run Jack wrote to say he'd picked up work with a touring company. He'd be moving along the south coast for the next six weeks. The question in Lizzie's mind was whether Amy would be moving with him.

★ ★ ★

The war entered its fourth year in August. There was still no sign of peace but Lizzie began to look forward to both Harry and Matt being granted leave before the year was out. Her heart soared when, sooner than she'd allowed herself to expect it, Harry wrote to say he was due in London in four days' time.

Waiting for his arrival, Lizzie bubbled with happy anticipation, but every now and then uncertainty crept onto her horizon. Their feelings had survived one year apart but the war had battered him down for a further year since then and who knew how that might have affected him? His letters were full of love, but it was the British way to show a stiff upper lip to the world. Beneath the surface . . .

The day before he was due back in England another letter arrived from him that sent Lizzie's emotions into a different sort of whirl. *I've had an idea and I hope you'll approve of it*, he wrote. *I'd like to take you to stay with my family in Surrey for a few days. Do say you'll come, darling girl.*

It was kind of him to invite her, but how would his parents feel about an unexpected guest? How would they feel about Lizzie? She'd heard enough about them to know that they inhabited a much more luxurious world than she did. Their idea of a suitable young woman for their son might be different indeed from a girl who worked for her living and had only a few pounds in a Post Office savings account to her name.

Lizzie had always known that, if her romance with Harry continued, she'd have to meet his family sooner or later. But just now she didn't feel ready.

30

The first thing Harry did was to hold Lizzie close in a way that left her in no doubt that his feelings for her were as strong as ever — as hers were for him. A kiss followed. Another hug. Another kiss. And then the laughter of relief that the first nervous moment of meeting was behind them.

They moved into the music room where a fire burnt brightly in Harry's honour. 'Is Miss Penrose not at home?' he asked.

'Out visiting.' Margaret was growing more tactful with every year that passed and her absence undoubtedly owed more to a wish to give Harry and Lizzie time alone than to a need to see Cordelia.

'In that case . . . ' Harry sat in an armchair and lifted Lizzie onto his lap.

She snuggled into his chest.

'What do you think of my idea of spending a few days in Surrey?' he asked.

'It's kind of you to invite me.'

'But?' He pulled back to study her. 'You're not *worried* about meeting my family?'

'Perhaps a little.'

'They'll adore you,' Harry promised. 'You're kind, beautiful, intelligent and most important of all — to them anyway — you make me happy.'

Lizzie wasn't convinced. Harry loved her. His family didn't. They might not even give her a chance to let them see what sort of person she was.

But Lizzie had no grounds for suspecting that Harry's family were snobs beyond the fact that his parents were wealthy and his sisters had all married into comfortable circumstances. 'Perhaps I'm being silly.'

'It would be ungallant of me to agree that you're silly,' Harry said, smiling. 'Let's just agree that you're becomingly modest. You'll come to Surrey tomorrow? Assuming your teaching and concert commitments allow it?'

'I'll come, but I can only manage one night. You'll thank your parents for inviting me?'

Harry was travelling down to Surrey later that day. 'Of course.'

Lizzie would have been happy to take the train the following morning but Harry insisted on driving up to London to collect her in his father's car. 'It'll give us more time together, darling.'

He came early so they could reach Surrey in time for lunch. The drive was pleasant and Lizzie warmed to the leafy green of Harry's home county. 'It's peaceful and pretty here,' she remarked, admiring trees, hedgerows, and lovely houses set in extensive gardens.

'We're all very fond of it. Don't imagine we always live quietly, though. Dinners, parties, tennis, golf . . . We're all rather social. My mother and sisters do charitable work too, so time never hangs heavily.'

A sign announced that they were entering the village of Beechfield Green. 'Nearly there,' Harry said.

Lizzie's nerves fluttered as the car passed between tall gateposts and came to a halt outside a rambling house of great loveliness. Her old home in Witherton had been substantial, but this house was both bigger and grander, with numerous gables across the front and climbing plants growing around an oak-timbered porch.

'Home,' Harry said.

He helped her out of the car but put a hand on her arm when she moved towards her case. 'Robert will see to it.'

Robert? The front door opened and a maid in traditional black dress, white cap and apron stood waiting. She must have been on the watch for them. 'Thank you, Bridget,' Harry said, leading Lizzie towards her. 'Where is everyone?'

'In the family sitting room, sir.'

A young manservant entered the hall. 'Ah, Robert,' Harry said. 'Could you see to Miss Kellaway's luggage and take the car around the back?'

'Certainly, sir.'

Bridget took their coats and Harry guided Lizzie across a large wood-panelled hall to one of the doors. 'We're here!' he announced, throwing it open.

'Harry, darling!' A fair-haired, middle-aged woman dripping lace and pearls rose to her feet.

Maria Benedict, Lizzie supposed. Harry's mother.

'This must be Miss Kellaway. Welcome, my dear. We're most happy to meet you.' Mrs Benedict tilted her cheek for Harry to kiss then offered a hand to Lizzie. It was soft and feminine.

A man came forward. Doubtless Harry's father, Giles. He was dark-haired like his son. 'Delighted,' he said, shaking her hand with a much firmer grip.

Lizzie was introduced to Harry's sisters who were just as he'd described them. Eleanor, the eldest, was tall and imposing. Alicia was a little less so, while Charlotte, the youngest, was soft and round. All were fair, and all appeared to be friendly.

'These are the grandchildren,' Mrs Benedict said then.

'We don't expect you to remember all their names,' Charlotte added.

'Well, let's see.' Lizzie bent to shake hands with all eight children, listening as each one gave their name. Straightening again, she pointed to each child in turn. 'Thomas, Albert, Celia, Matilda, Ralph, Louisa, Edmund, and Letitia, the latest addition to the family. Letty for short.'

'You've been coaching her, Harry,' Charlotte suggested.

'Not me.'

'Remembering children's names is a knack that comes from teaching piano,' Lizzie explained.

She felt better for this early chance to be open about the fact that she worked for a living. She wasn't ashamed of it.

'You're clever!' Edmund declared, and everyone laughed, their friendliness undimmed.

'Sherry?' Mr Benedict suggested.

This sherry was nothing like the awful stuff Margaret bought. It was smooth and probably expensive.

Lizzie wanted to look around the room but resisted the temptation, not wishing to appear rude. She still formed an impression of French windows curtained with heavy brocade, a large marble fireplace, several sofas, chairs and side tables, and numerous photographs in silver frames.

'Do sit,' Eleanor invited, patting the seat next to her, but at that moment there was a stir at the door and three men entered in golfing clothes.

The sisters' husbands, Lizzie assumed, and she was duly introduced to Frank, Paul and Jonathan. All three men appeared to be friendly too.

'I hope you'll excuse us turning up straight from

the golf course, Miss Kellaway,' Frank said.

'Certainly.'

'Who won?' Eleanor asked.

'The honours went to Jonathan,' he told her. 'Paul's ball was stuck in a bunker for an age and I just couldn't hit straight today. Next time we'll give the blighter a decent challenge, though. Eh, Paul?'

'Indeed. You've been warned, Jon.'

Jonathan grinned.

'What time's lunch?' Frank asked then. 'Eighteen holes make a chap hungry. You must be famished too after the drive, Miss Kellaway.'

Before she could reply Bridget appeared to announce that luncheon was ready in the dining room.

'Full house today, what?' Frank remarked, as they settled around the capacious table.

There was soup followed by poached salmon then a fruit compote. All of the food was delicious and so was the wine.

Maria Benedict had placed Lizzie at her side. 'We don't always have wine with luncheon but we wanted your welcome to feel special.'

'Fear not, Miss Kellaway,' Eleanor said from across the table. 'We're crowding you today but you'll have a quieter day tomorrow.'

'I'm grateful for the chance to meet you all,' Lizzie said. She paused, then added, 'Please call me Lizzie.'

Harry's sisters and brothers-in-law were all happy to be called by their Christian names. No one suggested she should call his parents Maria and Giles but Lizzie wouldn't have felt comfortable with that anyway. Not yet.

The conversation mostly flitted between family concerns about dentists, cooks, food supplies and neighbours, but sometimes Lizzie was asked about her life in London. She guessed the questions were driven partly by a wish to include her, and partly by a wish to probe into her suitability for Harry.

She'd expected it and decided not to mind. It was natural for them to be curious about the girl Harry loved. Besides, she was proud when she talked about Margaret, their teaching and the concerts they performed.

'These are amateur concerts?' Mrs Benedict asked.

'Oh, yes. They're our small contribution to the war effort.'

'Doubtless much appreciated by your audiences.' Mrs Benedict paused then added, musingly. 'Teaching music is a respectable way for a young woman to occupy her time until she settles down.'

'My girls are learning the piano,' Eleanor told Lizzie. 'Their teacher is terribly strict, though. No sense of humour. I'm sure my girls would rather have a teacher like you.'

'My Louisa won't be ready to learn for another year or two,' Charlotte said. 'Perhaps Lizzie will be able to teach her then.'

Did this mean that Lizzie had passed muster with this family? She rather thought she had, especially when Harry sent her a glowing look of approval.

After lunch, the men took the children into the garden for a run-around, Paul limping due to his foot injury but doing his best to keep up. Lizzie returned to the family sitting room with the women. They told her about their own war efforts — knitting, rolling bandages and organising parcels for the troops. Eleanor also took flowers into the local hospital each week and all four Benedict women served on charity committees.

'We lead full lives here in Surrey,' Mrs Benedict said.

'We're never dull,' Charlotte agreed.

Looking through the window, Lizzie watched Harry chase the children across the lawn. He was a thoroughly nice man as well as a handsome one, and Lizzie felt a burst of love for him. How lucky she was to have his love in return.

Later, after his sisters had left and Lizzie had seen the room she'd been allocated — a delightful room overlooking the extensive garden — Harry took her aside and drew her into his arms. 'I hope you don't want to run all the way back to London after having the entire family foisted onto you,' he said.

'I like them.'

'They like you.'

He smiled then kissed her. With a sigh of contentment, Lizzie kissed him back.

The next morning, she attended church with Harry and his parents. Luncheon followed, then Harry suggested taking Lizzie for a drive.

'Good idea,' his father said. 'You young things shouldn't be with old people like us all day.'

'Show Lizzie something of the area,' his mother suggested.

Harry did so, and the more Lizzie saw of lush, green Surrey the more she liked it. 'That looks pretty,' she said, pointing to a wood they were passing.

'The perfect place for a walk,' Harry agreed.

He drew the car to a halt and they entered the wood arm in arm, following a path that rambled between oaks, sycamores, hornbeams, beeches and alders. Squirrels leapt from branch to branch above them.

Birds flitted in trees. 'I can hear a woodpecker,' Harry remarked.

Listening, Lizzie heard it too. She smiled up at him and he turned to face her, releasing her arm to cup her face. 'I love you so much, dearest girl. I know that if you add up the hours we've spent together, they're relatively few. But we've been writing for almost two years now and those letters — those many letters — have helped us to get to know each other and grow closer. Months of separation might have seen a weaker courtship wither. My feelings for you only grow stronger. So I hope you don't feel I'm being premature when I ask you a question. It doesn't feel premature to me. It feels right. Darling Lizzie, will you do me the very great honour of becoming my wife?'

Was it foolish to feel so taken by surprise? Yes, she and Harry were in love. Yes, he'd introduced her to his family. But Lizzie had seen being in love and meeting Harry's family as stepping stones on the way to a shared future that would only come to pass once the war was over, Harry was safely at home and they were seeing more of each other.

'You think it's too soon?' Disappointment shadowed Harry's face and it grieved her to see him hurting.

'I just wasn't expecting this. It's knocked the wind out of my sails.'

Thoughts raced through Lizzie's head and a matching maelstrom of emotions raced through her heart. Why was she hesitating when there was no doubt in her mind that she loved Harry and he loved her?

Was it because she feared jinxing the future if she started to plan it?

Or because she feared their feelings might change once the war ended and they were living ordinary lives that were no longer shadowed by the constant fear of tragedy?

Or was Lizzie worried that Margaret might think it too soon?

All of those reasons, perhaps. But only an idiot would let superstition influence her decision and wasn't life always full of risk?

'You're not sure you love me deeply enough, is that it?' Harry asked.

'Not at all! Of course I'll marry you!'

Lizzie threw her arms around his neck and kissed him, relieved to see warmth and joy re-enter his face. She'd have hated to send him back to the war a dejected man.

'No proposal is complete without a ring,' he said, and he drew a small box from his pocket.

Inside was a ring. A diamond solitaire. Beautiful, but as he slid it onto her finger, they realised it was too loose. 'I'll write to the jewellers in London and warn them to expect you to return the ring for alteration,' Harry said. 'They'll need to measure your finger, of course.'

'Tell them we'll return it together when you're next on leave. I'd like you to be the first person to put the ring on my finger once it's been altered.'

'That means you won't be able to wear it in the meantime.'

'Yes, I will.' Lizzie reached up to unfasten the silver chain on which she'd hung her mother's ring. She slid Harry's ring alongside it. 'It makes me happy to think of your ring hanging next my mother's,' she told him. 'She'd have been overwhelmed with joy to know I'm marrying a man as wonderful as you.'

Lizzie turned serious suddenly. 'We must cling to our happiness, Harry. To hope, too.'

Harry nodded, smiled and kissed her. 'Shall we go back and share our good news?'

'Yes, let's,' Lizzie said, though with trepidation. Harry's family had been welcoming so far, but perhaps they'd decided on tolerance because they expected that time and distance would put an end to their son's interest in her eventually so it wasn't worth kicking up a fuss of opposition.

She was pleasantly surprised by their obvious delight. 'It's so lovely to see our dear boy happy!' Mrs Benedict declared.

'It certainly is,' Giles Benedict agreed. 'There's some champagne in the cellar that I've been saving for a special occasion, and occasions don't come more special than this. Ring the bell, Maria. Let's have it brought up.'

'Have you given any thought to the wedding?' Mrs Benedict asked, but her husband laughed.

'Maria, they've only been engaged for half an hour.'

'I know. I suppose I'm just excited. I so much enjoyed our daughters' weddings.'

'I doubt we'll make any plans until Harry's next at home,' Lizzie said.

'Very sensible, my dear. It's a pity you have to return to London today. I could talk about weddings forever.'

'I know!' Giles Benedict rolled his eyes comically.

It wasn't long before Lizzie had to leave as she was teaching the following morning and squeezing a concert into the afternoon. Once again, Harry insisted on driving her.

'Happy?' he asked, after they'd waved goodbye to his parents and driven through the gateposts onto the road.

'Very.'

'So am I.'

He looked deeply satisfied, and Lizzie was glad.

But she was thoughtful on the journey home. For all that she thought superstition was nonsense, she couldn't quite dismiss the feeling that she shouldn't jinx the future by announcing to the world what she expected it to hold. She decided to tell only Margaret, Polly and Cordelia about her engagement.

She told her godmother the news first. Margaret went quiet for a moment but when she spoke her voice was deep with emotion and sincerity. 'Congratulations, Lizzie. You deserve to be happy.'

Happier than Margaret had been? Lizzie still hadn't written to Mr Grafton, unable to decide if she'd be doing the right thing or not. Every now and then she'd take out pen and paper to write to him, but each time she returned it to the drawer with a sigh. Maybe one day . . .

Lizzie was worried that the engagement might remind Polly all too painfully of being rejected by Davie, but she should have known better. Polly's soft heart was as generous as ever. 'Don't look so fearful, Lizzie,' she said. 'I don't begrudge you your happiness. Far from it. No one deserves happiness more than you.'

Cordelia was equally sincere. 'I haven't met your soldier, Lizzie, but I like the sound of him. I'm flattered to be taken into your confidence and you can rely on my discretion. I quite understand that you don't want to tempt fate by making too much of an uncertain future.'

Clearly, Lizzie wasn't the only one to feel superstition hovering.

She thought about writing to Matt about her engagement but decided to tell him when she saw him next, which would surely be soon.

Between her teaching and the concert Lizzie hadn't time to see Harry the next day but, thanks to Margaret covering some lessons and rearranging others, she managed to spend the whole of the following day with him. In the evening she invited Margaret and Polly to share a celebratory dinner with them in the rarely used dining room.

'Let's open a bottle of my sherry so we can toast your happiness,' Margaret said, but Harry spared them the ordeal by bringing champagne.

'He's lovely,' Polly whispered. 'Handsome too!'

The last day of Harry's leave was spent quietly with another walk, this time in Regent's Park. When it began to rain, they sheltered under a tree. 'It looks like the rain's settling in,' Harry said, after a while. 'Shall we make a dash for the street and find somewhere to have lunch? We may get a little wet but it beats starving ourselves into skeletons here.'

He was grinning, his dark eyes bright, and Lizzie felt tenderness wash over her along with grief because Harry was so alive yet would be returning to the front within hours. 'Lunch it is!'

She set off running. Harry caught her up, took hold of her hand and together they ran to a tea shop.

She cried after they parted, but, as ever, she could only get on with life as best she could. She had teaching and concerts to keep her busy. Friends too. And hopefully it wouldn't be long before Matt was home.

News of Matt came soon. But it wasn't the news Lizzie wanted.

31

Lizzie's head reeled in dismay when she read Edith's letter. Words leapt out at her. *Injured, hospital, wounds . . .*

Fighting down panic, she read the letter again. Matt was in hospital. His wounds were healing . . . That was good, wasn't it? But what was the nature of his injuries?

Broken ribs and tissue damage, she read. Bad enough, but at least he was whole. Or so Lizzie assumed. Edith promised to let her know as soon as she had more information.

Another letter arrived two days later. Edith had spoken to the hospital matron and heard that Matt was doing well.

A week passed then Matt was moved to a convalescent home and Lizzie was excited to receive a letter from Matt himself. He assured her that he was fine, but then he wasn't the man to make a fuss. A further fortnight passed and Edith had somehow arranged for Matt to finish his convalescence at home. Joe was fetching him by taxi and train.

Matt wrote again to tell Lizzie that he'd arrived at the farm and was enjoying being with the family. He wondered if Lizzie might visit for a few days?

Lizzie was thrilled to accept the invitation and a week later took the train to Stafford. *You'll be met,* Matt's latest letter had said, but it hadn't specified by whom.

Walking out of the station, Lizzie had no trouble

recognising Joe Warren as he stood waiting beside a horse and cart. 'You've grown,' she told him. He was almost as tall as Matt, though he still had the irrepressible grin he'd had as a boy.

'So have you,' he said.

'Yes, I'm quite the young lady these days,' Lizzie teased.

'Too fine for us country folk?'

'I may be young but I don't think I'll ever be fine.'

He smiled back at her, took her bag and hauled it onto the cart. 'Need a hand getting up?'

'I'll manage.'

She climbed up easily while Joe walked around to the driver's side and sprang up with athletic ease. 'This is Hector, isn't it?' She gestured towards the horse.

'Yes, he's old but at least we still have him. A lot of horses have been requisitioned for hauling artillery and supplies.'

'I'm glad Hector's safe at home.' Lizzie paused then asked, 'How's Matt? Is he really going to recover fully?' She was desperate to see for herself that he was healing well.

'So the doctors say. Matt's certainly not the man to malinger.'

'No.' Lizzie smiled. 'I can't imagine Matt malingering.'

Joe was easy to talk to, happy to chat about the farm he loved as the cart rumbled along the roads. 'Did you ever get a tractor?' Lizzie asked.

'Not yet. Tractors are expensive. Hopefully one day . . .'

Looking around as they moved into the countryside, Lizzie saw little to stir her memory, but she'd

286

been ill when Matt had first taken her to the farm, and sick with worry when they'd set off for London a few days later.

The countryside here was pretty, lush fields being bordered by hedgerows among which campion, knapweed and rosebay willow herb flowered.

Lizzie sat up straighter when she saw a white-painted wooden signpost bearing the words *Sorrel's Lee 3 miles* on one of its arms. This was the farm's nearest village. Soon she saw the roof of the farmhouse in the distance. How idyllic it looked, though Lizzie knew that the farm involved a great deal of hard work.

Joe turned the cart down a lane and, after another few minutes, steered them between gateposts into the yard. One of those gateposts bore the name Sorrel's Patch. What a pity Lizzie had missed it all those years ago. Still, she was here now.

A small boy stood looking out for them. He waved to Joe then ran off towards the kitchen door shouting, 'They're here!'

Edith came out carrying her little daughter as Joe brought the cart to halt. She was followed by Mikey and Molly, easy to recognise despite the fact that time had given them height and taken the babyishness from their features. Lizzie jumped down and found herself wrapped in Edith's free arm while the others crowded round.

What a lovely family the Warrens were.

Edith made rapid introductions. 'Mikey, Molly, Thomas, Rose . . . Come inside. I expect you're in dire need of a cup of tea. Matt's keen to see you too.'

'How is he?' Lizzie searched Edith's face for the truth.

'We were desperately worried when we heard he'd been hurt, but he really is doing well. Come and see for yourself.'

Matt was propped in an armchair by the kitchen fire. 'You'll excuse me if I don't get up?' he joked.

The familiar smile curved his mouth but the lines around his eyes were deeper and he'd lost weight again. Lizzie felt the prickle of tears and an urge to throw herself against his chest and howl. How emotional she was these days! Wanting neither to hurt him nor look ridiculous, she bent to kiss his cheek instead. 'I'm so glad you're on the mend.'

'A farmer's constitution comes in handy.'

He held her in his gaze for a moment. 'You're a sight for sore eyes, Lizzie,' he added then. 'A picture of health.'

'She's pretty,' Molly said, and Lizzie was glad to be able to swallow down the excess emotion and laugh.

'It's true,' Molly insisted.

'Then let me return the compliment. You're pretty too.'

Molly was a willowy girl with soft honey-coloured hair and gentle green eyes. She blushed endearingly at the praise.

Edith passed her daughter to Matt. 'Will you hold Rose while I make tea? Lizzie, I know you said you'd pack a lunch to eat on the train but you must have room for cake.'

'Cake would be welcome, but only a small piece.' She didn't want to rob this growing family of their food.

'We're all having cake,' Edith's son, Thomas, said. 'It smells gorgeous but we weren't allowed to eat it until you came. We've been waiting for hours!'

Edith scolded him for bad manners but Lizzie only laughed again. 'It's lucky the train was on time, otherwise you might have starved.'

'I might,' he agreed sombrely, though he was clearly far from starving.

'Tell me how old you and your sister are,' Lizzie invited.

Thomas was five. 'Rose is just a baby but my dad is a hundred.'

Molly rolled her eyes. 'Fibber.'

'Tea's ready,' Edith announced.

'You're allowed to sit with Uncle Matt,' Thomas told Lizzie. Clearly it was a treat not to sit at the table.

'I'm honoured.'

She sat in the armchair opposite Matt's and Edith brought them tea and cherry cake, doubtless made with cherries from the orchard.

The kitchen door opened and two men came in — Joe, and a fair-haired, gentle-looking man who had to be Edith's husband, an impression he confirmed by walking up to her, kissing her and smiling at her with deep affection. What a happy marriage this was.

Peter was shy, Lizzie realised, but he asked kindly about her journey and said, 'Good, good,' when she told him it had been uneventful.

The children made up for his quietness by chattering about the farm, its animals, their favourite things and Lizzie's luck in riding on a train, an adventure none of the younger children had experienced yet.

Contentment radiated from Edith and Peter. Life on the farm was exactly what they wanted. Joe too had the satisfied air of someone who was following the perfect path for him. Even Molly spoke of the chickens and cows with such enthusiasm that she appeared destined to live the rest of her life on one farm or another.

Mikey had always been different. All of the Warrens enjoyed reading, but Mikey was the one with the taste for indoor study. 'Do you miss the pottery?' Lizzie asked.

'Sometimes, but I'm glad to be home and we've plenty of books here now.'

Matt looked proud of all his brothers and sisters, and Lizzie was struck again by how much he'd sacrificed to keep them safe and happy.

'Enough,' Edith finally announced. 'I'm going to give Lizzie a break from all this noise by taking her up to her room.'

There were cries of disappointment.

'We'll talk again soon,' Lizzie promised.

'You're sleeping in my room,' Molly said. 'I'm sleeping in the boys' room with Thomas.'

'Oh?' Lizzie assumed Edith and Peter must have Matt's old room so where did that leave Joe, Mikey and Matt himself?

'Joe and Mikey are sleeping in the barn!' Thomas cried. 'I wish I was allowed to sleep in the barn.'

'When you're older,' Edith told him.

'I'm not allowed to sleep in the barn either,' Matt said, green eyes glinting humour. 'I'm sleeping next to the piano.'

'I've inconvenienced you all,' Lizzie said guiltily.

'Not at all,' Matt insisted. 'We want you here. And I was already sleeping next to the piano so I don't have to manage the stairs.'

Joe had picked up Lizzie's bag but she took it from him. 'I've kept you from your work long enough.'

She was touched to see that flowers from the garden had been placed in her room. The purple Michaelmas daisies added to the impression of freshness and cleanliness. 'I'm afraid the children aren't going to leave you alone if they can help it,' Edith said. 'Do feel free to tell them to quieten down or go away.'

'They're lovely.'

'But noisy too.' Edith opened the top drawer of the old chest of drawers. 'I've emptied out this drawer for your things.'

'Thank you.'

'Come down when you're ready, but don't feel you have to rush.' Edith headed for the door.

Lizzie unpacked her bag, leaving out the gifts she'd brought — sweets, crayons and drawing paper for the children, two bottles of wine for the grown-ups and a set of lace-edged handkerchiefs for Edith. Lizzie doubted Edith had the time or the money to buy pretty things for herself.

Opening the window, Lizzie leant out to take in the view of gently rolling farmland, grasses and crops in myriad shades of green with animals grazing contentedly in the pastures. How soothing it was here, hard work notwithstanding.

She didn't linger long, though. This time with the Warrens was too precious to be idled away.

The children's eyes widened when they saw Lizzie enter carrying gifts. 'Barley sugars,' she told them, putting the sweets on the table. They'd been hard to find, given the sugar shortages, but the children's excitement made the search feel worthwhile. 'Crayons and paper too.'

'Thank you, thank you!' Thomas cried.

'Yes, thank you,' Molly said, rubbing his hair.

She took the wine to Matt and the handkerchiefs to Edith.

'How pretty!' Edith cried. 'I'll save these for best.'

'You're very generous, Lizzie,' Matt said, approvingly.

'May we have the sweets now?' Thomas asked.

'After your dinner,' Peter told them.

Edith made one of her fragrant stews for their meal, the mutton and vegetables cooked to perfection and the flavours brought out with fresh herbs. There was rhubarb pie and custard for dessert.

At Matt's suggestion Peter opened the bottles of wine so the meal had a festive air. Everyone was interested in the Penrose Players and Singers, with questions being thrown at Lizzie thick and fast.

'Do you ever get scared?'

'Or forget the words?'

'Or sing the wrong notes?'

Lizzie answered all of the questions then said, 'I was nervous at first but it's heartening to see how much the men enjoy our concerts.'

'What you're doing is wonderful,' Matt said.

Lizzie thought about how much he must be suffering, being separated from the home and family he loved. From his piano too. 'You must miss being without music.'

'I'm not without it all of the time. In rest periods we can sometimes go into nearby towns and villages. There are cafés — estaminets, they call them — and I've been allowed to play the piano in a few of them.'

'I'm glad.'

Lizzie became aware of whispering among the children.

292

'Do you know a song called 'Those Golden Fields'?' Molly finally asked.

'Actually, yes. I heard it being played in a music shop and liked it. A patient at one of our concerts requested it too, so I'll be buying the sheet music soon. Why? Is it one of your favourites?'

'Yes!' Molly cried, and there were smiles all round.

'It's Uncle Matt's song,' Thomas said.

Lizzie turned to Matt in wonder. 'You've had a song published?'

'Mmm, I taught myself to read music so I could record the notes on paper.'

'We're so proud of him,' Edith said.

'Of course you are!' Lizzie said. 'It's an incredible achievement.'

Molly went into the parlour and returned with the sheet music. The cover showed rolling fields with a copse of dusky trees in the background and a hedgerow with flowers, birds and butterflies in the foreground. Doubtless the song had been inspired by living here at the farm.

'I hope you'll play it for me,' Lizzie told Matt. 'If you're well enough?'

'He's well enough,' Molly said. 'He's played it for us lots of times. He said we shouldn't show off to you about his song but I don't see what's wrong with showing off when you've done something so utterly fantastic. I'd show off if I'd written a song.'

Everyone laughed.

'I'd love to hear Matt's song but let me help to clear up after this delicious meal first,' Lizzie said.

Edith wouldn't hear of Lizzie helping after her long journey. Instead, the Warrens leapt into action with well-practised precision, everyone except little Rose contributing something, whether it was carrying plates to the sink, sweeping the floor or wiping the table.

'Shall we?' Matt asked Lizzie, with a gesture towards the parlour.

They both got up — Matt stiffly — and walked into the other room. It had been turned into a bedroom for Matt but the piano stood in the same place as before. Placing their wine glasses on small mats on the piano top, they sat side by side on the stool. 'This is like old times,' Matt said, smiling.

He raised the piano lid and played a few notes with fluid ease. 'Just warming up,' he said.

The other Warrens filed in and gathered round. 'All right,' Matt said then, and he began to play, singing the lyrics in the low-pitched crooning voice she remembered so well. '*Golden in the sunshine and graceful in the breeze . . .*'

It was the sort of voice that was neither perfect nor professional. It even had a catch in it here and there. But it was an intimate, hypnotic voice that drew the listener in.

'That was utterly mesmerising,' Lizzie said, afterwards. 'May I play it?'

'I'd rather you sang while I played,' Matt said.

Lizzie read the words through twice then nodded to show she was ready. Wanting to do justice to Matt's song, she put all of her heart into singing it. When she finished, she saw Matt had a satisfied smile on his face. She raised a questioning eyebrow.

'I remember how you used to think your voice wasn't up to your friend, Polly's. I liked your voice when you were child and I like it even more now. It's full of emotion.'

Hadn't Cordelia said much the same? Lizzie's cheeks felt warm. 'I don't know about that.'

'I do.'

'Matt's right about your voice, Lizzie,' Edith said. 'It's beautiful.'

'Sing more songs!' Thomas pleaded, and, seeing that everyone else seemed keen for her to continue, Lizzie obliged until Edith insisted she take a breather.

'Is 'Those Golden Fields' the first song you've written?' Lizzie asked Matt.

Molly answered for him. 'He's written lots.'

'Several, anyway,' Matt confirmed.

He played and sang four more songs, three dreamy and one a lively, humorous song called 'My Pillow Waits' about wanting to go to sleep but having to stay up to oil his rifle, pile sandbags on top of the trench, chase rats away and pick lice out of his uniform.

'That's the best song,' Thomas declared. 'Especially the verse about the lice.'

'You're disgusting,' Molly told him affectionately.

'Are all the songs going to be published?' Lizzie asked Matt, for, without exception, they were excellent.

'That's the plan.'

'It's getting late,' Edith announced. 'It's long past bedtime for you younger ones and we older ones need to be thinking about settling down too.'

Life on the farm meant early to bed and early to rise, but there was also a plea for understanding in the look Edith gave Lizzie. Edith wanted to ensure Matt rested while he could.

'I'm tired after my journey so an early night will suit me perfectly,' Lizzie said.

It still took some time to settle the children. Lizzie

was invited to read bedtime stories, which she enjoyed, then she tucked the little ones in before going out to the barn to admire the camp that had been set up in the hayloft. 'I feel guilty for making you change sleeping arrangements,' Lizzie said again, only to be shouted down with cried of, 'This is much more fun!'

Edith made the grown-ups a final cup of tea then they said their goodnights. 'I've enjoyed today,' Matt told Lizzie.

'So have I.'

Up in the small bedroom, Lizzie leant out of the window again. The air was cooler but still fragrant, and the moon was a silvery crescent in a star-filled velvet sky. With a sigh at the beauty of it all, Lizzie undressed and got into bed, wondering what the morning would bring.

32

She woke to brightness and the sound of voices down in the house and out in the yard. The Warrens had started the day without her.

'You needed the sleep,' Edith said, when, after washing and dressing hastily, Lizzie appeared in the kitchen.

'What can I do to help? After all that sleep you won't persuade me that I'm too tired.'

'You're still our guest.'

'I hope I'm more of a friend.'

'Of course you are. Well, then. Breakfast will be ready soon, so if you wouldn't mind slicing bread?'

Lizzie jumped to the task. Breakfast was a lively meal and a good one too with fresh milk and eggs. 'We have an advantage, producing our own,' Edith explained. 'I believe it's been difficult in the towns and cities with food being hard to come by.'

Lizzie confirmed it. 'It's usually egg substitute for us.'

'We're lucky, though even here in the countryside some people have struggled. In the early days of the war, we saw near-starving children looking for dandelion leaves to eat in sandwiches or soups as they'd nothing else. We gave them as much proper food as we could spare. It's got a little easier since the Food Controller was appointed to ration supplies, but it's still a struggle to get hold of things like tea and sugar with so many cargo ships being torpedoed.'

'Expensive too,' Lizzie agreed.

She spent the rest of the morning helping Edith and playing with the children, but in the afternoon, Edith insisted that Lizzie should have time to talk with Matt. They went outside to make the most of the fine September day, Matt insisting he was well enough to walk slowly.

They admired the apples, pears and plums then sat down on a wooden bench from where they could see the fields in which Peter, Joe and Mikey were working. They chatted for a while then quietness settled over them. A comfortable quietness. Matt's green eyes had narrowed against the sun as he drank in the scene and Lizzie guessed he was committing it to memory.

Birds flew overhead. 'Swallows,' Matt said. 'Here for the summer but soon they'll be going home to Africa or Arabia or even India.'

He'd be leaving home to go back to the front. Lizzie's stomach tightened with fear for him. 'Edith told me you'd been promoted to sergeant. She also told me about your Distinguished Conduct Medal.'

Matt grimaced, too modest to welcome praise for doing what he doubtless considered to be no more than his duty. 'Anyone would have done what I did.'

'Are you seriously suggesting that anyone would have continued a raid on a machine gun post while men were falling all around him? Then knocked it out of service, crawled to safety with an injured comrade on his back and crawled back to rescue two more?'

Matt shrugged.

'It was brave of you,' Lizzie insisted. 'But I hope you'll take care of your own life as well as the lives of your comrades.'

He turned to her with a wry smile. 'Has Edith put you up to this?'

'Can't I be concerned for you too?'

For a moment his expression was unreadable. 'I'm a lucky man having family and friends who care for me,' he said then. 'As I've already told Edith, I want to survive this war, so I've no intention of taking foolish risks.'

The trouble was that he wouldn't consider it foolish to risk his life to save others. He'd consider it a duty.

Just as had happened during her first visit as a child, Lizzie's days on the farm took on a pattern. Mornings were spent helping and playing with the children, while evenings were for gathering together for food and music. But every afternoon she spent time alone with Matt. Sometimes they talked, but at other times they simply looked out over the pastoral loveliness of the farm and the ever-changing sky above it, recapturing the old sense of comfort and companionship that wrapped Lizzie in inner warmth.

One wet afternoon she and Matt spent an hour at the piano after Lizzie had asked about his song-writing. 'It's hard to explain, but I'll try,' he said. 'I suppose I'm like a miner who digs deep for coal. I dig deep into how I feel about things, whether they're frivolous or more serious. The music comes from the mood and the words just follow. What do you do when you sing?'

'It depends. If I'm singing in a concert to cheer people up, I think about them and how I might make them smile. If I'm singing a slower song — a ballad, perhaps — I suppose I do as you do and get down the mine to dig out the emotion.'

He ran his fingers across the keys. 'I could write a song about you. 'Lizzie is busy' . . . '

'That makes me sound like a plant. A busy lizzie.'

'All right, let's think about other words that describe you. Intrepid, adventurous, principled, courageous . . . It's hard to make lyrics with those. Unless . . . Got it! 'Lizzie the Lionheart'!'

'Now you're being ridiculous,' Lizzie laughed. 'It reminds me of a song you played the first time I was here. What was it? Something about a lazy donkey?'

''Lazy Maisie',' Matt said. He began to play it and soon the younger children and Molly came to join in.

Much as she loved Margaret, Polly and her life in London, Lizzie felt emotion welling up inside her at the thought of leaving Sorrel's Patch and the lovely Warrens, her honorary brother, Matt, especially. No one had ever made her feel quite so safe or quite so understood, but perhaps that was the way of things with big brothers.

No one talked about the future beyond the war. Maybe superstition whispered in their ears too.

'Would you mind if we sang some of your songs at our concerts?' Lizzie asked Matt, when they were out on her last afternoon's walk at Sorrel's Patch, sitting on the bench again as Peter, Joe and Mikey worked in the fields.

'If you really think they'll entertain the men, I'll consider it an honour. I can give you a printed copy of 'Those Golden Fields' and I can write out the others if you think you can read my scrawl.'

'I'm sure I can.'

'Talking of handwriting — not that yours is a scrawl — I very much appreciate your letters. I hope you'll go on writing to me.'

'Of course I will.'

'You seem to know exactly what I like to read . . .

stories of your concerts and pupils that make me smile, and observations on the natural world that . . . ' He appeared to be thinking hard about how best to express himself. 'They soothe my soul, Lizzie,' he finally said.

His gaze was warm and sincere, and Lizzie felt another rush of emotion at the thought of this dear friend returning to the bleakness and horror of the war. She swallowed. 'I'm glad you like my letters.'

She was pleased when a butterfly settled on the path in front of her as it gave her a chance to turn the conversation to a subject that wouldn't make her cry. 'Red Admirals are so pretty.'

'Gorgeous,' Matt agreed.

The weather was warm for the time of year. Matt squinted as the sun came from behind tufts of white cloud to blaze down on them. He rolled his shirt sleeves to his elbows and Lizzie saw there was a recent scar on a forearm. She stared at it, a small red line in the curve of his muscle.

'Just a bit of shrapnel,' he said, when he noticed her looking. 'Warranted a couple of stitches, but no return to dear old Blighty. I had to wait for a more serious injury for that.'

Lizzie felt an urge to reach out and touch the scar — until a giggle from nearby jolted her out of her thoughts.

Thomas stepped from behind some bushes. 'Are you going to kiss Uncle Matt's arm better?' he asked her.

Lizzie was dismayed to feel a blush building.

'I kiss Uncle Matt's hurts better,' Thomas said, walking round to kiss the scar.

'That's because you're a little boy and my nephew,'

Matt told him.

'Mummy kisses my hurts better and she's a grown-up,' Thomas argued.

'She's also your mother,' Matt pointed out. 'Anyway, what are you doing here? Does your mother know you've come after us?'

'No, but I'm still on the farm, and I'm not talking to strangers.'

'Even so, I expect she told you not to make a nuisance of yourself.'

'I'm not making a nuisance of myself. I'm being friendly.' He paused, then, as though considering the question seriously, asked, 'Am I being a nuisance?'

'Your mother might think so. Best go back, eh?'

'Are you coming? Lizzie should come because she's getting sunburnt.'

'Perhaps it is rather warm,' Lizzie said, though it wasn't the sun that was making her cheeks flame.

She jumped to her feet, distressed and eager to get away, and they headed indoors with Thomas chattering all the way into the kitchen.

'You didn't disturb Uncle Matt and Lizzie?' Edith asked him.

'No,' Thomas said, though he looked at Matt and Lizzie uncertainly.

'We came in because we were feeling hot,' Lizzie said.

'I've just the thing,' Edith said. 'Barley water. No lemons, as we haven't seen lemons since the war started, but barley water with fresh mint is nice enough.'

Lizzie wanted only to be alone for a few minutes but she saw no way of refusing the barley water without her behaviour looking odd. She downed it quickly.

'Delicious,' she declared, then said, 'Would you mind if I went upstairs to pack? It'll save me from having to do it later.'

'Good idea,' Edith agreed, and Lizzie fled upstairs.

Reaching the little bedroom, she threw herself onto the bed and faced a truth that disturbed her deeply. She *had* wanted to kiss Matt's scar. She'd wanted to reach out and smooth her fingertips over its surface before touching her lips to it in gentle, healing kisses. And then she'd wanted to hold Matt close and kiss him too.

Well, why not? They were like brother and sister.

But, no. Lizzie's longing hadn't been at all sisterly. It had been . . . lover-like, she supposed, the very thought of it making her wince. It was unsettling. Upsetting. And she couldn't understand it.

How could she have felt such a powerful yearning for Matt when she loved Harry and was engaged to marry Harry? She had no business even thinking of another man, let alone craving the warmth, the closeness, the very essence of him.

Unless she'd misunderstood her feelings for Harry? A picture of his face came into her mind. Open and eager. Full of kindness and honour. Full of love too.

Feeling an answering tug of love for him, Lizzie knew that she hadn't mistaken her feelings for Harry Benedict. She liked him. Admired him. Loved him.

So why . . . ? She cringed again as guilt wracked through her. She might be unable to understand what was happening, but she knew it was wrong. Terribly wrong.

But in time an explanation occurred to her and gradually took shape in her mind. Lizzie was missing Harry dreadfully and longing to touch, to hold, to kiss him. Harry was away, though, while Matt was nearby. It had been a case of . . . Substitution seemed to be the most accurate description. Inappropriate, but now she understood it Lizzie would take care it didn't happen again. All things considered, no harm had been done except to her conscience.

Unless Matt had been aware of her wayward feelings? No, surely not. Those feelings had lasted for only a moment before Thomas appeared and Matt had given no sign of having noticed them. He'd chatted to his nephew as naturally as ever. To Edith too.

Lizzie breathed out slowly and gratefully, though her conscience continued to sting. Quite right too. She deserved it.

Getting off the bed, she packed her things, though packing them in the morning would have been the work of only two or three minutes. Then she swallowed hard and returned downstairs.

Lizzie was all smiles and helpfulness for the rest of the day, and, if she found it hard to meet Matt's shrewd gaze for long, she kept the fact to herself. She was just congratulating herself on having navigated the evening successfully when Thomas reached towards her throat.

'Why don't you wear your rings on your fingers?' he asked, and Lizzie realised her silver chain must have slipped out of the neckline of her dress.

'That's her mother's ring,' Edith said. Lizzie had mentioned in one of her letters.

'Both of them?' Thomas touched one ring and then another.

Lizzie's cheeks flamed again. 'Actually, only the emerald ring was my mother's. The diamond is mine. I'm . . . Well, I'm engaged to be married.'

'Engaged?' Edith looked taken aback. Confused too. 'Why didn't you mention it before?'

'This visit was about Matt being at home. It wasn't about me.' The explanation had felt reasonable when Lizzie had first arrived and decided she wouldn't share the news of her engagement just yet. Now it felt odd, even ridiculous. Lizzie couldn't understand it herself, so it was no wonder that Edith was surprised and perhaps even a little hurt.

Lizzie couldn't look at Matt but it was he who responded first.

'It was kind of you to let me be the centre of attention but there's plenty of attention to go around.' He walked to her side and kissed her cheek. 'Congratulations, Lizzie. This calls for a celebration. We don't have champagne, but we do have the brandy I brought home on my last leave.'

Edith gave a little shake as though waking herself up. 'Of course. What am I doing, standing here like a statue? It's lovely news.'

She stepped forward to hug Lizzie and soon the others were hugging her too.

Matt fetched the bottle from the pantry while Edith took glasses from a cupboard. 'I'm sure they're not the correct glasses for brandy but it's the thought that counts.'

'Can I have brandy?' Thomas asked.

'You can have extra milk.'

'Who's the lucky man?' Joe enquired.

Still feeling horribly self-conscious, Lizzie told them about Harry. They were all concerned when she mentioned how she'd met him after being caught in the Zeppelin raid, but it was hard to face their kindness when she'd treated them as virtual strangers who were unworthy of her confidences. 'It was Harry who found out which regiment you'd joined, Matt.'

'That was kind of him.'

'It was,' Edith agreed. 'We're glad he went to the trouble, otherwise we wouldn't have had the happiness of seeing you again, Lizzie.'

'He proposed just before he returned to the front but the ring is a little too big. That's why I wear it on the chain. I'll have it made smaller eventually.'

'Thomas is right. It's a very pretty ring,' Edith said, admiring it.

Lizzie felt even more uncomfortable, suspecting the diamond had cost what this family would consider a fortune. Perhaps it might even have equalled the price of a tractor or at least a substantial deposit on one.

Returning to Peter's side, Edith slipped her arm through his and sent him the sort of smile that said, 'Don't worry. Lizzie's ring may be spectacular and expensive, but I wouldn't swap you for all the diamonds on earth.'

Edith didn't have an engagement ring of any sort, and her wedding ring was a simple, slender band.

'I hope you'll be happy,' Peter said. 'If you're half as happy as I am with Edith, that means very happy indeed.'

'Thank you,' Lizzie said, then, anxious to turn the attention elsewhere, she added, 'It's my last night so we should have some music.'

She forced herself to be lively for the rest of the evening but when she went to bed, she lay wishing she wasn't ending her visit feeling she'd introduced a kind of awkwardness into her friendship with the Warrens. The thought kept her from sleep for hours.

Everyone hugged her when she was on the point of leaving the next morning, including Matt. She was touched, though she still felt uncomfortable. 'Thank you so much for having me to stay. I've enjoyed it immensely.'

'We've loved having you here,' Edith assured her. 'You must come again.'

'I'd like that.' Lizzie really would like that. It might give her a chance to make up for turning this visit sour. 'I'll see you when you're next in London?' she asked Matt.

Once she'd had a few days to let her feelings settle back into the old familiarity, she'd be desperate to see him again and know that all was well between them, though it grieved her to think that his presence in London would mean his return to the war.

Matt nodded. 'I hope so.'

With that she had to be content. She climbed into the cart, Joe clicked his tongue at Hector and the cart rumbled off. Lizzie waved until the Warrens were out of sight then turned to Joe. 'It's kind of you to take me to the station.'

'It's no bother.'

He wasn't the sort of man who needed to talk all the time and, after a few observations on the scenery they passed, Lizzie was relieved to be able to lapse into quietness.

''Til next time,' Joe said, when he left her at the station.

Lizzie spent the journey wishing she could start her visit to the Warrens again and manage it differently. Unfortunately, life didn't offer the chance to go backwards.

Back at home Lizzie wrote to Edith to thank her for

her hospitality, sending friendly messages to all the family, not least Matt. She duly received a letter in return, including equally friendly messages, not least from Matt.

But Edith's next letter struck a pang of dismay into Lizzie: *We were all so sad and worried to part from Matt. Did you manage to see him on his way back to the front?*

Lizzie hadn't seen him because he hadn't looked her up. He hadn't even let her know he was returning to the war.

Had she offended him by keeping quiet about her engagement? Lizzie couldn't believe he'd hold a grudge over that. Which left another, more mortifying, possibility. Matt had sensed that moment of attraction after all, but said nothing about it to spare them both from embarrassment. Perhaps it had even disgusted him, especially once he'd learnt that she was engaged to another man. Whatever his precise feelings, it appeared that he wanted to let their friendship drop.

Lizzie had never regretted a foolish moment more.

33

The postcard featured Bournemouth Pier. *I have a date for the next show*, Jack had written on the back. *December 10th, which means we can make it a Christmas show. I hope the date is convenient?*

Running out of space, he'd continued along the side. *Could you write and let me know?*

After checking with Margaret and Polly, Lizzie wrote back to confirm their availability. She was relieved to have the show on her horizon. She needed to keep busy in order to take her mind off the Matt-sized hole that had opened up in her life and the guilt she felt over darling Harry, twin hurts that she was keeping to herself.

Two weeks later Lizzie picked a letter off the door-mat and felt a jolt to her heart as she recognised Matt's handwriting on the envelope. Had he written to confirm that he no longer wished to be her friend? She tore the envelope open and pulled the letter out.

Dear Lizzie,
As you can see, I'm writing from France. Unfortunately, my train into London broke down and I had to spend the night in a siding so my plan of making time to see you evaporated.
It was a real pleasure to see you at the farm, however . . .

A broken-down train? Lizzie read the letter multiple times, trying to reach through the words to Matt himself. She supposed the story of the train might well be true, but the feeling that there'd been an alteration in their friendship wouldn't shift.

So why was he writing? Was it because he'd decided that it would look strange to his family if he dropped the friendship suddenly and he didn't want to explain his reasons? Matt might have lost his respect for Lizzie but he was too good a man to wish to humiliate her. The thought of it made her want to weep.

She spent a lot of time on the letter she wrote in reply, trying hard both to entertain him and to persuade him that she was still the Lizzie of old. Matt wrote again and their letters settled into a regular pattern.

Yet the unease persisted. Something had changed. Or appeared to have changed. Lizzie longed to see both Matt and Harry again so that everything in her world could fall back into its proper place.

In the meantime, she had other responsibilities — Margaret, Polly, her pupils, the sick and wounded servicemen she entertained . . . In navigating difficult times, discipline would be her friend.

★   ★   ★

Jack's next postcard featured the castle at Hastings. The message on the back was a hastily-written scrawl. *I'm making a flying visit to London on Wednesday and will call in the morning. I hope this will be convenient.*

Wednesday was today. Lizzie told Margaret that Jack would be visiting then rushed to the Post Office to telephone Polly at old Mrs Bishop's house. 'Can you come?'

Unfortunately, Mrs Bishop was struggling with her

arthritis and Polly felt obliged to stay with her. 'You'll tell Jack I'm sorry to miss him?'

'I certainly will.'

Margaret was giving a lesson when Jack arrived. 'No Polly?' he asked, obviously disappointed.

Lizzie passed on Polly's message. Did he believe it, though? It was frustrating as Polly had shown a lot of interest in Jack's postcards over the weeks of his absence and Lizzie had been hoping the interest extended to Jack himself.

He'd come to share the programme he'd drawn up for the Christmas show and to ask a favour. Would Lizzie mind overseeing the production of the leaflets and posters as she was on the spot in London and he'd be travelling around? 'I'll be glad to help,' she told him.

They talked about the show for a while longer but soon Jack had to rush off to another appointment. Having seen Amy's name in the list of performers, Lizzie hoped he wasn't meeting her. 'Polly really is sorry to miss you,' she said.

Jack smiled, but it was the sort of polite smile that suggested he imagined Polly was missing him no more than any absent friend.

He was giving up on her, just as Lizzie had feared.

Lizzie stood in an agony of indecision as she watched him walk away. It was one thing to hope that love blossomed between Polly and Jack. It was quite another to interfere. But Lizzie hated to think of her friend letting a chance for happiness pass her by. Talking to Polly herself still felt like a mistake, but perhaps Lizzie might do some good from a different direction.

'Jack!' She ran to catch him up.

'Did I forget something?'

'No, it's just . . . ' Oh, heavens.

'Just what?'

'Polly had a . . . disappointment. Her childhood sweetheart broke off with her when he went to the war and she needs to come to terms with that. Be patient with her, Jack. Perhaps I shouldn't have mentioned it, but —'

'It's helpful! So Polly had a childhood sweetheart. Did you meet him?'

'He was a friend when we were children.'

'But you think he was a fool to let Polly go. Of course you do. This war is doing strange things to people. They think they're going on a glorious adventure for King and country but the reality is . . . different. Even so, to disappoint Polly . . . '

He made it sound as though disappointing Polly was beyond his comprehension. 'You think I have a chance with her?'

'I don't know,' Lizzie said honestly. 'I think you might be happy together, but what matters is how you and Polly feel about each other.'

'There's no doubt about my feelings. It's Polly's feelings that are uncertain. But you've given me hope and I'm grateful. You're worried you've overstepped the mark in telling me about Polly's past, but I see it as trying to help a friend. You can be sure of my discretion.'

'Thank you.'

Still unsure if she'd done the right thing, Lizzie returned to the house. 'It's up to you now, Poll,' she muttered under her breath.

★ ★ ★

Jack returned to London from his tour looking bright-eyed and energetic. He threw himself into the arrangements for the show and was full of praise for what Lizzie, Polly and Margaret had planned, from Christmas carols to hats decorated with winter foliage. 'The Penrose Singers will do me proud,' he said.

'The Penrose Players and Singers,' Lizzie corrected, not wanting Margaret to feel her playing was being undervalued.

'Oh, no,' Margaret said. 'The Penrose Singers is . . . catchier, I believe is the appropriate word.'

Catchier? Margaret really was moving with the times.

Jack arranged for two rehearsals at the Merriment again — a general rehearsal, with a dress rehearsal one week later. Gathering together for the first rehearsal, Lizzie was pleased to meet the new performers — Sheldrick Rhodes, a flautist ('My real name is Stan Roberts, but it doesn't have the same ring,' he confided), Ernesto and Katerina who were opera singers, and Svetlana and Stefan who were dancers. She was also pleased to see the familiar faces of The Tierney Tenors, but not at all pleased to see Amy's predatory features, her jealous gaze following as Polly charmed her fellow performers with sparkle and sweetness.

In a break in the rehearsal one of the Tierney Tenors taught Polly some dance steps then spun her around at speed. When she almost overbalanced Jack caught her and set her upright. Polly looked up at him, laughing, and Lizzie was sure she saw something — a spark — pass between them. Certainly, Polly's cheeks glowed prettily pink and she spent the rest of the rehearsal looking as though she'd been struck by a revelation that made her feel happy, shy and thoughtful, all at the same time.

'Jack's fun, isn't he?' Polly remarked on the way home.

'A good person too,' Lizzie said.

Polly came to Margaret's house twice over the following week. Laughter burst from her in merry bubbles of joy and she moved with elastic lightness. She was quick to break into song too. Lizzie was delighted to think her friend might be climbing out of her rut at last.

Jack sent Lizzie a hopeful, enquiring look when he saw Polly again at the dress rehearsal. Lizzie sent him an encouraging smile in return but, wisely, Jack bided his time, letting Polly explore her changing feelings without pressure.

The show — called *Christmas Cavalcade* — was duly performed and Lizzie felt it was even better than the summer event. 'A superb evening,' Cordelia declared, coming backstage to leave champagne but declining to stay to drink it. 'I won't impose on your party and I have guests of my own to look after.'

More audience members came to congratulate them and Charlie Sparrow strutted like a contented turkey as he handed round glasses.

'I'm going to take this hat off before I have a drink,' Margaret announced.

The hats were not only cumbersome but also liable to be damaged so Lizzie and Polly followed her into the dressing-room to take their hats off too. Margaret put her hat into its bag with a satisfied sigh at no longer looking what she considered to be ridiculous. She didn't bother straightening her hair because it was scraped away from her face anyway, but strode straight off to the party. Lizzie and Polly lingered, having softer styles that needed attention.

Polly opened her bag to find her comb. 'Oh,' she said, then brought out an unopened letter. 'The post arrived just as I was setting out but I forgot all about it.'

She stared at the envelope as though trying to decide if she should open it now then said, 'I'll read it later. It's from my mother and I doubt she has any urgent news.' And the party was waiting.

She was returning the envelope to her bag when she paused, squeezing it between her fingers as though struck by its unexpected thickness. Mrs Meadows found writing difficult and rarely wrote more than a single page. Obviously curious now, Polly tore it open and pulled out both a letter and another, smaller envelope that made her grow pale and still.

'Poll?' Lizzie questioned, but Polly didn't appear to hear.

She opened the smaller envelope, read the letter that had been folded inside it then put a hand to her chest as though her heart was beating frantically.

'Polly?' Lizzie said again, worried now.

But when she turned to Lizzie at last, Polly's face was excited. 'It's from Davie. He says he made a terrible mistake in letting me go. He hopes I can forgive him and give him another chance.'

Lizzie realised someone was standing by the open doorway. Jack. He sent her a sorrowful look and walked away.

34

'Terrific party,' Sheldrick called as he half-walked, half-danced past Lizzie on his way to fetch another drink.

'Isn't it?' she said, though the enjoyment had gone out of it for her.

Poor Jack. He was trying so hard to be the life and soul of the evening but Lizzie could see that he was struggling. Polly was trying hard too but would clearly have preferred to be at home with her thoughts.

The party ended at last. Looking pale but sincere, Jack managed to thank Lizzie, Polly and Margaret for taking part in the show then excused himself to bid farewell to other departing performers.

'Tell me what you think about Davie,' Polly urged, drawing Lizzie aside as they put on their coats.

'It isn't for me to interfere, Poll.' Lizzie had interfered enough and probably cost Jack more pain by encouraging him to hope.

'I just want to know what you think.'

'I think you must do whatever makes you happy.'

'You sound doubtful. Don't you think Davie can make me happy again?'

'I'm not saying that.'

'You're not jumping up and down with joy either.'

'Davie hurt you before. I can't forget that.'

'He hurt me dreadfully, but he's apologised and tried to explain why he let me go. He says he began to feel cowardly for working on the farm instead of fighting, and once he'd joined up he got to know men who thought life was for laughing and larking instead of slaving on farms. He let them persuade him that there was a whole world of adventure waiting for those who hadn't tied themselves down too early. Not that he's blaming them. He's blaming his own weak-headedness. He says war does strange things to men. It twists their minds.'

Jack had said much the same thing.

'Davie's head is clear again now and he knows that what he wants is me and the life we always planned. He isn't just expecting to pick up where we left off, though. He realises we need to talk before he can hope to put his ring back on my finger. Obviously, we'll have to wait for his release before that's possible, but until then he wants us to write to try to get to know each other all over again through our letters.'

This was a more thoughtful Davie than the boy of old. Maybe he really was the man to make Polly happy for the rest of her life.

'If Davie can make you happy, then I couldn't be more pleased that he's come to his senses, though I'll be sorry to lose you to Witherton again. That's selfish of me, I know.'

'You're never selfish, Lizzie. You're the best friend anyone could have.'

Polly hugged her then stood back and said, 'Jack was quiet tonight.'

'Was he?'

'I've hurt him, haven't I?'

Lizzie couldn't deny it.

'Does he think I led him on? Do you think I led him on?'

'You'd never mislead anyone deliberately, Poll.'

'I hope not, but I still feel guilty. Jack and I were

never walking out together. We never even talked about it. But I let him think we were going in that direction.'

Polly paced the dressing room restlessly. 'I didn't realise how much he liked me until recently. I expect you noticed long before then, but after Davie rejected me, I closed my mind to anything romantic. It was the only way I could cope. But it gradually dawned on me that Jack had feelings for me and, much to my surprise, that I was beginning to have feelings for him. I like Jack. I might have grown to love him. But Davie . . . It's been Davie all my life.'

'I understand, Polly. I'm sure Jack's disappointed. But I'm also sure he doesn't hold a grudge. He wishes you happy.'

'I hope you don't lose his friendship because of me.'

'Jack has to do what's right for him, just as you must do what's right for you.'

'I wish I'd received this letter before I started letting Jack think there might be something between us. It could have saved him some pain.'

Sadly, life wasn't so convenient.

★ ★ ★

Lizzie told Margaret about Davie's letter the following morning. 'I'm glad he's written if he's the right man for Polly,' Margaret said, 'but Jack Lomax must be disappointed.'

It was her only comment, though a troubled look showed she felt Jack's pain.

Lizzie's concern for Jack prompted her to send a note to him, and just after Christmas they met over a cup of tea. Jack greeted her with a smile but she only had to see his bruised-looking eyes to know it had cost him an effort.

'Please don't think I resent Polly for preferring Davie. I could never resent her because I love her. I'm horribly disappointed, though.'

'I'm sorry, especially if I —'

'You did nothing wrong, Lizzie. You wanted Polly and me to be happy. I'm sure we *would* have been happy, if Davie hadn't written. But he did write and now I have to learn to face a different future.'

'You sound as though you've already made plans.' Lizzie feared she wasn't going to like them.

'I don't want to wallow in self-pity so I'm going to visit my family in Scotland then look for work in a provincial show. London feels too close to Polly just now.'

'You'll stay in touch?'

'Yes. But I know you're kind enough to allow me some weeks or months of silence first.'

'As long as it doesn't become permanent.'

'I'm not abandoning the fundraising concerts, in case you're wondering about them. Charlie and I hope to put on another one, possibly in the summer or next Christmas. By then I hope I'll be through the worst of my disappointment, because I'd like the Penrose Singers to perform again.'

'I'd like that too.' But even summer was six months away and by then Jack might be busy with other things.

'A new year begins tomorrow,' Jack said. 'It won't be the sort of year I had in mind, but I'll make the best of it. I shan't mope more than I can help.'

They parted soon afterwards. Watching him walk away, Lizzie wondered if she'd ever see him again.

Whatever happened, she wouldn't interfere in anyone's romantic life again. Not Polly's and not Margaret's. Lizzie couldn't even manage her own life.

35

January and February had never been Lizzie's favourite months. The winds were too mean, the cold too cutting and the daylight hours too short.

Impatient with her low spirits, Lizzie counted her blessings again and again. In her professional life she was able to feel useful through her teaching and concerts. In her personal life she was engaged to a wonderful man and had wonderful friends.

Edith remained one of those friends, as she still wrote regularly and appeared to have forgiven Lizzie for holding back about her engagement, though she didn't know about that inappropriate moment with Matt, of course.

Lizzie hadn't lost hope of keeping Matt as a friend too. At times she was convinced he was easing away from their friendship, especially after he'd once gone a whole month without writing. But at other times she felt they were drawing closer again, especially when he wrote about things he knew were dear to her heart.

Women have the vote at last, he wrote after Parliament had passed a law allowing it. *I know it only applies to certain women — those aged over thirty who own property, I believe — but it's a beginning, and I know you'll go on fighting for the equal treatment you deserve . . .*

Adding her blessings together, Lizzie knew that she was lucky. Yet she still couldn't shift the low mood completely.

She wasn't alone in that, of course. The war had

been raging for more than three years and, worryingly, the prospects of victory had been dealt a blow by developments in Russia. Revolution had resulted in political turmoil and Russia — formerly on the same side as Britain — had signed an armistice with the enemy. No longer needing to fight Russia in the east, Germany was moving thousands of soldiers to the western front. Lizzie had heard talk of more than a million soldiers being moved, and Britain was desperately seeking new recruits to fight them.

Britain was seeking money to pay for the war effort too. Cordelia was one of the many who went to Trafalgar Square in Tank Week early in March to buy a war bond from what they were calling a tank bank. 'The army tank is real,' she explained. 'A great metal monster. There are several of these tank banks across London.'

People were weary of the effects of war too — the constant anxiety over loved ones who were fighting or injured, the terror of air attacks, the daily grind of high prices and scarce food though compulsory rationing had been brought in to help ensure that everyone had at least something to eat. Not that it was always of good quality. Even bread had become coarse and mixed with grains or potatoes, though it had to be eaten anyway because the fines for wasting food were harsh.

The influenza had gone around too. Lizzie, Margaret and Polly had all escaped it, though the mothers of two pupils had been quite unwell for a while and there were reports of some poor souls having died.

Lizzie had declined an invitation to spend Christmas with Harry's family because she was committed to concerts on Christmas Eve and Boxing Day. She wouldn't have left Margaret in London anyway.

Lizzie had visited the Benedicts in January instead and been made to feel very welcome. Maria Benedict had shown her numerous photographs of Harry, beginning when he was a babe in a white shawl and finishing when he'd first put on his officer's uniform. 'Harry's been mentioned in despatches,' Giles told her. 'It's the second time. Did he tell you?'

'He didn't.'

'He didn't tell us either. We heard it from a friend.'

'Harry's too modest to boast,' Lizzie suggested, her emotions swelling with warmth for him.

If only the war would end soon. Once the men she cared about were home again, surely this restless anxiety would end and the world would look straight again?

Of course, there was a third man who was often in her thoughts. Jack Lomax. Lizzie had heard nothing from him and, as the year advanced, she wondered again if she ever would. She toyed with the idea of calling on Charlie Sparrow at the Merriment, but feared embarrassing him if Jack was planning another fundraiser but leaving the Penrose Singers out of it. Lizzie supposed she'd have to wait and see if Jack got in touch, but she had little patience with waiting these days.

Polly wanted news of Jack too. She gave Lizzie a questioning look every time they met but Lizzie had nothing to report.

At least Davie was writing often. 'He's desperate to get home to Witherton,' Polly reported. 'He can't believe he was stupid enough to think the sort of quiet, ordinary life we'll have there would be dull. Quiet and ordinary sound wonderful to him now.'

With the approach of spring the days lengthened and flowers appeared in gardens, though there were fewer in the parks, as many gardeners were away at the war and some flowerbeds had been turfed over. April brought lushness and energy to the season. Soft leaves unfurled, new grass shone, birds were busy, and women began to brave the still-cool air to venture out in lighter, more cheerful clothing.

Lizzie saw it and liked it, but still felt restless. It would be many months before she saw Harry and Matt again — if they survived the German assault on the front. Times had never been more worrying.

'Is there no summer fundraising show this year?' Cordelia asked.

'Not that I've heard,' Lizzie said.

'Pity.'

May arrived, bringing warmer days and small white flowers like confetti on the hawthorn bush in Margaret's back garden.

And one morning in May a letter fell onto the doormat. As always the arrival of the post gave Lizzie a sharp stab of anxiety in case bad news had arrived, but she picked this letter up to realise Jack had written at last. She stepped into the music room to read his letter.

Dear Lizzie,

I'm sorry I haven't written before but I trust you understand my reasons and won't judge me too harshly. You're well, I hope. Miss Penrose and Polly too. Please believe I'm sincere in wishing Polly happy.

324

Lizzie did believe it. To Jack love meant care instead of possession.

But enough of my feelings. There are many people nursing deeper sorrows than a bruised heart. This brings me to the subject of fundraising shows. I'll admit I thought long and hard about organising another one given the bittersweet memories of the previous shows. I decided that was selfish of me but when I got in touch with Charlie Sparrow to explore possible dates, I discovered the Merriment was out of commission due to water damage from a burst pipe. I've now heard that it's back in business and I've been offered June 17th. I'm sure you can guess that I'm inviting the Penrose Singers to take part.

Please be assured that I'll do everything in my power to avoid awkwardness. I wish there were more time for you to think about this invitation, but the date is close so I need to push for a decision. Forgive me.

Yours in hope and friendship,
Jack x

'Hmm,' Margaret said, after Lizzie had told her about the letter. 'I'm agreeable to taking part, but it might be uncomfortable for Polly.'

Polly's face certainly grew serious when she heard about the invitation, but she took a deep breath and said, 'Of course I'll take part. I owe it to Jack. I know you think I didn't encourage him, but I didn't discourage him either. If he needs my help, I'll give it willingly no matter how awkward it is.'

'I'm glad, Poll.'

Lizzie wrote straight back to Jack and a few days

later met him in a café around the corner from the Merriment. He greeted her as warmly as ever, though perhaps with a little less bounce. 'I'm fine,' he insisted, when he saw her concern. 'Thank you so much for agreeing to take part in the show.'

'Has it been hard to find performers at short notice?'

'Yes, but I'm pleased with the programme I've put together. Tell me what you think.'

He passed a sheet of paper over. 'Alfredo and Alberto are tenors like me. We're going to sing two songs together. Elise and Tamara are dancers. Modern, rather than classical ballerinas but there's nothing of the music hall about them to offend Miss Penrose. They wear floaty Grecian dresses and wave scarves about. It's all very artistic. Pierre is a violinist.'

'No Tierney Tenors this time?' Lizzie asked.

'Working in Newcastle. Stan — Sheldrick, I should say — is busy in Bristol.'

'And Amy?'

'Also busy elsewhere.'

Jack spoke airily but Lizzie suspected there was more to her absence than a work commitment. Perhaps she'd tried too hard to sink her painted fingernails into him. Whatever had happened, Lizzie was glad for Jack's sake. He deserved better.

'I'm having leaflets printed as usual,' he said. 'Could you pass some to your friends? Mrs Bishop, for one?'

'The human dynamo? If anyone can sell tickets, it's Cordelia and I'm sure she'll be only too happy to take some.'

'Good. I'd hate the show to flop.'

Jack sent leaflets as soon as they were printed. Lizzie gave some to Cordelia, handed more to pupils and posted others to the hospitals and convalescent homes where they'd performed.

As before, there was a Sunday rehearsal two weeks prior to the show. 'Sold out!' Jack told Lizzie when she arrived, his relief obvious.

Then he turned to Polly, seeing her for the first time in six months. His expression was gentle. 'It's so good of you to help out,' he said.

'Jack, I need your opinion,' Pierre called then.

Jack touched Polly's shoulder then walked away.

'There,' Margaret said with satisfaction. 'Everything comfortable. Now we can focus on our performance.'

Lizzie wasn't sure that Polly thought everything was quite comfortable yet. But she braced her shoulders and looked determined to keep any awkwardness to herself.

That first rehearsal was followed by a dress rehearsal on the next Sunday. For this show they'd decided to wear their smartest dresses. Lizzie's was blue, Polly's lemon and Margaret's grey, neither Lizzie nor Polly having had any luck in persuading her to try more cheerful colours. Margaret was thawing, however, and though she'd baulked at Polly's idea of wearing flowers in their hair, she finally consented to a very discreet arrangement at the back of her bun. Lizzie and Polly were being more flamboyant with their flowers.

The Penrose Singers were performing four songs, including one written by Matt. By now he'd sent several handwritten pieces of music through the post. Some were soft, lyrical pieces and she could imagine Matt singing them in that low, crooning voice of his. Others were livelier, including 'Pick Yourself Up', the one she'd chosen. It was about overcoming adversity, from spilt milk to a bombing raid, and just the sort of rousing, good-humoured piece she thought the audience would like.

The rehearsal got off to a bad start when Margaret had a sneezing fit just as she started to play. 'I'm terribly sorry,' she said, looking mortified at the way her body had betrayed her strong sense of discipline.

Everyone else smiled because it was unusual to see Margaret pink with embarrassment.

The rehearsal didn't improve but, having come through bad rehearsals to deliver successful shows before, Lizzie wasn't unduly worried.

The show was a great success, in fact, even though one of the dancers, Tamara, had gone down with the influenza that was going round again — this time more severely — and had to be replaced at the last moment by a friend. Once again there were drinks in the dressing rooms afterwards. 'Thank you, everyone!' Jack said, raising his glass in a toast.

He smiled round at all of them and if his gaze softened as it rested on Polly it soon moved on. He couldn't have done more to help Polly to feel at ease.

'These pins are digging in,' Polly said, putting a hand up to the flowers that Lizzie had pinned to her hair.

'Mine too. Flowers are pretty but the pins are lethal.'

They unpinned each other's headdresses. 'One of my roses is missing,' Polly noticed. 'I don't like to think of it dying on the stage for lack of water.'

She went to find it and Lizzie walked over to chat with Jack and Charlie. 'What comes next?' she asked them both.

The men exchanged looks and for a moment Lizzie wondered if she'd stumbled into a private conversation. Before she could excuse herself, Jack spoke with a smile. 'Actually, Charlie and I are talking of a joint venture. A partnership.'

'In a theatre?' Was Jack going to learn how to manage one?

'A nightclub.'

Lizzie had no idea what that meant.

'It's a place where people will come to hear music and to dance. Not waltzes or anything like that. Informal dances to informal music. We'll have drinks and food too, but mostly it'll be about having fun.'

'It sounds exciting.'

'The war is changing things,' Jack said. 'People are tired of gloom. They're going to want to grab at life once it's over. Men and women both.'

'I wish you the best of luck,' Lizzie said. A thought struck her. 'Does this mean there won't be a Christmas fundraiser?'

'We don't know if the nightclub venture is feasible yet. Even if we go ahead with it, a fundraiser might still be possible. Let's see what the next few months bring.'

Lizzie hoped they'd bring an end to the war.

After a while it occurred to her that Polly hadn't returned. Wondering if something had upset her, Lizzie went to the stage and saw Polly looking out across the empty auditorium.

'Are you all right, Poll?'

She turned. 'Yes, I'm fine. I suppose I'm just saying goodbye to all this. I've been terrified for much of the time we've been entertaining but, despite that, I've enjoyed it.' She paused, then added, 'You will come to see me when I'm back in Witherton?'

'Goodness, what's brought this on?'

'I've been thinking, that's all. Davie can't wait to return to some of the old places — the woods, the lanes and even the little clearing with the fallen log where we used to meet as children.'

'We taught each other songs there. And dances.'

'You're smiling because those were happy times. But you were mostly *un*happy in Witherton. Can you bear to go back?'

'I was happy when my mother was alive, and I'll always be grateful to Witherton for bringing you into my life, Poll.'

'So you'll come?'

'Just try and stop me. Now let's go and have a drink. Everyone's celebrating.'

'I didn't mean to be miserable. It's just . . . Oh, nothing really. Let's hope there's some champagne left.'

Everyone was thinking about the future, it seemed. Lizzie was desperate for some certainty in hers.

36

July came and some pupils left London to visit relations or have holidays. Others paused their lessons so they could avoid the deadly influenza by staying at home.

By August the worst of the influenza had passed again but still more pupils took holidays. With time on her hands, Lizzie went on long walks around London, feeling a little sad when she went to St James's Park and saw that the lake had been drained and crude office buildings erected on the lake bed to provide more offices for the war effort. At least children were having fun by balancing on the pipes that had been exposed and rolling down the bank to pretend to drown in the non-existent water. She also painted some of the faded woodwork in the house and even tried her hand at wallpapering.

There was better news from the war at last. The allies had rallied against the German offensive that had begun in March and Lizzie began to hope that Harry or Matt or, better still, both would soon have leave.

But one letter from Harry brought different news that made Lizzie feel dizzy with dread.

'He's been injured,' she burst out to Margaret. 'Shrapnel in the shoulder. A flesh wound, but it became infected.'

'If he's writing himself, he must be recovering well,' Margaret pointed out.

Lizzie realised that was true. 'Yes, of course.' She

331

read the letter through to the end. 'He writes that the doctors are pleased with his progress.'

Did that mean that the danger of infection had passed? She could only hope so. 'Gas gangrene can take a chap within hours,' a nurse had confided at one of the concerts. 'The doctors amputate when they can, but sometimes it isn't enough . . .'

'He's hoping to come home for a few days.'

But when Harry left the base hospital no one mentioned granting him leave. Ah well. He was healthy again. That was the important thing.

Lizzie reconciled herself to more waiting so was surprised to return from the shops one September morning to hear male laughter coming from the music room. Excitement thrilled through her. Could it be—

The next moment Harry was in the hall and Lizzie was in his arms.

'I'll just . . .' Margaret murmured, gliding past them and heading down to the kitchen to give them time alone.

'I'm sorry I didn't warn you I was coming,' Harry said. 'By the time I could organise a telegram I was already in London. I booked into my father's club for a wash and brush-up, and here I am. But what's this? Tears?'

Overwhelmed, Lizzie was sobbing against his chest. 'Sorry!' she croaked.

'Aren't you pleased to see me?'

'Of course I am!'

The sobs subsided and Lizzie was able to lift her head. Harry passed her a handkerchief so she could wipe her eyes and blow her nose. 'How are you?' she asked. 'How's your shoulder?'

'Better, thanks.'

They moved into the music room and sat on the sofa. Harry kissed her — very thoroughly — then Lizzie drew back so she could drink in every detail of his appearance. He was as handsome as ever but thinner and more lined. She reached out to stroke his cheek, overwhelmed by a rush of tenderness. 'Will this war ever end?'

'We feared the worst when we were so heavily outnumbered back in March, but we're fighting back. Don't get your hopes up for an early peace, but don't despair either. Enough of war talk, though. I only have a few days of leave and I want to enjoy them with you. Is that going to be possible?'

'I have to teach but not all of the time, and we've no concerts until Saturday.'

'Good food and company is just what I need. Is it too much to hope you're free for dinner tonight?'

'I'd love to have dinner with you tonight. But it's only just lunchtime. Have you eaten?'

'Not since breakfast.'

'You're welcome to join us for some soup.'

'I don't want to take your food.'

'We have plenty.' It was an exaggeration, but Lizzie would gladly accept a small portion and she was sure Margaret would feel the same. 'You won't mind eating in the kitchen?'

'It'll be a luxury after eating in a dug-out.'

They found Margaret skulking down there, clearly wondering how long she should leave the young couple together. 'Of course Harry must stay to lunch,' she said.

The soup was nothing special by Lizzie's reckoning — just vegetables bought cheaply and flavoured with herbs — but Harry ate it like a starving man.

'Delicious,' he declared.

'Better than army food?' Lizzie teased.

'Much better than army food, although that can be surprising sometimes. I don't mean surprisingly nice. Just surprising when the label has come off the tin and it turns out to contain corned beef instead of peaches.' Harry smiled as he spoke but Lizzie could see the fatigue in his eyes.

After they'd eaten, Margaret went upstairs to teach a lesson. Lizzie made tea and insisted that Harry should sit while she washed the dishes. She was deliberately quiet and when she turned back round she had her reward as Harry was sleeping, just as she'd intended.

She covered him with a blanket then left him in the kitchen and went up to teach her own pupils. When she returned more than two hours later Harry was awake and apologetic. 'I beg your pardon! Falling asleep was—'

'Perfectly understandable.'

'You're very kind.'

But she wasn't. Not always. It hadn't been kind to feel that moment of attraction to Matt. Yet looking at Harry now Lizzie was in no doubt that she loved him.

'I didn't like to go upstairs in case I disturbed the lessons,' he said, 'but now I must leave you in peace. I don't have my father's car, but I'll call for you in a taxi. What time suits you?'

'I'm teaching until seven-thirty. Will eight o'clock be too late?'

'It'll be perfect. I'll say goodbye here.'

Lizzie guessed he didn't want Margaret to catch them kissing on the doorstep.

It was an enthusiastic kiss and Lizzie felt flushed

when Harry released her. He smiled. 'Until later.'

They ate in a lovely restaurant near Trafalgar Square. 'You'll see your family while on leave?' Lizzie asked him.

'Of course. They've invited you to stay as well.'

'I won't be intruding?'

'They want to get to know you better. After all, you'll be joining the family soon. Are you able to come?'

'I'll look at my teaching diary when I get home.'

'I'm sorry you have to work for a living,' Harry said. 'I can't wait to give you the sort of life you deserve.'

Lizzie laughed. 'I like working. Most of the time.'

She managed to spend one night at Ashlyn and more time with Harry in London. But all too soon his leave was over.

'Stay safe,' she urged, when she saw him off at the station.

He held her to his chest, his ragged breathing leaving her in no doubt of how much he hated leaving her. 'I love you, Lizzie,' he said.

'I love you, Harry.'

Now what Lizzie needed was to see Matt and know he was back in his proper role in her life . . . a dear friend. Just not a romantic friend. But when Matt was granted leave, he didn't see her.

37

Lizzie heard that Matt was home in a letter from Edith.

> *Don't be alarmed but Peter has had an accident. He slipped in the yard and twisted his knee. He's going to be fine but can barely walk just now let alone work. Luckily Matt was given leave just after I'd written to tell him about Peter so came straight home to help out.*
>
> *It's typical of Matt to be generous with his time, but I'm afraid it means he's unlikely to be able to be to see you, Lizzie. I'm sure he'll write, though . . .*

Edith was telling the truth about the accident, Lizzie was sure, but had Matt seized on it as a chance to stay away?

Lizzie read the letter again and focused on the words, *unlikely to be able to meet you.*

Unlikely wasn't a definite no. But Matt had already returned to the front when he next wrote to Lizzie. *I'm sorry I couldn't see you but I know you'll understand I couldn't leave the family in the lurch . . .*

He described Peter's difficulties and how the farm had suffered as a result. *I hope I helped to get it back on target before I left.*

He went on to describe evening mists gathered in the hollows of the fields, the first hints of autumn colours on leaves, and a hedgehog he'd rescued after seeing it caught up in wire carelessly tossed aside by a neighbouring farmer or passer-by. *I worried I was too late to save it so my heart lifted when I saw its little face stir . . .*

He also wrote about music.

I was too busy to spend much time at the piano, but I found new melodies and lyrics entering my head as I worked. I hope I'll be able to find a piano to play on my next rest period so I can polish them into actual songs and send them to you.

Not that I expect you to include them in your concerts. I always appreciate what you do to promote my music, but I'd hate you to feel obliged . . .

Obligation didn't enter into it because Matt's songs were good. Lizzie would have included them in the concerts even if she hadn't known they were his.

I'll finish by saying again that I was sorry to miss you. I hope a year won't pass before I see you again.
With love,
Matt x

It couldn't have been a nicer letter. Yet Lizzie's uncertainties continued.

By October another wave of influenza — this one very grave indeed — was wreaking havoc. When the deaths from it climbed into the thousands Jack wrote to say that the Merriment was closing temporarily to avoid fostering the spread of disease. Sadly, this meant that the Christmas fundraiser was postponed. It was disappointing but sensible news.

Lizzie had heard children chanting a rhyme about the influenza.

I had a little bird,
It's name was Enza,
I opened the window,
And in-flu-enza

Fearful of catching the illness from her pupils, Lizzie had slightly different words in mind when she kept the window open during her lessons.

I had a little bird,
It's name was Enza,
I opened the window,
And out flu-enza.

Whether it was due to opening windows or simple good luck, Lizzie didn't know, but she stayed well and so did Margaret, Polly, Jack and all of the members of the women's group.

Across the English Channel the war continued, of course. Ever since it had begun Lizzie had heard rumours about its progress. Some had turned out to be true and others false, but as autumn advanced there really did seem to be electric expectation in the air.

Could it be that this time the war really was about to end? Lizzie hardly dared to hope so, but the buzz of anticipation intensified. People talked about peace in shops and out on the street. Pupils reported that their families were growing excited. Cordelia said her fingers were crossed.

Finally, Germany acknowledged defeat, and on 11 November an armistice was signed, bringing an end to hostilities.

'It's happened,' Lizzie told Margaret, rushing in

from the shops after hearing the news and finding her godmother in the music room. 'It's finally happened.'

Margaret nodded. Her nose turned pink and she got to her feet. 'I must . . . ' she began, only to hasten from the room, doubtless to give relief to her feelings in tears.

Lizzie felt tears forming in her own eyes. She sat down abruptly and gave into them, holding her face in her hands as sobs shook her shoulders. In time, she blew her nose and let thankfulness surge through her body like a tonic. The war was over. Harry and Matt had survived. Davie too. Lizzie refused even to consider that they might have been lost in the war's final days. Soon they'd be home again.

She went down to the kitchen to unpack the shopping. Margaret joined her, still pink about the nose but more in command of herself.

'I imagine our concerts will still be needed for a while,' she said. 'Some men will be in hospital or convalescing for months to come.'

The war had brought hardship and anxiety into their lives but it had also brought comradeship and opportunity. Lizzie realised that Margaret was going to miss the concerts when they finally stopped. They'd given her purpose and helped her to feel useful. Lizzie too.

But that was the thing with a changing world. It came with a mixed bag of emotions . . . relief, regret and also trepidation, for who knew what the future might hold? Certainly, no one would be quite the same as before, and alterations to people couldn't be put away like toys into boxes.

Sounds reached them from the street. Whoops, laughter and singing. 'People are out celebrating,'

Margaret said. 'Do go and join them if you wish, Lizzie.'

'I don't wish. But I do think we should celebrate.'

She poured them each a glass of sherry then raised her glass in a toast. 'To peace and a better world.'

'Peace and a better world,' Margaret echoed.

Someone knocked on the door. Polly. She looked pale and emotional. 'You've heard?' she asked.

'We're celebrating with sherry. Come and join us.'

Down in the kitchen Polly accepted a glass from Margaret. 'Isn't it wonderful? I don't know how long it'll be before the men are home, though.'

'It would be sensible to expect some delay,' Margaret suggested. 'There's plenty to keep us occupied in the meantime. Today, for example, we could run through our songs for Saturday's concert . . .'

Lizzie guessed that Margaret needed an outlet for her feelings. Perhaps they all did. 'Good idea.'

The next day Lizzie received a note from Jack, saying he was delighted that Harry would be returning home and also her friend, Matt. Polly received a note from him too, saying much the same about Davie. 'He hopes I'll have time for one last fundraising concert,' Polly said, and from the look on her face she knew that Jack was still hurting.

Davie was the first to return, travelling to Dover by ship then taking the train straight to London to see Polly.

'Oh, Lizzie, he's so thin!' Polly reported. 'And his poor hair looks like it's been cut with blunt gardening shears. He didn't want to upset me by telling me about the conditions in the camp but I insisted. They were awful! Two hundred and fifty men to a hut, bunks with only straw for mattresses, not enough blankets . . . The food was mostly soup made with oats or prunes or whatever else came to hand. The bread was made of bran and potatoes and was even worse than ours.'

'But he's home now and he's still your Davie?'

'Still the Davie of old,' Polly confirmed.

'More appreciative of you than when he went off to war, though?'

'He must have told me fifty times in an hour how much he regretted breaking off our engagement.'

'Then your marriage should be stronger as a result. How long is he staying in London?'

'He'll stay in a hostel tonight and tomorrow night, then travel up to Witherton to see his family.'

'They must be desperate to have him home.'

'Yes, he doesn't want to keep them waiting. But he'll return after a week or so, to spend more time with me.'

'Will I get to see him before he leaves?'

'Tomorrow, if that suits?'

'Bring him to dinner. By the sound of things, he needs feeding up.'

Polly duly brought Davie the following evening. 'I'm a walking skeleton but you're a beauty,' he said, walking up to Lizzie and kissing her cheek. 'It's good to see you again after so many years.'

Lizzie stood back to inspect him. 'You're not quite a skeleton, but you're certainly in need of a good meal.'

'Don't give me too much or it'll go to waste. My stomach has shrunk, though I'm sure it'll fill out again soon.'

He paused then added, 'Thank you for being such a good friend to Polly. I caused her a lot of heartache

341

and I'm glad she could turn to you for comfort.'

'Polly's been a good friend to me too.'

'Always generous, my Poll.' He reached out and took Polly's hand, smiling at her fondly across the table before turning back to Lizzie. 'You had so much more than we did when we were kids. Big house, smart clothes, good food . . . But my Poll still knew you were suffering. Do you remember how we used to sit in the den?'

'I do.'

'What were those songs you used to teach each other?'

The conversation slipped pleasantly along Memory Lane until Lizzie realised that Margaret could play no part in it and brought it to an end by getting up to clear the plates.

'What are your plans for the future?' Margaret asked Davie.

'Marriage to my darling Poll, of course.'

'And afterwards?'

'I'll work on the farm again. We'll live with my family at first, but hope to have a little house of our own before too long. There's a row of tumbledown cottages on the farm and I might be able to persuade the farmer to let me rent one if I knock it into shape myself. I'm not afraid of hard work.' He thought about it for a moment then grimaced. 'I can't believe I once turned my nose up at that sort of life. There's nothing I want more, now I'm seeing sense again.'

Lizzie hugged Polly close when they parted on the doorstep. 'I'm so happy for you.'

She hugged Davie too. 'I'll see you again when you're back from Witherton.'

'That'll be soon, I hope.'

Watching them walk down the street, Lizzie was pleased when Davie took Polly's arm as though he couldn't bear her to be even an inch away from her. They turned the corner out of sight but Lizzie didn't go straight back into the house. Instead she paused to look around her. The streetlights were clear again instead of half-smothered in dark paint. More lights spilt from windows now there was no fear of air raids or fines. Life was returning to normal. Or adjusting to a different sort of normal.

She was closing the door when her eye was caught by something. Or was it someone? A tall man standing in the passage between two terraces on the opposite side of the road? Standing and watching?

Matt's name leapt into Lizzie's mind and she stepped forward eagerly. But the shadows had swallowed him up.

If he'd been there at all. It was more likely that her imagination had played tricks because she was anxious to see him again. Matt wasn't the sort of man to skulk in shadows.

Jack called the following day. Margaret was out so Lizzie saw him alone. 'All well?' he asked, but seemed eager to move onto other business.

'Charlie is opening up the Merriment now this awful influenza seems to be easing off again. He's offered January 13th. I thought we could bill it as a new year, new beginnings sort of show. It's horribly short notice — again — but can I count on you to take part? You and Miss Penrose? I'll understand if Polly has other priorities, though I'd love her to be involved if she can spare the time.'

'You can certainly count on Margaret and I. As for Polly, I'll mention the show to her, though I don't

343

know when she'll return to Witherton.'

'Thank you.' He hesitated then said, 'Do you remember me telling you that Charlie and I had thoughts of opening a nightclub?'

'I do.'

'We've found premises. A basement off Piccadilly. It needs work, but we think it's going to be perfect. We're calling it the Velvet Slipper Club. Charlie is putting in most of the money so he'll be the senior partner, but he wants me to be the manager. Will you think seriously about singing for us, Lizzie? You'll be wonderful. I must dash now, I'm afraid.'

As Lizzie had expected, Margaret was keen to take part in the show. 'Now the war is over people may want to move on with their lives and forget all about the fallen and injured. We must raise funds for them while we can.'

Polly looked thoughtful when she heard about it. 'I'd like to take part, but perhaps it would be easier on Jack if I don't.'

'I won't pretend he's over you, Poll, but he doesn't hold a grudge and you could help to make the show successful for him. Besides, he has new plans to help him to move forward.' Lizzie told Polly about the Velvet Slipper Club and Jack's invitation to become a club singer.

'How exciting!' Polly said. 'Are you going to do it?'

'I can't plan anything until Harry returns.'

Instantly Polly set aside her own concerns to give Lizzie a hug. 'Hopefully that'll be soon.'

'Well,' Margaret said, when she heard about Polly's reaction. 'I hope we'll have her with us for a while longer, but we should prepare to do the show without her just in case she leaves soon.'

It was a sensible suggestion but Lizzie was going to miss Polly badly.

Margaret was practising a piece for the show a few days later when she made an unaccustomed mistake. She tutted, and tried again only to make another mistake. 'I don't know what's wrong with me today.'

'You do look flushed.' Lizzie stepped closer. 'Are you feeling unwell?'

'It's just a headache.'

'Then go and lie down. Sleep it off.'

'Perhaps I will.'

Margaret went up to her room and Lizzie took a glass of water into her. 'You're sure it's nothing more serious?'

'People are saying the worst of the influenza has passed now, thank goodness.'

But by morning Margaret was worse and Lizzie asked the doctor to call. 'It's the influenza all right,' he pronounced.

38

Lizzie felt the cutting edge of fear. The influenza had killed thousands. 'What can I do to help?'

The doctor gave instructions and Lizzie wrote them down with trembling fingers but also with determination to nurse Margaret back to health.

'You need to look after yourself too,' the doctor advised.

'I'm strong.'

'This flu has taken many a strong person. I can have Miss Penrose moved to a hospital so —'

'No! I mean no, thank you. My godmother would hate to be in hospital.'

She'd be mortified to find herself on a ward full of strangers, with more strangers tending to her bodily needs. It would affront her sense of dignity. Besides, Lizzie could give her total devotion while hospital nurses would be stretched in several directions.

'As you will, but if you change your mind . . . '

'I'll let you know. You'll call in again to see how Miss Penrose does?'

'I'll call in daily, and don't hesitate to fetch me if she takes a turn for the worse.'

Several times through the afternoon pupils called for lessons and Lizzie sent them away with her apologies. Eventually she tied a note to the door knocker.

Due to illness, lessons are cancelled for the time being. Kindly bear with us and we'll be in touch as soon as lessons can resume.
Miss L Kellaway.

346

Margaret's room was at the front of the house so Lizzie could hear voices outside when people came to the door. She was relieved that they sounded concerned rather than annoyed.

All through the night Lizzie sat with poor Margaret who was at times delirious and at other times able to speak a little. She hated to be a nuisance, she said. She was sure she could get up if only her limbs would stop aching . . . Lizzie should rest instead of tending to an old woman . . .

'You're hardly old.' Margaret was far too young to die now.

When morning arrived — greyness seeping into the darkness then lightening it to pearly white — Lizzie stood and stretched her cramped back. Margaret was sleeping so Lizzie went down to make tea and prepare a fresh bowl of cool water for soothing Margaret's face.

Three envelopes lay on the doormat. Lizzie was touched to find they contained letters from pupils and their parents, all expressing concern. Opening the door to bring the milk in, she was moved again to see flowers had been left outside.

Lizzie put them in a vase of water and took them into Margaret's room in the hope that they'd cheer her up.

'She's no worse,' the doctor said when he called, and with that Lizzie had to be content.

She was seeing him out when Polly arrived. 'What's going on?' Polly asked, as the doctor walked away.

Lizzie explained.

'You must let me help.' Polly moved forward to enter the house but Lizzie barred the way.

'If you catch the influenza, you could infect Mrs

347

Bishop. She's old and frail. It could kill her. You might infect Davie too. He couldn't fight it either, being so weak.'

Polly hesitated, clearly not liking Lizzie's argument but acknowledging the truth of it. Davie was due back in London that afternoon. 'All right. I won't come in, but you must let me help another way. Do you need any shopping?'

'Actually, yes.' Lizzie asked for bread and a few other things that sprang into her mind. 'Could you also tell Cordelia what's happened and ask her to pass the news on to our other friends?'

'Of course.' Polly returned with the shopping half an hour later. 'I'll come again tomorrow. Look after yourself, Lizzie. I'm worried about you as well as Margaret.'

Lizzie was tired but also thankful because Margaret was hanging on, managing to breathe and showing no sign of the blueness around the lips that signalled imminent danger. Not yet anyway. Knowing she needed to snatch rest where she could, Lizzie wrapped herself in a blanket and settled in the chair next to Margaret's bed.

The light was fading when Lizzie walked to the window to pull the curtains across. How gloomy these late November days could be.

She frowned suddenly, her heart beating faster because she thought she'd caught a glimpse of a figure in the passage again. But no, there were only shadows. Lizzie still had no news of Matt's return and it was preying on her mind.

She went downstairs for fresh water and cloths. More notes had been pushed through the door and more flowers left outside including a bouquet of late dahlias and an even larger bouquet of magnificent chrysanthemums that Lizzie supposed must be from Cordelia as she'd left a note to say she hoped her flowers would cheer Margaret a little.

The doctor came again in the morning. Margaret was still no worse but neither was she better. Polly came to the door too. 'I'm sorry to drag you away from Davie.' Lizzie said. 'Assuming he arrived safely yesterday?'

'Yes, I saw him last night and Mrs Bishop has kindly given me the afternoon off so I can see him again.'

'You'll give him my regards? My apologies too?'

'I'll pass on your regards but apologies aren't needed. Davie understands the situation. He wishes you and Margaret well.'

'I've another shopping list if you've time to fetch a few things for me?' Yesterday's list had been rushed and items had been missed from it.

'I'll make the time.'

Polly dropped the shopping off soon afterwards, so Lizzie was surprised to find her back on the doorstep in the afternoon. 'Poll, it's kind of you to call but you should be with Davie.'

'No, I shouldn't.'

Lizzie was tired. She didn't understand.

'Davie and I had a long talk earlier. He's been saying he made a mistake when he broke off our engagement, but I came to realise that he hadn't.'

What? Surely Polly couldn't mean . . .

'The war and that awful prisoner of war camp made him long for the old days, and I was a part of that life,' Polly explained. 'But the fact is that Davie was changing before he went to the war. And since then . . . Well, I've been changing too.'

Lizzie hadn't expected this.

'Change happens whether we choose it or not,' Polly continued. 'I still want the same things I've always wanted — a loving husband, children, a comfortable home — but I want other things alongside them. I suppose I've caught your sense of adventure at last, because I enjoy the excitement of stretching myself in unexpected ways. Like performing. I'll never be a lion like you, Lizzie. But I'm no longer such a passive little mouse.'

'Goodness, you've taken me by surprise.' But even as she spoke Lizzie realised Polly had indeed changed. Her confidence had grown. 'What does Davie think?'

'He argued at first, but finally . . . He understood, Lizzie. We parted as friends.'

'I'm glad about that.'

'There's something else. Someone else, I should say.'

'Someone else?' Suddenly the last piece of the puzzle fell into place. 'Jack?'

'You don't need to tell me I've been an idiot where Jack's concerned. I was a fool not to realise that he was falling for me when we first met, and I was an even bigger fool not to realise how deeply I was falling for him.'

'Does he know?'

'Certainly he knows. I went to his lodgings to tell him.'

'You did what?' Lizzie was shocked at Polly's brazenness.

Polly only looked smug. 'Terribly forward of me, but I'd wasted enough time.'

'You really have changed.'

'Mmm. I still need to protect old Mrs Bishop from

the influenza, but Jack doesn't.'

Polly half-turned and waved. When Jack appeared, Lizzie guessed he'd been waiting further down the street. His grin was wider than ever. 'I hope you're happy for us, Lizzie?'

'I couldn't be happier.'

'I've waited a long time for my darling.' He put his arm around Polly, drew her close and kissed her. 'We'll be getting married just as soon as possible. But until then I'm here to help. I know I can't do anything of a personal nature for Miss Penrose, but I can keep an eye on her so you can get some rest.'

'I don't know what to say.' Lizzie was overwhelmed.

'Say, 'Come along in, Jack,' and point me towards the kettle. I may be a man, but I can make a half-decent cup of tea.'

Polly blew kisses to both of them and left.

Jack proved he could indeed make a half-decent cup of tea. Unfortunately, it was also half-revolting, but Lizzie didn't mind because having Jack in the house was enormously comforting. Promising he wouldn't budge an inch from Margaret's side, he insisted that Lizzie should lie down in her bed and she felt much better for it.

Later in the evening when Margaret was still holding steady, Lizzie went out for a short walk, making a circuit of the terraces on the opposite side of the road. Frost shimmered on the pavements like scattered diamonds and the night-time air was crisp after the oppressiveness of Margaret's sickroom. Heaving the freshness into her lungs, Lizzie gave thanks for Margaret's survival so far and prayed for her recovery.

She was approaching the house again when she came to an abrupt halt. A tall man really was standing in the opening to the passage across the road and peering towards Margaret's house. Lizzie's imagination hadn't been playing tricks after all. 'Matt!' she called.

The man whirled around and she saw that he was a stranger, much older than Matt. The passage must be where he paused to catch his breath while out on a regular evening walk.

'I'm sorry,' Lizzie said. 'I mistook you for someone else.'

But she must have alarmed him because he hastened away at speed.

She'd let herself into the house and taken off her hat when a thought struck her. Running out again, she raced up the road in the direction the stranger had taken but he was nowhere to be seen. Vexed, she returned to the house.

'Are you all right?' Jack asked. 'I thought I heard you come in twice.'

'Yes, I . . . dropped a glove and went back to find it.'

It was a fib, but Lizzie needed to think before sharing her thoughts.

39

Lizzie insisted that Jack should go home to sleep but she was grateful for his promise to return in the morning. Having slept earlier, she wasn't tired as she sat through the night with Margaret, though she knew a moment of fear when the delirium worsened. Lizzie mopped Margaret's brow and eventually she subsided into sleep.

Margaret had a lucid moment towards morning. 'I'm sorry to be such a burden,' she croaked between sips of water.

'You're not a burden,' Lizzie insisted, then went on to explain that Jack would be coming. 'He sat with you for some time yesterday. Do you mind if he sits with you again?'

'Oh, dear. I must look such a fright. Illness is so undignified!'

Lizzie smiled. Margaret's body might be unwell but her personality hadn't changed. 'He won't sit with you if it makes you uncomfortable.'

'No, let him come. You need a break.' She paused then added, 'It was a happy day for me when you turned up at my door all those years ago.'

Lizzie's eyes filled with tears at the unexpected compliment but the fever soon reclaimed Margaret.

Jack duly arrived. Polly called too but didn't come in. 'I just want you to know I'm thinking of you.'

The doctor pronounced that there was still no change in Margaret's condition. 'But you're doing a good job of nursing her, young lady,' he said.

Once again, Lizzie's eyes filled with tears because there was nothing she wouldn't do for her beloved godmother.

More notes and gifts were left. Flowers, soup, and a basket of fruit. How kind people were.

Later in the afternoon, as twilight was casting its shroud of darkness over the day, Lizzie told Jack she was popping outside. 'A breath of fresh air will do you good,' Jack said.

It wasn't fresh air that Lizzie had in mind. Outside, she crossed the road to the passage where she'd seen the stranger and tied an envelope to the drainpipe. Surely anyone standing here would notice the white paper against the red brickwork, even in shadow?

They'd just finished dinner, eating in Margaret's room so she wouldn't be left alone, when a knock sounded on the door. 'I'll go,' Lizzie said.

The stranger was outside. Only he wasn't quite a stranger. He held up the envelope which Lizzie had addressed to *Mr George G Grafton*, and the note she'd placed inside it saying:

Dear Mr Grafton,
  You may have seen the notice on our front door advising callers that there's illness in the house. It's my godmother, Margaret Penrose, who is ill, but please ignore the notice and call if you wish to hear more.
  Yours sincerely,
  Lizzie Kellaway.

'Good evening, Mr Grafton.'

He nodded but looked too agitated to linger on social niceties. 'Your godmother is seriously ill?'

354

'She has influenza, but the doctor says she's holding her own.'

He swallowed, his Adam's apple bobbing in his throat like a boat on choppy water. 'I've no wish to intrude, but —'

'Come in, Mr Grafton. You're not intruding.'

She showed him into the music room. 'Please sit down. I'll make tea.'

She ran down to the kitchen to set the kettle on the stove then ran upstairs to Margaret's room. 'We have a visitor,' she told Jack. 'I'll explain later.'

Mr Grafton stood politely as she returned to the music room with the tea tray.

Now he was under the gaslight Lizzie could see that he was a handful of years older than Margaret, tall, thin, and going grey. His face was lean but intelligent, and Lizzie liked the kindness in his eyes. 'You knew my godmother many years ago,' Lizzie began, sitting down and pouring the tea.

He sat too and accepted a cup. 'With Miss Penrose ill, it feels too urgent a time to be dancing with words, Miss Kellaway. I fell in love with your godmother when we were young. She loved me too and would have married me, had it not been for her father. I was a musician but a poor one. Mr Penrose didn't admire my style of musical composition and thought I had no future. He was a stern man and doubtless he put his daughter under pressure to reject me on the grounds that to accept me would be to fail in her duty to him and bring disgrace to the Penrose name.'

Lizzie had guessed that something of the sort must have happened.

'When I realised my case was hopeless, I went to America where I proved to be rather more successful than Mr Penrose had anticipated. I tried hard to forget your godmother. I met other women and I hope you'll forgive me when I say that many of them were prettier than Margaret. More graceful and charming too, with a real sense of style in their dress. However, love may not be blind, Miss Kellaway, but it lifts a person above such considerations as appearance. For all their beauty and elegance none of those women were Margaret so none of them would do for me. So here I am, still yearning for a woman I haven't seen in more than twenty years.'

'It isn't for me to speak for my godmother, especially as she hasn't confided in me about your ... romance. But she never married either and she kept some music you wrote for her. 'The Girl —'

'—With Grey Eyes',' he finished, pleasure warming his eyes and bringing a whimsical smile to his lips.

'The reason I know you exist is because I stumbled upon that music when I was a child,' Lizzie explained. 'I never forgot it, and began making enquiries about you in music shops. That's how I learnt the address of your publishers.'

'And wrote to me care of those publishers.'

'To be honest, I thought my letter had gone astray as I lost it in the street.'

'Some kind soul must have picked it up and posted it. I'm very glad they did, though I had to wait until the end of the war before settling my affairs in New York and sailing across the Atlantic.'

'Why don't you play the song for her?'

'Now?' The suggestion surprised him.

'She sleeps for much of the time, but she has lucid moments and the music might reach through to her. I have the music here if you don't remember it.'

'Oh, I remember it.'

He moved to the piano and lifted the lid. Then he sat down and ran his fingers over the keys. 'It's well tuned.'

'Would you expect anything else from my god-mother?'

'She was always fastidious.'

'Allow me two minutes to get upstairs. I'd like to be with her when you play.'

Jack gave her a curious look when she entered Margaret's bedroom, but Lizzie hadn't time to give him an explanation now. 'Later,' she promised.

She sat beside Margaret's bed and soon the strains of 'The Girl With Grey Eyes' were floating through the house. It was a beautiful melody.

Margaret frowned and tossed from side to side. Her eyes fluttered open, looking confused.

'It's all right,' Lizzie said.

'That music . . . You shouldn't be playing it.'

'I'm not playing it.'

Margaret's befuddled brain realised it was true. 'I'm dead, aren't I? Or dying?'

'No, Margaret.'

'Hallucinating, then. Delirious.'

'You've had moments of delirium but this isn't one of them. It's George playing downstairs.'

'What?' Margaret looked shocked, delighted, afraid . . .

Lizzie explained how she'd contacted him. 'He's come specially to see you.'

'I can't see him like this!'

'Of course not. But unless I'm much mistaken you've turned a corner in your illness so perhaps in a day or two . . . '

357

'I haven't seen the man in twenty-five years. We're strangers to each other and just because we shared a . . . an interest in our younger years, it doesn't mean we share one now.'

'Perhaps not,' Lizzie soothed, 'but it doesn't hurt to talk.'

'I don't know about that.'

'I do.'

40

Margaret had indeed turned a corner and two days later prepared to receive George in her room. It was astonishing how a woman who'd cared little for appearances suddenly had a crisis of confidence over how she looked.

'You're going to wear this,' Polly said, now allowed into the sick room, and holding up a satin dressing-gown that old Mrs Bishop had insisted on lending for the occasion.

'It's pink! I never wear pink.'

'You always wear grey. But that was the old you. This is for the Margaret of the future.'

'It's also too short.'

'You'll be sitting in a chair with a blanket over your lap. No one will notice.'

Margaret finally consented to wear the pink dressing-gown and it was amazing how the colour added a glow to her skin and softened the granite features, especially when Polly arranged Margaret's hair in a looser, more feminine style than the scraped-back bun she usually favoured.

Even the blanket over Margaret's lap was chosen by Polly to present a picture of charm. A small cream satin eiderdown, it was another offering from Mrs Bishop.

'Oh, dear,' Margaret said again and again, nervousness making her bony fingers clutch at the fabric.

Lizzie went down to fetch George. He paused in the door to Margaret's room, but, as his gaze settled

359

on the woman he'd once hoped to marry, it was so full of tenderness that Lizzie knew he saw nothing to disappoint him.

Margaret's expression melted in return and Lizzie signalled to Polly that they should glide tactfully away. Margaret could ring the bell Lizzie had placed at her side if she wanted them to return.

An hour passed before they heard George's footsteps on the stairs. The change in him was remarkable. He was more upright, energetic, purposeful . . . 'I'm leaving now because I don't want to tire Margaret, but I'll return later.'

Lizzie smiled. 'I'm glad.'

She waved George off then went up to Margaret who was agitated but in an excited way. 'It's ridiculous to feel like this at my age! With a virtual stranger too!'

'George isn't a stranger.'

'He should be after all these years, but he isn't. That's odd, isn't it?'

'Love endures.'

'Love!' Margaret said, as though it was too absurd an idea for her to contemplate, but the girl with grey eyes had a sparkle in them.

The doctor announced himself to be deeply gratified by Margaret's progress. 'I wish all my patients had your powers of recovery, Miss Penrose. I declare your illness has made you look ten years younger.'

It wasn't the illness. It was George.

He came every day to talk, laugh and play the piano. As soon as Margaret was allowed downstairs, she played duets with him, wearing one of the new dresses she'd asked Polly to buy on her behalf after deciding her dull, ancient clothes weren't fit to be seen. 'Nothing gaudy, though,' she'd warned Polly. 'Something befitting a woman of my age.'

Polly had bought a pale blue dress and a lilac dress, and although Margaret had fussed that they were too frivolous . . . 'Ribbons and lace? What were you thinking, Polly?' . . . she'd been persuaded to try them on and gone strangely quiet.

'Elegant, not frivolous,' Polly had said.

'I suppose it would be a bother to return them . . .'

'Margaret and George should play a duet at the show,' Jack suggested, one evening.

He'd dropped the formal name of Miss Penrose as it no longer felt right with this softer woman.

'It would be an honour,' George told him.

Jack's plans for the show were coming along well. He and Polly were to sing a duet and Polly was also to sing with Lizzie. It warmed Lizzie's heart to see the two happy couples so full of joy but she couldn't help feeling the contrast with her own loneliness. It was beginning to look as though neither Harry nor Matt would be in England for Christmas.

Another Christmas overseas! Harry wrote. *I was so looking forward to spending our first Christmas together but I'm trying not to be down-hearted. After all, we're at peace now so it can't be long before I'm home . . .*

Matt didn't mention Christmas. *Just a quick note to say I was pleased to hear that women can now stand for election to Parliament. Congratulations. It's good to see all those years of campaigning paying off again . . .*

Lizzie read Matt's letter often. It was short, a scribbled note on a subject he knew was dear to her heart, but she wished he'd written more. It was impossible to know what he was thinking and feeling when there were only a few lines to interpret. A sense of foreboding took root inside her, but perhaps her imagination was simply running a little wild.

They were rehearsing one morning when Lizzie answered a knock at the door to find Matt outside in his stained brown army greatcoat with his pack slung over his shoulder. For a moment she was so dizzy with joy that she could neither speak nor move.

'Hello, Lizzie,' he said.

He looked leaner than ever. And very tired. Lizzie's muscles were unlocked by an urge to run to him. But she got no further than a single step. Matt's green eyes were sombre. Something was wrong.

Dread kicked inside her chest. Was he here to tell her that it had been nice to exchange letters in the war but now their lives were going in different directions? In other words, was he here finally to put an end to their friendship because she'd crossed a boundary that day on the farm?

'It's so good to see you,' she said. 'Come in, Matt.'

'I have a train to catch, but I didn't want to pass through London without seeing you.'

'You'll come again? Or I could —'

'I came to say goodbye as well as hello. I'm going to spend a few weeks on the farm, but then I'm going to try my luck in America.'

'America?' Lizzie was stunned.

'The farm no longer needs me and Peter is happy there with Edith. I'm free to try to do more with my music at last. I'm told America is a great place for aspiring musicians.'

But it was thousands of miles away. 'You're coming back?'

'I'll see how things turn out.'

'Please, Matt. Come in and talk about it.' Lizzie

was distressed beyond words.

'It's a wonderful opportunity for me.' Clearly his mind was made up and there was no room for discussion. He mounted the steps at speed, kissed her cheek, then stepped away. 'Goodbye, Lizzie. Be happy.'

He walked off without once looking back.

Lizzie closed the door but leant against it, too upset to return to the others. 'I'm going to make tea,' she called, and stumbled down to the kitchen for a few minutes alone.

She wanted what was best for Matt. Of course, she did. But America? Musicians might well thrive there, but they could thrive in England too. She could understand that he wanted to get away from *her*, but not the family who'd been looking forward to spending time with him now the war was over. They'd miss him terribly.

But perhaps the war was partly to blame. Matt might have been more deeply affected than he'd liked to admit. Lizzie thought of the poor unfortunates she'd seen at some of the concerts — men whose nerves had been shot to pieces the way other men's bodies had been shot to pieces. She remembered trembling fingers, the terror of unexpected noises, and eyes staring into space as though disconnected from the world. Matt hadn't appeared quite so damaged on the surface, but underneath . . .

Something he'd said gave her a glimmer of hope. He was returning to the farm before travelling to America. Once there he might find the healing he needed. Lizzie shouldn't despair yet. Even so she felt distraught.

Time was passing, though. Her friends would be wondering where she was and Lizzie wished to keep her distress to herself.

'That was Matt at the door,' she said, when she returned to the music room.

Everyone looked behind her, expecting to see him.

'He had a train to catch but wanted to say hello first. It was nice of him to come out of his way.' Lizzie busied herself with tea pouring so no one could see her face.

'Hopefully he'll return to London soon or you could visit the farm,' Polly suggested.

'Actually, he's thinking of trying his music in America.' There. Lizzie had said it, and she hadn't broken down in tears. Not yet, anyway. 'You've heard Matt's music, George. Do you think he'll do well over there?'

'A young man of his talent should do well anywhere.'

George told them about New York's shows and clubs, and Lizzie slumped with the relief of having got through the moment.

A few days later a letter came from Edith. Lizzie tore it open.

As you can imagine we're all in a tizzy about Matt's plans. It's only fair that he should have the chance to see what he can do with his music after he's sacrificed so much for the family, but we'll miss him horribly!

We're trying to persuade him to wait for three months but we're not having much luck . . .

Matt really was keen to be gone. Once he got to America he might settle there permanently and Lizzie might never see him again. The thought was unbearable.

That same day a telegram arrived. Throwing her

hopes into good new of Harry, Lizzie ripped it open. *Home next week*, Harry advised.

Thank goodness! Surely now the world would stop feeling as though it had tipped off its axis?

41

Polly, Margaret, George and Jack were thrilled to hear about Harry's return. 'If he should invite you to spend Christmas with his family, don't refuse on my account,' Margaret said. 'There'll be four of us here, so I shan't be starved of company.'

'His family may want to keep Harry to themselves for a few days.'

'They might. But if the offer is made . . .'

The wait for Harry's return felt endless but time passed as time always does. He sent another telegram to advise his expected arrival time and as soon as Lizzie heard his knock she flung the door open and threw herself against his chest.

Harry laughed. 'That's a nice welcome!'

'I've missed you so much.' Lizzie realised she was crying. Again.

'I've missed you too, my darling.'

She looked up at him and grimaced through her tears. 'I wanted to look nice for you but now my eyes must be red.'

'You're as beautiful as ever.'

They went into the music room where a fire had been lit so Harry would be comfortable. Like Matt, Harry looked thinner and sharper-boned but that was to be expected, given the horrors of the war. Lizzie supposed that all men who'd fought would carry the scars of dark memories all their lives. Doubtless Harry was tired too but Lizzie was relieved to see that his eyes were as warm as ever when he looked at her. The war might have battered him, but it hadn't defeated him.

Margaret came to welcome him and introduce George but after serving sherry to celebrate Harry's homecoming, the older couple tactfully withdrew.

'We can make plans for our future now I'm back,' Harry said. 'We can visit the jeweller for one thing. It's time my engagement ring was on your finger. We should look at wedding rings at the same time because I hope you'll marry me soon, Lizzie. First things first, though. It's Christmas Eve tomorrow so this is terribly short notice, but will you come down to Ashlyn and spend Christmas with my family?'

'Your family shouldn't feel obliged to invite me, Harry. I'll understand if they don't want to share you for a while. As long as you come back to me, of course.'

'My parents suggested inviting you. They want to see us both, but be prepared for a lot of questions about the sort of wedding we'd like.'

They travelled to Surrey by train after Lizzie had spent the morning shopping for gifts. Giles Benedict met them at the station in the car. He shook Harry's hand then pulled him into a quick hug before hugging Lizzie too. 'This is the best Christmas treat we could have asked for,' he said.

Mr Benedict spent the short drive telling them how much his wife was looking forward to seeing them, and how she'd cajoled the cook into cooking the finest feast possible, given that food supplies still hadn't returned to pre-war levels.

Maria rushed out of the drawing room as soon as they arrived. She was tearful at the sight of Harry and hugged him several times before she collected herself enough to turn to Lizzie. 'Forgive me, dear. I was a

367

little overwhelmed but it was rude to leave you standing there.'

Lizzie assured her that she understood and walked into the drawing-room arm-in-arm with her future mother-in-law.

Harry's sisters and their husbands came to dinner, and Lizzie fielded numerous questions about the forthcoming wedding. 'Our church, St Michael's, is charming,' Harry's mother said.

'I remember it.'

'You could have the service there and the wedding breakfast here, but only if you wish. It's a bride's privilege to choose where she marries, and your godmother may have her own ideas about the wedding. We just want you to know that we'd be happy to host the celebrations.'

'It's kind of you,' Lizzie assured her. 'I'm sure Harry and I will be thinking about the arrangements soon.' After all, there was no need to fear jinxing the future now Harry was safely at home.

'Of course. Poor Harry has barely had chance to draw breath since returning.'

'I won't be able to draw breath at all after this feast,' Harry said. 'It's a splendid dinner, Mother.'

Maria Benedict couldn't have looked more pleased.

The following morning, they attended the service at St Michael's — Maria Benedict watching Lizzie as though hopeful that the surroundings would impress her favourably as a venue for the wedding ceremony — then returned to the house for drinks, gifts and Christmas lunch. Harry's sister, Charlotte, was spending the day with her husband's family but Eleanor and Alicia came with their families and Lizzie enjoyed the children's excitement as they talked about the oranges, sweets and toys Father Christmas had left in their stockings.

Charades were traditionally played in the Benedict household but first Giles said, 'Why don't you take Lizzie out for a drive, Harry? You haven't had five minutes alone together today.'

Harry jumped up enthusiastically and soon they were motoring along Surrey's peaceful roads. 'It's green here even in winter,' Harry said.

He was right. Many of the trees had shed their leaves but evergreens and still-lush grasses compensated for any starkness.

'There's something I want to show you,' he added.

Turning a corner, he pulled up next to a grassy verge. 'What do you think?'

He was looking down a drive towards a house. It wasn't as large as Ashlyn but it was pretty with an oak door set into a timbered porch and windows made from diamond-shaped glass panes criss-crossed by silver leadwork. Beside the drive an estate agent's board announced, *For Sale*.

'Can we afford this?' Lizzie asked. The house had four bedrooms at least, and the gardens were large. 'I've very little money put by and —'

'I'm not marrying you for money, Lizzie. I have money saved from before the war as well as my army service gratuity, and my father has offered a large sum as a wedding gift. I'll be earning a good income too, once I'm back at work. We can't look inside the house now, but perhaps in a week or two?'

'It's gorgeous,' Lizzie said. 'Are you sure you want to live here, though? Straight away, I mean. If we live in London for a while, you'll be nearer to your office. I can continue working too.'

'I don't expect my wife to work.' Harry looked as though that would make him a terrible husband.

'I enjoy my work.'

'You could teach my sisters' children, and perhaps some of the children of our friends. Just as a hobby.'

'I enjoy my singing too.'

'Singing is allowed in Surrey, darling. We have a lively social life and I'm sure our friends would love to hear you play and sing.'

'Jack's opening a nightclub. He'd like me to sing for him.'

'Nightclub singing?' Harry blinked, clearly appalled. 'Jack can't realise what he's asking.'

'I haven't agreed to it. The club isn't even open yet. But don't you like London, Harry?'

'I lived there for about a year when I'd just started at the bank, but it was too bustling and impersonal for me. I was much happier when I returned here. Please don't think Surrey will be dull. We live very social lives, yet we also have tranquillity and space.'

Perhaps Harry craved tranquillity and space after his experiences in the trenches.

'If you really don't like the thought of living here, we can think about London,' Harry said, beginning to look worried. 'I want you to be happy, darling girl.'

Lizzie wanted him to be happy too, and clearly London wouldn't make him so. 'Surrey is beautiful.'

'And only a short train journey away from London,' he pointed out, cheerful again. 'You'll be able to see your godmother and friends often. You can shop in London too, and we can go to the theatre sometimes.'

Lizzie smiled then looked back at the house. It really was lovely.

42

Lizzie returned to London the next morning, unable to stay longer because the show was fast approaching and she needed to rehearse. Harry insisted on driving her, even though he was staying in Surrey for a while longer. He was generous with his time as well as his money. He'd given Lizzie a gold bracelet for Christmas but expressed himself delighted with her more modest gifts of a diary and a leather-bound volume of *Just So Stories*, his favourite book.

'The first entry in the diary is going to be the date of the show,' he told her. 'I can't wait to see you perform in one of your charity fundraisers at last.'

They parted with a kiss. 'I love you, soon-to-be Mrs Benedict,' Harry said. He paused, then added, 'I hope you like that name?' His brown eyes were eager.

'It's a wonderful name.'

Rehearsals for the Penrose Singers — the ranks swelled by George — began as soon as Lizzie returned. It was to be her last public performance and, wanting it to be memorable, she was pleased when Cordelia arrived with several yards of silver gauze. 'It happened to come my way and struck me as being useful for your costumes.'

'It's perfect,' Lizzie assured her.

They were to wear their hats again, this time trimmed with ivy. The silver gauze would look striking wound into the greenery and cascading down behind them. Perhaps there'd be enough gauze for a sash for George.

Every day Lizzie lived in dread of receiving a letter from Edith telling her that Matt had left for America, so when a letter arrived with Edith's handwriting on the envelope, Lizzie opened it with a dry mouth and a tumult in her stomach. The contents took her by surprise.

I'm coming to see your show! Edith wrote.

Matt leaves for America the day after the show and I told him that, if he wouldn't stay longer, the least he could do was to give me a treat of my choosing. He told me he'd be glad to give me a treat so naturally I chose a trip to London with tickets to your show.

We're catching the train down in the morning, staying in a small hotel and then catching the train back the following morning. I hope to fit in one or two of the London sights — Buckingham Palace especially — as well as the show. I can't tell you how excited I am. I've never been on a train before. I've never stayed in a hotel either. I've never even been out of Staffordshire.

Lizzie reeled. She'd have a chance to see Matt again and restore their friendship even if . . . Well, even if he still left for America because, with the friendship restored, she could stay in touch and hope to meet him again at some time in the future. It grieved her sorely to think that any such meeting might be many years away. But perhaps it was inevitable that the changing world would bring loss as well as joy in the shape of marriage to Harry.

Singing was going to be another loss. Singing in public, that was. Lizzie felt sad when she seized a quiet moment to stand on the stage in the hour before the show was due to begin, but also determined to perform better than ever before. For the sake of Matt, Edith, Harry, Jack, her fellow performers and all the people who'd receive the funds they raised, Lizzie vowed to sing her heart out.

Harry came backstage just before the performance, bringing flowers and champagne as a contribution to the after-show celebrations. Lizzie hoped Matt and Edith would join the party too. She'd written to invite them but, not having seen them yet, could only trust that they'd arrived in London safely and were sitting in the audience.

Margaret and George opened the show with a piano duet. It was sublime. The notes rose into the air like messengers of joy and the audience loved it. The tone for the evening was set and Lizzie realised she wasn't alone in wanting this to be the best show of all.

The Penrose Singers performed two songs next, including one of Matt's more humorous compositions. Lizzie hoped he'd think they'd done justice to it. Certainly the audience enjoyed it.

More acts followed, then, after an interval, Polly and Jack sang a love song. Watching from the wings, Lizzie saw their eyes sparkling with love and knew that their singing couldn't have been more sincere. The Penrose Singers performed again towards the end of the evening, bringing the show to a close with Lizzie and Polly encouraging the audience to join in. The standing ovation they received couldn't have been bettered.

Backstage the champagne flowed but Lizzie's attention was on the door. Harry arrived first. 'Darling, you were spell-binding!' he said, folding her into his arms.

Edith appeared in the doorway next, looking shy. Lizzie smiled and beckoned her into the dressing room, her heart kicking inside her chest as her gaze lifted to the tall man who entered behind her. Matt, of course. He was clean-shaven and dressed in civilian clothes, carrying them with the careless elegance of a man in the peak of physical fitness, even if he was still rather thin.

He looked back at her, his green eyes unfathomable, then stepped forward to kiss her cheek. 'Congratulations on a truly magical evening.'

She'd hoped for the ease of old to settle back over them but instead she felt jangled-up inside. Brittle. 'I hope you liked the way we performed your song?'

'It was perfect.'

Lizzie had no fault to find with his words. Nor with the way he said them. But she still felt awkward. Almost tearful.

Polly and Jack came over. Margaret and George too. Introductions were made and congratulations offered on both the show and the forthcoming weddings. Watching Matt speak to the others so kindly, Lizzie wondered how she could put things right but soon Matt was deep in conversation with George and her chance of a few minutes alone with him began to fade away.

Frustrated, she turned to Edith who was as fresh and sweet as ever as she spoke of her excitement in coming to London and seeing the show. 'I'm so glad you got to see Buckingham Palace,' Lizzie said.

'It was wonderful! Did I tell you that Matt's buying a tractor for us from the money he's earning from his songs?'

'You didn't. But it sounds just like Matt.'

'He's a special man,' Edith said.

The party was getting crowded, so someone suggested taking it onto the stage. The piano Margaret and George had used stood there still, and people began to plead for music. Once Matt's identity became known a clamour went up for him to perform some of his best-known songs.

He began with 'Pick Yourself Up' and everyone sang along. Then he sang a ballad by himself, his low voice drawing them in with its hypnotic quality.

'You should come and sing in The Velvet Slipper Club,' Jack called.

Matt smiled politely then said, 'This is a new song. I've called it 'Distance'.'

He played the introductory notes then began to sing.

There's a distance between us, a stretch of blue sea,
Storm-tossed or still, it keeps us apart.
With no way to cross it, together to be,
I stand on the shore with bruised, broken heart.

Lizzie found her own heartbeat had quickened.

'I've done all I can,' Edith whispered in her ear.

'What?' Startled, Lizzie whirled around to face her but Edith was already weaving through the crowd towards Polly.

'All right?' Harry murmured, placing his arm around Lizzie's shoulder.

She nodded but felt more unsettled than ever. The remaining words of the song washed over her and, with her thoughts turned inwards, she forgot to applaud at the end until she realised everyone else was clapping.

George played next. He started with 'The Girl With Grey Eyes', which had Margaret blushing adorably, then moved onto some lively tunes that had people dancing. Even Margaret shuffled from foot to foot for probably the first time in her life.

Harry whisked Lizzie into a twirl and she forced a laugh, hating the thought of worrying him with her strange mood. 'It's been a fabulous evening, hasn't it?' he asked.

'The best!'

She laughed again as Jack grabbed her for another twirl. No one was dancing formally. They were simply jigging and whirling about. Someone whistled at Margaret and she responded by throwing her arms into the air with merry abandon to a round of cheers from everyone else.

Matt danced too. With Edith, and then with Margaret. But he didn't approach Lizzie.

Polly claimed Harry for a dance and at that moment Lizzie saw Matt talking to Edith and gesturing to his watch. Lizzie hastened over. 'You're not leaving already?'

'It's been a lovely evening but we have a train to catch at ten tomorrow and we both have busy days ahead,' Matt explained. 'Edith needs to be back at the farm and I'm travelling on to Liverpool to catch the boat.'

'I'll fetch my bag,' Edith said, gliding away.

Lizzie looked up at Matt and felt physical pain. 'I wish you weren't going to America.'

'I have to go.'

'You can do well with your music here.'

'My music has nothing to do with it. Surely you know why I have to go, Lizzie?'

She stared at him, confused. Yet not entirely confused.

'Staying here . . . Being with you and seeing what we could do with our music . . . Writing more songs . . . Perhaps even performing in Jack's club . . . It would be incredible. But you love another man,' he said. 'I need to go away or I won't be able to bear it.'

With that he left her to say his goodbyes to the others.

Dazed, Lizzie followed and stood by as he shook hands with Harry.

'Have a safe journey home and I hope America turns out well for you,' Harry said.

Matt nodded. 'You'll look after Lizzie?' He glanced at her with a wounded softness that cut into her like broken glass.

Harry squeezed her close. 'I'll guard her with my life.'

'You'll write?' Lizzie begged Matt.

He smiled and gave something that might have been a nod but might equally have been evasion.

Edith looked troubled. She too shook Harry's hand and kissed Lizzie but said nothing more than a murmured goodbye, perhaps because she didn't know what to say.

Had she guessed that Matt had feelings for Lizzie? Of course she had. Her trip to London made sense now. She'd been playing the matchmaker. But Matt was right. Lizzie loved Harry. She was going to marry him.

Lizzie watched brother and sister leave the party then Harry whisked her into the dance again. She smiled up at him but her throat felt horribly tight as though it were holding back a flood of grief.

She could hide from the truth no longer. Yes, she loved Harry. But she also loved Matt and not just as a friend. Lizzie didn't know how it was possible to love two men at the same time. It was wrong. Shameful in fact. But undeniable.

'It's going to be a busy year with three weddings,' Harry said. 'We really must start planning ours soon.'

'Yes,' Lizzie answered. 'We must.'

He beamed down at her. 'I never knew I was capable of so much happiness until I met you, darling girl.'

43

Lizzie was exhausted by the time the party ended, desperate to be alone to sort through her shattered feelings. But first there were glasses and bottles to clear. Lizzie threw herself into the work with as many smiles as she could muster.

Afterwards Harry drove her home along with Margaret and Polly, who was staying the night in Marchmont Row.

He waited until Margaret and Polly had gone into the house then said, 'May I call tomorrow?'

'I'd like that.'

'Until tomorrow, then.' He took her into his arms and kissed her.

Lizzie kissed him back but tears threatened again, and, when he released her, she couldn't meet his gaze. Harry was wonderful in every way. The guilt of loving Matt too was awful.

'You're tired,' Harry said kindly. 'I'll see you in the morning.'

Gallant as ever, he walked her to the door then left.

Margaret and Polly were in the kitchen. 'I don't know about you two, but I want my bed,' Lizzie announced, needing to flee from them urgently.

'You don't want a cup of tea first?' Polly asked.

'Not on top of all that champagne. What a terrific show it was. Terrific party too.'

Unable to say more, Lizzie bolted upstairs and threw herself onto her bed. When had she fallen in love with Matt? She supposed the love she'd felt for

379

him as a child — that extraordinary closeness and sense of being at one with him — had simply grown up as she had. But by the time she'd met him again as a woman she'd been committed to Harry. So, she'd labelled her feelings as friendship — until that day on the farm when they'd crept out to show they actually had a different identity. Even then she'd tried to argue them away by blaming them on missing Harry.

Clearly Matt had fallen in love with her too. He'd behaved honourably by retreating from her. But he was hurting. After tonight Lizzie had no doubt of that.

She buried her face in her pillow and sobbed.

Lizzie felt wretched when she went downstairs the following morning. She was glad when Polly had to rush off early while Margaret had to sort through some music for George, sparing Lizzie the necessity of pretending all was well. She only hoped she could put on a show of good cheer when Harry came later.

She didn't expect him to arrive early and assumed the milkman had called to collect his weekly payment when a knock sounded on the door at nine o'clock. But it was Harry on the step. 'Will you come for a drive?' he asked. 'Blow the cobwebs away after last night's partying?'

'Of course.' Lizzie dug inside herself for some energy. 'Come in while I get ready.'

She went up to her room to put on her coat and hat, pausing to breathe in deeply before re-joining Harry with a smile. 'Where are we going?'

'It's a surprise.'

Were they going down to Surrey to see inside the house he'd pointed out to her? Lizzie felt weak at the thought of a long journey but, wanting Harry to enjoy his surprise, she kept her dread to herself. She couldn't sit in silence, though. 'I was impressed by your dancing last night,' she said.

Harry looked pleased. 'I'm not a natural dancer like you, but it was fun. I was so proud of you and all the money you raised. I saw many men fall in the war and few of them were wealthy. I know their families receive pensions, but they don't go far. Your fundraising should help to relieve real hardship.'

They continued to talk of the show until Lizzie realised Harry had come to a halt outside Euston station.

'We're here,' he announced.

Oh, no. Had he brought her here to wave off Matt and Edith? Lizzie wasn't sure she could see Matt again. Not without breaking down.

'Go to him,' Harry said. 'Go to Matt.'

'I don't think—' She broke off, frowning.

Harry wasn't smiling now. He looked serious. A little sad. It confused her.

'He loves you and you love him,' Harry added gently.

What? Lizzie stared at him. Shocked. Dismayed. 'Harry, I'm engaged to *you*. Committed to *you*. Not out of obligation, but because I love you.' And she hated to see the pain that had entered the kind brown eyes.

'I believe you do love me. But the way you love Matt is . . . different.'

'I —'

'Matt is your soulmate, Lizzie. I'm not.'

She shook her head to deny it, but his words acted on her like a revelation, understanding bursting into her mind like a firework lighting up darkness. Her feelings made sense now. Much as she cared for Harry,

381

she and Matt were two halves of a whole. Soulmates indeed.

'You're a special person, Lizzie,' Harry said. 'I realise how hard you've tried to love only me, and I'll always be grateful for the time we had together. Your letters comforted me enormously when I was in France and your smiles warmed me when I was on leave. But I think I've always known it wasn't to be. We're different people who want different things. I want the sort of steady life my parents have in leafy Surrey. But keeping you there would be like caging up an exotic bird which thrives in sunnier climes. We'd both do our best to make our marriage work, but it wouldn't make either of us feel happy and fulfilled. Not in the long term.'

He pulled a rueful face. 'I never took you to the jewellers to have the ring made smaller, did I? Perhaps I always knew deep down that you'd never wear my ring.'

'Harry, I'm sorry.'

'Don't be. My life's richer for having met you, and I'll never regret digging you out of the rubble of that bombsite. Now it's time for us to part, but we'll do so as friends. You deserve to be happy, Lizzie.'

'So do you!'

'I've every intention of being happy, and I'm sure there's a girl out there who'll want nothing more than to settle down to a domestic life with me in Surrey. But that girl isn't you, Lizzie. Go now. Chase your own happiness before it sails away to America. And don't worry about my family. They'll understand.'

Lizzie hesitated then threw her arms around him. He let her hold him close for a moment then tilted her chin so she was looking up at him. 'There's no need for tears, darling girl. We're both going to be fine.'

'You're an amazing man, Harry Benedict.'

She took his ring from the silver chain around her neck and gave it back to him. Then she got out of the car, blew him a final kiss and raced into the station.

It was busy. So very busy.

But there they were. One tall, manly figure. One slight and feminine.

'Matt!' she called. 'Edith!'

Both figures turned. Edith smiled first. Matt looked as though he couldn't quite believe Lizzie was here. Couldn't quite believe what he must be seeing in her expression.

But then a look of wonder passed over his face and was followed by a smile. He put down his suitcase to hold out his arms. And Lizzie ran to him. The one true love of her life. Her soulmate.

Acknowledgements

Like most writers, I rely on some amazing people to help make my books possible and this book is no exception. Special thanks are due to my lovely editor Hannah Todd and all at Team Aria, to Kate and the gang at the excellent Kate Nash Literary Agency, to my friends and gorgeous daughters who keep me going, and to all my fabulous readers.

We do hope that you have enjoyed
reading this large print book.

Did you know that all of our titles
are available for purchase?

We publish a wide range of high
quality large print books including:
Romances, Mysteries, Classics
General Fiction
Non Fiction and Westerns

Special interest titles available in
large print are:
The Little Oxford Dictionary
Music Book, Song Book
Hymn Book, Service Book

Also available from us courtesy of
Oxford University Press:
Young Readers' Dictionary
(large print edition)
Young Readers' Thesaurus
(large print edition)

For further information or a free
brochure, please contact us at:
Ulverscroft Large Print Books Ltd.,
The Green, Bradgate Road, Anstey,
Leicester, LE7 7FU, England.
Tel: (00 44) **0116 236 4325**
Fax: (00 44) **0116 234 0205**

Other titles published by Ulverscroft:

THE ORPHAN TWINS

Lesley Eames

London, 1910. Lily is ten years old when she realises her grandmother, a washerwoman, is seriously ill. She's determined to do what she can to help and keep her grandmother's illness a secret — even from her beloved twin, Artie. When tragedy strikes and the twins are faced with the prospect of a workhouse or an orphanage, a benefactor offers to take Artie in and educate him. All Artie's needs will be taken care of — but the gentleman has no use for a girl. As the orphan twins grow up and take different paths, their new lives are beyond anything they could have imagined. Will they ever find a way to be together again?

THE BRIGHTON GUEST HOUSE GIRLS

Lesley Eames

Thea's loathsome stepbrother is trying to trick her out of her inheritance of her parents' beautiful house in the seaside town of Brighton by means of a will which Thea believes to be forged. Anna is pregnant and grieving, her explorer fiancé lost at sea. Her violent father drives her from the family home in the backstreets of London's Bermondsey and her fiance's upper-class relatives cruelly reject her. Daisy is in search of independence, running from a man she doesn't want to marry. Together the three girls set up Thea's home as a guest house and embark on a mission to outwit her stepbrother by proving his fraud.

A SONGBIRD IN WARTIME

Karen Dickson

Shaftesbury, 1936. Mansfield House Hotel has been a refuge for Emily ever since she was orphaned at the age of 16. Not only did they give her employment as a chambermaid, but it's also where she met her fiancé Tom.

When theatre agent Roland stays at the hotel and hears Emily singing, he hatches a plan to get Emily away from Tom and make her a star.

Six years later, Emily has made a name for herself as 'The Bristol Songbird'. Her love for Tom is still as strong as ever, but she's not heard from him since that fateful night so long ago . . . And with the world enveloped in a war, it seems unlikely the two will ever meet again.

Will Emily and Tom find their way back to one another? Or will the war — and Roland — keep them apart?